KING MAKERS

GRADUATION

SOPHIE LARK

Bloom books

Published by Bloom Books, an imprint of Sourcebooks
P.O. Box 4410, Naperville, Illinois 60567-4410
(630) 961-3900
sourcebooks.com

Originally self-published as *The Savage* in 2022 by Sophie Lark.

Cataloging-in-Publication data is on file with the Library of Congress.

Printed and bound in the United States of America.
WOZ 10 9 8 7 6 5 4 3 2 1

ALSO BY SOPHIE LARK

Minx

Brutal Birthright
Brutal Prince
Stolen Heir
Savage Lover
Bloody Heart
Broken Vow
Heavy Crown

Sinners Duet
There Are No Saints
There Is No Devil

Grimstone
Grimstone
Monarch

Kingmakers
Kingmakers: Year One
Kingmakers: Year Two
Kingmakers: Year Three
Kingmakers: Year Four
Kingmakers: Graduation

This one's for my bad girls 🐆
Xoxo

Sophie Lark

SOUNDTRACK

"When I'm Small"—Phantogram

"Girls"—Zella Day

"Goddess"—Jaira Burns

"All the Things She Said"—Poppy

"Company"—Tinashe

"La Vie En Rose"—Emily Watts

"American Money"—BØRNS

"Bad Girls"—M.I.A.

"Heartless"—Kanye West

"Don't Blame Me"—Taylor Swift

 Spotify

 Apple Music

CONTENT WARNING

The Kingmakers series is a dark Mafia romance in a university academic setting. Expect all the violence and plotting a bunch of conniving young adults from crime families will commit. *Graduation* also contains consensual multiple-partner sex, including female/female sexual acts and male/female/female sex. Due to violence and sexual content, these books are intended for mature readers.

This book may contain, but is not limited to, the following potential triggers:

- Violence, including violent fighting
- Murder
- Drug manufacturing
- Drug use

Previously On Kingmakers:

What's the price tag for family loyalty?
With love on the line, the Spy makes a heartbreaking choice.
Leo's risky plan to help his friend puts Sabrina Gallo
in the path of the infamous Adrik Petrov.

An ancient blood feud spills over school grounds. When the dust
settles, not everyone is left standing...

This Year:

Sabrina is supposed to return to Kingmakers
for her sophomore year.
But a visit from Adrik offers new temptation...

KINGMAKERS

GRADUATION

ADRIK

SABRINA

JASPER

NIX

RAFE

ANDREI

HAKIM

VLAD

ILSA

CHIEF

ENZO GALLO

GIANNA LUCAS

DANTE GALLO · SIMONE SOLOMON · NERO GALLO · CAMILLE RIVERA · SEBASTIAN GALLO · YELENA YENINA · CALLUM GRIFFIN · AIDA GALLO

HENRY GALLO

SABRINA GALLO

LEO GALLO

MILES GRIFFIN

SERENA GALLO · DAMIAN GALLO · NATASHA GALLO · CALEB GRIFFIN

DARIO GALLO

NOELLE GRIFFIN

GALLO
Family Tree

FERGUS GRIFFIN — IMOGEN FITZGERALD

CALLUM GRIFFIN — AIDA GALLO   RAYLAN BOONE — RIONA GRIFFIN   NESSA GRIFFIN — MIKOLAJ WILK

MILES GRIFFIN   MARSHALL BOONE   COLE BOONE   CREED BOONE   TEDDY BOONE   ANNA WILK

CALEB GRIFFIN   CARA WILK

NOELLE GRIFFIN   WHELAN WILK

GRIFFIN
Family Tree

ALEXEI YENIN

ANASTASIA ZAITSEVA

ADRIAN YENIN

ROSE COPELAND

SEBASTIAN GALLO

YELENA YENINA

DEAN YENIN

LEO GALLO

NATASHA GALLO

YENIN
Family Tree

CHAPTER 1
SABRINA GALLO

I LEAN AGAINST THE SHIP'S RAILING, LETTING THE COLD SALT SPRAY hit me in the face.

On the broiling deck, this is the only way to cool off. My hair will go insane, but I don't mind.

I'm deliberately ignoring Ilsa Markov playing street craps against the base of the mast with a cluster of Enforcers. Likewise, she's pretending not to notice how each bob of the ship tosses my skirt a little farther up my thighs.

We broke up last night.

She said it was because she's graduating. She'll be joining her sister, Neve, in Moscow, while I'm stuck at school three more years.

We both know that's not the real reason.

The last time we fought, she said, "I don't think you're cut out for a relationship."

That stung. Technically, we were never "in a relationship," but we'd been hooking up on and off all year long, and besides that, I actually liked her.

Ilsa's one of the only female Enforcers and the only student who can knock me on my ass in sparring. She gave me a black eye that covered half my face; I looked like the Phantom of the Opera. I like to count that as our first date.

Right now, she's fleecing Archie Chan for every dollar he's

got left in his pockets. She's rolling so well that Archie mutters something about loaded dice. Ilsa shoots him a stare that shuts his mouth fast.

Ilsa would sooner cut off her own pinkie than cheat. I call her "Diana" not just because she looks like Wonder Woman but because her code of honor is as hard-plated and immovable as Amazonian armor.

I don't know if she likes the nickname. Ilsa doesn't always love my jokes. Probably another reason we split up.

I don't have control over what comes out of my mouth.

The worse the situation, the funnier I find it.

My dad says I get that from my aunt Aida.

Nobody's strangled Aida yet, though not for lack of trying.

I'm not sure I'll be that lucky.

I'm not blessed with my aunt's sunny disposition. In fact, at the moment, I'm in a foul fucking mood.

Half my cousins are graduating along with Ilsa or already have. Miles is gone, and Leo and Anna are leaving.

I hate being younger.

I was excited to come to Kingmakers, but it's impossible to catch up to the cousins who are already moving on again, starting their lives in the real world. I'm hot with jealousy.

The strict rules of the island grate on me, not to mention the humiliating "homework" and the relentless exams. The best part of the year was when we stole the chancellor's boat for an unauthorized field trip to Kazakhstan.

I hitch half a smile, remembering the one night I wholeheartedly enjoyed.

The night I met Adrik Petrov.

I already knew him by reputation. Adrik is a legend at Kingmakers. He was forming his Wolfpack before he ever graduated, a clique of students so ruthless that even the professors were afraid of them.

He had my back on that little adventure. Don't think that means I owe him one. I helped break his uncle out of a prison fortress, so we're more than square.

Adrik ordered me to meet him on the dock in Dubrovnik on the last day of school.

I can't decide whether it would be more fun to take a spin with Russia's bad boy or to disappoint him.

Unfortunately, the ship only goes one place, so I don't have much choice unless I fancy jumping the rail and swimming the last mile to shore.

He might not even be waiting.

Men don't keep their promises when they live in the same house as you. I'm not arrogant enough to think he's been mooning over me the last four months while I've been trapped on a tiny island in the middle of nowhere.

He might not even remember gripping my wrist so hard it left a bruise in the shape of his thumb.

I will see you again. I was simply offering you the courtesy of choosing the time and place...

Like I was one of his Wolfpack.

Like I had to obey.

He doesn't know me very well.

I don't even like men.

Is Adrik a man? Or an animal?

I grin, wondering how to test him.

I've got at least another hour before I see if he showed up.

The journey back to shore seems interminable.

Wilting in the heat, the students strip off their uniforms, leaving button-up shirts and knee socks scattered all over the deck.

My own uniform is much the worse for wear. It takes a beating when our classes take place anywhere but the classroom: Marksmanship, Combat, Surveillance, Torture Techniques, Stealth and Infiltration...

The hem of my plaid skirt is distinctly bedraggled, stained with something dark—grease or old blood. My socks have long since lost their elastic, puddled around my ankles.

I'd like to burn the lot, and maybe I should when I get home. God knows this set of uniforms won't last another three years.

"What are you scowling about?" Cara Wilk leans against the rail with a notebook tucked under her arm.

It's not schoolwork. Cara's always scribbling. She wants to be a writer. I suspect she only came to Kingmakers so she could get material for her novel. She's not criminally minded, which won't matter. Her sister, Anna, is heir.

Cara's as dark as Anna is fair. With her large, sad eyes and pale, pointed face, she looks like a Victorian ghost child. That suits—the Gothic mansion in which she grew up is almost certainly haunted.

"I'm sick of these clothes," I tell her.

Cara's uniform is still perfectly pressed. She's the only person on the deck not sweating profusely. The Irish students resemble lobsters fresh out of the pot.

"Aren't you hot?" I demand.

"Mind over matter." Serenely, she turns her face into the breeze.

Even the chancellor looks uncomfortable in his dark suit and thick black beard.

He's probably peeved that he has to take the ship back to shore with the rest of us plebs. Word got out about his private cruiser. All his secrets are leaking out. Nothing stays hidden in the Mafia world, unless everyone who knows is dead.

Big bad Luther Hugo got a slap on the wrist. Now he has to pretend to be on his best behavior. If the Hugos weren't richer than God, he'd have been sacked from the school with a knife in the spine as a retirement gift.

I know better than to think he's actually changed. He stands in the shade of the mainmast, his beetle-black eyes crawling over me.

I return the stare.

Men have looked at me like this since I was eleven years old. It doesn't faze me. Their lust is their weakness and my strength.

"I loathe him," Cara murmurs.

Harsh words from my gentlest cousin. I can't resist teasing her.

"I dunno. He's pretty hot for an old man."

This is true. Age hasn't reduced Hugo's height or dulled the devilish cast of his sharp features.

"Sabrina!" Cara turns on me, disgusted. "That's Hedeon's father!"

"So? He's not *my* father."

"He fucked a student!"

"I wish he would."

Cara shakes her head, refusing to smile.

Switching tactics, I nod toward Hedeon Gray, pitching my voice low and insinuating. "If you're so worried about poor illegitimate Hedeon, how come you're not sitting with him?"

Hedeon is already surrounded by Anna, Leo, and our cousin Caleb. The only place to sit would be directly on his lap.

Cara catches my drift. Her cheeks glow pink as a china lamp.

"Don't call him 'illegitimate.'"

"Sorry." I dip my head in apology. "I meant 'bastard.'"

Now she's genuinely angry, knuckles whitening on the spine of her notebook.

Ever the wordsmith, Cara fashions her retort like a dart and hurls it straight at my heart.

"Don't take it out on me just because Ilsa dumped you."

Sometimes you want to get punched in the face.

Sometimes you'll goad anybody to do it.

I laugh at my own success.

"You're a feisty little bitch today, aren't you? You must really like Hedeon."

"Oh, fuck off." Cara walks away.

She's had enough of me. Just like Ilsa.

Everybody thinks they want Sabrina. The dose is the poison.

Cara drops down next to Anna, her cheeks still stained with pink. Anna shoots me a sharp look from under the encircling comfort of Leo's arm.

I wink at her.

Heavily tattooed, ice-blond, and moody, Anna is just my type. Leo's lucky I *am* younger. If I were their same age, I wouldn't have lost out on Anna like a little bitch.

Don't worry. We're only cousins by marriage. This isn't *Game of Thrones.*

Then again, who knows what might tempt me? The more I'm not supposed to have something, the more I want it.

My mood slightly elevated by depressing Cara's, I gaze out across the dark blue water. At last, I spot the wheeling gulls and white sails that herald Dubrovnik. In another ten minutes, the distinctive rust-colored roofs of Old Town rise into view.

The crowded dock gives no hint if Adrik Petrov is waiting.

I tell myself I don't care either way.

Still, my heart beats a little faster, the sharp scents of diesel and salt seeming to promise that *something* exciting will happen today.

I snatch up my backpack, slinging it over my shoulder. I've got a change of clothes in there, just in case.

As we queue up to descend the gangplank, Ilsa approaches me, tossing back her mane of black hair, saying in her forthright way, "No hard feelings. Look me up if you're ever in Moscow."

She holds out her hand to me, nails blunt and unpolished—something I always appreciated when she slid those fingers inside me.

"Don't shake my hand, you asshole." I pull her into a hug.

I rest my cheek against the side of her neck, inhaling the clean scent of soap and fresh laundry laced with gunpowder. Ilsa ranked first in the final Marksmanship exam.

She hugs me back, allowing her hand to rest briefly on my lower back before she lets go of me.

"See ya around, kid," she says, just to infuriate me.

I smile instead. It's the closest she's ever gotten to a term of endearment.

"Good luck," I tell her.

Ilsa is about to take her position as her sister's lieutenant, an unheard-of arrangement in the Russian Mafia. The Markovs control one of the richest slices of Moscow, or at least they did before the high table imploded. There's a civil war among the Bratva. Who knows who will take control when the dust settles?

As I descend to the dock, Adrik Petrov is nowhere to be seen.

Probably for the best. I'm sure my mom's anxious to see me back in Chicago.

I sigh, unexcited for the long flight home and the even longer summer stretching ahead of me. My dad will run me ragged as he expands his empire all up and down the I-80 corridor.

I suppose it's my empire too. I'm his heir, but sometimes I think my little brother, Damien, is better suited to that role.

The Gallos have gone legitimate. I ought to get my contractor's license instead of attending Kingmakers. It would certainly make my mom happier.

She worries about me. Everyone does.

They want me safe at home.

Safe is boring. Safe feels like a hundred pounds of steel chains wrapped around my limbs.

Born and raised in Chicago, I've barely seen the world. Vacations don't count—resorts and hotels are playpens for tourists.

I thought Kingmakers would scratch my itch, but it's just another prison, even more cut off from everything interesting.

Anna doesn't agree with me.

"I'll miss Kingmakers," she sighs, having stepped off the ship for the last time.

"Not me!" Leo replies gleefully.

"Yes, you will," Anna says, confident that she knows Leo better than he knows himself.

A deckhand tosses my suitcase down on the dock so hard it almost bounces into the water.

"Hey!" I holler up at him. "Is that how your mother dropped you on your head?"

He shouts something back at me in Croatian.

"Why do you always escalate?" Leo laughs at me.

I haul the suitcase upright, one of the wheels wonky and refusing to spin.

"Motherfucker," I mutter, glancing back to see if the deckhand is still in sight for further chastisement.

"Come on." Anna grabs my arm and hauls me along. "No time for that."

Cara and Caleb are already waiting for us at the end of the dock, their suitcases among the first to be unloaded.

I follow my cousins toward the taxi stand, trailing behind, the promise of the day failing to materialize.

Before I can cross the cobbled concourse between the dock and the queues of battered taxis, a black Ducati skids to a halt in front of me, a cloud of exhaust billowing up around us. The chrome muffler sparkles in the sun, the bike radiating heat like a living thing.

It's the Superleggera V4, the fastest superbike in production. Ducati only made five hundred of them, so I've never actually seen one in person.

My eyes slide down the sleek carbon-fiber frame, the engine settling to a low growl that thrills my bones. It's fucking gorgeous.

The rider yanks off his helmet, shaking out a head of thick, coarse hair. He's tanned darker than the last time I saw him, almost as brown as me. His narrow blue eyes, pale as a husky, flick up to meet mine.

His bare forearms are dusty from the cobbled streets, clear tracks of sweat cutting down. The hand gripping the helmet is battered, deep cuts across the knuckles.

Adrik Petrov, in the flesh.

"You're late," I tell him.

"I'd say I'm right on time."

His English is flawless, the masculine bite of the Slavic accent edging each word.

Adrik jerks his head toward Leo and Anna. "Good to see you."

You'd never guess Adrik ever needed our help. I doubt he'd admit that he did.

He's as arrogant as ever, tossing his black hair back out of his face, radiating as much heat as that bike. He's not quite as tall as Leo but broader in the body, with a tight, compressed energy that makes the veins stand out on the backs of his hands.

Like the engine revving to leave, Adrik is impatient.

"You coming or not?"

I'd like to say "not," just to wipe the smirk off his face. But I can't take my eyes off that bike. If *Thou shalt not covet* is a real commandment, I'm going straight to hell.

"If she won't come, I will," Caleb says, drooling over the Ducati.

My brain runs a dozen swift calculations.

"I'll come." I push my suitcase toward Cara, who has to catch it quickly so it doesn't topple over on its wonky wheel. "Take that home for me, will you?"

Cara glances between Adrik and me. She doesn't love this idea.

"What am I supposed to tell your dad?" Leo demands.

"Tell him I'll catch a flight tomorrow."

Leo blocks my path, arms crossed over his chest. "If you get yourself in trouble—"

"Oh, save it," I snap. "After the year you had!"

Leo grins, well aware that he's being a filthy hypocrite. "Alright. I'll carry your damn bag. Don't make Cara lug it around."

Cara passes it to him.

My cousins file off toward the taxi stand, Anna lingering behind for one last warning glance.

I turn my back on her.

I fucking hate when they baby me.

Alone with Adrik, the air feels thick as honey.

"What's the plan?" I ask him.

His bright blue eyes flash across me, head to foot, taking in the uniform he probably remembers even better than I do. A ghost of a smile crosses his lips.

"You hungry?" he growls.

His voice is low and rough. I can smell the heat of his body, mixed with ocean salt and the bike's exhaust. The tip of his tongue rests against the sharp point of his incisor as he waits for my response, eyes slitted against the dazzle of sun on water.

"Always."

"I got us a table at Coco."

He's trying to impress me. Coco is the bougiest joint in southeast Europe—fancy enough that even the Mafia brats have a tough time getting a table.

"Get on," Adrik says, holding out his helmet to me.

God, I'd love to throw my leg over that seat.

But even rule breakers have lines they won't cross.

"I don't ride bitch on bikes."

He scoffs. "Then have fun walking."

I turn on the heel of my sneaker, marching off in the direction of the Artemis Hotel. Adrik stares after me, clearly thinking he was calling my bluff.

I don't bluff.

A line of mopeds and motorcycles is parked against the curb. I scan the rank, looking for the best option.

A candy-red Kawasaki stands out like a racehorse among ponies. It's nowhere near as boss as Adrik's bike, but it's leaner and potentially faster in the narrow medieval streets of Old Town. As long as it has the right rider.

I grab my knife from my pocket, flicking out the blade. In seconds, I've popped the ignition cap and spliced the wires beneath. Clenching the clutch, I spark the wires until the engine roars to life.

Without glancing back at Adrik, I roar off down the street.

The wind whips my hair back. The throbbing engine between my legs sends vivid vibrations all the way through my body, up to my fingertips, and down to my toes.

I fucking love this feeling.

It's been eight long months since I rode a bike—worse than celibacy.

The motorcycle brings me alive, sending blood rushing through my veins. It sparks every neuron until the cobblestones stand out in high definition, until I hear the shouts of fishmongers in the open-air market of Gundulićeva Poljana and smell the tantalizing scents of home-grown truffles and olive oil as I whip past the Gligora wine and cheese shop.

I only spent a day in Dubrovnik back in September, but if my father and I have one thing in common, it's an eye for detail. I'm not just a pretty face—everything I see, I memorize. I remember every street I walked and every shop I passed the night before I caught the ship to Kingmakers.

I know exactly where Coco is located and how to get there.

In fact, I might know a faster route than Adrik.

Avoiding the crowded thoroughfare of Stradun, congested with tourists, sidewalk cafés, and overburdened carts of kitsch, I take a hard right through an alleyway, then several more twists and turns through narrow residential streets.

Adrik's bike howls as he speeds after me.

He's trying to catch me.

His bike is faster, no question. If this were a track, he'd blow past me in a single lap.

But we're not on a track. The more we have to stop and start and the sharper the corners we navigate, the more I can make use of the light frame and zippy 650 cc engine on the Ninja.

I expect to leave him in the dust.

Tossing a look back over my shoulder, I see Adrik bent low on the bike, cutting the space between us.

He handles the machine like a pro, slicing through turns with surgical precision, slowly gaining ground on me.

Adrik doesn't just know how to ride. He knows how to race.

Racing is all about taking lines. It's strategy. That's why the best brain wins over hundreds of laps. You have to shave off fractions of a second each turn, each lap more perfect than the last.

I'm taking my turns at maximum speed, coming in hot, turning as tightly as possible.

Adrik's bike is bigger; he has to slow at the corners. But he's calculating his angles like fucking Pythagoras, flattening the curve, bringing the bike to a straight line as soon as possible so the Ducati can make full use of its monstrous 998 cc engine.

Adrik is sacrificing entry velocity for exit speed.

It's a math equation. I know that—and apparently he does too.

I speed through a tight roundabout, leaning so hard that my bare knee almost scrapes the road and my hair trails in the dust.

I started this race, and I'm damn sure going to win it.

My bike sounds like a lawn mower compared to the leonine roar of the Ducati. I rise up off the seat, feinting like I'm going to turn right out of the roundabout, then juking left instead, shooting the gap between a delivery van and a Fiat. The delivery driver lays on his horn, and the Fiat's owner shouts furiously out his window. I cackle with triumph, pulling away from Adrik.

Not being entirely familiar with the area, I fetch up against a stone staircase so tight that the handlebars of my bike scrape the plaster walls on either side as I bump down. Terrible on the shocks, but who cares? It's not my bike.

I almost collide with an old woman in a flowered headscarf who gives a startled squawk.

"*Oprosti!*" I call to her cheerfully.

She shakes a fist at me, then begins her shaky ascent of the stairs, a basket of bread, jam, and fresh-cut flowers tucked over her arm.

Adrik is forced to stop at the top of the stairs, watching as she painstakingly makes the climb.

Laughing madly, I zip through the Buža Gate while a furious uniformed attendant shouts something in Croatian.

Adrik will never catch me now.

I pass under the bright orange cable cars ascending to the top of Srd Hill. We could have ridden the cars, but I'd much rather take this winding road on the bike, roaring up the Mediterranean hillside, the ocean flat and glittering below me.

Clouds of dust billow up behind me like smoke. I speed faster and faster, reckless and thrilled, chasing the swallows that dart and swoop across my path. I'm not racing Adrik anymore—I'm challenging the voice that tells me to slow down before I take a curve too hard and tumble off the cliff or collide with a tour bus driving the opposite direction.

Sense is never as strong as the impulse for more.

There's no angel on my shoulder, only a devil that whispers, "Faster, faster...fucking fly!"

I'm reaching the peak.

There's no more road ahead of me, only the dazzling view of the harbor and the ancient crescent of Old Town far below.

My all-time favorite movie scene is when Thelma and Louise drive their '66 Thunderbird off the rim of the Grand Canyon. I've never seen anything more beautiful than that baby blue car soaring into space.

I'll never die an old woman in bed. My last memory will be something so beautiful it will echo through eternity.

Someday...not today.

I turn the bike into a shaded courtyard, at the end of which stands the entryway to the restaurant, the double doors topped by an old-fashioned awning on which the ornate scroll of *Coco* is painted in gold script.

I stop short in front of the valet.

"I'll park it myself," I tell him, hoping he won't notice the gaping hole that ought to be an ignition switch.

As I pull the bike into its berth, I hesitate.

I look at the twisted wires, the ends spliced together.

Taking my knife from my pocket, I cut them off short.

Then, dusty and sweating, I march up to the host, already planning how I'll get a table.

CHAPTER 2
ADRIK PETROV

I CAME ALL THE WAY TO CROATIA FOR SABRINA GALLO.

This might seem like madness, having met her only once before. I guess you could say she made an impression on me.

She haunted me like a piece of music that wouldn't stop playing in my head. Even when I thought I was thinking of something else, I could hear that husky laugh of hers, wild and mocking, echoing through my brain.

I'm used to being the most outrageous person in the room—the one who will go the furthest and do the most.

I was the electricity.

Until Sabrina crashed down in front of me, like a hundred million volts of lightning right at my feet.

She forced her way into my rescue mission, stubborn and unapologetic. I didn't want the Gallos with us; it was supposed to be a family affair. I soon saw she was more than capable—downright ingenious. At the end of one single night in her company, I knew I'd never seen anything like her and might never again.

So I demanded that she meet me on the dock on the last day of school.

I wanted a day alone with her—to take her apart like a pocket watch and see what makes her tick.

I'm good at reading people. Really fucking good.

Once you understand how people think, you know what they'll do.

I did not predict that within five minutes of meeting her, a schoolgirl who barely comes up to my chin would roar away from me on a stolen bike.

Even less did I guess that Sabrina would beat me to the restaurant, securing her own table right by the window without even accessing my reservation.

"How did you get in here?" I demand, dropping down on the empty seat next to hers.

I'd rather not give her the satisfaction of seeing how sweaty and dirty I became chasing her up here, but without the benefit of a helmet, Sabrina is even worse. She's halfway to a chimney sweep, her face streaked with dust and her button-up blouse the color of weak tea.

"Nobody turns me away at the door," she says.

Conceited but probably true. Sabrina Gallo is the most beautiful woman I've ever seen. She has the kind of beauty that's almost upsetting, because it jolts you every single time. You keep waiting for something to humanize her—an unflattering angle or an ugly expression. It never comes.

Even the dirt only serves to highlight the brilliant whites of her eyes and the flash of her teeth as she grins. Her skin looks toasted, as if she's been singed over a fire. She licks the dust off her lips, their dusky pink the color of Himalayan salt.

Sabrina crackles with energy, the tiny hairs all around her head glowing gold in the sunshine like filaments. If I touch her, she might electrocute me. Yet I'm aching to get my hands on her.

I've never chased down a woman before.

I don't give a fuck about dinner—I want her back on that bike. This time, I'm going to catch her.

Sabrina has other plans. She pores over the menu, declaring, "I'm fucking starving. They don't feed us on the ship. What's good here?"

"Everything," I say, plucking the menu from her hands. "But we're not sitting here."

A tiny line forms between her eyebrows as she frowns. This only increases her attractiveness, like a vein of gold in kintsugi pottery.

"Why not?"

"Because my table is better," I say, taking her arm and pulling her to her feet.

This is an excuse to touch her. Her flesh burns against my palm, warm from the sun and the exertion of operating the bike.

People who've never ridden a motorcycle have no idea how much strength it requires. I'm not surprised to feel hard muscle beneath the smooth skin of her forearm.

"Why don't you clean up first?" I say. "The bathroom's over there."

"I will after I order. I told you, I'm starving," she says, obstinate and perfectly satisfied with her current appearance.

She likes opposing me.

She'll learn soon enough that I get what I want.

There are a hundred ways to bend a person to your will. Not only brute force, which is the crudest tool. I'm infinitely adaptable and fucking relentless.

So I smile at Sabrina and say, "I love a woman with an appetite."

Her thick lashes flick up at me like a fan, exposing the direct stare of those smoky eyes. A smile tugs at the edge of her lips.

"I bet you do."

Because she doesn't know where my table is located and she really is hungry, I have the pleasure of watching her follow me upstairs, docile as a kitten—for the moment at least.

I've reserved the entire rooftop patio. Sheltered from the heat by a thick pergola of lemon trees, the citrus-scented air is cool and fresh. The sun is just beginning to dip down into the water. The cloudless sky glows like a flaming brand, brief but brilliant.

Sabrina raises one soot-black eyebrow, impressed despite herself.

"Alright, it is a better table," she admits.

Our server hurries over, a crisp white cloth folded over his forearm. His dark hair is pulled back in a bun at the base of his neck, and young as he is, he can't help staring at Sabrina, even though he knows I'll be the one paying the tip.

"Can I offer you a drink to start?" he stammers.

"Do you have Vietti?" Sabrina inquiries.

"White or red?"

"Always white," she declares. "Fuck red wine."

Unsure how to respond to this heresy, the waiter lets out a nervous chuckle, then turns to me. "And you, sir?"

"The same."

I don't share Sabrina's prejudice against red wine, but I want to drink what she's drinking.

The silence that follows the waiter's departure could be awkward. Not for me—I've never felt awkward in my life—but perhaps for Sabrina.

She leans back in her chair, arm slung over the back rungs, legs apart, though not quite enough to show her underwear—deliberately irreverent. I assume she wore her uniform to show me how little effort she's putting into this meeting.

If she were polite, she would ask after my uncle.

Instead, she asks, "What's going on in Moscow?"

"You'll have to be more specific. It's a big city."

Sabrina lets out an impatient snort. "Ivan Petrov has moved his holdings to America. Your father took control of St. Petersburg. I'm wondering who's going to fill the vacuum in Moscow. Especially now that Danyl Kuznetsov is dead."

My hand twitches under the table—with excitement, not irritation.

"It sounds like you know more about it than I do."

"The fuck I do." Sabrina narrows her eyes. She doesn't like me playing games.

The Petrovs have kept St. Petersburg as our stronghold for the last twenty years. Still, keeping a foothold in Moscow is essential, as it's the seat of the high table. My father sent me there to secure our place. I intend to do much more than that.

"Maybe *I'll* take Moscow," I say idly.

"How much of it?"

"All of it."

Sabrina bites the edge of her lip, grinning.

"What about the Markovs?"

Now it's me who raises an eyebrow. The Markovs own the largest territory in Moscow. Nikolai Markov has only daughters. The high table will not readily accept a female heir with only with her sister as lieutenant. Nor will the other *pakhany*. Neve Markov will be lucky to last a year.

The arrival of the wine interrupts us.

Sabrina seizes her glass, taking an eager draught before I can propose a toast.

"*Poyékhali*," I say drily, holding up my wine.

Sabrina clinks hers against mine so robustly that she almost cracks the glass.

"*Poyékhali*," she imitates with surprisingly good inflection.

I take a sip.

"*Blyad!*" I scoff. "It's pure sugar!"

"I like my wine to taste like cotton candy," Sabrina laughs.

It's sweet, but on second taste, not cloying. Actually, clear and refreshing, with a tart pop and slight carbonation. Sabrina grins as I drink a little more.

"You like it," she says.

"It's not terrible," I admit.

Sweets are not among my vices.

Salt on the other hand…

I zero in on the girl sitting across from me.

"Why are you interested in the business of the Bratva?"

"Only one Bratva."

"Which one?"

"I used to fuck Ilsa Markov," Sabrina says mischievously.

She's trying to make me jealous. She should have picked a less-attractive object. I know Ilsa Markov—while she's too bullish for my taste, the idea of her in bed with Sabrina sends a rush of blood straight to my cock.

"When was that?" I inquire.

"Oh, up until about…last night." Sabrina smiles wickedly.

I finish the rest of the wine in one swallow.

"And just when I thought I knew everything there was to know about Ilsa…"

"You didn't know she's gay?"

"I didn't know she had such good taste."

That gets a laugh from Sabrina, so low and delighted that my cock swells to uncomfortable proportions, no longer fitting within my jeans.

This girl is much more intoxicating than the wine. I can't remember the last time I got hard from conversation alone.

"Would you like to order?" the waiter asks, reappearing with irritating promptness.

I turn a blazing look on him that makes him take a step backward. I'd like to tell him to fuck off for the next several hours, but Sabrina wants food.

"Bring us the *fritule*," I say.

"After that, I'll have the filet," Sabrina interjects before I can order her entrée as well.

"I'll have the same." I pass him our menus.

"I don't know if I like *fritule*," Sabrina says with an edge of annoyance.

"You will."

"How do you know?"

"Because they're delicious. And much like Ilsa, I trust your taste."

That mollifies her slightly. The arrival of our appetizer thaws her entirely. The hot, crisp little pastries are stuffed with raisins, fresh-grated orange rind, and a dash of rum. Sabrina devours them in two bites each.

"Fucking fantastic," she says, willing to admit when I'm right.

Of all the things I like about her, this is one of her best traits.

CHAPTER 3
SABRINA

For once, the hype is justified. The food is fantastic at Coco, and Adrik is just as impressive as everyone says.

I keep looking for a hole in his persona—something he thinks he knows that I know he's wrong about. Some cringey joke. Some moment where I puncture his ego, and like every other man I've ever met, he can't handle it and his temper flares. That's what I expect to happen, because that's what's always happened when I've tried to date men.

They hate when you disagree with them, especially when you're right.

They hate when you don't fawn over them.

And most of all, they hate when you're different from the picture of you they created in their mind.

That happens to me most of all.

Men look at me and see liquid sex poured into the body of their dreams. They want me so bad that they can't possibly imagine that what's inside that package might not appeal to them quite as much as the exterior.

They say I'm everything they ever wanted, then they want to change everything about me.

How I dress, how I talk, what I like, how I behave…

And that's before the jealousy kicks in.

The more they want you, the less they can stand for anyone else to look at you.

Our waiter is trying to behave himself, but even he can't resist a furtive glance down the front of my shirt as he drops off the entrées.

I check to see if Adrik noticed.

Adrik leans back in his chair, his wineglass balancing lightly between his middle and ring fingers.

His expression is as relaxed as ever, no hint of irritation drawing those thick black brows together.

The moment the waiter leaves, he says, "Has anyone ever been able to resist you?"

I smile. "Not yet."

Adrik pours a little more Vietti into my glass, keeping his eyes locked on mine, no need to watch what he's doing. "Then I guess I'm just like everyone else."

Of all the things I expected from Adrik Petrov, self-deprecation wasn't one of them.

He throws me off balance. Those ice-chip eyes narrowed in on me, that rough growl, but the words themselves are flirtatious and complimentary. The man has layers to him.

He sparks my curiosity. Also my impulse for mischief.

I ignore the freshly filled wineglass, wanting to keep my senses sharp. I've got plans for about thirty minutes from now. I can't get tipsy.

Adrik picks up his steak knife, tendons standing out on his bare forearm, the bicep above as round as a softball. His hands are large, the fingers gripping the handle thick and square-tipped.

"Have you ever been to Russia?" he asks me.

"No."

"Would you like to?"

I take my time cutting into the perfectly grilled filet so I can measure how serious an invitation he's offering.

I thought Adrik was here for sex.

But he's already put more effort into the hunt than I expected. He didn't get that bike in Croatia—he rode it here or shipped it. He knew it would impress me. He knows how I feel about anything on wheels.

And not because I told him. He's done his research.

I don't know how I feel about that.

Adrik wants something. Not just my body—something else.

I look up at him.

He's waiting and watching, his own steak untouched.

"What's Moscow like?" I ask him.

"Well…you know when a thousand kinds of people poured into America, and it was chaotic and lawless, and fortunes could be made and lost in a day?"

"Yes."

"That's what it's like. It's the wild, wild East."

I take a bite of the filet, licking the juice from my lips.

"That sounds…intriguing."

Adrik grins back at me, his teeth white and strong. He has a wicked smile and a stare that makes you feel naked. There's nothing sweet about him, nothing gentle. I could see him in a fur coat and boots in a Siberian castle, snow howling all around…

He was made for a harsher climate than this.

The leather jacket slung over the back of his chair is heavy and battered. The body it revealed is tight, sleek, and flawlessly maintained. I admire when a man takes care of himself. I can tell a lot about Adrik from the way he treats his body and his bike.

He's less tattooed than the average Bratva. Out of school for several years, I would have expected his arms and hands to already bear record of his accomplishments. One of the only tattoos I can see is a large patch on his right arm: the head of a black wolf in woodcut style. I've heard all his Wolfpack wear the brand, more reminiscent of a military group than Bratva.

Still, I suspect that if I could see Adrik without his shirt on,

I'd find his shoulders stamped with the traditional stars of his organization.

I saw what Adrik was willing to do to save his uncle. He's loyal.

There's much to admire in Adrik Petrov. He's calculated, intelligent. He doesn't fail to notice things; he doesn't guess wrong. That's how you become a legend: consistency.

I'm almost intimidated.

And I'm sure as fuck attracted to him.

Every time he shifts in his seat, I catch a waft of his cologne, mixed with his own feral scent. It makes my stomach clench up in a knot.

I've never felt this kind of arousal toward a man.

Men are inherently flawed. They have so many weaknesses— overcome by ruthlessness and brute power.

There are exceptions. My father is an exception. My brother, my cousins. You'd think with all these good examples, I'd have a positive view of men. But I'm talking about the mass of men, the balance of them. It's a simple equation: men have the power. If men were good, the world would be good.

"What's running around in that head?" Adrik asks me.

He's examining me like one of those puzzles you have to turn over and over to find the right angle of attack.

"I was wondering if you wanted dessert."

"I don't eat sweets."

"I bet you don't."

Adrik gives a shrug of his shoulders, no doubt intended to shift the slabs of muscle beneath his tight black T-shirt.

"I don't want to overeat. In case I need to exert myself later."

Unlike the waiter, his eyes stay fixed on mine—no crude up and down over my body. But the hunger is all over his face. He wants me.

I'll admit—I'm tempted too.

Adrik and that Ducati sitting outside have a lot in common.

Both exotic and powerful, with enough octane to blast me into space. A ride like no other.

"Let's get out of here," I say, no longer interested in my steak.

Like Adrik, I don't want anything weighing me down.

I stand up from the table, the cool ocean breeze lifting the hem of my skirt, dancing it around my thighs.

This time, Adrik can't help looking.

While he's distracted, I take a quick glance over the outline of his jeans. I see plenty to catch my interest but not what I'm looking for.

"It's getting cold," I say.

The sun has long since sunk below the ocean, plunging Old Town into a deep, purplish twilight. The lamps along the sea wall glow like a hundred golden globes strung on a long, thin wire.

Adrik lifts his jacket off the back of his chair, throwing it over my shoulders. Its weight surprises me. I'm enveloped in the rich, wild scent of him, mingled with gasoline fumes from his bike. Like the gasoline, Adrik's aroma carries a wicked edge: head-spinning, heart-racing, incendiary.

I slip my hands in the pockets of his jacket, searching.

My fingertips find only air.

"Where are we headed now?" I ask Adrik.

"Culture Club. Have you been there?"

I nod.

Before I boarded the ship to Kingmakers, I spent my last night in Dubrovnik dancing at Culture Club until four in the morning.

Adrik throws down cash on the table, not waiting for our server to return.

I stride ahead of him, down the stairs, out to the courtyard where the strings of lights suspended over the cobblestones glitter off the windshields of the many expensive cars parked by the valets and the long berth of bikes and mopeds capped by the Ducati that outshines them all.

Dangling from the ignition, I spy what I was looking for.

Motherfucker left the keys in it. Fucking *tempting* someone to try to handle this bike.

I hear Adrik's heavy tread behind me.

Turning, I say, "You just leave the keys?"

Adrik smirks. "I'd like to see someone try to steal that bike."

He's not wrong.

There's a saying for the young bucks who think they're going to hop on the biggest engine they can find: *too much bike.*

You have to practice on the old mare before you can ride the bronco.

If this particular bronco bucks you off, you'll be nothing but a smear on the pavement.

I saunter over to the bike, running my fingertip lightly down the frame.

Adrik watches me, hands in his pockets, chin upraised.

I throw him a flirtatious look. "You're not worried someone's gonna see this gorgeous, gleaming piece of machinery glowing in the moonlight and feel an irresistible urge to swing her leg over the seat?"

I do exactly that, straddling the plush leather of the bike, skirt riding all the way up on my thighs.

Tossing my hair back over my shoulder, I settle my hips in place on the seat, leaning forward, arching my back, really letting him see how much I'm enjoying mounting this monster.

Adrik knows exactly what I'm doing. He can't keep the grin off his face. He loves that I'm shameless.

"You like the way that feels?" he growls.

"Almost," I say, leaning forward and twisting the keys.

The engine roars to life, instantly awake, instantly warming.

"Ahhh," I sigh. "Much better."

The vibration drums through my bones. I press against it until every cell in my body thrums at the same frequency. I'm perfectly in tune, a note suspended in the air.

I sit up, silhouetted against the sky, fully aware of how stunning I look to Adrik in this moment—a prize he'll do anything to obtain.

I twist the throttle, revving the engine, smiling at him over my shoulder.

He starts to grin back, so happy he could die.

Until dawning horror wipes the smirk off his face.

I haven't squeezed the clutch yet—haven't even begun to make my move. But Adrik knows exactly what I'm about to do.

He takes a step forward, his expression dark enough to stop a coward's heart dead in their chest.

Low and savage, he whispers, "Sabrina...*don't you fucking do it.*"

I don't even hesitate.

I pull in the clutch and put the bike into gear.

Exhaust fills my mouth, coating my tongue.

I'm tasting it now.

I want it.

I fucking *need* it.

Still, I know better than to roar off like Evel Knievel. I just threw a rope around the neck of a stampeding bull—no need to apply the cattle prod.

Gently, I let out the clutch, easing down the accelerator at half the speed I would usually use.

The engine responds like I blew in a gust of pure octane. The asphalt beneath the back tire seems to melt away into black glass as the wheel fishtails, slick and frictionless. I'm not heavy enough. I'm not holding it down.

I drop my ass as low as I can to counterbalance, the bike surging forward with shocking speed, an animal released from its pen. I thought it would run. It's already at a gallop.

Adrik is sprinting toward me, much too late. The bike tears out of the lot, almost flattening a uniformed valet who has to leap into the bushes to save his skin.

Adrik shouts something after me, his words whipped away by the wind and drowned in the howl of the engine.

With my weight shifted back, the front wheel rears up wild, trying to flip me off its back. I throw myself forward, lying down on it, hugging it with all my might. Determined that no matter what happens, I won't be thrown off.

I've got to get low, cover the whole thing. Not to be pervy, but it really is like fucking someone—someone trying to throw you off with all their might. This particular someone is a hell of a lot stronger than me.

I am *barely* holding it together coming toward the first curve of the mountain.

I take that turn on the widest possible line, and still I'm riding the edge of the cliff, a dizzying drop inches to the right of my wheel. I see the dark glint of the ocean far below me, my foot dangling over air, before I can wrench myself back onto the road.

My heart thunders so fast it's one continuous clench. I'm drunk on terror and the power of this machine.

I'm on the razor's edge, balanced over a thousand different ways to die.

The stars ignite one by one all around me. No streetlamps to drown them, only the single headlight of the bike, glaring ahead like an eye in the darkness.

Clear as a vision, I remember how Adrik handled this bike—like it was trained to his command. Like it was part of him.

He rode this bike with grace.

I'm not Adrik. Not yet.

The Ducati is on fire between my legs, the engine burning hotter and hotter like it's about to explode. Each imperfection in the road sends a ripple of motion through us both. I'm a surfer just barely regaining balance as I rip across the wave.

I'm tamping this beast down through sheer force of will. Actually, that's not true—there's nothing mystical about it. I'm making a thousand calculations a second to maintain a modicum of control. My blood is pure adrenaline, thin and fine as soda pop bubbling through my veins.

This thing is a rocket, and the only way to ride it is to hold on.

Halfway down the mountain, I come to a straightaway long enough that I dare to touch the accelerator again, giving it a light burst of juice. The Ducati roars and surges forward like it was standing still before, throwing me back, my stomach in my throat.

I let out a shriek of pure glee, instantly whipped out of my mouth.

I've never hit g-force like this.

It's addicting. Even as I slow for the next turn, I already want more.

I spare one second's thought for poor Adrik Petrov, left standing in the courtyard of the restaurant.

I wonder if he's found a ride yet.

CHAPTER 4
ADRIK

I NEED TO ADJUST MY CALCULATIONS WITH THIS WOMAN.

I keep looking for boundaries. I don't think she has any.

Which means the possibilities are limitless.

I grin to myself, glad to know this little excursion won't be a waste. Sabrina is just what I hoped.

She's clever and tricky, with balls of steel. There's not a man in Moscow who would steal a pen from me, let alone my fucking bike.

But she's no good to me dead.

Sabrina seems determined to ride the divide between wild and utterly insane. One push, and she could plummet into the abyss. I don't know if I can hold her steady.

Whether I can or not, one thing is certain: I've got her number now. She won't surprise me again.

I walk over to her bike, not hurrying, because I'll catch her easily, even on this piece of shit Kawasaki.

The way she fishtailed out of here, there's no way she even made it out of that first turn. I'm going to have to ride down there and scrape her up off the pavement, if she's not already over the cliff.

I swing my leg over the Ninja's seat, planning to reignite the engine hot-wired by that little kleptomaniac.

When I flick the switch, nothing happens.

I yank the wires out of the ignition. They're no longer spliced but cut off short.

She cut the wires the moment she got here.

She was planning to steal my bike the whole damn dinner.

All the time we were laughing and talking, drinking that cotton candy wine and eating those eighty-dollar steaks, she was fantasizing about flying down the mountain on my Ducati.

I've never been fooled by a woman. Sabrina Gallo has done it to me three times in one night.

I don't know whether to congratulate her or tie her up and throw her in my trunk.

———

Twenty-two minutes later, I roll up next to Sabrina at the red light at the bottom of Srd Hill.

Her arms are shaking, sweat streaming down her face, her hair in ropes, and her tattered schoolgirl uniform more gray than any of its former colors.

Her body looks like it was made for that bike. Her expression tells me the bike was made for her.

Eyes shining like silver, her chest rises and falls with hectic happiness.

"I'm never giving it back," she pants.

Steam rises off my shoulders in the cold night air. Taking a man's bike is one thing. Stealing his jacket along with it is pure evil.

"I ought to put you over my knee and whip your fucking ass," I tell her.

She grins, utterly unrepentant, twisting her wrist, revving the engine of the bike as a deliberate provocation. "You'll have to catch me first."

The rickety Honda I'm riding coughs and sputters next to the low purr of the Ducati.

Sabrina eyes my bike, unable to contain her glee.

"Where'd you get that thing?"

Barely reining in my urge to throttle her, I hiss, "I had to fucking buy it."

Her lips split into a smile so irresistible that I can't help but enjoy it, even when it's at my expense.

"How much did you pay for it?"

"Seven thousand dollars, you fucking asshole."

She can't stop laughing. "For that piece of shit?"

"I wasn't negotiating. I was trying to catch you before you incinerated yourself."

She shrugs, remarking, "For seven thousand dollars, I would have bought the BMW. Or at least the Yamaha."

"It wasn't a fucking bazaar!" I explode. "I had to take what I could get."

Sabrina looks me up and down, eyebrow cocked. "Huh. Well, if that means you only have three thousand left in your pocket, I guess we're not gonna have the kind of night I thought we'd have."

The. Fucking. Audacity.

I shake my head at her, letting her think what she wants to think. I'm not the kind of bitch who pulls out his bankroll.

The cross light turns yellow.

With moments until we see our green, I jerk my head at the girl still mounted proudly on my bike.

"Alright. Let's see what you got."

I gave her permission, but Sabrina isn't waiting for it. She's already crouched low over the handlebars, staring forward, a cat with its eye on the bird.

The light goes green, and she pounces.

This time, she's ready for the power of the clutch. She holds it tight so it can't pop back, turning her wrist for a smooth, steady increase in speed.

Barely, just barely, she manages to hold the back end steady as she pulls away at 70 percent speed, with only a tiny wobble of the back tire.

Not perfect. But pretty fucking impressive. She's a fast learner.

I hang back so I can watch her ride.

I'm not racing anymore…just admiring.

I pull up to the Culture Club one minute behind Sabrina. The Ducati is still blazing, almost panting as it rests on its stand, the engine giving off light ticks as it slowly calms. The keys dangle from the ignition.

Sabrina has already disappeared inside, neatly hopping the line that snakes down the massive stone staircase. I pass the bouncer a folded $100 bill to do the same.

I assume she's headed to the bathrooms to clean up. I wash my own face and hands, then dunk my head under the faucet to get all the dust out of my hair.

My hair looks almost the same wet or dry—thick and black as fur, springing up in unruly directions. I shake it out, spattering the mirror with water droplets.

It takes Sabrina longer to emerge. I wait under the stone archway leading to the dance floor, the show from the DJ booth sending patterns of shadow and light shooting across the opposite wall, tinting the white stone violet.

Sabrina steps out of the bathroom like Venus rising from the sea: hair brushed to a glossy sheen, skin washed and glowing like amber, skintight dress hugging curves a surgeon couldn't dream of creating. She's traded her sneakers for six-inch heels and lined her eyes with smoky kohl.

Whatever she brought in that little backpack is nothing less than transformative; she looks like she flew in here on a private jet instead of riding a rocket.

I guess she cares after all.

Heads turn in her direction, men and women alike staring with their mouths open.

I have the distinct pleasure of witnessing their disappointment as Sabrina strides up to me instead.

"You ready to party?" she says.

"Who am I partying with? This can't be the girl who just stole my bike."

Sabrina shrugs. "Why be one thing when you can be everything?"

When you can manipulate reality, life is a game.

I know this game. I play it all the time. I've just never played it with anyone else.

"I can't get used to you," I tell her. "Every time I see you, it's a slap in the face."

Sabrina smiles. "You like getting slapped?"

I bring my hand down hard on her ass, giving it a sharp smack. Her ass is full and firm beneath my palm, the impact rippling across her flesh.

"Not as much as I like doing the slapping."

Sabrina doesn't flinch. She looks up into my face, softly saying, "Then I guess we'll see who hits the hardest."

I pull her onto the dance floor.

The pounding bass bounces off stone walls so thick that the club stays cool as a refrigerator, even in the density of bodies pressing in from all sides. Streams of light shoot off in all directions from the DJ booth, cutting across the dance floor, illuminating Sabrina in vivid bursts of violet and blue.

She raises her hands overhead, showing off her sinuous length. She writhes like a snake, a cobra under the hypnotist's charm, swaying to the music.

I press against her, her back against my chest, our hips moving together. I run my hands down her sides, feeling those outrageous curves, feeling the heat radiating out of her body into mine.

The music pounds harder and harder. Sabrina dances faster, full of wild energy, a star that blazes bright in the sky, believing it will never burn out. She holds nothing back, saves no energy for later.

We dance until we're sweating all over, pressed together down every inch of our frames, moving as one.

The bartenders line up a hundred shot glasses down the length of the bar, setting them ablaze with a roar of heat.

"You want a drink?" I ask Sabrina.

"I want several drinks."

We push our way over to the bar. Sabrina takes two shot glasses. Instead of passing one to me, she tosses the first down her throat, then the second, wiping her mouth on the back of her hand.

I grab my own drink, swallowing the liquor that burns all the way down my throat as if it were still aflame.

Then I seize Sabrina, gripping a handful of her hair and yanking her toward me, kissing her ferociously, tasting the liquor in her mouth.

Her lips are full and lush beneath mine. She doesn't shrink beneath the kiss but opens her mouth, taking my tongue all the way inside.

I love the way she leans into me. I want her, and she wants more.

When we break apart, she says, "Gimme another shot."

I motion to the bartender.

Sabrina is looking in the opposite direction at the two girls standing on a raised platform at the corner of the bar, dressed in chaps and fringed bras, their liquor bottles in holsters on their hips.

The taller of the two, a redhead with a nose piercing and a tattoo of a bison skull on her thigh, crooks a finger at Sabrina, motioning her closer. She crouches down. Sabrina bends backward over the girl's knee, the back of her neck resting against the tattoo. The girl pours the shot directly into Sabrina's mouth, then passes a slice of lime from her lips to Sabrina's.

Sabrina whispers something in the redhead's ear while she slips a folded bill into the girl's bikini top.

When Sabrina returns, she's flushed and giddy, her lips swollen as she sucks on the lime.

"You like that?" I ask her.

"Who wouldn't?" Sabrina casts an appreciative look back at the redhead.

"Have you been to the private rooms upstairs?"

"No." She glances toward the back staircase, blocked by two bouncers and a velvet rope. "What's up there?"

"The best part of the club."

Taking her hand, I pull her toward the staircase.

I peel a thick wad of bills off my roll, passing a couple grand to the bouncer, saying, "We need a table and bottle service."

The bouncer unhooks the rope to let us pass.

"Upstairs and to the right," he grunts.

Sabrina follows me up, all eyes and ears, looking everywhere at once.

Turquoise light shimmers across the domed ceiling overhead, as if we've plunged underwater.

Up here, the private tables are surrounded by high-backed booths. Each booth faces a shower, enclosed in glass, in which dancers undulate beneath the pounding spray.

"Which table?" I say to Sabrina.

What I really mean is *which girl?*

Sabrina examines her choices before pointing. "That one."

We sit at the table facing a blond girl in a white bikini, the straps of her bathing suit wrapped around her waist, crisscrossing her body. The girl's hair is pulled up in a high ponytail, her sharp cheekbones and narrow green eyes giving her an almost alien appearance.

I put my arm around Sabrina's shoulders, watching her watch the girl dance.

The pane separating us is tinted a smoky gray, the transparent box filled with steam, but the girl can see us just like we can see her. She leans against the glass wall, letting the shower pour down on her breasts, the white material of her bikini top turning translucent as it soaks through. She looks over at Sabrina, biting her lip.

Sabrina's cheeks flush. Her hand tightens on my thigh.

"Is she your type?" I murmur in Sabrina's ear.

"My type is hot."

"And is that hot to you?"

Sabrina laughs. "What do you think?"

Leaning over so my lips are right against her ear, I growl, "I think I'd love to watch you peel that bikini off her body."

Concealed by the table, I slide my hand up Sabrina's thigh. I meet the hem of her dress and keep going, up to the heat and warmth of the furnace between her thighs. My fingertips find her pussy lips. Sabrina isn't wearing any underwear.

She shivers when I touch her. Her eyes meet mine, and she licks her lips. Then she turns back to the girl, spreading her thighs an inch wider to give me more space.

Holding Sabrina's gaze, the blond reaches up and unfastens the tie behind her neck. Slowly, languorously, she lowers the bikini top, revealing a pair of magnificent breasts with pale pink nipples. She shakes her tits lightly, letting them sway and then settle back into place.

Sabrina is hypnotized.

I slide my fingers up and down the cleft of her pussy lips. She's fucking soaked.

I slip one finger inside her. Sabrina groans, her eyes locked on the girl. The blond presses her palms against the glass, running her tongue through the condensation in one long lick.

With my arm around Sabrina's shoulders, my right hand hangs above her breast. I let my fingertips brush against the material of her dress. Sabrina's nipple stiffens, her chest rising and falling as if she's running.

I trace the outline of her nipple with my middle finger, watching as it stands upright in a hard point, straining against the tight black dress. Sabrina breathes faster and faster, almost panting.

I caress her breast, pulling and squeezing on her nipple through the dress. Sabrina arches her back, moaning softly.

The blond dances directly against the glass, swaying her hips, watching us. She runs her hands over her breasts, lifting and dropping them, pinching her nipples in imitation of what I'm doing to Sabrina.

Sabrina can't tear her eyes off the girl. She darts a few quick looks in my direction, cheeks burning, embarrassed that I'm seeing her in this state. She can't hide her arousal. She knows I can see it. She knows how vulnerable it makes her.

Sure enough, she doesn't even flinch as I yank down the front of her dress, exposing her breasts to the blond. All she can do is let out a sigh of longing, fingers digging into my thigh.

I feel like I just uncovered a golden idol. I'm blinded by brightness.

Sabrina's breasts are fucking spectacular. She's all-natural, brown as the other girl is pale, her nipples dark as chocolate. I want to attack her like a wild animal, I want to lick and suck on every part of her. But I restrain myself, running my fingertips over her nipples light and teasing, flicking them into hard points without giving her the relief she craves.

Sabrina writhes against the plush seat of the booth, biting her lip, looking back and forth from me to the blond.

"You want to fuck her?" I whisper in her ear, pushing two fingers inside her.

"*Ughhh,*" Sabrina moans, her eyes rolling back.

"Answer me."

"Maybe," she hisses, stubborn as ever.

"Take her home, then."

Sabrina lifts her chin, giving me a haughty look.

"If I take that girl home, it's to fuck her the way I want, not to put on a show for you."

I pinch Sabrina's nipple hard, making her gasp.

"One thing you need to learn about me...I make everything better. If you want to fuck that girl and you bring me along, you're gonna have the best night of your life."

I slide my thumb across her clit, up and down, with just the right pressure to bring her up to the edge, to make her clamp her thighs around my hand and press desperately against me.

Her breath comes in ragged gasps. She's dying for more.

Still Sabrina hesitates, glancing between me and the blond. I know she wants that girl, and I know she wants me too. But she's torn.

"You've never had a threesome?" I ask her.

Sabrina narrows her eyes at me, annoyed that I guessed right.

"I never wanted to."

"You like women?"

"Yes."

"And you like men?"

"Occasionally."

"Then what are you waiting for?"

Sabrina swallows, her throat tightening.

I pull her against my side, murmuring in her ear, "All I want to do is give you what you want."

She looks up at me, our faces inches apart.

"I want it all."

My arm tightens around her.

"Go and get it, then."

I see the decision on her face before she speaks.

"Alright. I'll ask her."

I laugh, watching the blond press against the glass like a puppy at the pound.

"I think she's already saying yes."

An hour later, when the blond has finished her shift in the showers and I've sent her a hefty tip via the bouncers, she emerges from the staff room, dressed in a pale-blue sheath and sky-high heels, her hair loose down her back, large diamond hoops dangling from her ears.

She perches herself on a stool over by the bar, crossing her legs in front of her, casting a furtive glance in our direction as she orders her drink.

"You want me to pick her up for you?" I tease Sabrina.

"The day I need a wingman is the day I throw myself off a cliff," she snarls.

"Perfect. I'll meet you out front with the car."

Sabrina pauses, casting a suspicious glance back over her shoulder. "What car? We rode here on bikes."

I shake my head. "When will you stop underestimating me? I've had four months to plan this date. Of course I have a car."

A smile plays over her lips. She likes surprises.

"Alright then. See you in a minute."

I head toward the stairs, pausing halfway down so I can watch Sabrina work.

She slides onto the stool next to the blond, raising a finger to the bartender to order a drink of her own.

Then she leans on her elbow, frankly looking the blond up and down, paying some compliment that makes the girl laugh, pink in her cheeks.

I'm hit with a rush of heat, watching Sabrina radiate her raw sexual energy at full blast.

Everything Sabrina does is charged—each lift of her eyebrow, each flash of her teeth, the way she sits, the way she stands, the way she crosses her legs. Everything about her is hot as hell, and that's when she's not even trying.

Now I'm watching her exert herself, bringing all her powers to play. It's fucking mesmerizing.

She takes her drink from the bartender, plucking the stick of olives from her martini and sliding one in her mouth. She chews slowly, then dips the olives back into the gin before removing another with her teeth.

Sabrina has the quality certain actors possess, compelling you to watch her every move. She can sexualize even the simplest of actions.

The blond can hardly meet her eye. She's nervous now, with no glass wall between them. She's blushing, fidgeting on her stool.

Sabrina murmurs something, holding out her drink for the girl to take a sip. Obediently, the blond bends her head and drinks from Sabrina's glass. When a little vodka clings to her lower lip, Sabrina catches it with the ball of her thumb. Their faces are close together, their mouths inches apart.

Sabrina licks the vodka off her thumb, slowly, sensuously, holding the girl's gaze. She lowers her hand, letting it rest on the blond's bare thigh.

The women mirror each other down the length of their bodies, leaning in close, eyes locked. I can't hear what they're saying, but from the expression on Sabrina's face, it's something naughty.

The blond blushes harder than ever, giggling. She nods.

I head down the stairs, smiling to myself.

CHAPTER 5
SABRINA

THE DANCER'S NAME IS KYLIE, AND SHE'S FROM AUSTRALIA. SHE'S been working in clubs across Europe, in Ibiza at first, then Cannes, now Dubrovnik.

"I'll work through the summer, then head home in the fall." She downs the last of her drink. "Well, it won't be fall in Melbourne. I guess I'll have two summers in a row."

I order us another round for the road, since Adrik will be the one driving.

"It's on me," I tell Kylie as she reaches for her purse.

"My god, you're gorgeous," Kylie remarks. "You should be a model. I tried when I came to Spain, but I wasn't tall enough."

"You look pretty fucking perfect to me," I tell her.

Kylie blushes, pleased and already a little tipsy. I don't think I was the first person to buy her a drink tonight.

"That guy you were with—"

"Adrik."

"Is he your boyfriend?"

"It's our first date."

Kylie laughs. "You're a wild one."

"You have no idea."

The music thuds around us. I'm enveloped in her sweet floral scent.

"What's that perfume?"

"Very Irresistible."

"It certainly is."

She giggles, covering her mouth with her hand. Her teeth are crooked, the incisors overlapping the ones in front. I think it's adorable.

I lean forward.

"Why don't you come home with me so I can see if you taste as good as you smell?"

Kylie blushes redder than ever. "Is your hotel close by?" she murmurs.

"Fuck if I know."

Seizing her by the hand, I pull her to her feet. Her heels are even taller than mine, putting us at almost the same height. The blue dress clings to her body. All I can think is how badly I want to uncover those soft breasts again and press them against mine.

"Come on," I say, pulling her toward the stairs.

Adrik is already waiting when we exit the club, pulled up to the curb in a vintage Alfa Romeo, black with cream interior.

I stare at the car, more startled than impressed.

The '65 Alfa Romeo Giulia Spider is one of my all-time favorite cars. My father used to have one.

I don't believe for a second this is a coincidence. Adrik did his homework.

The man has gone all-out for our date. I brought an outfit in a backpack—he shipped two vehicles halfway around the world. I researched the Petrovs, Adrik did his research on *me*.

I'm beginning to realize that I'm in way over my head.

Adrik leans his elbow on the doorframe, window rolled down.

"Get in," he orders.

Kylie jumps to attention like she's been spanked, hurrying over to the car and sliding in the back seat.

I follow at a slower pace, my eyes running down the sleek lines of the car.

"I thought you'd like it," Adrik says, rightfully smug.

He keeps dangling toy after toy in front of me. If this is the bait, then where's the trap?

I could turn around and walk away right now. Maybe I should.

But Kylie is already in the back seat, looking up at me, that blue dress riding up on her thighs, those perfect tits stretching the limits of modern textiles.

Adrik fills the whole of the front seat, drumming his fingers impatiently on the wheel, his masculine scent drowning out Kylie's perfume.

I want a dozen different things in this moment, and I want them desperately. My heart races, my chest tight, an anxious throbbing in my guts.

My own words echo in my head: *I want it all.*

Climbing into the back seat beside Kylie, I say, "Let's go."

CHAPTER 6
ADRIK

I DRIVE DOWN IZA GRADA TOWARD THE KAZBEK, WHERE I'VE booked the most expensive of the thirteen unique rooms within the boutique hotel.

I planned to come back here with Sabrina alone, but I can't say I'm disappointed with the turn the night is taking.

I want Sabrina at maximum arousal, and I don't give a fuck what's turning her on: it could be me, the car, or the girl. I don't give a shit, so long as I have her at level 1000.

I watch in the rearview mirror as she starts kissing the Australian dancer. Sabrina has the fullest lips I've ever touched. Watching them entwine with lips almost as full, almost as soft, watching delicate pink tongues lapping at each other and slim, feminine hands running over skin smooth as butter, curves like a Botticelli painting...I've never seen anything so right.

They kiss for a long time, longer than a man would have patience for. Their soft moans and giggles sound like every cheerleaders' locker room, every slumber party of male fantasy.

Sabrina pulls down the front of Kylie's dress, taking her breast in her mouth. Kylie leans against the car door, head thrown back, moaning as she thrusts her hands into Sabrina's thick, dark hair, pressing Sabrina's face against her chest.

Neither of the girls are buckled. Nor am I. If we crash, we're all going down in flames together.

What a way to die, watching the hottest thing I've ever seen unfold behind me in little snippets via the mirror.

Sabrina is aggressive, and she knows what she's doing. She's putting on a master class back there, alternately licking and sucking on Kylie's neck, playing with her breasts, all while sliding her smooth thigh between Kylie's so she can grind her pussy against Sabrina's leg.

When she has the blond panting and moaning, Sabrina slides down the leather seat, putting her head under Kylie's skirt, pulling her underwear to the side, licking that soaking pussy until Kylie makes frantic whimpering sounds, a steady, "Huh, huh, huh, huh, huh," that melts into a long, drawn-out, "*Uhhhhhhhhhhh!*" as she starts to come.

She's got a quick trigger, or Sabrina has a talented tongue.

The moans of the two girls is a symphony in the back seat. It draws me back irresistibly until I'm hardly sparing a glance for the road.

The long, winding highway is dimly lit. I really should pay attention to the cars that fly by with no respect for the speed limit, but there's no fucking way I can tear my eyes off what's happening directly behind me.

The sweet scent of the girls' perfume fills the car, as does the even sweeter scent of their arousal.

Sabrina's eyes flash up, meeting mine in the mirror. She gives me a wicked smile, her lips swollen, her mouth shining with Kylie's wetness.

She leans between the two front seats, seizing me by the face and kissing me so I can taste Kylie's pussy in her mouth.

She holds me in place, kissing me wildly, while the car whips through the night.

I grab her with my right hand, growling in her ear, "You taste like a slut."

"And you fucking love it." Sabrina swipes her tongue in one long lick up the side of my neck, seizing my earlobe between her teeth and biting down hard.

I stomp the accelerator, more motivated to get to this fucking hotel than I've ever been to arrive anywhere.

I'm going to rip that dress off Sabrina and throw her down on the bed hard enough to leave a dent in the mattress.

Sabrina's still nibbling on the side of my neck like she did to Kylie. She's running her tongue around the rim of my ear, then plunging it inside. She's an animal, a cat in heat, more feral by the minute.

Kylie gets on her knees behind Sabrina, pulling her skirt up around her waist. I already know Sabrina isn't wearing underwear. Kylie grips Sabrina by the hips and starts eating her pussy from behind.

Sabrina lets out a moan right into my ear, so sensual and aching that goose bumps erupt across every inch of my skin. My cock is hard enough to punch through cement. I've got half a mind to pull over right now and leap over the seat. I'd do it if the hotel were even a mile farther away.

But I need a private room and a bed and a shit ton of drinks to enact my plans. Sabrina is going to scream my name over and over and over until she forgets how to say any other word.

She ran me ragged tonight, chasing her all over this goddamn city. Now she's going to pay for every arrogant look, every rowdy remark, every minute she tried to defy me.

She's going to learn the difference between what she wants and what she needs.

I don't give a shit about this blond except as an accessory. I'll use her to give Sabrina an experience like none she's had before. Sabrina thinks she can get whatever she wants. I'll show her that I can give her more.

After what feels like an eternity, we pull up to the wrought-iron gates of the sprawling baroque hotel.

The Kazbek was built in 1573 as a summer residence for nobility. Ivy swarms the ancient stone walls, the ranks of windows positioned to overlook the private beach. Thickets of citrus trees perfume the air, and cascades of hot pink bougainvillea drop their petals in a carpet on the cobblestones.

I toss the keys to the valet, who can only stare open-mouthed as Sabrina and Kylie tumble out of the back seat, flushed and disheveled, their arms around each other's waists.

I already checked in this morning, the brass key to our suite safe in my pocket.

I lead the girls up the grand staircase to the upper level, then down the long hallway to our room.

Kylie looks around in wonder. "This is a hotel? It looks like a castle."

"Everything looks like a castle in this city," Sabrina laughs. "I don't think they've built anything new in five hundred years."

"But they know how to decorate," I say, throwing open the double doors.

The sumptuous suite is adorned in dark wood, burgundy, and pale gold, the drapes falling twenty feet from the exposed beams of the ceiling all the way to the floor. A massive fireplace takes up the majority of the far wall, with a sitting room and a full bar in between the entryway and the master suite. The bedroom leads out to a private deck with an infinity pool that seems to connect to the endless expanse of ocean beyond.

It's all gorgeous, but at this moment, I have eyes for one thing only: Sabrina Gallo.

"Get those fucking clothes off your body," I order, ready to tear her dress to shreds if she hesitates.

"You want to watch me take my clothes off?" Sabrina teases me, one black brow raised like a question mark.

"*I* do," Kylie assures her.

Sabrina grabs a chair and drags it into the center of the room.

"You sit here," she says to Kylie. Then to me, "Pour us a drink, and I'll get some music playing."

She saunters over to the stereo system, scrolling through her phone for a playlist. She's moving deliberately slowly, throwing me a saucy glance over her shoulder.

Everything is a game to her. A test to see how far she can push me before I snap.

I pour the drinks impatiently, shoveling ice into the glasses, a double shot of Belvedere for each of us, a splash of soda and lime for the girls, straight up for me. Vodka needs no augmentation—it goes down easy as water as long as it's chilled.

I press the drink into Sabrina's palm, gripping her hip with my free hand, letting my fingers sink into her flesh to let her know I'm displeased that she's keeping me waiting.

Sabrina drains her glass in three gulps, setting it down hard on the windowsill.

Then she starts the music.

She turns her attention on Kylie, who freezes in place on the chair, caught in Sabrina's gaze.

When Sabrina fixes you with that steely stare, your heart rate triples. She's not even looking at me, and I'm still baking in reflected heat.

I lean up against the wall, sipping my vodka, watching Sabrina sway to the music.

She prowls around the chair, never taking her eyes off Kylie, letting her fingertips trail along the seat back. As she comes around the front again, she whips her hair so the wild dark waves flow like a waterfall down her back, dropping to the carpet, crawling over on hands and knees.

There's nothing subservient about this movement. Sabrina's stalking like a tiger. Kylie sits back in the chair, breathing heavily, her eyes fixed on Sabrina's face.

I can see Sabrina's ass cheeks exposed beneath the short skirt and the marquise shape of her neat, little pussy glistening in the lamplight. Like her nipples, her pussy is darker than her skin, which strikes me as undeniably womanly and erotic, especially when contrasted with the baby-pink paleness of the blond in the chair.

Sabrina reaches Kylie. She sits back on her haunches, pushing up Kylie's skirt. She seizes the band of Kylie's thong in her teeth and pulls it down the length of her legs, spitting it aside.

Then she stands once more, pulling her own dress overhead, baring her nude body.

My jaw drops.

I've imagined Sabrina naked a thousand times.

Never once did I get it right.

I could never dream up a body like hers. Curves like a Stradivarius, skin glowing like bronze, every millimeter of her designed with lust in mind.

This is no angel fallen from heaven; the devil made Sabrina, and he knew what he was doing.

Sabrina sits down on Kylie's lap, grinding her ass against the other girl. She lifts Kylie's hands and places them on her breasts like she's a stripper at a club giving permission to a john.

Kylie touches her with reverence. She runs her hands over smooth brown skin that gleams like silk, down to Sabrina's tight waist, and then to those exaggerated hips that make me want to throw Sabrina over the bed and mount her like an animal.

I'm storing up every second of this, because I know I'm going to run it through my head over and over and over again.

My mouth is salivating, my balls boiling.

Sabrina reaches down between her legs and finds Kylie's pussy. She rubs the shell-pink pussy as if it were her own, her delicate fingertips drawing exquisite pants and moans from the other girl.

I watch exactly how she touches the other girl so I can imitate it later. I watch how lightly she dances her fingertips over the exposed clit, how slowly and sensually she builds the waves of pleasure, how she varies her touch, never staying too long in one place.

The sounds she draws out of Kylie are insanely erotic. She has complete control of the other girl. Kylie's head is thrown back, her eyes half-closed, lids fluttering. The moans coming out of her are low and guttural, shooting up into high whimpers and pleading.

"*Oh yes, baby. Yes, baby, pleeeeease.... Ohhh, exactly like that...*"

Kylie cups Sabrina's breasts in her hands, pulling on her nipples. Sabrina leans her head back against Kylie's shoulder, eyes closed in ecstasy, grinding with sinuous grace.

The doubling effect of two beautiful women stacked on each other is warping my mind. Sabrina looks like some arcane deity, four arms and four legs, glowing like a goddess. I want to fall on my knees and worship her.

I cross the space between us in two steps, dropping in front of her and burying my face in that perfect pussy. Her taste and scent fill my mouth, rich and intoxicating.

Sabrina lets out a long groan, arching her back so her breasts press harder against Kylie's palms.

I slip my fingers inside Kylie, using my hand on one girl and my mouth on the other. I can hear them moaning together, Kylie soft and light, Sabrina low and husky.

I lick Sabrina's pussy in slow, measured strokes, softly lapping at her clit. Building her pleasure in layers, like a pearl. Listening for each gasp and groan, finding exactly what she likes and then hitting it again and again and again.

"*Ahhh!*" Sabrina gasps. "Don't stop!"

I wouldn't stop if this whole hotel were burning down around us. I'm not stopping till she fucking explodes.

Sabrina starts shaking like she's hooked up to a generator. Thrusting both hands into my hair, she presses my face against her pussy, grinding against my tongue, crying out, "*Ohhhhhh my fucking god!*"

I keep licking until she lets go of me, until she slumps back against Kylie, limp and weak.

I scoop her up, carrying her over to the bed and throwing her down on top of it.

Then I grab Kylie and lift her out of the chair, setting her down directly on top of Sabrina.

Kylie pulls her dress over her head so she's naked too. I brought her to the edge with my fingers, but I was focused on Sabrina, and now she's frantic, grinding against Sabrina, sliding between Sabrina's thighs so she can scissor.

Lying on her back, Sabrina spreads her legs wider so Kylie can slot their pussies tighter together. Kylie kneels on top of her, facing sideways, rolling her hips in a rocking motion, riding Sabrina like a saddle.

The girls are so aroused that they gasp at every touch of skin. They roll together, shifting the angle of their hips, finding just the right spot and sliding against each other, eyes rolled back at the delicate friction of silk against silk.

Sabrina is voracious. Even though she just came, she's already trying for another, bucking her hips against Kylie, biting the edge of her lip, her eyes narrowed in focus.

I want her focused on *me*.

Coming around to her head, I stand next to the bed and unzip my jeans, letting my cock spring free. It stands straight out from my body, dark and congested with blood, veins swollen and head throbbing.

I'm so hard that I might need medical attention. It looks like I took a fistful of Viagra.

Sabrina's the Viagra. I've never seen anything so gorgeous or so erotic. Kylie wants to fuck her. I want to fuck her. It's a competition to see who can get our hands all over her quicker.

I've been waiting too long.

I smack my cock against Sabrina's cheek to get her attention.

"Get to work," I order.

Sabrina's eyes flash up at me. Her lips part, showing a glint of teeth.

The voice of warning tells me to be careful—this little psychopath might just take a bite out of me.

But the drive to slide my cock between those pillowy lips is irresistible. I push my cock into her mouth.

I sink into pure, liquid heaven. My eyes roll back in my head, my knees buckling beneath me.

Sabrina's mouth is warm and swollen. She sucks cock the way she kisses—like she's starving. It's like she's trying to suck the come out of me from the moment her lips close around the head.

It feels way too fucking good.

My balls contract, and I feel a rush of pleasure, too much too soon. I have to rip my cock out of her mouth and squeeze the head hard in my hand to stop from coming.

Sabrina gives a wicked laugh, which morphs into a moan as Kylie presses against her.

I shove my cock back in her mouth. The moan vibrates around my cock, sending shivers up and down my spine.

Kylie grinds against Sabrina. With each roll of her hips, I thrust my cock deeper into Sabrina's mouth. We're fucking her from both sides, sharing her, but not generously. We both want as much as we can get.

Kylie is scissoring so hard that it's pushing Sabrina to the edge of the bed, until her head hangs off. Her chin tilts up, letting me push my cock all the way down her throat. I can see the bulge above her Adam's apple every time I thrust.

Kylie is reaching a fever pitch, her soaking pussy sliding against Sabrina's in short, frantic strokes. Her breasts bounce on her chest, her head thrown back and her blond hair—still damp from the shower—trailing down her back. She starts to come, longer than she did in the car, with a drawn-out moan that sounds almost painful.

I push my cock all the way into Sabrina's mouth, holding it there while it twitches with pleasure. I pull it out again, glistening and wet.

Kylie sits up, panting, giving it a hungry look. She leans forward, mouth open.

I glance at Sabrina.

She sits up too, kneeling on the bed next to Kylie, passing my cock to the other girl like she's sharing her favorite lollipop.

Kylie runs her tongue up one side of my cock while Sabrina slides her tongue down the other side. They move their mouths up and down, back and forth, their tongues licking and sliding and lapping from all angles. My cock is on fire between them. I've never seen such a beautiful sight.

The girls meet at the top, kissing and sucking around the head, their tongues entwined, their mouths closing over me from both sides.

They're making out around my cock, treating it like a meal they have to consume to get to each other.

Playfully, they take turns with it, showing each other what they can do.

Kylie closes her mouth over the entirety of my cock, bobbing her head up and down aggressively, showing Sabrina how deep she can take it.

When it's Sabrina's turn, she dances her tongue around the head, swirling it around and around, then licking the underside with the flat of her tongue over and over until I can't help but groan, my knees shaking beneath me.

The girls laugh, determined to torture me, determined to make me blow.

They team up against me, Sabrina sucking the head while Kylie licks the shaft and strokes my balls with her hand. They work together, vigorous and intent. I close my eyes, letting the sensation of their individual hands and mouths blend into one.

The girls swap positions several times.

Even blind, I can tell when Sabrina's mouth envelops the head of my cock. Her lips are so warm and lush that there's no mistaking them.

My cock is aching, throbbing, dying to explode directly into her mouth. I let each wave of pleasure hit me like a blast from a fire hose, refusing to let go, clinging to my last shred of control.

CHAPTER 7
SABRINA

ADRIK PUSHES KYLIE DOWN ON THE BED AND SETS ME ON TOP OF her. He's stronger than both of us put together, so he can lift and move us effortlessly.

Kylie is slim and soft beneath me, her blond hair still smelling slightly of chlorine, her skin fresh and sweet.

By contrast, Adrik is hard as mahogany, aggressive and demanding, salty with sweat.

The combination of masculine and feminine, dominant and delicate, is almost more than I can handle. It's an all-you-can-eat buffet, and I'm gorging myself sick.

I kiss Kylie, her mouth tasting of Adrik's cock, her breasts pressed against mine, her hands light and soft on either side of my face.

Adrik grabs my throat from behind, pulling me upright, growling in my ear, "I know you like pussy. But don't you even try to lie and tell me you don't like cock."

I can feel his erection against the small of my back, burning hot and throbbing hard.

He grips the base of his cock, bending it down, thrusting it inside me from behind.

The sound that comes out of me is no sound I've made before. I'm impaled, filled all the way up in a single stroke.

Adrik releases his grip on my throat, letting me collapse on top of Kylie, but that barely helps. I turn my face against her, nibbling and sucking the side of her neck, letting out helpless moans every time Adrik thrusts into me. I've never seen a cock like his, let alone fucked one. It's stretching and filling and tearing me apart, way too much to handle—if I believed in the concept of "too much."

The combination of Kylie's scent and Adrik's cock is brain-bending. I'm kissing her and fucking him, a woman's lips and a man's cock, the best of both worlds.

Kylie has her legs wrapped around my waist. Each of Adrik's thrusts pushes me against her, grinding me against her clit.

I imagine it's her cock I'm riding. I imagine her and Adrik blended together as one person, everything I like and everything I want in one package.

Then I imagine that I have a cock like Adrik's, that I can fuck a pretty girl as hard and as long as I want. I love giving girls pleasure. I'd love to have another tool to do it.

I imagine I can climax like a man can, exploding everywhere, come pouring out of me...

I start to come in a way I never have before, each stroke of Adrik's cock a mini orgasm, one after another. Every time he thrusts into me, I moan, helplessly limp on top of the other girl, clinging to her, groaning against her neck.

Kylie is flushed deeply pink all over her body, across her chest, down her thighs. Her eyes are glazed, her lids heavy.

"That sounds fun," she whispers in my ear. "You mind if I take a ride on that?"

"Help yourself."

I'm not a jealous person. Sex is recreation as far as I'm concerned, and I'm happy to share.

Besides, Kylie is gorgeous; the thought of her on top of Adrik turns me the fuck on.

Obligingly, Adrik lies down on the bed. Kylie straddles him, lowering herself down on his cock.

"Holy shit," she groans as it slides inside her. "God, you're thick."

Adrik is a specimen, no question. His body is inhumanly hard, with slabs of muscle on his chest, back, and thighs. His legs are powerful, twice as thick as mine. Yet there's a beauty to his proportions, a cleanness to his lines, like a dancer.

Kylie looks slim and willowy on top of him, pale next to his tan. She starts to ride him, her body rolling on his, her lips parted, mouth open. Her waist looks impossibly small with his large hands gripped around it.

I could watch this forever, but Adrik isn't looking at Kylie. His eyes are fixed on me.

"Get over here," he orders, grabbing my wrist and pulling me toward him. He makes me straddle his face.

I'm facing Kylie now, her on Adrik's cock and me on his lips.

She leans forward to kiss me, moaning into my mouth.

Sitting on someone's face can be uncomfortable if you're scared of smothering them. Adrik is too big to worry about that and too indestructible. He wraps his hands around my waist, pulling me harder against his mouth, thrusting his tongue inside me.

His oral is aggressive, the slight stubble on his face providing a friction that rides the line between pleasure and pain. His mouth on my pussy and Kylie's mouth against mine makes me writhe against them both, locked in a triangle of opposites, with me as the fulcrum.

I'm loving the gluttony of this, the outrageous naughtiness. I'm getting everything I like and everything I want. Kylie's sweetness and softness, mixed with Adrik's aggression and heat. Her lovely breasts and his thick cock. I kiss her and kiss her, never wanting this to be over. Never planning to stop.

I start to come without meaning to, without even realizing it's happening. It's hard for me to come from oral, but I can press down on Adrik's tongue as hard as I want. I'm not worried about hurting him. I ride his face exactly how I like it, legs spread wide, each roll of my hips plunging me down into an endless well of pleasure.

The orgasm goes on and on like it's never going to stop. It's so long that I actually think to myself, *Holy shit, it's still fucking going.*

I come back to consciousness, looking at the windows, almost expecting to see morning.

I can hear from Kylie's whimpers that she's building to orgasm too.

I guess I am jealous after all, because I fucking love making her come, and I'm too greedy to let Adrik have all the fun.

Rolling off Adrik, I move around behind Kylie, straddling Adrik's legs, my chest against her back. I cup her breasts in both hands, massaging her tits in time with each stroke as she rides Adrik's cock.

"*Yes, yes, yes!*" she cries, her body undulating like a wave, my fingers tugging and pulling on her nipples, sparking pleasure with every stroke.

I kiss her neck. I murmur filthy shit in her ear.

Adrik has his hands on her hips. He's driving her down hard on his cock, every muscle flexed in his stomach, his chest, his arms. Our eyes meet over Kylie's shoulder. We can't help grinning at each other, because Kylie has passed beyond words. She's babbling in tongues like a Pentecostalist, and we're making her climax together, harder than any she's had before.

She lets out one long scream, her head thrown back against my shoulder, her body arced. Then she collapses sideways on the mattress, panting and sweating, her blond hair plastered to her face.

Adrik seizes me and pulls me on top of him, his cock sliding right into me, soaked from Kylie's pussy.

I'm far from a virgin, and I have a whole collection of toys at home, but I've never felt anything like this cock. It throbs and pulses inside me, warm and thick and alive, relentlessly driving in and out of me.

If I had access to this thing twenty-four seven, I could never keep my hands off it. Like Adrik's bike, I'd do anything for a ride.

I experiment with different speeds, different angles, leaning forward with my hands on his chest, leaning back so his cock rubs that spot inside me on the inner wall. Each stroke is heavenly. I'm floating on pleasure, a river carrying me along to some unknown place. Bright sparks pop in front of my eyes, blue, green, and purple.

Some men just lie there when you're on top. Adrik grabs hold of me and fucks me from the bottom up, following my motion, adding intensity to every stroke.

I ride him harder and harder, sweat running down my body, my tits bouncing on my chest.

Each swell of pleasure is stronger than the one before, waves that roll higher and higher, until I know the next one will break.

I lean forward, grinding into him, looking down into his face.

Adrik looks up at me, hands locked on my hips, teeth bared. His hair is wet as ink, his body glistening. His eyes hold mine, a kind of madness in them: he's going to fuck me till I come or die trying.

A part of me wants to hold back, to refuse to give him what he wants so desperately.

As if he can read my mind, he hisses, "*Give it to me.* You come on that cock *right fucking now.*"

There's no choice about it. The orgasm detonates inside me, as if Adrik had his finger on the trigger. It blasts outward from my belly, exploding through every inch of me, obliterating everything in its path. I lose my sight, my hearing, and my balance. I collapse next to Kylie, falling so far that it feels like I've sunk through the mattress and all the way into the floor.

Time passes, how long I have no idea.

Then, in a dreamy voice, Kylie says, "Fuck, that was fun."

CHAPTER 8
ADRIK

I WAKE UP ON THE BED, NO BLANKETS ON TOP OF ME BECAUSE they're all knotted up in a twisted mess on the floor.

Light streams in from the balcony, slicing across the empty mattress that no longer contains Sabrina or the blond Australian.

I sit up, looking around the empty suite.

I see the pile of wet towels from when we all took a dip in the infinity pool sometime after midnight.

In the living room, dozens of empty dishes scatter across the table from our three a.m. room service. We gorged ourselves on fresh fruit, french fries, bacon sandwiches, and chocolate cake, then piled back in the bed for another round of sex.

Sometime around sunrise, we all fell asleep, curled up in a pile like puppies who played too long.

I don't care that Kylie left. It stings that Sabrina did too.

I thought…I guess I thought we connected last night. Enough that she'd still be here in the morning.

I swing my legs over the side of the bed, a headache throbbing in my temples. The water bottles next to the bed have all been drained.

Fuck.

The disappointment settling on my shoulders is heavy and dull. I'm trying not to let myself feel it, but it's impossible to ignore. My night with Sabrina went far beyond what I'd anticipated. I wasn't ready for it to end.

I'm irritated with myself for falling asleep so hard. I should have heard her get up. I wanted to talk to her.

Our night together is already fading, too intense to be real. The day before me is solid and dreary, the magic disappearing along with Sabrina.

I don't want to get up, but what else is there to do?

The logistics of shipping my car and my bike back home, of paying for the room and booking a flight for myself, seem tedious in the extreme. I sigh, head in my hands, trying not to think about it.

Before I can push myself up from the mattress, I hear the scrape of a key in the lock.

The door swings open. Sabrina backs in, carrying a coffee in each hand, a brown paper bag clenched in her teeth. She sets one coffee down and hands me the other, taking the bag out of her mouth so she can speak.

"I got you cream with no sugar," she says. "Did I guess right?"

"Yeah." I nod. "You did."

"It's a gift." Sabrina grins.

The wave of warmth that washes over me at the sight of her is almost embarrassing. I hadn't realized how low I was feeling until she buoyed me up again.

She's wearing the same black dress from the night before, with my leather jacket thrown over it. The way the jacket hangs down halfway to her knees, the sleeves partly covering her hands, is incredibly endearing. It reminds me how much smaller Sabrina is. She's vulnerable, more than she would want anyone to perceive.

I like the way my jacket looks on her. I like that she chose to wear it again.

"I thought you left," I admit.

Sabrina pauses in the process of opening up the brown paper bag. She looks at me, her expression serious.

"Would you have been disappointed if I did?"

I could play it cool. Shrug or say something callous like, "Your loss." Instead, I answer honestly.

"For the first time ever…yeah. I would be."

She fumbles with the bag, removing a couple of pastries, laying them on a clean napkin on the bed. Color stains her cheeks the same dusty rose of her lips.

"I was just taking Kylie down to her cab. I didn't want her to have to do the walk of shame alone."

Catching her wrist, I pull her toward me.

"There's no walk of shame when you're shameless."

Sabrina laughs. "Not everyone's as evolved as me."

I take her face between my hands and kiss her. Her skin is warm from the morning sunshine, her mouth tasting of coffee and vanilla. We're standing in the wedge of light pouring in through the glass doors. It illuminates the edges of Sabrina's skin, like she's filigreed in gold.

When we break apart, her eyes sweep down my naked body. She lets out a snort of amusement.

"That didn't take much, did it?"

There's no hiding the effect her kiss has on me. My cock juts straight up between us, fully hard and demanding attention.

Sabrina slides her hand softly up and down its length, her fingers light and cool, my cock throbbing against her palm.

"Hm," I grunt. "That feels good."

Sabrina gets that look of mischief I'm already coming to know so well. She keeps running her hand up and down my length, light and teasing, making the head ache each time her fingertips dance over it.

"What feels better?" she says. "This? Or this?"

Dropping to her knees, she runs her tongue all the way from base to tip. She lightly mouths the head, enclosing it within those pillowy lips, flicking at it with her wet, soft tongue.

The groan that wrenches out of me is all the answer she needs.

I'd like to spend the next several hours doing exactly this, but mindful of the activities of the night before, I stop Sabrina, saying, "Let's get in the shower. I need to clean up."

"I'd rather swim," Sabrina says. "It's a gorgeous day. I don't want to be inside."

"You don't have a swimsuit," I point out.

We skinny-dipped last night, but it's full daylight now, and the deck is visible from the beach below.

"Who gives a shit?" Sabrina says.

She slips out of my jacket, laying it carefully over the back of a chair. Then she shimmies out of her dress just as easily, letting it fall in a puddle on the floor.

I don't know if I'll ever get used to the look of her naked. She's got a body like a Maserati, sleek and exotic and expensive.

I stand watching as she pulls open the double doors, striding out to the infinity pool and slipping into the cool blue water without a hint of shyness.

I follow after her, noticing how much louder it is now that the city is awake all around us. I hear the rumble of trucks through the narrow streets, the screech of gulls, and distant shouts from the outdoor market. Below that, the steady rush of the ocean.

Sunlight sparkles across the infinity pool in a thousand diamond points of light. Sabrina dives beneath the surface, her hair floating around her in a dark cloud. When she pops up again, her hair shines like an oil spill down her back, nipples hard and purplish from the cold water.

I drop in next to her, letting the water close over my head. I keep my eyes open, wanting to see how Sabrina looks underwater, that phenomenal body floating and twisting in space.

She's a mermaid cast in bronze, silvery spiderwebs of light flickering across her skin.

Sabrina sinks down beside me, her hair floating up again, twisting around her like tentacles.

She kisses me underwater, bubbles passing between our lips, tickling my face.

We're cut off from Old Town, no sound down here. Only the muffled fluttering of our legs and the thud of my heartbeat in my ears. The sun beats down brilliantly, the water cool. Sabrina's flesh slides beneath my hands, slippery and firm.

When we surface, we're still kissing, hungry as if it's our first time.

I want to fuck her so bad it's like I haven't done it yet. Maybe I haven't, because my attention was divided before. I want it all focused on Sabrina.

I pull her down on my cock, sliding inside her beneath the water, her legs wrapped around my waist, her arms around my neck.

The water slows my pace, makes me fuck her steady and deep, each stroke bobbing her a little in and out of the water, her breasts floating on the surface.

We're weightless together, rotating in the water, the endless view of the ocean swapping positions with the ornate facade of the hotel.

There's no friction between us, both of us slick as seals. It feels good, but it won't be enough to make Sabrina come.

Carrying her over to the steps out of the pool, I sit on the lowest stair, turning Sabrina around so she's sitting on my lap with her back against my chest. I grip my cock and slide it back inside her, parting her legs so her calves are hooked around the outsides of my thighs.

With her thighs spread wide open, her clit is exposed. I reach around with my hand, rubbing her clit with the flat of my fingers, thrusting up inside her so the head of my cock rubs against her from the inside, my hand on the outside.

With my other hand, I pluck and tease her nipples, moving back and forth between her breasts.

Sabrina is trapped in place on top of me, legs spread open, chest exposed. She's a butterfly pinned to a mat, all her beauty on full display for anyone to see. I wish I had a camera set up in front of her.

Her clit is fully exposed, almost too sensitive to touch. She gasps and squirms, but I keep her legs spread wide over mine, my fingers relentlessly stroking that little nub as it gets firmer and warmer, engorging with blood in much the same way as my cock inside her.

Sabrina is panting, rocking her hips in the limited range of motion she can manage.

She reaches back with both hands, cupping the back of my head, thrusting her fingers into my hair, scratching her nails against my scalp. I turn my mouth toward her, sucking on the side of her neck, sucking hard and rough, not giving a fuck if I mark her. I *want* to mark her. I want to leave a bruise that lasts for a month.

With every thrust, I stroke her clit—short, steady rubs that imitate the sensation of her riding on top of me, the way her clit rubs against my lower stomach. That's what made her come hardest last night.

I imagine how good this would look on camera, to put Sabrina in this position and fuck her like this, spread wide open, put on display.

The thought is so erotic that I can feel my balls swelling, even in the cold water.

I bounce her harder on my cock, pressing against her clit with my hand, listening to her gasps and moans as they grow deeper, more frantic.

"Right there," she groans. "That's the spot...hit it...hit it...hit it...*ahhhhhhhhhh*!"

The sound of her coming makes me explode. My balls squeeze like a fist, and I erupt inside her, spurt after spurt that feels hotter than lava in the chilly pool.

She's light and floating in my arms. It's easy to turn her around to face me, to kiss her again, the taste of arousal thick in her mouth, her body limp and warm as she curls up against me, her head on my shoulder.

The sun bathes us both, the water laps against us, and the waves crash far below.

All I can think is how glad I am that she came back.

CHAPTER 9
SABRINA

It takes several more attempts for Adrik and me to actually put our clothes on. We fuck again in the shower and once more on the bed, so ineffective at making ourselves presentable that it's almost dinnertime before we're fit to leave the hotel.

We each buy a fresh outfit at the shops along Stradun, Old Town's main street.

Adrik is now wearing a loose linen shirt, rolled up at the sleeves, with his same battered jeans. The shirt should make him look casual and summery, but it doesn't.

Adrik's features—like the markings on certain husky dogs—always seem to be scowling. His narrow blue eyes and thick black brows are ferocious, his body language so pugnacious that he could never resemble anything as benign as a tourist.

His charm can be disarming, but the moment he's not smiling at me or turning me into putty with those dangerously talented hands of his, I remember that he's Bratva and that he ran train at Kingmakers long before any of my cousins showed up. There's a ferocity to him, an edge of viciousness I like.

I'm also wearing cosplay of a kind—a twelve-dollar sundress bought from a kiosk run by a little old lady whose face was as wrinkled as a paper bag from long hours spent squinting into the Mediterranean sunshine. The dress is white eyelet lace, ruffled at the skirt and shoulders, which makes me look as sweet as a daisy. Underneath, I'm still poison ivy.

I sit across from Adrik at a café table overlooking St. Saviour Church. The waiter has brought each of us a glass of the local plum brandy, and I'm about to order a shit ton of food, because I burned a lot of calories with all this marathon fucking.

"So," I say, fixing Adrik with a cool stare. "When are you going to tell me why you're really here?"

If I've surprised Adrik, he gives no sign of it. He simply smiles, lifting his brandy and swirling it gently so the amber liquid rotates lazily within the glass.

"Why do you think?" he asks.

I consider the options.

At first, I assumed he was here to fuck me, but he's put in too much effort.

I don't believe in anything as stupid as love at first sight, and even if I did, the Bratva aren't romantic.

Which leaves only one possibility, as surprising as I find it...

"You want me to join you in Moscow," I say.

Adrik smiles, pleased that I understood so quickly. "That's right."

"Why?"

"I see something in you."

"What?"

"Talent," he says simply. "I want you with me. I want the best by my side."

My face feels hot, the brandy already going to straight to my head. It's been a long time since I devoured those pastries this morning. My stomach is empty, my body wrung out.

"So this is a job interview."

Adrik shrugs, a heavy raise and drop of his shoulders. "If that's how you want to look at it."

I poke my fingertip through the holes in my lace skirt. "I don't need a job."

"Everyone needs a job."

"I'm still in school. I've got three more years at Kingmakers."

We're interrupted by the waiter, who deposits a basket of fresh-baked flatbread directly between us.

Adrik and I reach for the bread at the same time, our knuckles brushing together with a static spark. Every time he touches me, even as casually as this, it upsets my heart rate.

I take an enormous bite out of the bread, chewing hard.

Adrik holds his in his hand, eyes fixed on my face.

"In three years' time, I'll own half of Moscow. The time to get in is on the ground floor. Like a start-up." He smiles, enjoying his comparison. "That's the American dream, isn't it? It's no good buying Apple stock now. You want to be Jobs and Wozniak, building circuit boards in a garage."

I swallow my mouthful, only half-chewed. The bread scrapes its way down my throat.

"I don't need to work in a garage. I'm an heir, in case you forgot. I've got an empire waiting for me, already built."

"Sure," Adrik says carelessly. "If you want to be a realtor."

I'd like to throw my drink in his face. He's being deliberately insulting, trying to goad me.

That's what he wants—to make me lose my temper.

So I keep an iron grip on my calm.

"I think you know better than that."

Adrik sets his bread on his plate and leans forward, eyes burning into mine.

"I know exactly what your father is up to. He bought dozens of distressed retail spaces in the so-called Magnificent Mile in the aftermath of the pandemic. Now he's buying up property along the I-80 and I-55 corridors, building warehouses, filling the need for supply-chain distribution. In another five years, he'll be the single largest holder of commercial real estate in all of Chicago."

My mouth is open, no words coming out. Adrik is describing my father's operations as accurately as I could myself.

"Your uncle Callum is gearing up for another run at the governor's mansion, Dante lives in Paris with his wife and children, and your uncle Sebastian handles the less legal side of the Gallo empire." Adrik ticks off my relatives on his fingers. "Your younger brother is only sixteen and technically not your father's heir, but by all accounts, he's more deeply involved in the family business than you've ever been."

Now my face is flaming, because that's also true—Damien may appear quiet and reserved, but he has a brilliant criminal mind. He's been running my father's books since his twelfth birthday. They spend hours together analyzing potential acquisitions, running the numbers on the properties for which my father negotiates with ruthless aggression.

I'm always invited to these meetings, but they don't interest me the same way they do Damien.

Truth be told, I'd rather work with Uncle Seb. But even there, the Gallos have been divesting our most egregious illegal activities. Each year that passes, we clean up our books, a larger percentage of our income coming from legitimate sources.

"What's your point?" I snap.

"My point is this," Adrik says patiently. "I don't think you want to be Nero's heir. I think you want to be a fucking gangster. You don't want to inherit an empire. You want to build one."

I lift my brandy, taking several swift swallows.

Even though the sun is sinking, the stone walls of Old Town still reflect the heat of the day. The air is still and muggy, no breeze off the ocean.

I'm hot and flustered. I feel cornered by Adrik, attacked by him.

But also…flattered.

He came a long way to make this pitch. He pulled out all the stops. It feels good to be courted—professionally, not just sexually.

I set down my glass.

"If I was going to build an empire, it would be for me, not you."

"No one builds an empire alone," Adrik says. "Not even you or me."

I'm not exactly a team player. I barely get along with my own family.

They think they know my strengths and weaknesses better than I do. They think I need their caution and their advice.

I don't.

I'm the smartest of any of them, not just some pretty face, not just some fucking kid.

Adrik met me once, and he saw me for what I am: valuable.

He came to scout me, like a VP of the Cubs who just saw a kid with a ninety-eight-mile-per-hour fastball.

"I don't know shit about Russia," I say. "I've never even been there."

"So come visit."

I pick up my drink, taking a long, slow sip.

"I'll think about it."

Adrik drives me to the airport in Barcelona, a journey that takes us three days in the open-top Alfa Romeo, stopping in Piran to walk the sea wall, in Milan to shop in the Piazza del Duomo, and in Monaco to bet the last of our cash on black.

I've never spent so much uninterrupted time with someone. Usually, by the end of a date, no matter how well it went, I heave a sigh of relief when I'm alone again, free to eat what I like, read what I like, and wander through my own thoughts without interruption.

Even with Ilsa, spending too much time together was sure to end in an argument. Every one of our fights occurred because I was bored and started acting like a jackass, teasing her about things she takes too seriously or challenging her in a way I knew was sure to wind her up. Or just flirting right in front of her.

Adrik has a thick skin. It's hard to offend him. He has a level of confidence impervious to minor slights like me turning my head to get a better look at a stunning redhead sauntering by.

"You want to go talk to her?" he inquires without a hint of jealousy.

"Maybe," I say. "I love gingers."

"I know," he laughs. "I've met Nix. I don't think you offered to room with her out of the goodness of your heart."

"I don't perv on my roommates," I inform him. "I only watched her change at most three or four times. Maybe five. But not more than six."

Adrik chuckles. "If we're not drawn to beauty, then why have eyes?"

"My thoughts exactly. Good food is for eating, fast cars are for driving, and beautiful women deserve to be ravished."

"Life is for living," Adrik concurs. "Take all you can get while there's breath in your lungs."

We're in agreement on this topic and many others.

The only point on which we differ is whether I should join my fate to Adrik's for the foreseeable future.

He hasn't brought it up again since our last dinner in Dubrovnik. Yet I know his offer is on both our minds all the time.

Nix isn't my roommate anymore. She left Kingmakers to move to Oregon to be with Adrik's cousin Rafe.

Adrik wants me to do the same: abandon my schooling and my ambitions in favor of his.

Everything within me rebels against the idea.

Yet when he drops me off at the Barcelona airport and I turn to see him standing by the Alfa, arms crossed over his chest, dark hair blowing in the breeze…for the first time, there's no relief in the feeling of being alone again.

CHAPTER 10
ADRIK

THREE MONTHS LATER

I'VE COME TO CANNON BEACH, OSTENSIBLY TO VISIT MY UNCLE AND cousins but really to see Sabrina.

We've kept in touch over the summer.

She's been working with her father and brother during the day, at night rebuilding a vintage Indian motorcycle with her mother.

She sent me photos of the bike and one or two of herself, though not the kind of pictures I'd request if I had my way...

I'm kicking myself for not filming any part of our three days together. I'd give a kidney to be able to watch Sabrina's breathtaking body participating in those activities at which she is so phenomenally talented. I've run through my own memories so many times that I hardly know if I can believe them anymore. They seem dreamlike and too fantastical to possibly be real.

After our trip, I went through withdrawal.

My first two weeks back in Moscow were miserable. I snapped at Jasper and Vlad, drank too much, and felt bored of my own plans, the ones I'd been formulating before I ever went to Dubrovnik.

Then Sabrina sent me the first picture of herself. Nothing sexy or posed. In fact, she was dressed in steel-blue coveralls and work boots, grease up to her elbows and a smear across one cheek. She was crouched down at the wheel of the bike, working a wrench, her forearm taut and tendons standing out on the back of her hand. She glanced back over her shoulder, probably as someone called her name—that's when the photo was taken.

The fact that she sent me this picture over any other pleased me in a way I can hardly explain. It was a photo of her in her favorite place, doing what she loves. She sent me a picture of the real Sabrina, which is who I most want to know.

And yes, I have jerked off to that picture, though it isn't a nude. Because that's how attracted I am to this girl. That's how badly I want her. I'm more aroused by a candid shot of her than the raunchiest porn.

The flight to America felt like it took years. We flew commercial. Even though we had those Delta One seats where you can lie down entirely in an enclosed pod like you're having an MRI taken, I still couldn't sleep a minute. I wanted to see Sabrina with a hunger that kept me awake all through the night.

We had been texting more and more frequently.

She kept me updated on her activities, and I told her how I'd found a house for me and the Wolfpack, a base of operations to begin our business in Moscow.

Sabrina pretended only a casual level of interest, but her questions were probing enough for me to assume that she hadn't forgotten my offer, nor entirely dismissed it.

We each have our excuse for this visit.

She's here to see Nix, her old roommate. Nix is living in a mansion on the cliffs above a cold northern beach, the mansion that now houses my uncle Ivan and his wife, my cousins Rafe and Freya, and several of my uncle's men.

My own mother and father have come along with me and also my brother, Kade. To have the Petrov family whole again is so deeply satisfying that we've taken every opportunity to visit.

I'm relieved to see Ivan and Sloane looking something like

themselves again. Though Ivan was the one trapped in a windowless cell in the bottom of a mine, the physical toll on his wife was almost as severe. She grew thin and worn with every day that passed until she became a shadow of herself. If Ivan had died before we found him, she might have died too—by her own hand or by the kind of medical accident that really is no mystery at all if one understands the effects of stress on the body.

Rafe is also himself once more, in the sense that I can call him by his name and acknowledge him as my cousin.

The lies we had to tell to protect our family have cost us all.

The high table hasn't forgotten that we concealed my uncle's capture from the Bratva. They pretend that they would have helped us, but we know the form their "help" would have taken. They would have descended on us like hyenas, ripping apart the carcass of our empire and dividing it among themselves. Putting Sloane under house arrest for her own "protection." Impeding my father from paying the monthly ransom that kept Ivan alive.

The Bratva are friends of convenience. As in any animal pack, if the dominant male can't fight off his challengers, he's soon deposed. He cannot rule in absentia.

Ivan's empire was already fracturing as he shifted his focus to his holdings in America. Sloane was first to recognize the vast potential of the legalization of marijuana in Washington and Colorado. Before the legislation had even passed, she and Ivan bought up land for farming and prime real estate for dispensaries. The money that poured in was a blessing and a curse, because it made them rich beyond measure but also attracted the attention of old enemies.

Parted from Russia for three years, it seems my uncle has no desire to return. He's made his home here on the West Coast, gifting the monastery in St. Petersburg to my father. Now my father is *pakhan* of St. Petersburg, subordinate no longer.

I could stay at the monastery with him. But to my mind, St.

Petersburg is for the younger brother. Kade can inherit when my father retires. Moscow is the prize.

Moscow has never been controlled by one man. At best, it's been divided in four portions, with the Markovs taking the largest share. Currently, a dozen bosses vie for power in the vacuum created by my father's absence and the death of several key players.

It's all up for grabs. And I want it all.

I'm not arrogant enough to think I can do it alone.

I've already assembled my Wolfpack, handpicked and trained by me alone. Sabrina is the last piece.

It might seem like madness to bring a woman into the mix, but I can see the equation in its entirety, the fullness of what we need to succeed. Sabrina is crucial. She's the seasoning on the steak. The ingredient that no one else possesses.

I don't need more men created in my image.

I need something different.

Someone who challenges me. Someone with their own mind and their own ideas. Someone shaped in an entirely separate world.

This is my vision, and I'm here to make it a reality.

When I see her in the flesh, everything I planned to say evaporates from my mind, leaving me speechless.

She's standing next to Nix and Rafe, wearing an old pair of denim shorts and a flannel shirt, barefooted. So radiant in the summer sunshine that she could almost blind me.

I feel my mother glance from Sabrina to me, intuiting the connection between us or else tipped off by my brother.

Sabrina likewise sweeps her eyes across my family. I'm pleased to see that she's robbed of a fraction of her usual cheek, enough that she introduces herself politely to my parents and gives Kade a surprisingly civil, "Good to see you again."

When her eyes meet mine, she says nothing at all. Her face reddens, and her chest rises and falls a little too quickly beneath the flannel shirt.

I'm wondering if she's afflicted with the same thickness in her throat and the same pounding heart that seem to have attacked me without warning. Everything is quiet on the outside, while inside is chaos and confusion.

"Hello, Sabrina."

"Hello, Adrik."

That low voice operates on me like Pavlov's bell. I'm sweating, salivating, and a host of other reactions that I'd rather not experience with my mother two feet away from me.

What the fuck is happening?

You'd think I was sixteen again.

You'd think I'd never seen a woman before.

"Did you have a good flight?" Nix pipes up, her voice high and strained.

If anyone is more uncomfortable than me in this moment, it's Nix Moroz. Her father was the one who imprisoned Ivan. While Ivan and Sloane have obviously forgiven her, she's not as certain of her reception with the rest of us.

I couldn't give two shits who she's related to.

If Ivan doesn't mind his son sleeping with the enemy, far be it from me to raise a fuss about it. What better revenge for Rafe than to cut Marko's throat and steal his daughter? Sounds like justice to me.

Apparently my mother feels the same, because she immediately replies, "It was lovely, thank you. I'm Lara, by the way. Are you Nix? I've heard so much about you from Kade!"

My mother is kindhearted. In this instance, she probably feels especially charitable. Her own father was a sadistic piece of shit who threw her mother out a window. So she knows a little something about family drama.

"She hasn't heard 'so much' about you," Kade assures Nix. "Just a normal amount. Sabrina, on the other hand..."

"What's that supposed to mean?" Sabrina says, coloring.

"He's only teasing," my mother says, putting her arms companionably around both girls' waists. "We're indebted to you both for the assistance you gave our family."

"I don't know about that." Nix winces.

"We're all here now," my mother says firmly. "That's what matters."

She heads inside the house with Nix and Sabrina, my father following along behind her at a slower pace, burdened by several suitcases.

"I'll take those." I heft the two largest. "You help too, you lazy shit," I say to Kade.

"I've got 'em," Rafe says, taking the other two suitcases.

He's lingering behind on purpose.

Sure enough, as soon as my father and Kade are a few steps ahead, he shoots me a sly look and mutters, "How was Dubrovnik?"

Not knowing what Sabrina told them, I respond with, "Sunny."

Rafe snorts. "Alright. Keep your secrets."

"Don't quote that fucking movie at me."

Since we were kids, Rafe has homed in with unerring precision on the most irritating lines from every film we've watched together, then deployed them relentlessly.

"What movie?" he says innocently.

"I liked you better when you were depressed," I tell him.

"Then you shouldn't have brought Dad home, should you? Next time, think ahead."

"Don't think 'cause we're the same height now I won't beat the shit out of you."

Rafe cocks an eyebrow at me.

"Same height? I've got an inch on you at least."

"Just fucking try me," I snarl. "It was a long flight. I'm dying for some exercise."

"No thanks," Rafe says. "I got enough of that at Kingmakers."

I sigh. "Those were the days. You were always sure of knocking someone out in the course of a week."

"Sometimes several people."

"Almost makes me miss it."

"Don't worry. I'm sure there'll be plenty of opportunities for mayhem in Moscow."

"He's not going there for mayhem," my father calls back over his shoulder. He's got the ears of a bat—always has.

"*Konechno net, otets,*" I say. *Of course not, Father.* "I'll follow all your orders to the letter. Just like you did at my age."

Fully cognizant of his own bad behavior, my father turns around and fixes me with a steely stare.

"Now is not the time for levity, boys. We have many more enemies than friends. Especially in Moscow."

"I know. There's a lot of people trying to kill us," I say. And then, so quietly that not even my father can hear, I mutter to Rafe, "And some of us keep fucking those people."

Struggling to keep a straight face, Rafe whispers back, "*Nix* was never trying to kill us. Just her dad."

"Well, give her time. She doesn't know you as well as I do."

Rafe grins. "When has a Petrov married someone safe?"

My gaze fixes on Sabrina, stepping through the front doors of the mansion.

She pauses, looking back over her shoulder. In the gloom of the house, her face is in shadow, her eyes glinting like a jungle cat.

"Who the fuck wants to be safe?" I say.

It takes an excruciating fourteen minutes of chitchat to finish greeting every goddamn person I'm here to visit before I can isolate Sabrina from the group.

"We don't have enough rooms," Sloane says to me without apology. "You'll have to bunk with Rafe."

"That's fine." I lift my bag again. "Sabrina can show me the way."

No one remarks on my choice of escort, though I catch the twitch of my aunt's lips that tells me she understands perfectly well what I'm up to.

You have to be pretty fucking sly to get anything past Sloane.

My aunt has always been my favorite relative because she's blunt and unsentimental, as ruthless as a man and as calculated as myself. She taught me how to shoot in the woods behind the monastery.

"Marksmanship is meditation," she told me. "You have to clear your mind of everything but the shot. A sniper is a monk. He separates his mind from his body. Cold can't touch him, nor wind, nor time. He'll wait three days with no food or water if that's how long it takes for the target to enter the kill zone. When you pull the trigger, it's your mind that moves, not your finger."

"Ivan's lucky you chose poison and not a rifle when you came for his head."

Even at ten years old, I already knew the story of how my uncle and aunt first met.

Sloane looked at me, no trace of amusement on her face.

"I would have destroyed all my happiness in a moment without ever knowing what I'd done."

"Maybe you would have been happy either way."

"No," she said, still unsmiling. "I would have been nothing at all."

I didn't quite understand her. I didn't understand what "nothing" meant.

Sabrina leads me up the stairs to Rafe's room.

I'm close enough to touch her, though I haven't yet. I'm simply admiring the way her bare calves flex as she ascends the stairs and the pleasing tension in the arches of her bare feet. She bounds up like she's made of springs, full of restless energy.

I follow after her, the suitcase weightless in my hand.

The moment we're inside Rafe's room, I toss it aside and push the door shut.

Sabrina turns to face me, cheeks glowing, lips parted.

Before she can speak, before she can even take a breath, I seize her face in both hands and kiss her like I haven't seen her in a hundred years. My hands are all over her body, ripping open her shirt, yanking down her shorts, lifting her up and slamming her against the wall without one thought for the noise that might be overheard by the people downstairs.

She's clawing at me just as eagerly, pulling up my shirt so she can put her bare chest against mine, shoving her hand down the front of my shorts to grip my cock. She lets out a groan when she touches it, desperate to have it inside her.

"Hurry," she pants in my ear. "I'm fucking dying for you..."

Clothes half on and half off, I thrust inside her, burying my cock eight inches deep in that soaking wet pussy, already warm, already throbbing for me.

I'm fucking her hard, and it's still not enough. She wraps her arms around my neck, slamming herself up and down on my cock, biting at the side of my neck, panting into my mouth, kissing me so roughly that I taste blood—mine or hers, I really couldn't give a shit.

There's no thought of foreplay or drawing this out as long as possible. We're hurtling headlong toward climax, each of us desperate for relief.

It's not a race—more like a free fall. We're plummeting toward an inevitable conclusion, no more able to stop than we could sprout wings and fly.

Whether she hits it first or I do, I can't tell. All I know is I'm bursting inside her, a creature splitting its skin. What will emerge from the carapace, I have no idea. I can't possibly be the same person before and after this.

The pleasure is blinding, the room less than nothing around me. All that exists is Sabrina and whatever I become when I'm with her.

It's all over in minutes. She collapses against me, no longer able to hold herself up. I have to set her down because I'm shaking, but I won't let go of her, not for a second.

We look at each other, frightened of this thing between us, over which neither of us has any control.

When she can speak again, Sabrina says, "I needed that."

"Me too. I thought I knew how bad I wanted it. But it was... more."

We're staring at each other, still breathing heavily.

Only minutes have passed, but everything feels different between us. Whatever separation of time and distance existed, we blasted it apart. Sex connects us in a way I've never felt before.

"How have you been liking it here?" I ask her.

She's been staying with my aunt and uncle for three days already.

What I really mean is *How do you like my family?*

"Sloane is intense," Sabrina says. "Ivan too, but I expected that. I knew Sloane as Ms. Robin at Kingmakers—she was our librarian. I know her, but I don't know her. Same with Rafe, actually. It's a little disorienting. Worse for Nix, I'm sure."

"Sloane is hard to know under any circumstance. Her father was insane. He raised her like a child soldier."

"Nix told me." Sabrina nods. "She was a killer for hire?"

"One of the best. Two hundred commissions—only missed once."

"Ivan."

"That's right."

Sabrina squints at me, slowly buttoning her shirt.

"The Petrovs are forgiving."

"You know how it is in our world. Everyone is a rival, ally or not. Your only true friends are your family. And the inverse is true—family are friends, whatever they might have been before."

The last two buttons ripped off and bounced somewhere under the bed. Sabrina ties the bottom of her shirt in a knot instead.

"Family can hurt you. My father was shot six times at my uncle's wedding."

"But not by your uncle."

"No." She smiles. "Though I'm sure he thought about it a time or two."

"None of us know the span of our life. You have to trust somebody. I'd rather be stabbed in the back by a friend than have no friends at all."

Sabrina is quiet a moment. "I'm not sure I agree."

I hold her gaze. "Then you've never had a friend like me."

"Is that what we are?" she says softly.

"We're going to be something. I can promise you that."

The corner of her mouth tilts up. "Whether I want it or not?"

"There's no choice about it. From the moment I saw you, I knew our paths would converge."

Sabrina smooths her hair down with both hands, an action that does little because her hair seems as intent on insubordination as my own, especially this close to the ocean.

"You fascinated me before we ever met," she admits.

"I heard about you too."

"From who?"

"Kade. The first week of school, he told me he'd never seen a girl so beautiful."

"Hm," Sabrina says.

"He's not very observant."

She laughs. "What does that mean?"

"Your looks are the least interesting thing about you."

Color comes into her cheeks. I understand that this is the compliment Sabrina most wants to hear. She's been told she's beautiful all her life. You might as well observe that the sky is blue or water is wet.

I grip her upper arm and pull her close.

"If he took five minutes to look closer, he'd have told me that you're brilliant and bold and that you were made for me in every possible way."

She tilts her face up to me, but she doesn't kiss me, only looking straight into my eyes.

"You won't like everything about me," she warns.

I kiss her, long and deep.

"Yes, I will. I want all of you, Sabrina. Every single fucking thing."

CHAPTER 11
SABRINA

I'VE GOT A SERIOUS PROBLEM.

I'm only supposed to stay in Oregon for a week. Then I'm headed back to Kingmakers, catching the ship in Dubrovnik on September first, trapped on Visine Dvorca until the fifteenth of May. No laptops, no cell phones, and no visitors.

I came to Cannon Beach to get one last hit of Adrik Petrov before an eight-month detox.

Now I'm realizing I'm a full-blown addict.

Each day that passes, it only gets worse.

With him in Rafe's room and me in Nix's and neither of us admitting that we're actually dating, we have to sneak away to get our fix.

We've fucked down on the beach, in Rafe's car, in the shower, in the basement gym, and even in the kitchen at two o'clock in the morning.

It's never enough.

Each time, I tell myself it's the last time. Then I fuck him even sooner. The spaces when we're apart grow shorter and shorter, and I need more and more of him to satisfy me. The second we're done fucking, before I've even put all my clothes back on, I already want him again.

This is classic addict behavior. I'm sneaking around, lying to Nix, and god knows I'd cheat, borrow, and steal to get more of him.

When I can't get it, I'm fidgety and irritable. I don't want food or entertainment. I only want Adrik.

No one has ever had this kind of power over me. It scares me. I almost hate it.

How I feel is irrelevant, because I'm not in control. I make promises to myself, then break them the next minute. Resistance is pain, and giving in is the deepest of pleasures.

There's never been a drug on the planet that felt as good as this. The more I cross my own lines, the better it feels.

I suck his cock like I need his come to live.

I let him spank me till my ass is red and choke me until all I can do is mouth the word "more."

The rougher the sex, the more I like it. I've never let a man leave a mark on me before, and now I'm wearing hoodies in the summer to cover the hickeys on my neck and the bruises on my wrists.

I've never been with someone wilder than me or more aggressive. It's an escalating arms race with no end in sight. Even Adrik seems shocked at himself when I slap him across the face and he slaps me right back. We stare at each other, wide-eyed and panting, before I leap on him again. He flips me over and shoves me face down in the sand, fucking me until my whole chest is scraped raw, my bikini top washed away by the tide.

I sneak back to the house as the sun rises, red and sore, covered all over in wet sand. I rinse off at the outdoor shower, already regretting that I promised Nix we'd go shopping in town.

I want to spend time with her—of course I do—but I'd prefer an activity that Rafe and Adrik might join, or at least something at the house where I might catch a glimpse of Adrik reading a book in the hammock or smell his cologne as I pass by Rafe's room.

I only have two more days before I'm supposed to fly to Dubrovnik. I'm a kid desperately trying to ride every last ride before Disneyland closes.

It's madness. I'm strung-out, pathetic, a goddamn embarrassment. What would my father say if he could see me?

He knew something was up, with all my texting and how secretive I became with my phone. He's a goddamn detective. I knew if he spied so much as Adrik's name on the screen, he'd never stop hounding me about it.

He didn't believe my bullshit story about why I was three days late coming home from Dubrovnik. To my cousins' credit, they kept their mouths shut under what I'm sure was intense interrogation—even Cara, who's allergic to lying to the point where she will literally break out in hives.

I told my brother the truth. Damien always has my back. All he said was, "You know how Dad feels about Russians."

Luckily the Petrovs don't seem to share the same prejudice against Americans.

Adrik's mother Lara has been nothing but warm to me. She has the thickest accent of any of the Petrovs, and unlike Sloane, she doesn't seem to take part in the family business. She has Adrik's coloring—olive skin, blue-black hair—but her features are softer, her voice gentler, her movements slow and almost dream-like.

She goes for long walks down on the beach in the mornings, carrying a little sketchbook with a nub of a pencil tucked in the spine. The pages are already filling up with drawings of the view off the cliffs, the black-and-white oystercatchers that pick their way down the beach, and the seals that roll out of the waves to sun themselves on the rocks.

She's immensely affectionate to her boys, rarely passing Kade or Adrik without ruffling a hand through their hair, dropping down on her husband's lap on the sofa instead of sitting beside him, curled up against him in a little ball as if she were still a kid herself.

She reminds me of my own mom—steady and calm.

Dominik Petrov is nothing like my dad. He strikes me as

someone who never would have chosen this life at all if he hadn't been born a Petrov.

His respect for Ivan is obvious. I suppose loyalty to his brother has been his motivation all this time. The jagged scar down his cheek is one of the many pieces of evidence of the cost of this service. The lines of exhaustion on his face in moments of repose make me think he would rather rest than rule. But maybe the people best suited to lead are always the most reluctant.

Neither of them has Adrik's ferocity. There's an extremism in Adrik that draws me. We share the same abhorrence for rules and restrictions or even reasonable restraints. I want to find the edge, even if I risk flying over it. I'll never trust what can and can't be done until I try for myself.

I head upstairs for a proper shower, then dress in shorts and an old Cubbies jersey that only partly covers the scrapes on my chest and arms. Nix eyes the marks when she comes in from her own shower but doesn't say anything, roughly drying her flaming hair with one of the faded beach towels from the linen closet.

She steps into a pair of ragged cutoffs, the long muscles of her thighs flexing. Nix is built like an Olympian. I'm jealous of her athleticism. Physical disadvantage is the one aspect of femininity I loathe. Nix is the only woman I know as strong as most men.

Well, maybe Ilsa too. She certainly held her own among the Enforcers at Kingmakers. I don't know how she stood living in the gatehouse with all those overgrown frat boys. I would have perished from the smell alone.

"You'll like the shopping on Hemlock Street," Nix says. "They've got some cool little boutiques. Lots of coastal shit—knit bikinis and straw visors and jewelry made out of shark's teeth."

"Sounds great," I say.

Catching the lack of enthusiasm, Nix glances up from the floor where she sat down to pull on her sneakers. "What's wrong? I thought you liked shopping."

"I do."

"Well, god knows I'm not doing it for me. If you'd rather go somewhere else, none of that bougie shit's gonna fit me anyway."

I shrug. "I just wanna hang out with you. Doesn't matter to me what we do."

"Yeah?" Nix looks up at me from under the cloud of her already frizzing hair. Nix's hair is the texture of cabled yarn, with each strand curling in a different direction. This close to the ocean, she gets Diana Ross volume in a shade somewhere between Fanta and a fresh tangerine. "You don't wanna ask the guys if they want to come with us?"

I keep my face expressionless and my voice casual. "I dunno. I guess we could if you want."

"*Only if you want,*" Nix says, imitating my blasé attitude. "*Makes no difference to me whether I get to scam on Adrik all afternoon…*"

I laugh. "Invite them, then. Is that what you want to hear?"

"No," Nix says, grinning at me mischievously. "I want to hear what kind of heat Adrik is packing to have you waking up before seven a.m. to sneak out of our room."

"Who said we're fucking?"

"Unless you took up roller skating, it's pretty obvious," Nix says, shooting a pointed glance at my skinned knees. "That and your guilty fucking face."

"What's guilt?" I say airily. "Never heard of it."

"I'll write out some definitions for you," Nix says. "A few words you should learn: 'moderation,' 'safety standards,' and 'I'm sorry.'"

"Sounds like pure Chinese."

"Chinese isn't a language."

"And 'I'm sorry' isn't a word. It's a phrase," I say sweetly.

"Just when I thought I missed you…" Nix hauls herself to her feet, a long way from the ground to her full height.

"Don't miss me. Come back to school with me. It's miserable without you."

"I'm happy here," Nix says simply.

I can see that for myself. She seems perfectly at home with Rafe's family and happy in America, though it's six thousand miles from what she knew before.

The Petrov ring glints on her left hand. Ivan gave it to her, a placeholder until Rafe could buy her an engagement ring. But Nix doesn't want a diamond. She likes the family ring. She wants to be accepted as a Petrov, as one of them.

She isn't afraid to uproot her life and change her plans at a moment's notice.

Is she braver than me? Or only more certain of what she wants?

"You want to go down to Seaside?" Nix asks me. "There's an arcade by the pier."

"Sure." I shrug. "I like games."

"Me too." Nix grins, already alight with competitive fire. "I wanna play you at Skee-Ball."

Rafe jumps at the chance to take Nix to the arcade. Adrik agrees with the same level of nonchalance I was attempting, but he shoots me a look with so much heat that morning sunshine feels weak and watery by comparison.

As we climb in the back seat of Rafe's Mustang, I spy a pair of my underwear crumpled up on the floorboards from when Adrik and I borrowed the car to "go for ice cream" the night before. I kick the black lace thong under Nix's seat, hearing Adrik's soft hiss of amusement as he catches me hiding the evidence.

"Remember when we used to play *Super Smash Bros.*?" Rafe says to Adrik, resting his arm across the back of Nix's seat so he can turn and reverse down the long, winding driveway through the thickets of spruce shielding the Petrov mansion from view of the road.

"I still play with Andrei and Hakim," Adrik says. "It's an easy way to remind them who's boss."

Andrei and Hakim are two of Adrik's Wolfpack—he's got five in all living in his rented house in Moscow. The only one I know is Jasper Webb, and only by reputation.

"You should try playing *Halo* against Zima," Rafe says, naming the youngest of Ivan's men, a skinny guy who speaks his own pidgin of English slang and rapid Russian, never wakes up before noon, then works late into the night on the Petrovs' security systems.

"I love *Halo*," I pipe up.

Adrik looks at me, interested. "We should play at the arcade."

"Sure." I shrug.

I've been playing video games with Leo and Miles since I was old enough to hold a controller. You have to bring your A game to match Leo's reflexes or Miles's strategy. I guess that's the one advantage of being younger—I've been sprinting to catch up all my life.

Adrik's hand rests on the bench seat, his fingers inches from my bare thigh. The sun beats down on us in the open back seat of the convertible, the fresh salt air whipping against our faces as Rafe pulls onto the main road leading down to Seaside.

Adrik's black hair ruffles in the wind, long and shaggy, so thick that when I sink my hands in it, all my fingers disappear.

I want to touch him now. Sitting this close is like lurking around the kitchen when you're starving. Every time I catch his scent, it makes my mouth water.

The edge of his pinkie brushes against my thigh.

The sun is hot, and his hand is hotter.

I let my thighs fall open so my leg rests on the back of his hand. Each jolt of the car sparks our skin together, rock against flint.

The Mustang flies down the open road, Rafe steering easily with one hand on top of the wheel. His other palm rests on Nix's leg, his thumb softly kneading her thigh.

They don't have to hide anything. Not anymore.

Why should Adrik and I hide? Who are we trying to fool?

I look at his profile: the sharp Roman nose, the stern jaw, the narrow, slanting eyes with that look of wildness lurking in them. No matter how disciplined Adrik pretends to be, he can't fool me. Like calls to like. He has a demon inside, just as wicked as mine.

Adrik feels me looking. He turns to face me, the wind swirling our hair around our faces like we're caught in a tiny typhoon, closed off from anything around us, even our friends in the front seat.

Time seems to stretch between us, the song on the radio playing at quarter speed, the car's engine humming up and down my spine.

Adrik mouths, "*I want you.*"

I whisper back, "*Then take me.*"

Adrik's parents know why he's really here. Nix knows too. Who am I lying to?

Only myself.

I know exactly what I want. I just can't admit it.

It's crazy. I know it's crazy.

But why shouldn't I want crazy things? Why shouldn't I take a chance?

I've never cared for security or even happiness…

I want what I want, even if it's all wrong for me.

CHAPTER 12
ADRIK

THE ARCADE IS A PLAYFUL CACOPHONY OF LIGHT AND COLOR—THE old-school eight-bit graphics of *Pac-Man* and *Centipede* bleeping and blaring next to the thunderous surround sound of a brand-new *Transformers* game.

Rafe loads up a couple of cards with credits, passing one to Sabrina and one to Nix so they can swipe at will.

Nix runs directly over to *Tomb Raider*, swiping for all four of us.

Sabrina lifts her plastic gun, connected to the console with a long, thin cord. She racks the slide like she's ejecting a cartridge from a Glock, peering down the sight with a practiced eye.

"Take it easy, Lara Croft," I tease her. "The game hasn't even started."

"You better take it seriously," she says. "I will be judging you."

I already know Sabrina well enough to recognize that most things that come out of her mouth sounding like jokes are nothing less than the absolute truth. She watches every move I make. There's a tally in her head where she scores what she thinks of me.

I'm not afraid to perform under pressure.

I rack my own slide, gun pointed at the screen, counting down the seconds until the game starts.

It's a melee from the moment we begin. Rafe, Nix, and Sabrina are fresh out of Marksmanship class, and I hit the range three times a week. We're obliterating bad guys before they've halfway popped their heads up on-screen, the scores tallying so rapidly that the numbers flow by like a ticker tape.

Rafe is steady and relentless, Nix aggressive and utterly locked in. Most of my attention is on Sabrina—she flicks her gun across the screen so fast I can hardly follow her, anticipating the movement patterns of the characters, focusing on headshots for the highest point value.

She doesn't know this game as well as I do. The little gold relics are key to scoring bonus points. Sabrina hits three, but I nail six in total, beating her score by two hundred.

This angers her. As playful as Sabrina can be, in competition she's deadly serious.

"Let's play again," she barks.

"There's a billion other games," Nix says, pulling Sabrina along so she's forced to drop her plastic gun. "Come on, I wanna race in *Mario*."

Sabrina takes the first round of *Mario Kart*, ruthlessly nailing Nix with an exploding blue turtle shell an inch from the finish line and zipping past her with a cackle that shows her complete lack of remorse. Rafe wins the next round, via some bullshit with a POW block.

Then Nix takes us to school on a carnival-style game where you throw plastic balls at ugly grinning clowns that pop up from all corners of the marquee.

When we switch to *Walking Dead*, it's my time to shine. It's a two-player game, so Rafe and Nix split off to shoot dinosaurs on *Jurassic World* while Sabrina and I slaughter zombies head-to-head.

Sabrina is good at shooter games, but she's not as familiar with the crossbow console. She hisses in fury as I sweep the first round, obliterating 128 zombies to her paltry 96.

"Next chapter," she orders, swiping our cards again.

This time, she's locked in, finger curled on the trigger, nailing zombies dead between the eyes the instant they appear on-screen. She's so aggressive that each zombie is a race to see which of us can strike first, the shambling figures lighting up in blue or green depending on whose arrow hit home first.

I start out ahead. As the level progresses, she creeps up on me—28 to 21. Then 44 to 39. Then 60 to 58...

"I'm gonna get you, motherfucker," Sabrina mutters, sparing no glance away from the screen.

She's about to pass me when the NPC jumps directly in the way, taking an arrow to the head that Sabrina intended for a SWAT zombie in riot gear.

"You dumb bitch!" Sabrina shrieks at the hapless avatar.

The game deducts points for executing a human, and I get the credit for the SWAT zombie instead.

"Aww, so close," I say as our round ends 132 to 131.

Sabrina is pissed. She wants to win every minute, all the time. And she particularly wants to beat *me*.

I fucking love it. There's no on and off switch in my head either—I'm full throttle. I'd never take it easy on her. I'd never let her win. I couldn't be with someone who would expect that of me.

"*Halo*?" I say.

Sabrina doesn't answer. She snatches up our card and marches directly over to the *Halo* consoles.

There are two types of game on offer: classic arcade or team battle, where you can access the online database and play with anyone from all over the world.

I'm pleased to see that Sabrina selects the latter. Team battle is more complex and challenging. You're not just shooting aliens—there's real strategy involved.

"Should we play together?" I ask Sabrina.

"You fucking wish," she says, swiping our card.

As the game loads, I cast a quick glance at Sabrina, separated from me by a partial barrier that prevents me looking at her screen.

I can still see the curve of her back and the long fall of her hair, densely black like coal, thick and textured.

She's nothing like a Russian girl. In spirit, she's all American—boisterous, overconfident, ambitious. In looks, she's a citizen of nowhere. I've never seen anything quite like her, not even at Kingmakers where students hail from all over the globe.

Sabrina was judging my reflexes. Now I'm running an evaluation of my own.

Video games are more useful than an IQ test. Assuming everyone knows how to play, the smartest person wins. That's how I first met Chief—I watched him run train against Andrei and Hakim in *Halo*. Despite his awkwardness and the wardrobe literally picked out by his mother, I could see how brilliant he is. I called him Master Chief after the main character in the game. He loves the nickname. Guys like him don't always get the respect they deserve.

"First to fifty kills wins," I call to Sabrina to annoy her.

"*I'm aware*," she hisses.

It's four vs. four, each of us paired up with three random teammates.

From the moment we spawn, I'm hunting for Sabrina.

In *Halo*, the key to winning is to have a high kill-to-death ratio. You want to murder as many members of the opposing team as possible before taking a bullet yourself.

I'm staying in close proximity to my teammates, because smart teams stick together.

As soon as we spot the opposing team, I start hurling grenades. You can chuck them before you get close enough to shoot, and if you're precise enough, you can bounce grenades off objects and even around corners.

I hear Sabrina curse, and I know I must have hit her shield. She's not dead, though. Before I can close in and shoot her with my pistol, she bolts and disappears.

Sneaky little bastard. She knows it's a battle she can't win, two against one with my teammate close by.

She's a fucking shadow, not sticking with her team at all but running across the map solo, constantly changing positions, picking off stragglers, then melting away again.

My team is still winning. We're up 24–20, because I'm leading the group like a phalanx. I get the gravity hammer and rack up six kills in a row, though none are the person I most want to smash.

"Where are you hiding?" I mutter.

Sabrina can hear me—we're only two feet apart. But she stays silent, only the clicks of her sticks telling me that she's in motion, not hunkered down somewhere.

I see a shimmer of red out of the corner of my eye. Sabrina bursts from cover, ambushing me under the protection of an overshield. Impervious to my hammer blast, she shoots me twice in the face.

I'm out for ten seconds—the longest ten seconds of my life. Sabrina uses my absence to go on a fucking rampage. She kills two of my teammates in the first three seconds, an achievement the game commemorates by declaring "Double kill!" at top volume.

"You hear that?" Sabrina calls.

I grit my teeth, watching the seconds count down until I'm back in the game.

"Triple kill!" the game announces as Sabrina murders my last remaining teammate.

"I think that was all of you," Sabrina says, so smugly that I have to restrain myself from karate-kicking the barrier between us.

The moment I'm back in the game, I sprint for Sabrina. I'm determined to blast her shield off and send her to purgatory in revenge. Catching sight of her, I lob the most beautiful grenade right at her feet, bouncing it straight into her shield, cracking it off like a cantaloupe.

Now she's back to normal, unprotected, me against her. I'd

planned to follow up that grenade with a pistol shot to the face, but Sabrina is a fucking jumping bean. She won't stay still for even an instant, leaping and darting through 3D space, up and backward and around, using her grappling hook to yank herself around like Spider-Man.

"What the fuck are you doing?" I laugh, trying to blast her.

Sabrina responds by grappling directly over me and shooting me in the back.

I can't fucking believe it.

I'm out again. Sabrina celebrates by raining terror on my hapless team for ten excruciating seconds.

This time when I respawn, I'm determined to get the overshield myself. It's due to regenerate in twenty seconds, and I know exactly where to find it. I jog to the spot, arriving precisely when the game announces, "Overshield incoming."

I crouch under cover, knowing better than to run out in the open before it appears, counting down silently in my head.

With two seconds remaining, I break cover.

Only for Sabrina to catapult down from the ramparts and land right on top of me, smashing me in the back of the head with her rifle.

Instant kill.

From behind the barrier, I hear her soft chuckle.

"I knew you'd go for that shield."

I could kill her right now. Not in *Halo*—in real life.

When I spawn again, I hunt for Sabrina with a fury I've never known. I abandon my teammates to their fates, searching the map for the one and only person I want to see. Finally, I spot her in my peripheral, but I don't turn my character toward her. I keep running on a straight axis like I have no idea she's there.

As soon as we reach a junction point, I double back. Sabrina throws her grenades where I should have been.

When I run up behind her, she's already got her gun up, waiting for me to round the corner, thinking she's going to shoot me in the face.

"Looking for someone?" I chortle, hitting her in the back and killing her instantly.

Before she can respawn, the game ends, 50–46. Sabrina's team wins.

She pokes her head around the barrier, eyes blazing with fury, no hint of celebration on her face.

"Again," she demands.

"Only if we play together."

She pauses, considering.

"Alright."

The game that follows is the most enjoyable round of *Halo* I've ever played. Now that I don't have to worry about Sabrina murdering me, it's Christmas Day. We snatch up every superweapon, raining terror on the opposing team, killing everyone in sight like we're invincible and they're standing still.

Her play is so elegant that I have to stop for a moment just to observe. I'm watching a symphony composed on-screen in front of me. Sabrina tracks the other team, triangulating with me, running to where she thinks the other players will respawn before they even appear, killing them before they can look around.

She uses her weapons in a cascade, swapping through one after another for maximum efficiency and speed. She memorizes the map, taking shortcuts, popping up where you'd least expect her.

Most of all, it's a fucking clinic of headshots. If you miss a headshot, you get nothing, so a smart gamer starts at the chest and works up to the head. Sabrina is headshots *only*. She misses on occasion, but her accuracy is so high that her total points double anyone on the opposing team.

She's better than me.

I don't like to admit that, and I sure as fuck don't say it lightly. But she's a little more talented at *Halo* and maybe even just a little bit smarter than me.

When we lay our controllers down, Sabrina turns, face flushed in triumph.

"So?" she says. "What do you think?"

"I think I always want you on my team."

CHAPTER 13
SABRINA

WE'RE EATING DINNER ON THE PETROVS' BACK DECK, THE ONLY dinner we've all eaten together and probably the only one we will. Someone or other is always absent at mealtimes, and soon I'll leave.

Adrik generally contrives to sit near me. Tonight, through Freya's insistence on an immediate refill of ice, I've ended up next to Ivan, with Adrik across the table and two seats down.

The table groans under the weight of a feast cooked by Timo, who used to be one of Ivan's *bratki* but has graduated to the position of head chef via an extensive education culled from *Pitmasters* and *The Great British Bake Off*.

Tonight he's dazzling us with smoked tri-tip and a salad made of ripe peaches and candied hazelnuts. Dominik fills our glasses with Shiraz. Freya carries in a browned and braided loaf of challah, which Zima seizes before she's even set down the platter.

"You made this?" he asks Freya, tearing off a chunk of bread.

"Kade helped."

"Oh," he says with much less enthusiasm.

"You live off Zoodles," Kade scoffs. "I could crack an egg in your mouth, and it would be high cuisine compared to the shit you eat."

"Crack an egg in my mouth?" Zima makes a disgusted face. "What kind of porn are you watching? Never mind. I'll check your browser history."

Kade laughs while looking alarmed that Zima might follow through on that threat.

Ivan clears his throat, throwing a quelling look down the table. "Manners," he says.

"Dad's right," Rafe agrees. "It's ten minutes into dinner, and we're already discussing Kade's taste in pornography. Have some class. Save it for dessert."

I can't help laughing, and I'm relieved that Sloane smiles as well. She's sitting at the other end of the table, wearing a black blouse and cigarette pants, her hair twisted up in a loose chignon. It's strange to see her with her natural dark hair color and even stranger to see her real expression, wicked and sly as a fox. I had no idea how much she was acting as Ms. Robin. The real Sloane is sharp and sarcastic and frankly terrifying.

I'm keyed up, talking hectically to Nix, laughing too loud. I'm full of nervous energy, building up inside me like a pressure cooker with no release.

Across the table, Adrik sits silently, not joining in the conversation. I've tried to catch his eye several times without success. Then, as soon as I speak to anyone else, I feel his stare burning into me.

Ivan is an intimidating presence on my other side. He's a beast of a man with a brutal-looking face, a rough, rasping voice, and a gravity only occasionally punctured by his wife. Even when he addresses me politely, it sends shivers down my spine.

"You have only two more days with us?"

I wish I hadn't just taken a massive bite of tri-tip. I chew and swallow as quickly as possible, half choking myself.

"Yes," I gasp. "I fly out Friday morning."

"You'll be missed," he says with a polite nod.

There's something courtly in his manners. I know he must have been barbarous beyond belief to claw his way to the top of the heap in St. Petersburg, but Ivan Petrov has a formality and a dignity that remind me more of a king than a Mafia boss.

There's a reason this family follows him. A reason they were willing to risk everything to bring him home.

Ivan says, "I hope you have an excellent second year, without any interruptions."

He means this as an apology of sorts or a thank-you.

With full honesty, I reply, "The interruption was the best part of the year."

"If we don't make trouble for Sabrina, she'll make her own," Rafe says from the other side of Nix. "She's probably already plotting how she'll land herself right back in the chancellor's office on the first day of school. That's why she's so extra tonight."

This reference to my first ship ride over to the island is not as cheering as Rafe intended. It only reminds me that Nix won't be with me this time.

"Yeah," I say. "I guess that's why I'm so lively."

"You're happy to be going back," Adrik states, his voice cutting across the table.

"I didn't say happy."

"Lively, happy, what's the difference?"

"Well, lively isn't the same as happy. Is it?" Sloane says. She's looking at me, not Adrik. And even though she's smiling, there's a stillness in her eyes that makes me think she understands exactly what I mean.

"Happy is harder to attain," I say.

"Impossible for some," Sloane remarks.

This doesn't feel directed at me, not exactly. But it might be for my benefit. I wish she weren't sitting so far away. I'd like to ask her what she means.

Instead, I have to say what can be said in front of the whole group.

"Impossible hardly seems like a barrier in this house. Can I ask you all something?"

"Of course." Ivan inclines his head, listening.

"What was the code you used over the phone to tell Dominik and the others where to find you?"

Ivan smiles. "A simple cypher, one Dom and I used when we were boys avoiding trouble with our father. The first letter of each word forms the message."

"So nobody expected any kamikaze youngsters?" I say, composing my own example on the fly.

I'm showing off for Adrik. He rewards me with a small smile, the first of the night.

The real message is

So

Nobody

Expected

Any

Kamikaze

Youngsters.

Sloane catches the code just as quickly, and so does Zima, sitting at the far end of the table. Mouth full of bread, he lets out a snort that spews crumbs across Freya's plate.

"It took me a lot longer to come up with them," Ivan says gravely.

Sloane teases him, "*I see snow* was not your best work. How about some coordinates next time?"

Ivan is too used to his wife's ribbing to rise to the bait. "I wanted to make sure you weren't looking for me in the desert, my love. I know how you hate sand."

Dominik scoffs. "Yeah, it was super helpful. We crossed Fiji off the map."

Ivan is unperturbed. "You did find me in the end."

"It was a dark time," Lara says quietly. "We're in brighter days now."

She casts a quick smile at Nix, letting her know she's part of those brighter days and not blamed for what came before.

Nix has fallen silent beside me. I want to smack myself for

bringing this up. I was curious and not considering how it would make her feel.

"*Sorry,*" I whisper, squeezing her leg under the table.

Nix takes a slow breath, lips pale but face composed.

"The sun sets on one life and rises on another."

"For all of us," Freya agrees.

Ivan's return marks a turning point for everyone. Freya won't have to run the Petrovs' dispensaries anymore; she's headed off to Cambridge to complete her long-postponed economics degree. Dominik is *pakhan* in St. Petersburg. Adrik is free to pursue his own goals with the Wolfpack. Rafe can be himself again—he'll marry Nix in the spring, and he's already confided to me that he's been scouting houses to surprise her.

You have to literally chain a Petrov in a cell to stop them chasing what they want.

I envy them all.

CHAPTER 14
ADRIK

AFTER DINNER, EVERYONE HELPS CARRY THE DISHES BACK INTO the kitchen.

Sloane and I linger at the table the longest, me gathering up the empty wineglasses and her folding the tablecloth with all its crumbs so she can shake it out over the railing of the deck.

The sun is going down. Pale moths flutter around the strings of lights suspended over the hammocks. The honeysuckle in the yard smells sweeter now than it did in the daytime.

"She's very clever," Sloane says.

I smile, pleased that Sloane noticed how quickly Sabrina rattled off that quip in Ivan's code.

There's no point pretending. I'm sure Sloane already knows twice what I think she does.

"I'm glad you could meet her," I say.

Sloane is not maternal, not in the usual way. She's my aunt, but she's been more like an older sister to me or a friend. I want her approval, hers and Ivan's. I always have.

Sloane gives the tablecloth a brisk snap, tossing the crumbs across the lawn for the delight of all the robins and sparrows in the morning.

"I knew you'd never pick some pretty little idiot," she says.

I shake my head. "That would bore me."

Sloane refolds the tablecloth, crisply, intricately, like a flag, even though she's only taking it to be washed.

"She'll be an asset to you," she acknowledges.

I'm not sure I like the term "asset." It's a word Sloane's father would have used. Sabrina is valuable to me, and potentially useful. But she's much more than a tool or a means to an end.

Sloane continues, "And a liability too."

I pause, a bouquet of wineglasses in each hand, the dregs of Shiraz streaky and dark.

"What do you mean?"

"She's unstable."

"How do you know?"

"Because it takes one to know one."

I frown, irritated that Sloane is passing judgment on Sabrina when she hardly knows her at all.

"She's young. That's all."

"Some people form at an early age. That was you, Adrik—you've been the same practically since you were a baby. I taught you, but I never changed you. You are who you are. Other people are more malleable. You can shape them and hone them, like a sword. You can wield them for your own purpose. And some people...some people are bombs. When they go off, they tear everything apart, including themselves."

"Which one are you?" I demand.

"I've been a sword and a bomb."

"Then you grew up."

"*No*," Sloane says sharply. "I changed. It's not the same thing."

"Do you like her or not?" I say coldly. "I can't really tell."

"Of course I like her. But you're my nephew. I have a responsibility to you."

"And you think you need to warn me."

"Yes, I do."

"Of what exactly?"

"You think you're invincible. You think you're in control. But you've never been in love before. Love makes fools of us all."

"I thought love saved you!" I'm hot in the face. "Didn't you say that? That all your happiness came from Ivan?"

"It did," Sloane agrees. "It still does. But don't think that's the only way it can go."

"I appreciate the concern." I pick up the last glass. "But I can handle myself. And I can definitely handle Sabrina."

Sloane gives her maddening smile, smoothing out the last wrinkle in the tight packet of the tablecloth.

"Sure, Adrik," she says, light and calm. "Just remember...when a bomb explodes, it destroys whoever stands closest."

CHAPTER 15
SABRINA

I'M SUPPOSED TO FLY TO DUBROVNIK TOMORROW. I HAVE MY suitcase with me, full of a fresh batch of uniforms, and I already said goodbye to my parents and Damien back in Chicago.

Nix can tell I'm in a funk about leaving. She's so honest that she ignores social niceties and the bullshit people say, cutting right to the heart of what she sees: "You don't want to go back to school."

We're lying on the back deck of the Petrovs' house. The wooden beams are warped and graying from the constant salt spray tossed up from the beach below. In the large hammock, we can lie side by side, head to foot. Nix's red hair sprawls across my brown arm, my dark hair across her pale one. From above, we must look like a yin-yang symbol.

The breeze is strong enough to keep us rocking, though neither of us is pushing.

Adrik has gone on some errand with Kade and Rafe and Rafe's sister, Freya, something to do with the dispensaries. I didn't ask Adrik for details, because there've been people all around us today, and the things we actually want to talk about can only be said in private.

"I like school," I say to Nix.

That's mostly true. I spent years yearning to go to Kingmakers. Once I arrived, the classes and training and ferocious competition were everything I'd dreamed.

It was a fire hose of information straight to my brain. I guzzled it down, always with more and more and more coming, no end of everything to learn.

But the rules, the strictures, the monotony of it...

I don't want to be on someone else's schedule. I don't want to be chastised. I don't want to be a student.

I've always felt older than my years. I like Kade and Cara and most of my classmates. But the one who feels like my equal is Adrik. I want to be eight years ahead. My mind is already there. I'm ready.

"That's not what I said." Nix pushes off the closest post with her bare foot, sending the hammock into a dramatic swoop. "I said you don't want to go back."

"No," I admit after a moment. "I don't."

"Because of Adrik?"

It's the first time she's said it out loud.

She knows that we're involved. But Nix is never one to pry. She flows like water and allows everyone else the same luxury. She accepts us all as we are.

It's probably the only way anyone can be close to me.

Ilsa wanted me to be better than I am, leading to endless disappointment.

"I don't know if it's because of Adrik or because of what he makes me want."

"What does he make you want?"

"He makes me want to follow my impulses."

"And that's a bad thing?"

I look at the long stretch of sand below us, pocked by countless footprints, then perfectly smooth where the waves have washed them away.

"Historically, yes."

Nix laughs softly. "Sometimes bad decisions take us to the best places."

I sit up a little so I can see her face. Her eyes are closed, her red-gold lashes lying against cheeks dusted with freckles finer than sand.

"Not everyone's story ends as well as yours."

Without opening her eyes, Nix replies, "My story isn't over. It's been painful along the way...but I can accept anything if it's my choice. Regret comes from what you wish you did. You can't regret what you know was right."

She's thinking of her father, I'm sure. She loved her father more than anything. He was her whole world—until she met Rafe.

Nix chose the Petrovs. Because Rafe was what she wanted.

"I *thought* I wanted to go to Kingmakers. Maybe I'm one of those people who's never satisfied."

Nix tilts her face up, catching more of the sunshine. She takes a deep breath and lets it out. I feel the sigh more than I hear it, our bodies pressed together all the way down our sides.

"I don't think Rafe and I will stay here forever," she says. "But it's where we want to be right now."

"You're saying I don't have to plan so far ahead."

Now Nix does open her eyes, and I see the sympathy in them, her desire to help me, not to push me in any direction. She takes my hand and squeezes it.

"I'm not saying anything, except I'll miss you wherever you go."

My face is hot with the discomfort that comes whenever anyone is kind to me. Aggression is easier to match.

"My dad always says in our world, you're dead if you can't think eight steps ahead."

"Well...I don't want to fight with your dad," Nix says, lazily swinging the hammock again. "But life isn't chess. You're not looking down on an open board. No one can actually see the future. Sometimes you just...jump."

She digs under her thigh, retrieving her phone.

"Look," she says, scrolling. "You look pretty happy to me."

She holds up the screen for me to see. It's a picture of the four of us at the arcade. Nix is eating cotton candy, Rafe has his arms wrapped around her waist from behind, and I'm holding a giant teddy bear that Adrik won at the shooting gallery. We could all have won bears if the barker hadn't banned us from the game after Adrik dented half his targets.

That bear's sitting up in Nix's room right now. Like an idiot, I'm wishing it could fit in my suitcase.

"Did you post that pic?" I ask Nix.

Adrik is standing right next to me—not touching me but close enough that it's pretty clear we're on a double date.

"Yeah," Nix says, "but don't worry. My account's private. I've only got, like, twenty-eight followers including you."

Nix wasn't exactly popular at Kingmakers. That's probably what drew me to her in the first place. If I were a gardener, I'd only grow cacti.

I hear the commotion in the house that can only mean that Adrik and the others have returned. The dogs bark with joyful excitement. Rafe tells them to shut the fuck up much too nicely for them to actually obey.

Rafe comes out on the porch, hunting for Nix. She jumps out of the hammock, almost swinging me out on my ass so she can throw her arms around his neck and kiss him.

Adrik stands in the doorway, dark and unsmiling.

The urge to jump up like Nix and put my hands on him is almost overwhelming. I can't not look at him when he's close. I can't stop this burning all over my skin, this anxious churning in my guts. It's lust and it's need and it's something else I can't put into words because I don't understand it. I don't understand how it can be so strong when we've only spent a dozen days together, spread out over months.

How has he become so essential to me?

I don't like this at all.

I'm vulnerable. Cracked open like one of those crabs down on the beach, exposed to any gull that wants to drive its beak through my heart.

"Do you want to go for a drive?" Adrik asks me.

I should say no. I'm only making this harder on myself.

Instead, I'm already on my feet.

We take Rafe's car, which he's lent repeatedly without question. Rafe knows what it's like to keep secrets. To want something you're not supposed to have. To sneak away again and again for a taste of it, promising yourself each time that this will be the end, you'll finally be satisfied...

I let Adrik drive because it's his cousin's car.

My rules about cars aren't as strict as bikes. Even so, I don't sit in the passenger seat unless I'm confident in the driver.

Adrik operates the Mustang smoothly and efficiently. He knows competence is more impressive than speed.

The road unspools beneath us, his arm resting lightly across the back of the bench seat.

"You leave tomorrow," he says.

It's not a question; we both know this already. The silent clock has been counting down in his mind as much as mine.

"Seven a.m."

"I'll drive you to the airport."

I want to say *thanks,* but I can't trust my voice. It might break or come out in an embarrassing squeak. Better to say nothing.

Why does this feel like we're parting forever? Why am I so upset?

The sun sinks down heavy and red ahead of us, casting long shadows from every tree and post.

Because no one knows how many days they have or how many chances. Everything changes. No one stays the same.

Adrik pulls into a lookout point high above the Pacific. The beach below is dark rock, no sand and no sunbathers. We're surrounded on two sides by towering fir trees and Ponderosa pine. The sunset is bloody—vivid and angry.

Adrik kills the engine, turning to me. For once, he doesn't seize me and kiss me but only looks at my face, eyes narrowed, jaw stiff. He runs a hand through his thick shock of hair. His fingers are like claws, his shoulders hunched.

"I don't want you to go."

"That's insane."

"Yes, I'm insane. I'm crazy for you. I'm not afraid to say it."

His heat and candor are like nothing I've known from a man. No posturing—only the truth, given freely.

My heart hammers, and my hands twist in my lap.

"You think I'm afraid?"

"Yes." His eyes burn like blue gas flame. He won't smile even a little. "You're afraid to come to Russia. You're afraid to be alone with me. You want the protection of your family or your school, even when you hate how they chain you."

"I know nothing about Russia, and we've only been dating a week! I'd be a lunatic to come live in your house with your Wolfpack. A bunch of guys all together and then me. How the fuck does that work?"

"It works how I say it will."

"Because you're the boss."

"That's right."

"I don't want to be your soldier. I want freedom, not a new master."

"You'll be my partner."

I make an impatient hissing sound. Everyone knows when there's a king and a queen, the final word comes from the king.

"Let me show you," Adrik says, enclosing my hand in his much larger one. "Come to Moscow. See what it's like."

I try to pull my hand back, but he won't let me. Without even trying, he holds me trapped.

"I can't just roll up to Kingmakers a week late. If I miss the ship, I miss the year."

He won't stop looking at me. He won't give me an inch of space.

"Come with me. You won't regret it."

But I might. How can I know?

"*Come with me.*"

He overpowers me like a wave. He wants to swallow me up in him, to make us one and the same.

Fighting his pull is miserable. I'm in physical pain.

I want to cry with frustration, with confusion, but I won't let myself, never, never, never.

Instead, I fling myself on him. I silence him with my mouth. I show him with my body how badly I want him, how wild he makes me. I straddle his lap, ripping off my clothes and his, not caring who might drive in here or who might see us.

Adrik responds as I knew he would—pulling up my skirt, tearing my underwear, shoving his cock inside me. Letting me know that he understands our purest, truest communication is always our bodies together, giving in to what we both want with equal passion, equal need.

We can never be misunderstood when we're in each other's arms. Our words could never match our bodies. This is what's real. This is what matters.

I fuck him in the scent of leather and gasoline, the bloodred sun beating on the dashboard, glinting off the chrome dials and the sparkling glass.

This is where I want to be. I'd trade my whole life for this moment, and I'd trade this for nothing, not anything that exists.

In this moment, we are one person. We are one thought. And the thought is this:

This is right. I'm supposed to be with you. I don't care about anything else. I don't care what I believed before I met you or what I planned. You smashed what I was, and you made me something new.

Is it love or is it madness?

I accept either one.

My climax is a rush of chemicals and light, my body an engine and Adrik the fuel. We burn and burn and burn together.

When it's over, I cling to him for hours, until the sun sinks all the way down, the air turns cold, and my fingers are chilly against his warm neck. I curl up against him like a child. All I want is his arms around me forever.

———————

We drive home slowly, trying to stretch out each moment. I haven't given him my promise, but I want to. The words are in my throat, waiting to be spoken aloud.

As we near the entrance to the long, winding driveway up to the Petrov house, I see a car parked at the side of the road. Right where the mailbox would be if it weren't blocked by the front wing.

My heart stops in my chest.

The streetlamps are far apart on this lonely stretch of road. The man stands in shadow, his face indistinguishable. Still, the lean body is all too familiar to me. Even if I could see nothing of him, the vehicle itself is too distinct to mistake.

My father is waiting.

CHAPTER 16
ADRIK

SABRINA'S VOICE IS TIGHT AS SHE ORDERS, "PULL OVER HERE."

It only takes a glance for me to understand what's happening. In the glare of our headlights, I see a spare figure dressed all in black, arms crossed over his chest, leaning against the boot of a Hellcat.

We pull up behind him. He stands and ambles toward us, moving slowly, gingerly—old scars, old injuries. His body is as battered as the boots on his feet, his face much the same. Still, you can see the traces of a powerful beauty. Like an aged rock star, he retains a dark glamour that time can't erase.

Sabrina steps from the car, her sneakers crunching across gravel. I exit as well, unwilling to lurk in the driver's seat.

"Hi, Dad."

"Hello, Sabrina."

I would give a great deal to be able to smooth down Sabrina's hair without him noticing or rebutton her shirt the right way.

His eyes pass over the evidence of what I've done to his daughter, then fix on my face.

It seems feeble to introduce myself. If Nero is here, he already knows who I am.

Instead, I nod my head toward the Hellcat, its engine long cooled, its black body gleaming in the night.

"Nice car."

Nero says, "Would you like a drive in it?"

I can feel Sabrina's tension. If I look at her, she might shake her head.

Nothing will prevent me from accepting the invitation. I'm no coward.

"Sure."

"Wait in the Mustang," Nero orders his daughter.

He wants to keep this confrontation out here on the road, away from Ivan's property.

Sabrina opens her mouth to give a fiery retort. It's me who shoots her a look, asking her for once in her life not to argue.

"We'll be back in a minute," I say.

I hope that's true.

I slip in the passenger seat of Nero's car, leaving the seat belt unbuckled. I don't want to be restrained, not on this ride.

Nero climbs in behind the wheel—slower, stiffer. His face gives no hint of pain, but he must feel it every day.

He pulls away from the curb smoothly, one hand on the wheel. He drives like a professional, with a precision that can only be obtained by years of focused practice.

In the dark and silent car, I ponder how to begin this conversation. Nero's presence means he already knows some of what is passing between me and Sabrina. Maybe all of it. I don't know what she's told him or what he's discovered.

Nero suffers no such hesitation. He's as quick as his daughter.

He says, "Why do they call you the Legend?"

Sabrina told me the Gallos love to play chess. I suppose we could call this the King's Gambit—Nero offers a benign, even generous opening. If I take it, he's sure to spring a trap.

I try to deflect.

"It's just an old nickname from school. We were the first class to win three years of the Quartum Bellum. I doubt anyone would use it anymore—not since your nephew won all four."

People absolutely still say it, but I'm downplaying what now sounds ridiculous and immature in the small space of the car, coming out of the mouth of the man known as the Moriarty of Chicago.

Hoping to disarm him, I end with a statement, not a question, volleying the conversation back at him.

Nero is far from disarmed.

In a silky tone of politeness, he says, "That's right. I forgot that you knew Leo. Well enough that you convinced him and my daughter to leave school in the middle of the night and attack an armed fortress of Malina."

Fuck me.

Nero knows everything. And he's not pleased.

I appeal to common ground. "Leo and Sabrina were never supposed to be a part of that. I'm sure you can understand how far I would go to bring a family member home and how impossible it is to prevent your daughter from doing anything she's set her mind to."

The ties of family loyalty are as powerful to the Gallos as they are to the Petrovs. And Nero knows Sabrina better than I do, for better or worse.

Nero turns into the canyon, a drive I would hesitate to take at night, especially with no reduction in speed. He's accelerating, the car flying down the dark and winding road cut deep through the mountain peaks.

"I understand," he says, his voice cool and rational. "But understand *me* now. You are a gravitational pull toward danger and chaos, and you are pulling on my daughter. Starting with the night she met you. In fact, I'll wager that you've already planted the idea of her coming to Russia once she's finished school."

Nero sees inside my head. He has the right idea, wrong timeline. I haven't planted a seed—I've grown a tree. Sabrina wants to come. I know she does. But Nero's influence is powerful. He's here to chop that tree to the ground.

As I remain silent, the speedometer creeps up—eighty-five, then ninety. There's no jerk of the wheels under Nero's steady hand and no hint of emotion on his face.

In Russia, we have a saying: *In the still water, the devil dwells.* I've never met a man with water stiller than this. Nero is ice-cold, driving a hundred miles per hour through the canyon. His breath is unchanging. No pulse in his throat. He is not afraid—not of me or the car or the grim reaper sitting in the back seat with his scythe hanging over our heads.

I want to stay as calm as him. I want it desperately, but heat rises up my neck, sweat prickling my palms.

I blurt out, "Russia is no different from Chicago if you're living the life we live."

For the first time, I see anger on his face. A darkness that suffuses his features like ink in water, obscuring all but the words he throws at me like poisoned darts.

"You wear no sheep's clothing with me. You think I don't know the Bratva? I know you very well."

The Gallos' dealings with my countrymen were familiar to me before Sabrina relayed any part of it. Nero stole the Winter Diamond, the prize of the Bratva, igniting a firestorm that almost burned the Gallos to the ground.

He hisses, "You gave us your word. You signed a contract with my father. Then you shot him in the face and put six bullets in my back that were aimed at my wife. If your people had their way, Sabrina wouldn't exist."

I can't deny the betrayal of the blood oath, a crime even the Bratva blush to remember. Alexei Yenin signed his print in blood, then launched a massacre at the wedding of his own daughter and Sebastian Gallo.

All I can say in defense is "That wasn't me, and that wasn't my family."

"No?" Nero sneers. "Then show me your shoulders."

I don't hesitate. I wrench down the shoulder of my shirt, baring nothing but flesh.

Instead, I point at the wolf on my arm. "I wear my own brand. Mine and no other. I have no quarrel with the Gallos." With a flash of teeth, I add, "I'd like to keep it that way."

I won't be intimidated by Nero.

He looks at the wolf, rapid thought flickering behind those dark eyes. He resembles his daughter so strongly that I feel the strangest mix of connection and confusion. Nero stole the diamond. I want to steal the thing most precious to him.

"I would never hurt Sabrina," I tell him. "I'd do anything to keep her safe."

"Anything? I'm sure you think so…"

The speedometer is up to 120. We're racing down a dark road meant for less than half that speed. Each curve presents us with a sheer rock face, rushing toward us at sickening pace.

Eyes as black as that stone, Nero says, "I would drive us into a wall this moment before I would risk you hurting her."

I don't think he's bluffing. Like father, like daughter. Nero will take this way past the line. He'll risk anything to extort a promise from me.

I won't be robbed—not of Sabrina and not of my word. He'll have to pry her from my cold dead hands.

My voice is as steady as his. "I'm not the one taking your daughter from you. Sabrina won't be caged. She'll bite her own arm off before she'll let either of us tell her what to do."

I see him flinch—just a twitch of his thumb on the wheel, but the clear sign that my arrow hit home.

Slowly, incrementally, the speedometer sinks. We're still flying down the road but no longer hurtling to our deaths.

Nero's eyes stayed fixed on the road, his final threat spoken more to himself than to me: "We'll see about that."

CHAPTER 17
SABRINA

THE HOUR IN WHICH MY FATHER HAS ADRIK PRISONER IN HIS CAR is one of the most stressful of my life. I hate that I let them drive off together. If I wasn't afraid of making a scene a hundred yards from the Petrov house, I never would have allowed it.

When the Hellcat's headlights finally sweep across my car, I'm relieved to see that both Adrik and my dad are still in the front seats, alive and unbloodied.

Adrik may be a little more pale and somber than he was before. My father looks the same as always.

I jump out of the Mustang, half fury and half relief.

"Why didn't you just call me?" I demand of my dad.

"I find face-to-face conversation more honest."

I deserved that little slap. He knows I've been lying to him for months.

Equally, I know there's no point trying to avoid the tête-à-tête he drove all the way here to have. He took his shots at Adrik. Now it's my turn.

"I'll meet you back at the house," I say to Adrik.

He gives me a look I can't interpret, switching positions so he's back in the Mustang and I'm in the Hellcat.

Though it's only been a week since I saw my dad, the scent of his car and even his surly scowl put an ache in my chest. Why does home pull me and repel me with equal strength? Why is everything a battle? I wish I could choose like everyone else and be happy in my choice.

My father drives away from the house once more, but not far. We pull into the parking lot of a seaside café, the shop long shuttered, only a few scattered napkins blowing across the pavement like ghostly tumbleweeds.

Dad lets the engine run so the car will stay warm. He can see that I'm stiff with nerves. My arms are crossed over my chest, angry and defensive.

I thought he'd respond with anger himself or, at the very least, irritation.

Instead when he turns, I see fear in his eyes.

"Sabrina, you are so like me. I worry what that will mean for you."

This hurts and also reminds me that I came from this man, born of his flesh like Adam's rib. You can't forget your parents any more than they can forget you.

I pretend not to understand him.

"Why worry? You're happy enough."

He looks both older and younger in the dim light of the car—his face smooth, his eyes ancient.

"You can't imagine the darkness I lived in before I met your mother. I was cruel and violent. I hurt everyone around me. I had no control. I would have torn myself to pieces until there was nothing left."

My father has always been my mirror and me his. When we look at each other, we don't like what we see.

Stubbornly, I retort, "Maybe Adrik is my Camille."

"Don't insult your mother. Adrik is another Nero, not a Camille."

This isn't about Adrik. My father wishes *I* was more like my mother. But I'm not. Not even a little bit.

Fiercely, I say, "I like what I am. I'm not afraid to be more."

"You should be. You think restraint is the greatest evil—while you cut every rope that ties you to life."

I hate being lectured. Especially by him.

"You would never have taken advice at my age! You always took what you wanted."

"I want you to be better than me."

"Maybe I already am."

He shakes his head. "That's exactly what I would have said—when I was my most arrogant and foolish. Your mother changed me. She made me better. What will Adrik make you?"

I can't answer that. My father is the only person who can silence me, his arguments even quicker than mine.

All I can tell him is the truth. "I want to find out."

I've been angry. I've been frustrated. He stays as calm as the night around us. He looks in my eyes, steady and sad. "You won't survive every lesson."

He's not here out of pride or hatred of the Russians, I know that. He's here for my sake, not threatening but trying to reason with me.

I attempt to meet him on the same ground.

"Dad, I'm not exactly like you. We're similar, it's true. I struggle to be happy, really happy. You can understand that. You needed a Camille. Maybe I need someone more like me. Adrik sees me how I see myself. He's not another Nero. He's not my mother either, but he's not dark. He's not isolated. He commands friendship and loyalty. He grounds me more than you think."

This is the first time I've told anyone how I feel about Adrik. I haven't said it to Adrik or admitted it to myself.

My father is unconvinced.

"You're saying what you want to be true, not what you could actually know. You have a dream of what you think life would be like with him. So did Sebastian with Yelena. Reality is much more cruel."

I hate when he uses that as a weapon against me. His own worst mistake and our family's—an anvil around my neck that was forged before I was ever born.

My dad pushes on. "*I* see you for who you are, Sabrina. I know your intelligence, your passion, your potential. It won't flicker out like a candle. It will burn all your life. You have time. You don't have to rush. Get your schooling. Grow up a little more. Then I won't oppose you seeing Adrik."

This is a heavy compromise from him—more than I could have expected. It has an effect on me.

I hug him, something we don't do often. His arms are warmer than you'd think—not unlike my mom's.

I feel safe with him. I feel loved. I know how powerfully he needs to protect me, and for once, that doesn't feel like chains.

"Thank you for coming out here, Dad. I'm glad I got to see you again before I leave."

He kisses the top of my head, stroking his palm gently against my back.

"You'll understand someday how much I love you."

I'm torn in half, between the family I love and the man I want more than anything.

I turn my face against his shoulder to keep the tears back, because even with my father, I won't allow myself to cry.

CHAPTER 18
ADRIK

Because Sabrina has to leave so early in the morning, only Nix is up to say goodbye to her.

Sabrina trundles her suitcase down the front steps, looking ashen in the diluted light.

I take the suitcase from her, hoisting it into the back seat of Rafe's car.

Sabrina follows in uncharacteristic silence.

She's barely spoken to me since her drive with her father. Nero left directly afterward, his work done. She's going back to school. I won't see her again for eight months at least.

As I drive her to the very last place I want to take her, I want to argue again. Hell, I want to turn this car in the opposite direction and abduct her. But it would be pointless. I want Sabrina free and willing or not at all.

She leans against the car door as if she's exhausted. I've never seen her like this. Usually, she overflows with an energy so electric that it almost sears your retinas to look at her.

I understand the power of a father. I've had my conflicts with my own dad—times when I've bristled at his conservatism, his caution that can feel like wet mud I have to wade through on my way to anything new. He's a good leader, a good teacher. I emulate his methods with my own men. But he's always been willing to follow Ivan, while I refuse to be second to anyone.

Sabrina shares my hunger for independence. I know she does. That's why she's so tormented returning to Kingmakers.

But she's younger than me. She's not ready to shake off the weight of everyone else's expectations and advice. There's no point in trying to pile my own desires on the burden threatening to break her back.

Or...maybe she simply doesn't feel the way I do.

She's unhappy, I can see that...but actions tell the truth. She's leaving. What more do I need to know?

We pull up outside the airport in Portland.

I lift her suitcase out of the car, hating every part of that motion. I want to say something to her, and I consider several options, discarding each one in turn.

I'll miss you...pithy, insufficient.

I don't want you to go...already been said.

This was the best week of my life...true, but still not enough.

I'd give anything for more time...fucking pathetic.

I wrap my arms around her, crushing her against my chest, angry at her and at myself. I've never been like this before. I've always known what to do.

The impulse to snatch her up and throw her back in the car is overwhelming.

Instead, I let go, regretting it the moment I feel the cold emptiness between my arms.

Sabrina gives me one last look, her eyes huge and dark in her stiff face.

She pulls her suitcase away without either of us saying anything at all.

I stand by the car like a fucking fool, wondering how I got so attached.

I'm not some weak-willed romantic. Before I met Sabrina, I couldn't give a shit about women. All I cared about was building my business. All I needed was my brothers.

Then I saw her, and everything changed.

I came to Croatia to win her over, telling myself she could be an asset, just like Sloane said. And I still believe I was right about that. But that's not why I'm here. That's not why I want her to come with me.

All I want is Sabrina beside me.

I want that wild look in her eye, that quick wit, that fucking fire, the only flame I've encountered that burns hotter than mine.

Without her, I'm dull and unmotivated, unable to raise the slightest interest in my journey back home or what I'll do once I get there.

I stand by the car so long that the parking attendant passes by twice to chastise me. Still I stay, a fool till the end.

A jumbo jet rises in the air—Sabrina's airline, probably her plane. It soars up like a bird, glinting in the sun, hateful to me in every way.

Watching it shrink in size and fly away from me is one of the most painful things I've experienced.

I didn't think it would hurt this much. I thought I was ready.

I take several deep breaths, knowing I have to return to the house. I'll have to mask this sick churning in my guts while Rafe tries to rib me and my mother scans my face for the evidence of what she senses but is too kind to say out loud.

I should have hidden it better all along. I shouldn't have exposed myself like this.

It was impossible. I fell for Sabrina like a boulder tumbling off a cliff. The boulder was the size of a house. Now it's landed on my chest.

When the plane disappears in the clouds, I finally turn back to the car.

Only to hear my name screamed at top volume: "Adrik!!!"

If I could bottle the joy that bubbles up in me like pure, liquid sunshine, I'd be the richest man in the world.

Before I can even turn, she's leaping into my arms. She's

breathtaking. She literally steals the breath from my lungs, hair streaming behind her like a banner, face illuminated with radiant light, hands outstretched to me, skin flushed with sprinting. Her scent hits me—heady and warm, mocha and almond. I gulp it down, my whole head floating, high as a kite.

Nothing has ever felt better than her trembling body clasped tight in my arms.

She's shaking against me, clinging to me with all her strength, her arms around my neck, legs around my waist. She kisses me over and over, on my mouth, my cheeks, my forehead, my lips again.

I squeeze her too hard. I must be hurting her, but I can't stop.

She came back. She came back to me.

Sabrina presses her cheek against mine, saying fiercely, "It's crazy, and I don't care. I want to be crazy with you."

I hold her tight, making a promise I know I won't break:

"I'm never letting you walk away from me again."

CHAPTER 19
SABRINA

On September first, instead of boarding the ship in Dubrovnik, I fly to Moscow with Adrik.

I send my parents one single text:

Sabrina: I'm going to Russia

Then I shut off my phone so I don't have to deal with the fallout of that particular bomb.

I feel strangely calm all through the flight. Now that my decision is made, I'm no longer pulled apart at the seams. My confidence returns, and I fill with excitement.

Adrik likewise seems altered.

He's dressed in his usual way—T-shirt, jeans, boots, same battered leather jacket he wore the day he picked me up in Dubrovnik. Yet he's different here in the Moscow airport, among the throngs of people who look somewhat like Americans do but not quite the same.

There's enough dissimilarity in the style of suits and casual wear, amplified by the incomprehensible announcements over the loudspeakers and the Cyrillic signs, to remind me that I'm very much in a foreign country.

Eastern Europeans have their own characteristics—high cheekbones, narrow eyes, strong jaws, broad noses. Seeing Adrik next to

his countrymen seems to emphasize the dark exoticism of his looks.
He's never looked more brutish or more Russian.

I'm all nerves and anticipation. I wish I could read the signs—
I'll have to learn. I like learning new things.

"Where do we go first?" I ask Adrik once we've retrieved our
bags.

"Home. I want you to meet my brothers."

This is the part of the adventure that concerns me most. Adrik
lives with five other men. I know his actual brother, Kade, and we get
on well. But Kade is headed back to Kingmakers today. The five I'll
be meeting are strangers to me. I'll have to learn to work with them,
integrating into an already tightly bonded group.

I understand group dynamics well enough to assume that there's
already heavy competition for Adrik's favor. As the only woman—
and presumably the only one fucking him—I can expect a certain
level of animosity.

I don't enjoy frat-house fervor. Ilsa had to put up with it
constantly in the gatehouse. She didn't seem to mind it as much as
I would. She's not as fastidious about hygiene, and she has a brash
humor that served her well. She's as likely to pull a prank or start a
brawl as anyone.

Besides, she's an actual gold-star lesbian who's never even kissed
a man. The constant flirtation lobbed at her in her first year died off
when the guys finally accepted her adamant disinterest.

My situation is a little more complicated.

I don't have to wait until we arrive at the house Adrik jokingly
calls "the Den." One of his Wolfpack is waiting for us at the curb,
leaning out the open window of a black SUV. I can deduce his name
from the forearm and fist propped up against his jaw, tattoos of
skeletal bones superimposed on the flesh—this is Jasper Webb.

He graduated before I ever came to Kingmakers, but my cousins
described him in detail. He was an enemy to Miles and something of
a friend to Leo. I don't know what that makes the two of us.

"Take the front seat," Adrik says, throwing our suitcases in the trunk.

He doesn't want us both in the back with Jasper as chauffeur, nor does he want to relegate me to the back seat alone.

Adrik is cognizant of small social cues. Without any obvious effort, he's the oil that keeps the gears running smoothly when people come together.

Jasper turns his cool gaze on me. His unblinking eyes, pale and reptilian, offer no welcome. Grim skeleton tattoos run from his fingernails up the backs of his hands, over his arms and his shoulders, across his chest, and up his neck to his chin, visible through the thin material of his white shirt. If I could see through his jeans, I'd guess they run down his legs as well. Jasper doesn't look like a man who does things by halves.

The sides of his head are shaved, his shock of dark red hair falling down on the right side. His flesh is bone-white, his mouth thin and unsmiling.

"Sabrina," I say, holding out my hand.

With Adrik watching, he has to shake hands.

He squeezes hard. I squeeze back harder, holding his eye with none of the placating smiles women are taught to offer.

"Jasper," he says.

I could say *I know*, but I don't. I don't care what he thinks of my cousins or of me. I'll forge my own relationships here, on my own terms. None of us are at Kingmakers anymore.

"Good to have you back," Jasper says to Adrik, meeting his eyes in the rearview mirror before directing his attention to driving.

I notice Jasper doesn't use any term of address with Adrik—not *pakhan* or boss or *krestniy otets*.

"It's good to be back, brother," Adrik says, leaning forward to clap Jasper on the shoulder. "We'll talk tonight. I've been making plans in my absence."

I feel the frisson of excitement on Jasper's bare skin, though he only nods.

I'm lit with the same excitement myself. It's impossible not to be affected by Adrik's voice, deep and clear and confident. The Churchills and the Washingtons of the world have always had this quality—to stir the hearts of men when they speak.

As we pull onto the main roads of Moscow, I note the broadness of the avenues. The main artery of Kutuzovsky Prospekt spans ten lanes across. Still, the streets are clogged with cars, each red light interminable. In the midst of all this congestion, a black town car with a howling siren speeds down the highway in the opposite direction, forcing the cars to edge out of its way as it careens past.

"Was that a cop?" I ask.

Adrik laughs. "A politician. Top-ranking officials don't have to obey the traffic rules. They can speed all they like, drive on the wrong side of the road, cut off an ambulance or a fire truck... You better run for office, Jasper, or we'll never get anywhere."

Jasper spits out the open window. "Fucking parasites."

I smile to myself. The antipathy between criminals and politicians has always amused me, each of us disgusted at the corruption of the other. At least criminals are honest—we admit what we are.

"It didn't used to be this way," Adrik tells me. "The number of cars in Moscow has doubled in the last ten years."

The farther we drive into the center of the city, the more I'm astounded at its sprawling mass. Twelve million people live here. I looked it up before I came. The number gave me no idea of its real density—four times the size of Chicago and in some places just as modern in appearance. To the west, I see a forest of skyscrapers, gleaming glass towers to rival any at home.

But I'm not at home. The heavy brutalist architecture reminds me of that, the many cement tenements and, in the distance, the unmistakable red brick Kremlin and the colorful onion domes of the basilica.

The cars themselves are a bizarre mix of ultra-luxury Ferraris and beemers bumper to bumper with Ladas and Kias held together with wire and twine.

On the plane, I read that the average salary in Moscow is $1100 a month. Conversely, Moscow has more billionaires than London or San Francisco. I can see the dichotomy everywhere I look, the gated communities of the privileged jammed up against the cramped Soviet-era apartments of the worker ants.

"Where's the Den?" I ask Adrik.

"In Lyublino," he says. "Not much farther."

Jasper navigates a series of increasingly narrow streets, through concrete buildings that loom up on both sides, claustrophobically close. Everything in Moscow is built on a grandiose scale, thick and heavy and hulking. Each glimpse of a park is a relief, a breath of green in all this gray.

We've passed through countless strata of neighborhoods. Lyublino is on the seedier side—metal bars across the windows, graffiti in the alleyways. I see a mural of a woman with crow's wings growing out of her eyes and another of a Technicolor matryoshka doll.

At last, we reach the end of the road where Adrik's house sits. We pass through an iron gate running beneath a pointed archway topped by several spires, the crumbling stone blackened with soot and grime. Adrik's parents live in a monastery in St. Petersburg— perhaps his childhood home influenced his choice. The Den resembles a Gothic church, dark and ornate, with mats of crawling ivy attempting to pull down the dilapidated stones.

Jasper pulls the SUV into an alcove of cars, among which I see Adrik's bike and several others of similar style. I'll have to get a bike of my own. Fuck sitting in Moscow traffic.

"Come meet everyone," Adrik says, taking my hand.

He lets go before we enter the house, which I prefer. I don't want to be presented as his paramour. I'm here to work.

The interior of the Den is dim and cool, thankfully smelling only of damp and dust, not sweaty men. Tiny motes swim in the thin bands of watery sunshine crossing the hall.

The floors are bare stone, relieved by a few faded rugs. No art hangs on the wall, and the furniture I can see is sparse and shabby. I leave my suitcase by the door. Adrik does the same.

He leads me through a warren of narrow passageways, past a kitchen with two mismatched refrigerators and one vast farmhouse table, then down a short set of steps into a large common room.

Here we find the rest of the Wolfpack.

I hear the gruff laughter and shouting before we get close. Two are playing *Call of Duty*, sprawled out on beanbags on the floor. A thick-shouldered giant sits in an easy chair that groans beneath his weight, fucking around on his phone. The last wolf lies across the length of the couch, reading a paperback.

They're all much bigger than me, muscular and full of restless energy. As soon as we enter the room, their attention shifts, and silence falls.

The two video game players set down their controllers, swiftly shutting off the TV. No one jumps to their feet, but the sense of alertness is palpable. The reader lets his book fall to his lap, sitting up and grinning at Adrik. "Welcome back, boss. And you brought...a friend."

Five pairs of eyes fix on me—six if you count Jasper, who followed us into the house. I can feel his stare on my back.

"This is Sabrina Gallo," Adrik says, calm and pleasant, with no acknowledgment that this might be poorly received. "She's agreed to join us."

He points to each of the Wolfpack in turn, naming them: "That's Andrei, Hakim, Chief, and Vlad."

Andrei and Hakim are the gamers. Andrei is as blond and Slavic as one might expect, Hakim his direct opposite. Hakim might be Arab, his close-cropped hair dark and curly, his five-o'clock shadow black as paint.

Chief eyes me with interest as if we've already met, though I'm quite sure we haven't. He's not Russian either as far as I can tell—maybe Southeast Asian, with light brown hair and a golden cast to his skin. I'm not surprised to see him reading, since he was the one Adrik described as particularly intelligent.

Vlad, by contrast, is the biggest, the beefiest, and certainly the surliest. His close-shaved head with its grayish stubble resembles a rock sitting directly atop his hulking shoulders, and his small, dark eyes glitter like malachite as he glares at me with instant dislike. He's testing the structural integrity of the Affliction T-shirt stretched across pecs the size of dinner plates. I wonder if the shirt is ironic or if Affliction only just made its way to Russia.

Though the group's manner is casual, I'm cognizant of the ways in which they resemble a military unit. It's not just the matching tattoos on each of their arms. It's their deference to Adrik and the way communication passes between them in glances and inflections. I can imagine them storming a building with only a few gestures needed to coordinate an attack.

These are men who have bonded already. Worked together. Learned to trust one another.

I'm a stranger. An intruder.

They regard me silently.

I speak instead. "Adrik said you guys need some help opening jars."

It's not the world's greatest icebreaker, but it's enough to get a smirk out of Chief.

Not Vlad. "Why don't you help us decorate?" he sneers.

I feel Adrik stiffen, but I cut across him.

"Sure," I say easily. "Let's start with that shirt."

That gets a snort out of the two gamers, Andrei and Hakim.

Andrei pipes up. "A Gallo, huh? Was Leo busy?"

It's still insulting but not a bad sign. Ribbing is better than cold silence. If you can't take a few shots, you'll never fit in with men.

They really are pack animals, releasing their aggression publicly in front of the group so the group determines the appropriate behavior. They don't bottle shit up and bitch behind your back—or at least not often.

Andrei obviously knows Leo, but he's too old to be in the same year. So I know exactly how to respond.

"Yeah." I grin. "He's all tuckered out from running train on you at school."

This gets a laugh out of the gamers and Chief as well.

The chill in the room is warming, at least a few degrees.

Vlad isn't biting, hefty arms crossed, a scowl on his face. "I thought this house was patch-only."

He means the tattoos. It must be a rite of passage before entering the Wolfpack.

Adrik says, "This house was supposed to be brains only, but we let you in."

Now they're all laughing, and Vlad looks suitably stupid.

The tension is broken, as much as it needs to be for now. The real work will take place one-on-one as I get to know them individually.

Nobody welcomes change, but if I want you to like me, you're damn well going to like me. I'm as relentless as Adrik, in my own way.

"Do we need to clear out a room?" Chief asks.

"No," Adrik says. "She'll be staying with me."

Andrei and Hakim exchange a glance across the space between their beanbag chairs, but this is no more than they expected. The calm holds.

"Come on," Adrik says. "I'll show you the room."

We retrieve our suitcases, carrying them up the narrow staircase to the top floor.

I'm relieved everyone here speaks English. It's the lingua franca at Kingmakers and probably in this house too if Adrik gathered his Wolfpack from several countries.

I expect Adrik's room to be the largest and most luxurious. In actuality, it looks much like the others we passed on our way. A wide, low bed takes up most of the space, covered with a red cotton comforter in folk print. The bed is neatly made, the room cleaner than any other part of the house. I doubt this was for my benefit. Adrik is more disciplined than he looks and much more organized.

A wardrobe stands on one side of the room, a hefty bookshelf on the other, its shelves stuffed with tattered paperbacks.

"Did you bring those from home?" I ask Adrik.

He shakes his head. "I bought a crate of books in Danilovsky Market. I like to read to wind down. I'm not sure exactly what's in there actually—haven't had the chance to go through them all."

The singular window looks down over the small back garden. I peer through the bubbled glass, bisected by slender molded mullions, with a pretty pattern of decorative tracery at the top.

"Garden" was perhaps too generous a term; nobody has tended the jungle of vines and shrubs choking the trees, and half the ornamental plants are dead while the wildest weeds run rampant. You could hardly walk through to the high stone wall behind. Beyond that, a jigsaw of uneven tenement buildings, rectangular and ugly, with metal fire escapes crisscrossing down their sides.

"Not the best view," Adrik acknowledges.

"I'm not here for scenery." I set my suitcase down in the corner, turning to face Adrik.

"Then what are you here for?" he says, running a hand through his hair in a way that looks like it will smooth it but really makes it stick up in more directions than ever.

"Why don't you tell me? On our first date, you said you wanted to recruit me. What did you imagine I would do here? Where do I fit in with everyone else?"

Adrik shrugs, his heavy shoulders lifting and falling with almost audible weight.

"I told you, Sabrina. I don't plan to be your boss. I want you to run free. We'll see what you come up with."

A light heat spreads through my chest, and I let him see my smile. I worried that once I was here, he'd revert to some misogynistic Bratva and start barking orders at me. But it seems he really does intend to keep his word.

"Will you take me out tonight?" I ask. "Show me the city?"

"Of course." Adrik gestures to the room. "Does this suit you? Would you prefer your own space?"

I consider. I might like my own space, but I also know I'll be pulled into this bed every night like a magnet.

"This is good for now."

Adrik smiles. "That wasn't a real offer. I didn't fly you across the world to be roommates."

He opens the wardrobe.

"You can put your clothes in here. There should be plenty of space. I have to speak with some of the others. If you want to rest, there's at least an hour before dinner."

He leaves me to unpack, which takes little time since I brought only the single suitcase, mostly containing school uniforms that I toss straight in the trash.

Adrik wasn't joking when he said there was room for my things. He's got about six shirts in the wardrobe and not much else. He lives a minimalist life, that much is clear.

I'll have to adjust to all this tidiness. I've been known to toss my clothes on the floor when I roomed with Nix, but I won't do that here. It's time to grow up, like my dad said—in more ways than one.

We've got our own bathroom, thank god. I don't think I could stand sharing with Vlad.

I set my toiletries inside, my toothbrush next to Adrik's and my shampoo in the tiny box of the shower. The bathroom has been renovated somewhat more than the rest of the house, but it still looks thirty years out-of-date, its pedestal sink cracked on one side, the brass faucets rusted. The tub is made of oxidized copper so heavy that the floorboards sag beneath it.

Unpacking completed, I shove the empty suitcase under the bed, then stand and wait, wondering if I'll feel regret now that I'm settling into the reality of my situation.

Regret doesn't come. Only a deep sense of exhaustion.

I'd planned to make use of that cramped shower. Instead, I sink onto the bed, burying my face in Adrik's pillow. It smells of him—a scent I've tried a hundred times to isolate without ever being able to name it. It comes to me in waves like colors—dark like a deeply steeped tea, with notes of heady sweetness, burgundy wine or black cherry. Then that head-spinning chemical edge that compels you to inhale again and again, even if you know it might be bad for you or even toxic—testosterone like pure gasoline.

It's that scent that makes me feel at home in this room. That chains me to this bed with no desire to ever leave it.

I fall asleep breathing him in, over and over and over.

I wake to the clanging of a cowbell. It echoes through the house, bringing scuffling feet, scraping chairs, and jumbled conversation into the kitchen below.

If I hadn't been woken by the noise, the smell of beef stew might have done it. My gurgling stomach urges me out of the bed.

A glance in the mirror reveals smears of mascara under both eyes and a lopsided haystack of hair. I twist my hair up in a topknot and take a couple half-hearted swipes at my face with a damp cloth, too hungry for anything else.

By the time I get to the kitchen, everyone else is seated on the dual bench seats of the farmhouse table, including Adrik. He throws a look at Hakim, telling him to make room for me. I drop down between Andrei and Chief instead. I don't need Adrik's protection, not in this house.

Chief pushes me a basket of crusty bread, hard enough that it makes a sharp cracking sound when I tear off half a baguette. I dish stew from the tureen in the center of the table, ladling it into an earthenware bowl so heavy that I can hardly hold it in one hand. The stew is beef and vegetables, the broth thick as gravy.

"We take turns cooking," Adrik tells me.

"I don't cook."

"Neither do Vlad or Hakim, but we eat the shit they make, and we don't complain."

"Not even when Hakim makes goulash for the twenty-seventh time," Andrei says, grinning across the table at Hakim.

"Fuck off," Hakim grouses. "Took me long enough to learn to make that. I'm not fuckin' Gordon Ramsay, am I?"

"You're barely Sweeney Todd," Andrei laughs.

"I will be if you keep it up," Hakim says darkly. "You're getting fat enough to make a good pie out of you."

Andrei looks genuinely offended at this. "I'm not nearly as fat as Vlad. Am I, Vlad?"

He elbows his seatmate in his generous flank.

Vlad shoots Andrei a look of such malevolence that Andrei's grin morphs into a puckered mew, his blue eyes as round and startled as a schoolboy's. Andrei scoots several inches to the left, knocking my elbow and dislodging the delectable chunk of beef I'd gotten within an inch of my mouth. In retaliation, I steal the rest of Andrei's baguette.

While I loathe the idea of cooking for this pack of hyenas, I have to respect Adrik's insistence on family dinners. Eating is a bonding activity, and if we weren't forced to cook proper food, the house would soon become a wasteland of empty fast-food bags, with Andrei and Vlad as plump as Hakim claimed.

In truth, everyone at the table is admirably fit, ranging from

Jasper's lean and rangy muscle to Vlad's bulk. There must be a gym close by, maybe at the house. I wonder if Adrik makes everyone work out together.

It can't be worse than the workouts Ilsa used to put me through.

I catch Adrik's eye as he takes a second helping of stew. He grins, his teeth a flash of white in his tanned face. There is no head or foot to this table—also intentional, I'm sure. Adrik calls his men "brother." He avoids the appearance of authority. Yet they all wear his brand on their arm. They listen when he talks, and I assume they obey. Will he demand the same from me?

Conversation bounces back and forth across the table. Everyone here is younger than thirty, full of energy and crudity. Even Jasper smiles once or twice, though his chill is more complete than Vlad's, directed at everyone, not just at me.

Adrik passes out frosty bottles of Baltika from the fridge, popping their caps on the scarred edge of the table.

"Does the lady need a cosmo?" Andrei smirks at me.

"Is that what you use to get Hakim in bed?" I say, sweetly sipping my beer.

"He might be getting desperate enough," Hakim snorts. "You're on a dry spell, aren't you, Andrei?"

"I'd get laid every night if I was willing to take home the dogs you fuck," Andrei retorts.

"Can we talk business?" Chief pleads of Adrik. "Before I have to hear another recital of Hakim's conquests and the lies he has to tell to get them in bed."

"What lies?" Hakim protests.

"Did you or did you not tell some poor college student that you were Zayn Malik's cousin?"

Hakim shrugs. "I could be. I've got a lot of cousins."

"We can talk," Adrik says, silencing them all. "Who wants to tell me what you did while I was gone?"

"I will," Jasper says, composed and ready. "We sold off that load of ARs to the Slavs. They offered us ten keys coming in fresh from Bolivia. But they're asking fifty per, and I think we can get a better deal from Baldoski. We'll have to get a sample first and test it. There's rumors that he's cutting below forty percent."

Adrik nods, mentally tallying each point. I have no doubt he could repeat it all back verbatim if he wanted to. I know I could.

"And the books?"

"Up to date," Chief replies. "We took in twenty-eight K on the ARs, but I had to pay out twelve to the *musor*."

"Good," Adrik says. "I'm taking Sabrina out for a drink."

That's all. He gives no instructions. Dinner breaks up, Andrei washing the dishes because it's his turn.

As we exit the kitchen, I ask Adrik, "Don't you have any orders?"

"They know what they need to do. They'll come to me if they need help."

Interesting. This is unlike what I'm used to, even in relatively flexible Mafia organizations. Adrik offers an unusual level of autonomy to his men.

"What's the *musor*?" I ask him.

"The cops. Don't call 'em that to their face, though. It means *garbage*. They've been raking us over the coals with the bribes. I'm gonna have to figure out some kind of leverage besides money, or we'll never make a profit."

"Where are you taking me?" I ask him, wondering how to dress.

He smiles. "I'm gonna show you how we party in Moscow."

CHAPTER 20
ADRIK

Sabrina emerges from our room an hour later, wearing tight leather pants and a silky top I could crumple in one hand. Her hair, freshly washed and waved, floats around her like smoke. She's lined her eyes with so much kohl that she looks like an Egyptian princess, or maybe something more sinister—a vengeful goddess demanding sacrifice.

Having Sabrina here in my house is so fucking satisfying, I can't stop grinning.

I saw her, and I knew that I needed her—like a good-luck talisman or the aquila carried by the Roman legions. Not because Sabrina is a token but because she fills me with energy. She gives me power. I'm stronger with her here.

I'm determined to make her love Moscow. I want to show her its beauty and its potential.

I was never worried that she'd fit in at the house. Her introduction was exactly what I expected—Sabrina can handle herself. Like a cat surrounded by dogs, she knows how to give Vlad a slap on the nose if he growls at her.

In time, she'll come to know them all and respect them as I do. I haven't brought anyone into the Wolfpack without good reason—including Sabrina herself. They'll see her talent, and she'll see theirs.

My bigger concern is acclimating her to Russia in general. Moscow is a jungle with just as many hidden dangers as the Amazon.

"Are we gonna take the bikes?" Sabrina asks, looking eagerly out into the yard.

"Sure," I say. "You can take Jasper's old bike. Until we get you your own."

Sabrina makes no argument about taking the smaller, older Gold Wing. She knows we won't be racing through Moscow's congested streets.

We mount the bikes beneath the stone archway partially covering the parking pad.

I toss her a helmet.

"I don't need that."

Sabrina sets it down on the seat of Chief's bike.

"You don't wear a helmet?"

"The point of riding a bike is being out in the open. Feeling the air. Seeing what's around you."

"Until you crack your skull open on a curb. Don't you think that's kind of a stupid risk?"

Sabrina shrugs. "Everything we do is reckless. Everything's a risk."

Sabrina reminds me of a gambler intent on putting their entire stack on the line, just for the thrill of it.

Still, I set my own helmet down. It seems ungentlemanly to protect myself more than her.

The Ducati fires up with a low purr. I see Sabrina's eyes gleam. She remembers how that engine feels pressed up against her.

"Keep your mitts to yourself," I warn her.

She grins. "I will if you keep your keys in your pocket."

I pull out through the gates, leaning hard to take the corner. Sabrina follows after me, light, easy, relaxed. We swoop through the dark streets in tandem, two bats released into the night. I like riding with Sabrina close behind me, floating in and out of my peripheral with each curve in the road.

The night air feels cool and liquid, ruffling through my hair like fingers. Sabrina's right that it feels good to ride like this, unprotected and unbound. It's easy to call out to her at the lights, to point out Tagansky Park and the Novospassky Monastery as we pass by.

I take her to the Soho Rooms, one of the most exclusive nightclubs in Moscow, located right on the Moskva river so the purplish light pouring out from its windows wriggles across the dark water below.

A long line of guests waits outside the door. I don't have to pass a bribe to the "face master" before he waves Sabrina inside. He glances at the Vacheron Constantin on my wrist and allows me to pass along with her.

"Did you know him?" Sabrina asks me.

"It's *feyskontrol*—face control," I tell her. "Beauty is everything here. If you look wealthy, cultured, and gorgeous, you get in the club. If you don't, you won't."

The evidence is clear all around us—a mass of disproportionately stunning clubgoers, decked out in glittering minidresses and tight button-ups and slacks. Those who aren't young and beautiful are clearly wealthy, the older men in bespoke suits and enough gold chains, watches, and rings to attract their pick of the stunning young women flocking around them.

I brought Sabrina here because it's where the models and celebrities go. I thought she'd enjoy the glitz and glamour.

Dozens of disco balls reflect a flurry of purple speckles over the throng of drunken dancers. Once we've ordered our drinks, I take her up to the Summer Terrace, where a girl in a transparent bodysuit performs an aerial silks show. She floats through the air, twisted up in a long white swath, heedless of the fifty-foot drop to the dance floor below.

We take a seat at a small table with a good view of the room. Sabrina looks around at the stylish crowd, unsmiling.

"What's wrong?" I ask her.

"It's a tourist place."

"Not just for tourists."

She frowns. "This isn't where you would go—if it were just you or the Wolfpack."

"You don't like it?"

"I want you to show me what you do, how you live. I want to see the real Russia."

"It's not as posh."

She fixes me with that blazing stare, stubborn and demanding. "Take me where the Bratva go."

I smile, not displeased. "Alright. Come on."

We leave the club and wind through the darker, dingier roads leading into Danilovsky. Here the luxury cars pulled up to the curb look much more out of place, but no one would dare touch them, even if they were left unlocked.

There's no line outside Apothecary and no sign above the plain brick entryway other than a painted wooden board, the sort that might hang at an English pub, depicting a shot glass with an eerie green brew within.

I tell Sabrina, "It's neutral ground of sorts. No business here— just networking."

She nods, understanding.

We pass inside, through a dark and undecorated hallway, raw brick like the exterior.

Apothecary is smaller than the Soho Rooms and less crowded. It resembles an old speakeasy, with ancient plasterwork on the walls, stained by cigar smoke, and a dark wood bar, carved and scrolled, where dusty, unlabeled bottles line the shelves. The wrought-iron lamps let out a dim golden glow, casting pools of light distinct from the impenetrable gloom.

The tables are set far enough apart that conversations are unlikely to be overheard, especially under the steady thud of music pumped into the room.

The mostly male patrons are accompanied by women too tarty to leave any doubt of their profession. Sabrina—the only woman in pants and clearly foreign—draws plenty of eyes.

If the Soho Rooms differentiate on beauty and wealth, an entirely different principle operates here. Age and ethnicity are diverse, as is apparel: while some wear suits, jeans, trainers, and tracksuits are just as common. The real unifying characteristic is the sense that every person here has been battered by time and circumstance. Scars and injuries are common, the indelible marks of experience even more so. Even the youngest whores look old before their time, bearing the hollow expressions of those who have seen too much.

We order our drinks at the bar.

"Mykah," I say to the bartender, "this is Sabrina."

Mykah has the build of an enforcer—body like a refrigerator, hands like catcher's mitts—but his voice is soft and gentle. Whenever he's working, he wears a cloth beanie and an oilskin apron, a pair of spectacles perched low on his nose like a babushka.

"*Zdravstvuyte,*" he says, taking down the vodka for our drinks.

"*Dobryy vecher,*" Sabrina replies, trying out one of her newly learned greetings.

"Very good." Mykah nods his approval.

"It's shit," Sabrina sighs, "but I'll learn."

"Russian is very easy language," Mykah agrees. "It only take me three years to learn, and I was baby at time."

He roars with laughter, Sabrina laughing too, though more at Mykah himself than at his witticisms.

"What you do here with this one?" Mykah points his bar towel at me. "You know he is very bad guy."

"Adrik?" Sabrina says, eyebrows raised in mock surprise. "He told me he was an Elvis impersonator."

"Elvis!" Mykah chortles, spraying my arm with a little bit of spit. "Get me comb. I see it now."

He holds up his hands, framing my hair, squinting and picturing me with a pompadour. With his fingers spread, I can easily see the missing fingers on his right hand.

"Buy your own comb," I say, throwing down some cash and picking up our drinks.

"*Privet*," Mykah says, leaning in before I can leave. "Krystiyan *zdes'*." *Krystiyan is here.* He jerks his head in the appropriate direction without looking or pointing.

I glance the same way without letting my eyes rest on the group crammed into the far corner table.

"*Blagodaryu*," I murmur, turning away and leading Sabrina to our own table.

"What did he say to you?" she demands once we're seated.

"He was letting me know we've got an old friend in the house."

"The table in the corner?"

She doesn't miss a thing.

"Yeah. The pretty boy in the too-tight suit."

Sabrina laughs softly. "How do you know him?"

"From school. 'Friend' was an exaggeration. I fucking loathe him."

Sabrina looks at me with curiosity.

"What does it take to get on your bad side?"

"I told him something in confidence. When it got out, I knew he couldn't be trusted. That was the first reason. I've had plenty since."

"Well, don't worry," Sabrina says, giving me a sly smile. "Your secrets are safe with me."

"What secrets do you know?"

"Plenty. You talk in your sleep."

"What do I say?"

"I just promised not to tell anyone."

I take a sip of my drink. "That's probably for the best."

"Is everyone here Bratva?" Sabrina asks, letting her gaze shift around the room, the tables obscured by cigar and hookah smoke and the low light.

"Most of them."

She examines one table after another from under her lashes before pronouncing, "They don't look how I expected."

"What did you expect?"

She shrugs. "More tattoos."

"The old ways are dying out. You've got to blend in nowadays. It's better for business. If they have the marks, they keep them where a suit can cover."

"Not everyone," Sabrina says, looking at the man nursing a pint at the table next to ours, his shaved skull covered with a sprawling black widow spider.

"The first *vory v zakone* covered themselves in tattoos as a rejection of society. You know the history of the *vory*?" I ask Sabrina.

She shakes her head. "We don't study the Bratva till third year. In first year, we only did the 'Ndrangheta and Cosa Nostra."

I finish my Stoli and set it to the side, wanting both hands free while I explain.

"In imperial Russia, virtually everything belonged to the czar. The first group who formed the *vorovskoy mir*, the world of thieves, were revolutionaries of a sort. They had a code of honor—they shared their plunder equally and, like Robin Hood, distributed it among the people as well."

"How noble," Sabrina says with a saucy grin.

She knows as well as I do that spreading wealth is more strategy than altruism, buying the loyalty of those who surround you. I do the same thing in my own neighborhood, ensuring the silence of those who could report me if fear were insufficient to keep them quiet.

"When the Bolsheviks rose, the *vory v zakone* helped control the streets of Moscow," I continue. "That was when Mafia and government first became intertwined in Russia. It worked with Lenin, but when Stalin took control, he threw the *vory* into the gulags. There, the underworld truly took shape."

"Prison is the best recruiting ground," Sabrina says.

"That's right. The language and culture of the *vory* flourished in the gulags. Until the Germans marched on Moscow and Stalin was forced to use prisoners to swell the Russian army. He promised freedom if they would fight for their country. Many agreed, though it was against the code of the thieves to work for those who had imprisoned them. They fought and died for Russia. When the war was over, Stalin reneged on his promise and threw them right back in the gulag."

Sabrina gives a soft hiss of distaste, eyes narrowed. In our world, where there is no recourse to the courts, word is law and a promise a contract.

"The *vory* turned on each other. They called the ones who had fought *suki*, traitors, and they slaughtered everyone they could find. The prison guards did nothing. It meant fewer criminals to house and feed. In 1953, the prisons were finally emptied, eight million men turned out on the streets. The Bratva survived, but the old code was destroyed."

I indicate the man at the next table, every inch of visible skin decorated in tattoos.

"You see those crosses on his knuckles? The dagger on the back of his hand?"

Sabrina nods.

"There was a time when every tattoo had a meaning. If you put a mark on your body that you hadn't earned, the Bratva would cut it off you with a razor blade. Now it's decoration."

Sabrina's eyes glint with interest. She takes a hasty gulp of her drink, saying, "Tell me more."

Her face is bright and open, her attention intoxicating. I'd talk all night to amuse her.

"Then came the Soviet era. That was the age of corrupt Communist Party bosses and black-market millionaires. When the party fell, organized crime rose. The Bratva recruited from war veterans, the decimated police force, and even from desperate athletes and bodybuilders. You see that group over there?"

I jerk my head toward a table of *kachki*.

"They were bodybuilders?" Sabrina says.

It's not really a question. Even the oldest and most broken-down in the group still maintain enough of their mass to show that they were powerfully built men, filling out their oversize pullovers and zip-ups, acne scars on their cheeks and hair thin at the temples from rampant steroid use.

"That's right—all part of the Soviet sports machine. The one on the left, that's Boris Kominsky. He was a judo champion. The next one over, Nikolai Breznik, he was a wrestler, and Vladislav Aulov a Merited Master of Sport. Then all the funding dried up, and they went from hitting heavy bags to beating payments out of debtors. You see that one on the end, the ogre with the martini?"

The largest of a dozen big men is dressed in a kelly-green Adidas zip-up, a vodka martini delicately pinched in one monstrous hand.

"Hard to miss him."

"That's Ira Angeloff, better known as Cujo. Most of the *kachki* run their own rackets now, but you can still rent Cujo for your own personal attack dog if you've got the cash. They say he hits harder than Mike Tyson."

Sabrina casts a cool eye over Angeloff's knuckles, swollen and distended, a road map of scars.

"He looks good at his job."

"The best. His old boss got rich brokering bribes for oligarchs who wanted to buy the newly privatized state enterprises. The entire economy of Russia was up for grabs, and all the independent businesses popping up were ripe for extortion. Cujo made a lot of money for a lot of people, but I think most of it went up his nose. The house he lives in now is nothing special."

"Who runs the protection rackets now?"

"Everyone. *Krysha* is half the economy of Russia. Everyone pays protection money. It's part of business."

"Are you taking *krysha*?"

"Not yet. Most of the territory is already portioned out. We'll have to move in on someone else to take ground."

Sabrina scowls, trying to understand the current system.

"There's a high table," she says, "but the Bratva aren't one group."

I shake my head. "They never have been. There's no centralized authority, no head of the snake you can lop off. The high table represents a half-dozen of the biggest bosses in Moscow, but it's a loose alliance, and loyalties change all the time. It's supposed to prevent the outright warfare we had in the nineties."

"Chaos is bad for business," Sabrina says.

"That's right. Moscow was madness then. Every day, it was car bombs, drive-by shootings, boss after boss gunned down and then buried in monumental tombs that would cost a hundred years' wages for a normal Russian."

"I want to see them," Sabrina says.

"The tombs?"

"Yes."

I laugh. "If you're imagining white marble, think again."

"What do you mean?"

"Russian gangsters aren't exactly known for subtlety. The headstones are massive, glossy black, with life-size portraits of the dons. Sometimes with their favorite cars or their favorite women. Dripping in gold chains, drinking wine, and eating lobster."

"You're lying."

"I'm not even exaggerating. Whatever you're imaging, picture bigger, uglier, and tackier."

Sabrina laughs, delighted at the picture in her head.

"What stopped the wars?" she asks. "The cops cracked down?"

"They tried under Yeltsin without much success. Putin is smarter."

"How so?"

"He turns a blind eye to the Bratva as long as we remember that the Kremlin is the biggest gang in town. He'll even contract us from time to time."

"You work with the government?" Sabrina frowns.

"It's not a matter of choice. To use a term you Gallos would recognize, they make you an offer you can't refuse."

Sabrina considers this, fiddling with the straw in her drink.

"So you're saying of all the people you don't fuck with in Russia, the politicians are at the top of the heap."

"It's the underworld and the overworld. And all the normal people caught in the middle."

"So what's your angle?" she asks, her eyes fixed keenly on my face. "Where do you intend to stake your claim?"

I shrug. "That's the question, isn't it? Vice is a booming industry, competition everywhere you look. To expand in any particular area risks conflict with those already present."

I incline my head toward each table in turn, rattling off the names of gangsters and the territory they control.

"There's the Chechens over there. They've got a new boss, Ismaal Elbrus."

Sabrina eyes the fleshy figure in the center of the group.

"Did he eat the old boss?"

I let out a soft snort. "Don't let him hear you say that. Elbrus is vindictive as they come—all the Chechens are. Cross them, and they'll burn down your grandma's house and every house on her street."

"What do they do?"

"Illegal oil deals, bank fraud, counterfeiting... They've got a massive *obshchak* where they pool their funds, and they're connected in government, especially the Regional Department of Organized Crime."

Sabrina laughs at that little piece of irony.

"There's the Slavs on the other side of the room. They despise the Chechens. They're mostly arms dealers, and they've got as much heavy hardware as the Red Army—half of it stolen from the Red Army, actually. They're in local drug production, and they bring in cocaine from South America."

Sabrina nods, eyes flicking from table to table as she memorizes each face and each piece of information.

"You probably know her." I nod toward the table featuring the only other woman in the room not paid to be there. A beautiful brunette with a keen, intelligent face is speaking intently with a young man in an elegantly fitted suit. They look stylish enough that they would have easily breezed inside the Soho Rooms had they chosen to go there instead of here.

"Neve Markov," Sabrina says softly.

"See that rock on her finger? She just signed a marriage contract with Simon Severov, youngest son of Sanka Severov."

"She's engaged?"

"As of this week."

Sabrina examines Simon with fresh interest, stirring her straw around in her ice.

"You're wondering if Ilsa likes him?"

Sabrina smiles, unembarrassed by the mention of her ex. "I don't think she expected her sister to get married any time soon."

I shrug. "They say it's a love match."

Sabrina is already back to the business at hand. "You've been dealing ARs and blow," she says, remembering what Jasper reported.

"That's right. We have an agreement with Eban Franko to sell in his strip clubs. But the price of coke has been all over the map, and the molly we get from Amsterdam has been shit. We need a new supplier."

Sabrina frowns, thinking hard.

Her eyes roam the room, understanding that each group represents a center of power with which we will have to contend.

At last, she says, "What we need is a resource. They're fighting over what already exists. We could make something new."

"Make what?"

"The thing everyone wants…" Sabrina smiles. "A good time."

"The Slavs already make their own molly. They can buy in higher volume than us and undercut our price."

"If we can't compete on price, then we have to compete on quality. You said the stuff coming in from Amsterdam is shit?"

"Only one in three shipments tests pure."

"But you can get the raw materials?"

"I can get anything once I know where to look."

Sabrina bites the edge of her thumbnail. I see the wheels turning in her head as she sits across from me, scowling in concentration.

"We need something no one else can sell," she says softly. "Something unique…that we cook ourselves…"

"You want to be in charge of it?" I ask her.

She looks up, eyes large and luminous in her tanned face. I see her excitement, but she plays it cool as always. "Could be fun."

"You should bring Hakim on board. He took two years of biochemistry."

"Oh yeah?"

"His parents wanted him to be a pharmacist like his sisters."

Sabrina grins. "Then I guess it's time to make his parents proud."

CHAPTER 21
SABRINA

AFTER ANOTHER HOUR OR TWO OF DISCUSSION OF RAW MATERIALS and the best place to set up a lab, Adrik leans back in his seat, arm slung around my shoulders.

"How about another drink? So much work…must be time to play."

His large hand massages my shoulder, warm and heavy and pleasant.

Even in this room of strangers and criminals—the kind of people who would slip a knife between your ribs for an insultingly low sum of money—I feel comfortable, even safe.

Anything seems possible with Adrik. I'm full of wild energy and outrageous plans. I wish we could start this minute.

His hand dips lower, his fingers grazing the top of my breast. His arm is heavy around my shoulders, possessive. If I didn't like it, I'd shake it off. But it never feels wrong for Adrik to put a claim on me. Actually, it's flattering. With all the expensive escorts in the room, he'd only be human if his eyes wandered. Adrik only has eyes for me. His attention is addictive—the more I get, the more I want.

I lean against him, letting my own hand slide up his thigh over his jeans. Feeling the thickness and firmness of his thigh, how it radiates heat through the denim.

I look into his face. He's outrageously handsome—the kind of good looks that are even better up close. His skin is smooth and clear and brown, stretched tight over the sharp edge of his jaw. The shape of his lips makes me weak and melting.

"Two hours is a lot of work?" I tease.

"It's work keeping my hands off you long enough to have a conversation." He grabs a handful of my hair and pulls my head back, kissing me so deeply that I taste the vodka still burning in his throat.

My hand rides higher up his thigh. I can feel the swell of his cock pulling at his jeans. I press against the tight denim with my pinkie, tugging it against his cock. Adrik lets out a groan, pulling my hair to the left, turning my head so he can nuzzle against my neck.

I run my fingers lightly over his cock, just enough pressure for him to feel it through his jeans…

His heavy breath against my ear reminds me of an animal in a cave. A bear, a dragon even. Something you really shouldn't wake.

He puts his hand over mine, pressing my palm hard against his raging cock.

"You really are a bad girl…"

"I thought you were going to Soho?" a sharp voice interjects.

Jasper and Vlad drop down in the seats across from ours.

Vlad has swapped his Affliction T-shirt for one with the Chili Peppers' red star on the front. I hope it's because I hurt his feelings.

The moment we make eye contact, he's already glaring at me. I'm glaring right back, annoyed at the interruption.

Adrik makes room for them at the table, saying, "I'll get another round."

The three of us sit in silence, pretending to be comfortable while we wait for his return.

Jasper is paler than ever in the dim light, his skeletal tattoos shifting eerily through the fog of cigar smoke drifting around his lean frame. He lights up a cigarette with no filter, inhaling slowly, letting the curls of smoke leak out his nostrils.

"Can I have one of those?"

Benjamin Franklin said the best way to make a friend is to ask for a favor.

Jasper stares at me silently, then hold out his silver cigarette case. I take a roll-up and let him light it.

Jaspers flicks up the lid of his Zippo and creates a flame, all in one movement like a magician.

"Thanks," I say, puffing lightly.

He's mixed weed in the tobacco. The smoke singes my sinuses, sending a heady warmth through my brain.

"Settling in?" Jasper asks.

He's smarter than Vlad, smart enough not to show his animosity openly. But we both know the score. Jasper is Adrik's right-hand man. We're in direct competition for his attention.

Smiling, I say, "I already feel right at home."

"Oh yeah?" Jasper's upper lip curls, showing a glint of incisor. "Moscow is just like the suburbs of Chicago?"

"Sure." I shrug. "People are the same everywhere. The vodka's a little nicer."

I raise my glass to him, half friendly, half mocking, and take a drink.

Then, because it's not always my intention to be a dick, I ask him, "Where's home for you?"

It's the wrong question. Jasper's eyes narrow, his lips almost disappearing.

"This is it," he hisses. "I don't have another life waiting for me when I'm tired of playing gangster."

I consider quipping, *So there's no Mrs. Skeletor?* but I keep a lid on it, instead saying to Vlad, "How 'bout you, big boy? You an orphan too?"

"No," Vlad grunts. "My mother is alive. My father was killed trying to bring Ivan Petrov home."

Fuuuuuck me. When will I learn to do the tiniest bit of research before opening my mouth?

"Sorry," I say.

"Why? You didn't know him."

Aggression radiates out of the two of them, dull and heated from Vlad, sharp and cold from Jasper.

I'm not getting anywhere with chitchat. It might be time for some old-fashioned flattery.

"Leo told me about the boxing tournament at Kingmakers," I say to Jasper. "He said you almost won the whole thing. That you might have taken down Dean if you didn't have to fight Silas first."

Jasper has his roll-up tucked in the corner of his mouth, keeping his hands free so he can crack his knuckles swiftly and systematically. He runs down the fingers one by one, each pop as crisp as if his hands really were made of nothing but bone. When he's finished, he pinches the spliff between his thumb and index finger and lets out a vast cloud of smoke, through which his eyes glint, pale and green—an amphibian in murky water.

"I'd like to fight him again," he says.

That's how I'd feel too—I'd want another chance.

Grinning, I say, "Should we go find him? He lives here, doesn't he?"

Jasper shakes his head. "Dean went back to Kingmakers one more year—to teach."

"Professor Yenin?" I raise an eyebrow. "I wonder if he knows he's gonna have to answer questions and maybe say hello to people once in a while."

Jasper gives a ghost of a smile, crushing his roll-up into the ashtray with his bare thumb. "I doubt that's in his contract."

Adrik returns with four shots and four foaming mugs of beer, thumping them down on the table.

"Time to get serious."

The three guys hold their shots over the steins, counting down: *tri, dva, odin!* I drop my own shot into the foam, and we chug the mess down, warm and frothing, because Russians, like Europeans, haven't committed to chilling their beer.

Jasper finishes first, Adrik next, then me. The three of us pound the table with our fists, bellowing at Vlad as he sputters and spills, trying to get the last of it down the hatch.

"*Mocha, blyat,*" he grouses.

It doesn't taste great, but the liquor sends a wave of warmth surging through my body, aided by Jasper's spliff.

Adrik motions to the bartender for another round.

I know what he's doing—and it just might work. Vlad is already relaxing in his chair, his big legs sprawled out in front of him, his face flushed and mellow.

"You ever see them live?" I ask, nodding to his T-shirt.

"Once—in Berlin."

"My dad saw them play at Slane Castle."

"Oh yeah?" He leans forward, resting his beefy elbows on the table. "Some people say that was their best show."

"Are you one of those people?"

"No. I think it was Montreal in '06."

"How do you know?"

"'Cause I've watched every show they ever played on YouTube."

Vlad has a slow and simple way of speaking, but I'm realizing he's not an idiot. Or at least not all the time. We get in a mostly good-natured argument over whether you can judge a live show from a recording while Adrik quizzes Jasper about his new bike.

"How's the KTM?" Adrik asks Jasper.

"Something's rattling when I accelerate too hard."

"Chief look at it?"

"Yeah. He can't figure it out either."

"You gonna take it in?"

"I guess."

Adrik glances at me.

I could offer to fix it. But I don't know if I want to extend a favor to Jasper just yet. I stay silent, and Adrik doesn't suggest it for me.

The club is filling up, all the tables stuffed now as well as every seat along the bar. I've been keeping an eye on Neve Markov's party in case Ilsa happens to join them. I haven't told Ilsa that I'm in Moscow. I haven't told anyone yet, besides my parents.

A cluster of girls are dancing, slow and lazy, in the small space without tables that functions as a dance floor. I would guess they're escorts, judging from the skintight minidresses barely covering their ass cheeks. They're all so young and pretty that if I saw them in a club in LA, I would think they were models or actresses. But that's how it is here, as far as I can tell—too many stunning women everywhere you look, a common commodity, cheap as vodka.

Vlad watches the girls furtively.

The second round arrives. Vlad groans, but we bully him into chugging it down. By the time he's wiping the foam off his lip, he's tipsy enough to argue that the Chili Peppers just might be the greatest rock band of all time.

"When you count up…all the years they've been going…and all the hits they've had…not to mention…how fuckin' rad Anthony Kiedis is…it's indisputable…"

"Why'd you get him going on that?" Jasper says. "Now he'll never shut up."

Even Jasper is showing the effects of two boilermakers. The faintest tinge of pink has come into his pale cheeks, and he sounds amused instead of irritated as he tells Vlad that Anthony Kiedis doesn't hold a candle to Freddie Mercury, "Or Billie Joe Armstrong for that matter…"

Sensing his moment, Adrik says to Jasper, "Sabrina had an idea for a new product."

Jasper hesitates. "Is that right?"

Under the table, I hear a *snick* as he flicks his Zippo open.

"Yeah," Adrik says. "A party pill."

"Molly already exists," Vlad says.

"Leave it to a Russian to drink vodka out of a bottle and call it a cocktail," I say. "This will be a hybrid drug—already mixed for you. One pill, with a time-delay release."

Jasper's eyes sweep over my face. Under the table, the Zippo snaps shut again.

"One pill?" Vlad scoffs. "Why sell one when you can sell a whole bottle?"

"Because," I say, speaking clear and direct across the table, "everybody sells the same coke, the same molly, the same weed. This will be a custom experience. Exclusive to us."

Jasper's jaw shifts as if he's biting the inside of his mouth. He doesn't like that I'm already saying "*us.*" He doesn't want there to be an *us.*

"Who's gonna make it?"

"Me," I say. "And maybe Hakim."

Jasper perceives in a glance that Adrik is already on board with the idea, enthusiastic even. So he doesn't argue, though I'm sure he'd like to.

He shrugs, saying, "We can try it. We can sell it in the strip clubs."

"No." I shake my head. "It's a premium offering. We need to sell it in the Soho Rooms, in all the fanciest clubs. We brand it and stamp it—sell it to the models and the trust-fund babies. If they want it, then everyone will want it."

This is Jasper's chance to try to make me look stupid.

In the tone of an adult forced to explain physics to a toddler, he says. "Yuri Koslov sells in Soho. We can't just waltz in and peddle our product anywhere we want. We have agreements in the strip clubs, not in the nightclubs."

"Then we need new agreements," I say.

Jasper throws Adrik a look. It means *Get your bitch on a leash.*

Adrik ignores the look, considering the issue at hand, not the squabble.

At last, he says, "We'll start in the strip clubs."

Jasper smirks.

"In the private rooms, to the premium clients," Adrik says. "If it's popular, we'll expand from there."

"It will be popular—" I start, but Adrik holds up his hand to cut me off.

"Make it and test it first. Then we can talk about where to sell it."

"Sounds good to me," Jasper says, superior and satisfied.

He thinks he came out the winner in our first skirmish. And he's half-right.

I'm boiling with irritation, tossing down the remains of my tepid beer. I'm always going to be outvoted if it's me versus Adrik and the rest of the Wolfpack.

I push my chair away from the table.

"Where are you going?" Adrik asks.

"To dance," I say, stalking off through the thick fog of smoke.

I pass the table where the immensely fat Chechen boss is smoking from a three-foot brass hookah, a pair of gorgeous girls draped on either side of him, each puffing from their own slender pipe. The girls' eyes are glazed, their heads lolling against the don's beefy arms. As Elbrus lets out a chain of swirling smoke rings, I think how much he resembles the caterpillar in *Alice in Wonderland*, the two dazed girls befuddled butterflies flopped against him in their brightly patterned dresses.

I join the cluster of escorts dancing to the music pouring out of a stack of old speakers.

The girls make room for me at once, floating and resettling like a school of fish around a whale. They can see that I'm useful, either as a source of funds or as a way to draw business.

I bring more eyes their way. Elbrus is watching us, as are Adrik's frenemy, Krystiyan Kovalenko, and several other tables of gangsters who have yet to choose their female entertainment for the evening.

The eyes burning on my back hottest of all are Adrik's. I feel him watching while I twine in and out of the girls, sandwiched between them, sliding against their bodies.

I throw him a glance over my shoulder before sliding up behind the prettiest girl of all, her hair cut in blunt bangs and a bob, her lips a crimson bow.

I've been here a day, and I'm already getting tired of men—so much ego and so much insecurity in one hairy package. I want to be around smooth skin and soft voices. I want to be with the species who know that when a great song is playing, there's no fucking way you should be sitting in a chair.

My annoyance with Jasper leaks away as I sway with the beat, my hands on the other girl's hips, her ass pressed against me. Her perfume is light and sweet, and it makes me feel like I'm floating.

I've got a temper. It flares up fast and hot, but without fuel to keep it going, it burns out soon enough.

Already I'm willing to forgive Adrik for taking Jasper's side and even Jasper for turning it into a conflict in the first place.

I give Adrik another look, half a smile this time. He's still watching me while Jasper tries to pull him into conversation. I could lure him over here, show Jasper that he's going to have to become a whole lot more interesting if he wants to keep Adrik's attention. Really rub it in his face.

But I remember my mother's favorite saying: *You'll catch more bees with honey than with vinegar.*

I've got a whole lot of honey right here.

I ask the girls, "*Kto-nibud' iz vas govorit po-angliyski?*" *Any of you speak English?* I downloaded *Rosetta Stone*, but so far I've only memorized a dozen Russian sentences, and I doubt I'd understand the answers.

"I speak a little," the girl with the bob says.

"Me too," her blond friend chirps up.

I spend a few songs chatting them up, asking where they live and what they like to do. The brunette is a student at Moscow State

University; the blond lives in Balashikha with her mother. Their names are Polina and Olga.

"You come here often?" I ask them.

Polina shrugs. "Most weekends. The *mafiozi* tip well. I try to avoid the *kachki* though—they're too rough. The Slavs want to pay for pussy and then ask for anal."

"What are *kachki*?"

Adrik used that word as well. I thought it was the name of their group, but Polina says it like a descriptor.

Olga explains. "It means something like…pump up the muscles."

"Oh," I laugh. "Makes sense." I've still got about $800 in American bills. I slip the cash to Polina, saying, "Why don't you come sit with us? My friends are behaved. Better than the *kachki* at least." I nod toward the table where Adrik, Jasper, and Vlad lounge in their seats, throwing periodic glances in our direction while pretending not to.

"Not bad looking," Olga says, giving them a once-over. "I don't know about *Gospodin Skelet*." She wrinkles her nose at Jasper's tattoos.

Polina says, "I kind of like him."

"And you'll keep liking him." I grin. "As long as he doesn't talk."

I lead the girls back to the table, squishing in more chairs and ordering a fresh round of drinks. Soon we're passing shots around the circle and another of Jasper's roll-ups.

Olga is red-faced and giggling, clinging to Vlad's arm, asking him to flex so she can try crushing his bicep with both hands.

"*Eto kak kamen!*" she giggles. *It's like a rock!*

"Try like this…" Polina says to Jasper.

She takes a long inhale off the roll-up and then slowly exhales an inch from his mouth so he can breathe in the smoke all over again, straight from her lungs.

"Gets you twice as high," she murmurs, her red painted lips brushing against his mouth, her hand on his thigh.

Adrik pulls me onto his lap, murmuring into my ear, "You didn't bring anyone back for yourself."

His fingers grip my hips. His cock presses against my ass.

I shift on his lap, draping my arm around his neck and tickling the side of his face with my fingernails.

"I'm being generous," I say. "Sharing with your friends…"

I'm a Greek bearing gifts. The girls are the Trojan horse.

Even Jasper can't resist. Soon we're all laughing and drunk, Olga likewise sitting on Vlad's lap, Polina hanging on Jasper's shoulders.

We leave the bikes parked outside the club, sharing two cabs back to the Den.

Vlad throws Olga over his shoulder and carries her down to his room because she's too tipsy to navigate the stairs in her stilettos. Jasper and Polina have already disappeared.

Adrik rips my shirt off before we've even made it down the hallway. I kick off one shoe and then the other, but the leather pants defeat me. I'm hot and sweaty, so they're sticking to my skin.

Adrik throws me down on the bed, peeling me like a banana, stripping off the pants and flinging them across the room. He does the same with my underwear, jumping on me and shoving my legs apart, burying his face between my thighs. He licks my pussy like he's starving, his mouth warm and wet from drinking.

I'm too impatient for oral. I try to get up and kiss him again, but he shoves me down, thrusting his tongue in me, lapping at my clit like an animal.

"You love doing that," I say in a tone of wonder.

"It's my favorite thing."

"Your literal favorite? Over all the other things we do?"

I don't believe that for a second, but Adrik insists, "I'd rather eat your pussy than anything else. You taste like candy. When you're about to come, you taste even better."

"What's your favorite way to do it?"

"When you ride my face."

"You want me to do that now?"

"Can I film it?"

I've never let anyone film me having sex. I've never even sent a nude. It feels like giving a piece of myself away, something I can't get back again.

Adrik would love that video. He'd probably watch it a hundred times.

He's opened his whole life to me—his family, his house, his closest relationships. I want to give him something in return.

I prop his phone on the bookshelf, facing the bed. Then I press record.

Adrik lies back against his pillow.

I kneel on the pillow, my knees on either side of his face. Settling down on his mouth feels right. His chin is clean-shaven, his lips soft. Adrik is strong, so I don't have to worry about crushing him.

I rock my hips, sliding my pussy across his tongue. It feels slick and exquisitely warm. I can sink down on him, getting as much pressure as I want.

He latches on to my pussy, sucking gently on my clit. I lean forward, gripping the top of the headboard in both hands. It's just the right height that I can hold it for leverage. I'm drunk enough to need it.

I ride his face lightly at first, then harder.

He reaches up, caressing my breasts in both hands.

His hands are big and warm. Powerful too. The way they touch me is like nothing I've known. He can close his hand over my entire breast, squeezing and massaging. When he pulls at my nipples, it feels like I'm caught in some kind of machine, something bigger and stronger than myself. I'm locked in place on his face, gripping the headboard, his hands roaming over me. Everywhere he touches me sends warmth and pleasure pulsing through me in irresistible waves. I'm on top, but he's in control. He's making me feel everything he wants.

I start to come, and once I start, I can't stop. I'm clinging to the headboard like it's flotsam and I'm tossed around in a storm. I'm coming and coming all over his face, not tidy, not ladylike. Grinding on him like a hellion, making a mess.

When I flop down on the bed, the whole mattress feels like it's rocking, like it's a raft on the waves. My head won't clear.

Adrik sits up, wiping his mouth on his arm.

"See? It's fun."

I laugh. "Yeah, if you like waterboarding."

"Send me to Guantanamo," he says, kissing his way down my body again.

"No, no." I shove him off. "It's my turn."

Adrik lies back once more, me on my stomach between his thighs. His cock stands up thick and straight, the head mostly uncovered because he's aggressively hard right now. He's the first guy I've ever been with who isn't circumcised. I like the extra skin—it's soft and clean, providing a little extra friction when he's inside me.

I slide my hand down his shaft, retracting the last bit of foreskin. The head of his cock is slick and naked, slightly purplish, and so warm that I can feel the heat before I close my mouth around it.

I love sucking cock when I'm drunk. My mouth gets sloppy and wet, and everything tastes twice as good. My throat is so relaxed that I can take him deep right from the start, without warming up. His cock slides in so far that it's almost alarming. It glides all the way in like I'm a fucking sword swallower, like I'm the Houdini of dicks, making this thing disappear and bringing it right back again.

I look up at Adrik. His eyes are rolling back, like he might be having a seizure.

I grin and keep going.

I run my tongue up and down his shaft. I suck on his balls, which are smooth and tight and clean-shaven. I fit them both in my mouth, working his cock with my hand, making him groan like he's being tortured.

I tease him for a minute, swirling my tongue around the head, lapping at the underside, at that sensitive little notch where the head meets the shaft.

Adrik clutches at the bed, ripping up handfuls of sheet. When he can't stand it anymore, he grabs my head in both hands, thrusting his cock deep into my mouth.

I give him what he wants, bobbing my head up and down, using my mouth and hands in tandem. I'm sucking this cock like it's my full-time job, like my Christmas bonus depends on it.

After a minute, he can't hold on anymore. He lets out a roar, thrusting upward one last time, his cock jammed deep in my throat. I feel it twitching, but it's too far down for me to taste the come flooding out. I pull back just a little so I can feel it pulse right on the flat of my tongue. His come is slick and slippery. It fills my mouth, coating my tongue.

Before I can finish swallowing, he pulls me up and kisses me deeply.

"You filthy little whore," he growls. "I can taste my come in your mouth."

I've never let a man call me names before. With Adrik, it's a compliment. He wants me slutty. He wants me misbehaved. He wants the baddest bad girl. It's why he picked me in the first place.

Adrik can see that I'm thinking. When he's halfway in his right mind again, he asks, "You like when I call you a slut?"

"Yeah."

"Why? Because I'm dominating you?"

"No," I laugh. "Because you understand me."

I love sex. I always have. I'm not ashamed. Anyone who wants to be with me has to accept that part of me along with everything else.

"I don't know if I could be monogamous," I say to Adrik. "I didn't bring a girl home, but I might another night."

"Bring one home every night," Adrik says. "I don't care."

"It doesn't make you jealous?"

Adrik has rolled off the bed to grab hand towels for both of us.

He tosses me one, using the other to wipe down his body. He stands in the doorway, sweat gleaming on his body like a sculpture freshly cast in bronze. His cock swings heavy against his thigh. He's naked, powerful, unashamed. Taking a break for the moment but knowing he's going to fuck me again.

He fixes me with that blazing stare, pale and electric in his tanned face.

"I don't care who you fuck. I want your love and your loyalty, Sabrina. Can you give that to me?"

It's the first time either of us has said the word "love" out loud.

I've never said that word to anyone.

It makes me shiver, naked and exposed on the bed.

At the same time, I feel heat in my chest. The inferno that's been burning there for months, impossible to smother, impossible to control.

It's the reason I came here, even though it's dangerous, even though it's insane. I came here without any friends or family, without even knowing the language. For Adrik. Because I can't stand to be without him.

"Yes," I say quietly. "I love you. You and nobody else."

The surprise and delight that sweep his face are enough to make me laugh. He didn't think I would say it.

He throws aside the towel, leaping on me, the mattress groaning beneath our weight. He crushes me against his body, kissing me hard. I can feel his heart hammering against my bare chest.

"You love me?" he says. "Because I fucking love you. I love you, Sabrina."

"Since when?"

"The whole time. I didn't say it before because I didn't want to scare you off."

Elation bursts out of me as laughter. Adrik isn't offended—he understands what I'm feeling.

"You really love me too?" I say.

He looks in my eyes, serious. "I'm way past love. I'm obsessed."

I tell him the thing I didn't think I'd admit.

"It scares me. I feel desperate and crazy—way past normal. I feel like I was already on the edge, and then I met you, and I jumped right off the cliff."

"I know."

He's gripping me so hard that his fingers sink into my shoulders, and still I want more. When he's only holding me, I want him to kiss me, and when he's kissing me, I want to be fucked. It's never enough. I can't get full of him.

He says, "I'm used to being in control. With you...I'd trade anything for another minute."

We're kissing again, wild and hungry, eating each other alive. I'm filled with hot, soaring happiness. We finally said it out loud, and it feels so good to admit it.

This is real. The realest thing I've ever known.

If we're crazy, then we're crazy together.

CHAPTER 22
ADRIK

WITHIN A WEEK OF SABRINA'S IDEA, I'VE ALREADY FOUND HER THE perfect place for a lab. It's an old brewery in Nekrasovka—closed for the last eight years, surrounded by a cluster of textile plants pumping out fast fashion and the counterfeit purses that Russians love almost as much as the real thing.

With all the smog pouring out of the plants and the steam and noise of the dim sum shops and shawarma stands serving the workers, no one will notice if a couple more boilers fire to life in a squat brick building that ought to be empty. No one who matters anyway.

It's farther from the Den than I'd like, but I bought Sabrina her own bike. I park it right in front of the house so she sees it the moment she steps out the door.

It's the brand new Aprilia superbike, ultralight and sleek, black like mine. It amuses me to see the two bikes side by side, the difference in size mirroring the physical difference between Sabrina and me. Sabrina very much reminds me of a revved-up engine in a compact frame.

She can hardly contain herself when she sees it, dancing around the bike with many whoops and gasps as she examines the features. We've discussed her preferences enough times that I was fairly confident of picking right. Still, it was a risk surprising her. Her obvious delight repays every second of stress I had finding just the right motorcycle to suit her tastes.

"How are you so fucking smooth?" she says, kissing me again and again, then rushing back to the bike. "This is exactly what I wanted."

"I know." I grin. "I didn't exactly have to twist your arm for details. In fact, it would have been harder to get you to keep it to yourself."

Sabrina punches me on the arm hard enough to hurt.

"Oh yeah, were you wanting to discuss Proust? Shut the fuck up. You love talking bikes."

Her eyes are roaming over the chassis like it's a naked cheerleader.

"I can't wait to open it up and take a look at the engine."

"It's brand new! You're gonna mess with it already?"

"Of course!" She's laughing, bouncing on the balls of her feet like a kid on Christmas morning. "You guys have tools, a lift? Whaddaya got in that garage?"

I take her for a tour of what used to be a greenhouse, now functioning as a garage, tool shed, and general storage area.

Chief is already inside, working on Jasper's KMT. He's the best at repairs and fixes most things that break at the house. Not because he has any special knowledge of plumbing or air-conditioning units but because he has the patience to puzzle over diagrams online and then cobble together a fix until Vlad or Andrei fuck it up all over again.

Chief was in my year at Kingmakers, though not my dorm. He was an Accountant, me an Heir. In our finance classes, he was the only one who could calculate projections faster than me, and I was the only Heir who could do it faster than the other Accountants.

We were drawn together immediately because I could see how smart he was, and he could see that I could see it. I brought him into my circle. Some of the others gave him shit at first—especially Vlad. Chief has that vulnerable quality that draws the attention of a bully like Vlad, a wounded chick stumbling around the biggest rooster in the yard.

Defending him would only make it worse. I give him chances to shine, to show what he's best at. He makes himself useful around the house to make up for the fact that if we're ever rolling out strapped, he prefers to stay in the driver's seat while the rest of us handle business.

His real job is the books. He's a wizard with numbers, which I really fucking need at the moment, since we're operating on a razor-fine margin. I only have my own bankroll. I haven't taken a dime from my father or Ivan.

Sabrina wheels her bike in so she can show it off to Chief. He looks it over, all smiles and compliments, like he wasn't with me when I bought it.

He took to Sabrina at once. He's always ready to like what I like, and she's the prettiest girl who's spoken more than five sentences to him. Actually, Sabrina is more than cordial. She's warm and open, especially to anyone she sees as an underdog. Her sense of justice compels her to celebrate the unappreciated while puncturing the inflated egos of those at the top of the heap like Jasper or Vlad or sometimes yours truly.

Bubbling over with excitement, she's hitting Chief with a full blast of charm. He looks dazed, like he's taken a couple shots to the head. It's good for him. Sabrina is so overpowering that he forgets to be nervous, and he talks more like his real self.

Once she's borrowed his tools to open up the crankcase and they've both pored over the engine, she nods to Jasper's KMT, saying, "You working on the rattle?"

"Yeah. I dunno what's causing the issue, though. I took the whole engine apart and cleaned it and put it back together again. No fucking dice."

"Hm," Sabrina says, her sharp eyes flicking over Jasper's bike.

I'm sure she could fix it if she wanted to, but that's the spiteful side of her. Jasper hasn't exactly been friendly, and Sabrina has too much pride to extend the first olive branch.

It doesn't matter. She's finding her way in the house faster than I could have hoped. She's been gaming with Hakim and Andrei, and she cooked her first dinner with only a moderate level of misery. She dropped the platter of chicken and veggie skewers triumphantly in the middle of the table, her hair piled in a frazzled mess on top of her head, a streak of charcoal across her forehead from where she'd swiped away sweat with the back of her arm. She looked like she'd been through several world wars, but she was grinning.

"So? What do you think?"

Andrei was brave enough to take the first bite of the singed and strangely solid chicken breast.

"Hm," he said, chewing carefully. "It's…edible."

Vlad gave his chicken a pained look, but since he wasn't about to miss a meal for the first time in his life, he doused his skewers in hot sauce and shoveled it down.

Only Jasper refused to eat. He didn't say anything out loud, and neither did Sabrina, though I saw the color in her cheeks when she scraped his full plate in the trash. It pissed me off, but I stayed out of it because I know that's what Sabrina wants.

I finished all my chicken. Nothing bad happened after, which I counted as a victory.

Once Sabrina is finished showing off her bike and Hakim has stumbled out of bed—late as usual—we ride down to the old brewery.

Sabrina's already getting used to the vagaries of Moscow traffic. She zips neatly between the lines of cars, leading the way to Nekrasovka, only having to drop behind me once we pass out of the neighborhoods she recognizes.

Her ability to learn Cyrillic street signs reminds me of Sherlock Holmes when he bragged that he was the only person ever to memorize the immensely convoluted train schedule of Victorian

England. Sabrina's brain is like that—she sees something once and downloads it into her head.

She's riding faster than she needs to right now, excited to see her new workspace. Hakim can hardly keep up. He's probably still half asleep.

When we reach the brewery, Sabrina barely pauses to put the kickstand down on her bike before running inside.

The interior of the brewery smells strongly of hops and mold. Inches of thick gray dust have settled on the old tables and windowsills like the fallout from Chernobyl.

All the windows are high up on the walls, so tiny and beveled that the light leaks through in scattered shafts.

Weeds grow through the cracks in the moldering floorboards. Some are covered in prickled spikes, others in fragile, papery blooms.

Sabrina dashes around the brewery, her boots splashing through puddles of muddy water, her hair swirling as she spins around in the vast, open space.

"It's perfect!" she cries. "Fucking perfect!"

Hakim examines the space calmly but with no less interest. He's mostly checking the outlets, the water supply, and the drainage pipes.

"We've got full power?"

"Try the switch."

He flicks the uncovered switch on the wall. For a moment, nothing happens, and then with a rumble and a hum, a couple overhead bulbs illuminate. The others remain dark.

"Is that the wiring or the bulbs?" Hakim frowns.

"I dunno. I'll send Chief to take a look."

"Or someone who knows what they're doing…"

"I thought that was supposed to be you?" I grin.

Hakim scoffs. "Not even close. I've got a buddy I can call who went to school with me. He's been building hydroponic systems for basement grow ops. I'm not the only dropout turning tricks."

"Sure." I nod. "Keep it quiet otherwise. We don't want imitators before we've even started."

"Of course." Hakim nods.

Sabrina has completed her circuit of the space. She dashes back to us, flushed and bright-eyed.

"Let's get started already!" she shouts.

––––––––––

It takes another month to clear out the lab and get it operational. Everyone pitches in cleaning up the space, even Jasper and Vlad. I pay Hakim's friend a consulting fee to source the necessary equipment. We have to hire a professional to run fresh plumbing and install a new furnace and gas lines, but it's Vlad's uncle, so I'm not worried about loose lips. We don't explicitly tell him what we're doing, though I'm sure he can guess.

The most difficult part is finding the supplier for our raw materials.

We could buy from Amsterdam like the Slavs, but then our pills would be too expensive, even at the premium Sabrina thinks we can charge. Jasper wants me to approach Krystiyan Kovalenko. He's got access to the Ukrainians' drug pipeline that runs from Kyiv to Lisbon.

"No fucking way," I tell him flatly. "I'm not working with the Malina."

Those motherfuckers already stole three years of my life. I could own Moscow already if I hadn't been dancing on their puppet strings trying to keep Ivan alive.

"Krystiyan isn't Malina technically," Jasper says. "He's just related to them. Besides, Marko Moroz is dead."

"I know," I say coldly. "I watched Rafe hack him up like a ham. That doesn't mean I'm ready to buddy up with his second cousin twice removed or whatever the fuck Krystiyan is. Besides, you knew him at school. He's a fucking snake."

"What's your brilliant idea, then?" Jasper says, impatient.

"I don't have one yet...but I will."

The solution, when it finally presents itself, is far from ideal. I broker a deal with Lev Zakharov, a broker out of Rostov-on-Don, thirteen hours away on the edge of the Black Sea. Though several of the traditional smuggling routes have been cut off in recent years, his location allows him to bring materials through Romania, Georgia, Turkey, or Bulgaria, and he has connections to the cheapest manufacturers of raw materials in Thailand and China. Though he's only a small broker, he's known to be reliable and has no prior commitments in Moscow.

He happily agrees to work with us. But our agreement comes with a hell of a tax.

"He wants a five-percent cut," I tell Jasper and Sabrina. "He'll give the materials so cheap that we won't even notice it."

Now it's Sabrina who fires up, crying, "We don't need a partner! Just a supplier."

"He won't accept anything else."

"Find someone else then!"

"There isn't anyone else!" I snap. "It's not sugar and flour. They don't sell it in the baking aisle!"

Sabrina narrows her eyes at me, silenced but not at all satisfied. If she had a tail, it would be twitching behind her. She's pissed that I'm overriding her, but there really isn't any other option. None that I'll accept.

Getting the worst over with, I inform Jasper, "He's sending his son to Moscow. To protect their interests."

Jasper's so angry he's stiffened up like a corpse, arms crossed tightly over his chest.

"Zigor Zakharov is a fucking buffoon," he seethes.

"I'm aware. Once everything's running smooth, he'll back off. Or get bored. He'll be whoring it up at the brothels five nights a week. You'll barely see him."

Jasper and Sabrina respond with stony silence. I've managed to piss them off equally, for different reasons. Even in this shared state of annoyance, they're not looking at each other, their bodies angled in opposite directions.

"That's the deal for now," I tell them firmly. "Once we're rolling, we can reevaluate."

CHAPTER 23
SABRINA

COOKING DRUGS IS A LITTLE MORE COMPLICATED THAN I ANTICI-pated. Especially since this isn't a simple compound. It's a mix of MDMA, LSD, THC, and a dash of amphetamines. The MDMA is the base, providing the euphoria and the stamina to stay awake all night long. The amphetamines provide a tiny jolt on the front end, so the energy hits right away. The LSD makes music sound heavenly, so our partygoers will want to dance. And the THC acts like nitrous oxide in an engine, juicing the other drugs while mellowing out the jitters from the ex and the speed.

There's only so much information we can look up online. These are scheduled substances, and they haven't been studied in systematized trials, not to the degree they should have been. In the 1960s, MDMA was used in marital therapy, but the hysteria of the antidrug crackdown in the Reagan era put paid to all that. Only just now is the medical community finally acknowledging the benefits of psychedelics in treating depression and PTSD.

Hakim and I read everything we can, but at the end of the day, we're just a couple of mad scientists using our own bodies as guinea pigs. Or, more often, my body—Hakim is paranoid that we're going to fry our brains, and in any case, he's no use evaluating certain "side effects" I want to examine, as he has no girlfriend at the moment.

Still, he's just as brilliant as Adrik promised. He's the one who figures out the time-delay capsules so everything will hit at the right time. He's also got way more experience with lab equipment, so he finds us just the right painted light bulbs to make sure our lysergic acid doesn't degrade under UV light and constructs our respirators and ventilation hoods so we don't asphyxiate.

I'm the one who designs the pill itself: a lemon-yellow lightning bolt, the size of your pinkie nail.

"Can't we just stamp the pills?" Hakim complains when the custom casing proves devilishly tricky.

"No," I insist. "This will be easier to recognize, harder to counterfeit."

"You're stamping your logo all over a brand that doesn't exist yet."

"It will soon enough."

Hakim and I spend all day in the lab together, sometimes twelve or fourteen hours in a row, both of us sweating heavily inside our protective gear. The lab fills with a witch's brew of steam and smoke, shimmering and toxic. It's a relief when the temperature drops at the end of October, even though it makes the ride to and from the brewery much chillier. Adrik buys me a new set of leathers, thick and warm, with a black mink trim around the hood.

"A helmet would keep you warmer," he urges.

"It's the only fresh air I get," I say. "I spend my whole day inside goggles and a respirator."

As we near a finished product, Hakim and I work late into the night. The textile plants and purse factories run twenty-four seven. We often leave as the haggard workers change shifts, their conversation a babble of languages, their shoulders stooped from long hours hunched over machinery, attaching buttons and stitching straps.

Hakim and I don't eat while we're working—there's too much danger of cross contamination. Instead, we take breaks at the American diner on the other side of the purse factory.

The diner is located inside a chrome trailer shaped like a bullet.

The neon sign with its retro script reads *Shake Burgers* in good old English, the spelling accurate even if the syntax is a little jumbled.

I made Hakim come here the first dozen times because I missed American food more than I expected. The thick-cut fries and sizzling burgers with lacy, browned edges are a taste of home, even if they're cooked by a scowling Russian girl who seems to loathe everything about her own establishment.

Lately, however, Hakim has been suggesting Shake Burgers of his own volition, an alteration I credit to the miserable cook, who will only answer Hakim's questions in single-syllable grunts. On the other hand, she's got facial piercings and no eyebrows, Sharpie on her fingernails, and hair cut and dyed at home, possibly using the same Kool-Aid packets provided with the kid's meal. In short, she's just Hakim's type.

The cook's name is Alla. Her little sister is Misha.

Misha perches on a stool at the long Formica countertop, poring over her homework. She has a lot of homework for a twelve-year-old. I can't read the covers on her textbooks, but from the thickness of the spines and the complexity of the diagrams inside, I suspect she's in some kind of gifted program. And she's real uppity about it. She likes to fire questions at me, like "What was the most expensive war ever fought?" and "Why do you think Venus and Earth developed so differently?"

"I'm not doing your homework for you," I tell her.

"You just don't know the answers."

"Your questions are subjective. Or unknowable."

"Everything is knowable."

"Maybe in the future. Not today."

"Not for you, you mean."

I tap the cover of her astronomy textbook.

"If I read that thing, I'd remember everything in it. But guess what? I don't want to fill my head with a bunch of shit about exoplanets. I'm more interested in what I'm doing right here on earth."

Misha narrows her eyes behind the thick lenses of her granny glasses. Because these glasses magnify her eyes to double their actual size, the effect is something like an adorable little tree frog squinting at me from its perch on a branch.

"Which is…working at the purse factory," she says.

She knows damn well that's not what Hakim and I are doing.

I smile blandly. "I love purses."

"You don't even carry a purse."

"They won't let me when I'm working. I might steal other purses and put them in my purse."

Misha rolls her eyes, burying her nose in her textbook again.

We always sit at the counter so Hakim can harass Alla while she works.

"So…what do you do for fun?"

Alla ignores him.

"Can I get a chocolate shake?" I ask her.

"Misha," she barks. "Make shake."

Misha sets her pencil down in the crevice of her open textbook, sliding off her stool. With painstaking precision, she measures the ingredients for my shake into a steel tumbler and begins operating a machine so old and cantankerous that its sole intention seems to be to rip off one of her pipe-cleaner arms.

"Don't you have child labor laws in Russia?" I say to Alla.

"She is not child," Alla grunts. "She is demon."

Alla's English is about on par with the name of the diner—comprehensible but not exactly elegant. Since my Russian remains gibberish to anyone besides Adrik, I'm not one to judge.

Misha pushes her glasses up her nose, fixing her sister with a calm stare.

"It's not the medieval era. I'm not a demon just because I bathe every day."

"I bathe," Alla retorts.

"With *soap*?" Misha demands.

She looks like a fussy little schoolteacher with her oversize glasses and mousy braids. As far as I can tell, her family consists only of herself and her sister. She's here all the time because otherwise she'd be alone in whatever tiny apartment they share.

Once Misha has set a postcard-worthy shake in front of me, complete with a snowy peak of whipped cream and one garishly bright maraschino cherry, she scoots her stool a little closer. "Alla says I read too much and it makes me weird."

"Something made you weird," I say. "I dunno if it was the books."

"Do you read fiction?" she asks me.

"Yeah. When I can sit still long enough."

"What's your favorite book?"

I consider. "Well…when I was your age, it was *Ender's Game*."

"What's that?"

"It's about a kid, a really smart kid. He's trained by the military. You'd probably like it," I laugh. "He's weird too."

Misha nods solemnly. "I'll look for it at the library."

The bell over the door jingles as Adrik pushes his way inside. He comes to see me at the lab at least once a day and often meets me after work so we can ride home together.

Tonight there's a light dusting of rain on the shoulders of his leather jacket and tiny droplets glinting in his thick black hair.

"I didn't realize it was raining," I say.

He shakes his head like an animal, spattering my arm, then runs his hand through his hair in a rough motion that's become achingly familiar to me. It makes my stomach clench up. It makes my knees squeeze together under the counter.

"Not much," he assures me.

"*Vy golodniye?*" Alla says. *You hungry?*

Adrik is the only person she likes.

"I'd never say no to your food." He grins.

Alla really is an excellent cook, even though she hates her job with the fire of a thousand suns. Every time she lights the grill, I get the feeling she's about to toss the match on the floor and burn the whole trailer to the ground.

In less than ten minutes, she brings Adrik a plate of piping hot fries and a burger with grilled onions and extra mustard.

Despite having just finished a plate of my own, I'm seized by the impulse to take the biggest bite possible out of that burger.

"Go ahead." Adrik pushes me the plate. "You look hungrier than me."

I doubt that. Adrik is just as busy as Hakim and me, bringing in the first shipments of raw materials, liaising with Eban Franko, setting up our distribution channels, and bribing the appropriate cops.

It's not all work and no play, however. Not when we're testing the drugs.

"I've got a new formula for you," I murmur to Adrik.

"For tonight?"

"Yup."

He grabs my knee under the counter, hard, making a low rumble in his throat.

"Good. Let's get the fuck out of here."

"You haven't eaten."

"There's only one thing I want to eat."

"Gross," Hakim says from Adrik's other side.

"You better change your attitude," Adrik says, slapping Hakim on the shoulder as he stands. "Those are the words of a single man."

"You coming with us?" I ask Hakim.

"Go ahead. I'll come along when I'm finished."

He only has six fries left on his plate, but I'm guessing he's going to stretch them out as long as possible once he's alone with Alla. Well, as alone as you can be with a highly observant twelve-year-old three stools down.

"Can I have a box?" I ask Alla. "I'll eat this for breakfast."

She passes me a Styrofoam take-out container. I tip Adrik's burger inside, leaving her a wad of folded rubles as a tip.

"That's too much," Alla says, annoyed instead of gratified.

"That's how good the food is."

"Americans love to tip," Adrik says, smoothing over my unwanted generosity.

"They love to show off," Alla retorts, unsmoothed.

"Yeah." I shrug. "That's about right."

Alla doesn't want my charity, but Misha has holes in her shoes. Sometimes there's no right thing to do, just the lesser of two wrongs.

"What should we call it?" Adrik asks.

"Molniya. That's why I shaped it that way—it's lightning in a pill."

"Which version is this?"

"I dunno—6.0, maybe."

I hold up the little yellow bolt to pop in his mouth.

"How do I know you're getting the doses right?"

I scowl at him. "I don't remember you picking me up at the dock at MIT. I'm estimating."

Adrik laughs. "Fair enough. I have one more question, though. What if it makes the customers a little too content? What if they don't want to pay for lap dances? The strippers won't sell it if it doesn't help them make money."

I pretend to pout. "You don't have faith in me."

"This is business, not religion."

"What about a little wager, then?"

Adrik sits up straighter on the bed, a wolf catching scent of its favorite prey. He loves a good bet.

"What kind of wager?"

"How much cash do you have on you?"

He pulls a wad of bills out of his pocket, some rubles but mostly American Benjamins, the currency no Russian will refuse.

"A lot," he says.

"I'm going to charge you a thousand dollars a song," I tell him. "You try and keep as much as you can."

He smiles. "And what do I get if I can resist you?"

"I'll wear my helmet every time I ride my bike."

"Like a good girl."

"Like the best good girl," I say, trailing my finger down his chest. "And if *you* win?"

"I want a new gun. An expensive one."

"A John Wick gun?" he teases me.

Andrei and Hakim and I have been watching the trilogy, drooling over the endless supply of high-tech hardware John Wick seems to keep buried in every convenient basement.

"Yes. I want the actual gun Keanu Reeves held in his hand. Imagine how jealous Andrei would be."

"He might cry."

"God, I hope so."

"You have to win first…"

I laugh. "Baby, you just signed a deal with the devil. I've already won."

I put the pill on my tongue and lean forward, passing it into Adrik's mouth. He washes it down with a little water, passing me the glass so I can swallow my own pill.

"Now what?" he says.

"Now we wait."

Adrik lies back against the pillows, hands behind his head, looking up at the thick gray rain clouds filling the frame of our Gothic window.

I make a playlist on my phone—sexy songs I can dance to.

"Better keep that playlist short," Adrik says. "Two, three songs max. You ain't winning this bet."

I shake my head at him, adding my tenth song. "You're dreamin', babe."

Twenty minutes pass.

"I don't feel a thing," Adrik says. "You might need to up the dose. I weigh a lot more than you."

"Yeah, remember that you said that, and be glad I don't listen to you."

He laughs. "You're saying it's going to hit me hard?"

"Like a sledgehammer."

His voice has softened a little, and he's gazing up at the window with a dreamy, unfocused expression.

"You already hit me that way, baby girl…the moment I laid eyes on you. I thought I was in control. I thought I was ready. What a fucking fool I was…"

I love when his arms are up like that, showing off the thick bulges of forearm and bicep. I trace the lines of his muscles, below the sleeve of his T-shirt. Adrik lowers one arm, stretching it out so I can keep touching him. Though the hair on his head is so thick, Adrik has very little on his body. It makes his skin surprisingly smooth.

"Ho…lee…shit…" he breathes. "That feels incredible."

I'm mesmerized by the bluish veins beneath the rich brown skin, by the masculine proportions of his wrist and fingers. His fingers are thick and strong but beautifully shaped. His hands have become the most erotic thing about him, because of the way they look touching my body. Because of the way they make me feel…

"All my best and happiest memories involve those hands," I murmur.

"Are you happy here?" Adrik asks, his brilliant blue eyes searching my face. "I want you to be happy."

"I'm always happy when we're working together."

He smiles. "We're working so hard right now."

I laugh. "Someone give us a raise already."

"Okay. I think I feel it now. 'Cause I can't stand up."

"It hits the hardest the first time…maybe."

"If you got the dose wrong and I'm about to die, I'm completely fine with that."

"Fuck," I say. "I forgot to get a chair."

"Where are you going?"

I'm trying to push myself off the bed, but the floor keeps moving away under my feet.

"I gotta get one…"

"Those chairs are a thousand miles away. There's no possible way. You should give up and lie here with me."

"No, no, no. We have a bet. And I have to test some things."

"You're the best scientist. They're gonna give you a Nobel Prize."

"They really should. But these things are so political."

"It's like when *Saving Private Ryan* lost to *Shakespeare in Love*. So unfair…"

His voice is drifting away behind me as I stumble out of the room and down the hallway. Everything I look at seems magnified. I'm suddenly aware of the wood grain in the floorboards and the range of color in the dingy plastered walls—mauve and pink and dove gray mixed in what I thought was a simple cream.

When I come to the head of the stairs, I do the sensible thing and sit down on my butt, scooting down the steps one by one.

As I'm bumping along, Jasper comes up the other way, walking on two legs.

"What the fuck are you doing?" he says.

"These steps…are so tall…and so long. I think they were made for giants."

"These are totally normal steps."

"How would you know, Jasper?" I demand. "How many steps have you even seen?"

He squints at me. "Are you high?"

"I will ask the questions, comrade! And my question is…can you please get me a chair?"

He gives me another hard stare, then says, "What kind of chair?"

"Just like…a normal one."

With a sigh, he turns around, descending the steps once more. I can't tell if he's gone for a long time or a short time or if he'll ever be back again. In fact, I had a little bit forgotten what I was even waiting for when he returns with a folding chair.

"Thank you, Jasper," I say, overflowing with gratitude. "Seriously. I don't know how you did it."

He sets the chair against the wall at the top of the stairs.

"You gonna make it back to your room?"

"Probably."

Shaking his head, Jasper turns the other way down the hall.

I slowly drag the chair back to Adrik, which takes another hundred years.

He sits up on the bed, startled.

"Holy shit, I thought you died."

"This is you grieving? You were staring at the clouds."

"There's so many of them."

"Do you know they weigh a million pounds?"

"That's impossible."

"It's true."

"Don't…don't try and trick me with your made-up cloud facts."

"Here," I say, unfolding the chair. "Sit on this."

"But then I'd have to move."

"It's not that bad once you're doing it."

Adrik rolls off the bed, standing gingerly. "Oh. You're right."

He sinks down on the chair, grabbing my wrist and pulling me closer.

"Why are you so far away?"

"Hold on," I say. "I need better clothes."

Quickly, I change into high heels, a wrap skirt, and a top that ties in the front. These aren't things I would ever wear together as an outfit, but they'll be easy to take off.

When I return, even though it's only been a couple of minutes, the room is much darker. The sun is going down, sped by the thick blanket of clouds.

I start the music, "Company" by Tinashe.

"You got your cash?" I grin.

"I've got somebody's money," Adrik says, pulling it out of his pocket.

"Now remember," I say sternly, "you're trying to keep as much as you can."

"I already want to give it all to you."

I laugh. "But then you lose the bet."

Adrik frowns, trying to recover his competitive fire. "Okay. I'm gonna keep this money. No matter how tempting you look. No matter how sexy you are when you dance. Oh Jesus, this is so unfair."

I'm already swaying to the music, running my hands through my hair. My nails feel phenomenal against my scalp. Touching myself has never felt so good. I brush my hands down my chest, feeling my hard nipples against my palms, following the curves of my waist and hips, caressing my body.

In the dim room, I could almost believe I was in a strip club. I can't see Adrik's features as distinctly. He could be anyone. Just another john, here to spend money on me…

I can hear the separate parts of the music in a way I usually never notice—the beat going on and on in a complicated cycle, the glitchy synthesizer, the soft little exhalations the singer makes outside the actual singing.

I have to move. I *have* to. It's not a choice. Hitting the beat with my hips, my shoulders, feels intensely sensual and satisfying. Adrik's eyes follow every motion. Everywhere I touch myself, he stares, lips parted, the tip of his tongue dancing across his sharp white teeth.

I roll my hips toward him, showing a long slice of my thigh through the slit of the skirt. Adrik pulls a hundred-dollar bill off his roll, holding it out to me. Tempting me to come closer.

I step within his reach. He tucks the bill in the waistband of my skirt. His fingertips brush my skin.

I feel a wild thrill, like I'm broke as fuck and I really need the money.

I'm sinking into the fantasy. Believing in it. I feel like there could be people all around us watching, but I don't see them in the dark, and I don't care. All my focus is on the man in the chair. What I want from him...and what I plan to do to him...

I sway my ass right in front of his face, knowing it looks full and juicy from behind, the tight material of the skirt stretched across the cheeks.

Adrik groans. I feel his fingers fumbling as he tucks another bill in the back of the skirt.

I face him again, leaning forward so he can get a look at the round tops of my breasts, shoved up sky-high by the one and only push-up bra I own. This bra is the definition of catfishing—it makes me look like I have double Ds, like my tits are fake.

Adrik lets out a sound halfway between a rumble and a sigh, his eyes crawling over my breasts. He likes that they look like implants—it's perfect for the stripper fantasy. He tucks a hundred-dollar bill between them, letting his fingers slide across the top of my breasts. His fingers are warm and heavy, and even the money feels sensual brushing against my skin with papery softness.

Each bill he pushes into my underwear gives me a pulse of pleasure. It's a reward, and I'm highly motivated by rewards. I want more money. I'll do whatever it takes to get it.

Stepping back, I slowly untie the front of my shirt, swaying to the music. Adrik is mesmerized, his eyes glinting like blue diamonds. He shifts in the chair, his cock thick and swollen down the leg of his jeans.

I open my top like I'm unveiling a priceless work of art to his view. "*Fucking hell...*" he breathes.

The shirt slides down my right arm, dropping to the floor. I get down on my knees, presenting my breasts to him, now only covered by the bra, holding my hands over my head and posing. I turn side to side, slowly, sensuously, sliding one hand lightly down the side of my neck and over my left breast. I run the tip of my middle finger up and down the place where the cup of my bra meets my breast, teasing him, watching his face to see his reaction.

"You like what you see, Daddy?" I murmur in my softest baby girl voice.

"I fucking love it," Adrik growls.

"You want to see more?"

"*Yes.*"

Adrik tucks another bill in the shoulder strap of my bra. I have money all over me now. Instead of feeling cheapened, I'm expensive and valuable. This man will pay anything for a peek at another inch of skin.

I lift the tie at my hip and put it in Adrik's hand, inviting him to undo my skirt. He pulls at the bow, the flimsy skirt falling away from my hips. I'm in my bra and thong now and the sky-high heels on which I can barely walk, let alone dance, but Adrik doesn't notice any stumbles.

I turn around so he can get a good look at my ass, bisected by the string of the thong. I lean forward in a yoga pose, back arched, my bare cheeks presented to his view.

I'm understanding now why strippers dance and move and pose the way they do—it's all about offering up body parts to the man for his approval. Adrik likes what he sees. He rains money down on me, a handful of bills thrown over my back and ass so they float around me like falling leaves.

I twerk my ass, shaking it for him shamelessly. He throws another handful of money. I feel rich. I feel stunning. I feel glorious...

Adrik leans forward. His hand brushes against my ass furtively, like he knows he's not supposed to do it, tucking more money into my thong in apology. It's kinky as fuck that he's not supposed to touch. Each contact of fingers against flesh feels forbidden and thrilling. I'm seducing him, and he can't resist.

I roll over onto my back, giving him a quick flash as my legs pinwheel open and closed again. I lie on the floor in front of him, writhing with the music, rolling my hips. Pushing off against the stilettos, I lift my hips higher, enticing him to tuck more money in my thong.

He pushes bills into the waistband and then more into the front. Money is filthy, I know that, but the dirtiness of it, the cash against my bare skin, arouses me. He lifts my panties higher than he needs to so he can get a glimpse beneath. The back of his hand grazes that forbidden delta under my thong. My underwear is soaked, sticking to my skin.

He's Adrik, but he's also a stranger. His face looks different, hard with lust. All I see is his clenched jaw and the rigid muscle beneath his tight black T-shirt.

I want to be closer to that body. I want to feel his heat against my flesh.

I unclasp my bra, facing away from him so all he sees is my bare back at first. Then I turn, hands covering my breasts. I peel my fingers away, unveiling my breasts like he's never seen them before.

"Fucking spectacular," he groans.

He holds up a wad of bills, beckoning me closer.

I straddle his lap, the heels so high that I can easily rest my feet on the floor. I take the money and put his face between my bare breasts, my hand cradling the back of his head. His body is on fire. His head burns against my palm, and heat radiates from his chest. His cock presses against the damp material of my thong, his massive hands cradling my ass on both sides.

"Can I?" he says, opening his mouth.

"Yes, Daddy."

He closes his mouth around my breast, sucking hard.

I grind on his lap, sliding my pussy against the rigid rod of his cock, murmuring in his ear, "You gonna come see me every night, Daddy?"

"Yes…" he moans.

"Will you always ask for me? Your favorite baby girl?"

"God, yes."

I nuzzle against his ear, inhaling the richness of his skin and the animal scent of his hair.

"It feels like you have a big cock, Daddy."

"It's throbbing."

"It must be so tight in those pants. You want me to let it out for you?"

"Please, baby."

I slide off his lap, getting down on my knees once more. Slowly, prong by prong, I unzip his jeans. I slip my hand inside his boxer shorts, gripping the burning thickness of his cock, setting it free.

It stands straight up in his lap, dusky and monstrous in the dim light. I can almost see it pulsing, the skin stretched painfully tight.

Light as a feather, I float my fingertips across the head, wrenching a groan from deep in his chest.

"*Ty menyà prosto ubivayesh.*" *You're going to fucking kill me.*

Adrik never speaks Russian to me. The harshness of his voice and the fact that I can understand him give me a deep sexual thrill. It's the essential Adrik, raw and real. The gangster. The Bratva. The man who wants to take me to the darkest of places…

"You're working too hard, Daddy," I say softly. "You're under too much stress. Do you need your baby girl to take care of you?"

"*Da, pozhaluysta,*" he murmurs. *Yes, please.* His head is tilted back, his eyes half-closed. With absolute abandon, he pushes the rest of his cash at me.

I don't give a fuck that I just won the bet. I don't care about the money anymore. I want that cock in my mouth.

If I really were a stripper, I'd want the same thing. I wouldn't be able to grind against this body, to feel that massive cock throbbing under me, without wanting to play with it. I'd feel the same heat flushing through me. The same watering in my mouth. I'd risk anything to take him to a back room where no one could interrupt us...

Gently, I close my mouth around the head of his cock. His skin is velvet against my tongue, a texture I can taste as well as feel. It's cream and salt and sweetness all at once. I suck the head, fluttering my tongue against the underside, soaking it in my mouth.

Adrik makes a noise that vibrates in his chest.

I lift my head.

"More, Daddy?"

"*Ahhhhh...*" he moans.

Taking that as a yes, I close my mouth over the head again. My tongue is slippery, and it glides over the silky skin. I bob my head up and down, soaking his cock.

I pretend he's my favorite client and I'm pleasing him so he'll come back again and again. I pretend I have a crush on him, that I'm hoping someday he'll take me on a real date.

Fantasy and reality swirl inside my head. I'm not sure who I am or who he is. We can be anything and everything to each other. In the darkness of the room, in the sensual teasing of the music, all I know is that my pussy is on fire, aching, dying to be touched...

I reach down and touch myself while I suck his cock. My pussy slides against the flat of my fingers. I moan around his cock.

"Are you touching yourself?"

"Yes, Daddy."

"Come up here and feed it to me."

I straddle his lap once more, hovering over his cock. I touch his tongue, letting him taste my wetness. He closes his lips around my fingers, sucking gently.

"Nothing tastes as good as that pussy."

"You want to feel it, Daddy?"

"*Mmm...da...*"

I pull my thong to the side and lower down on his cock. It slides right inside me, wet from my mouth. I'm so soaked it feels like I poured a bottle of baby oil over us both. There's no roughness, no friction, only smooth, delicious pleasure.

It feels wrong and forbidden, like I could get caught any moment. Like I should make him wear a condom at least. But I'll die if I don't have his cock inside me, if I take it out for even a second.

He's still wearing his shirt and jeans. My thong rubs against me. The barrier of our clothing only make his bare cock in my pussy all the more erotic. All my focus is on our naked flesh, him touching me in the places that count most.

However I met Adrik, in any time or place, in any universe, this is how it would end. We're two elements that have to combine—we can't be kept apart. Are we sodium and chlorine or deuterium and tritium? Stable or explosive?

It doesn't matter. We can't keep our hands off each other. We never could. This is right, and anything that comes between us is wrong.

I ride his cock with more than lust—with a sense of cosmic purpose.

I'm grinding to the music, my body automatically following the beat. Dancing on his cock. That's how I know it takes exactly two lines for me to come.

My pussy clamps around his cock, my fingernails digging into his back.

"Adrik…Ohhh, Adrik…"

I'm coming and coming, warm and wet and melting all over his lap.

Adrik is coming too, deep inside me, his hand on the small of my back. He lets out a garbled roar in which I think he says, *Ya tebya lyublyu. Ya take sil'no tebya lyublyu… I love you. I love you so much…*

I'm flushed with every good chemical, the ones I dosed myself with and the ones that occur naturally when people touch, when they whisper in each other's ears, when they understand each other…

I murmur, "We're gonna be so fucking rich."

———————

We lie in bed afterward, my head on Adrik's chest, ear against his heart so I can hear it beating, deep and steady like a metronome.

I'm thinking how vivid the stripper fantasy became. That was a side effect I wasn't expecting. I wonder if it will happen every time on Molniya or if it was specific to what we were doing.

"I thought you said it was a party drug," Adrik says. "Felt more like a sex drug to me."

"Well, it would be different if we were at a club, obviously. It makes you want to do more of whatever you're doing. So if you were dancing, you'd want to keep dancing. If you're talking, you want to talk forever."

"Are you sure about that? You might start an orgy by accident…"

"You think I should dial it back a little?"

"No," Adrik says. "You're the artist. I trust your judgment."

My face is so hot with pleasure that I tuck my cheek against Adrik's neck so he won't notice. Nothing feels as good as his good opinion of me.

"That's not a bad idea…" I murmur.

"What?"

"A sex drug. I could make other formulas."

Adrik makes an amused sound. "I volunteer as a test subject."

I'm so lost in thought, imagining the possibilities, that his next sentence jolts me.

"I want you to start picking up some of the shipments with Jasper."

"What?" I say, sitting up, leaning on one elbow. "Why?"

"I know you want to be involved in more than just the manufacturing side."

I scan his face in the pale moonlight leaking in through the window.

"You're just trying to make Jasper talk to me."

Adrik chuckles. "Yeah, maybe."

"It's not gonna work. He can sit in silence for hours. I've timed him."

"It's not for you," Adrik says. "It's for him."

"What do you mean?"

"He's lonely. Depressed." Adrik trails his fingers lightly up and down my forearm. "You're my yellow sun. Jasper needs a little of that light."

"But…he fucking hates me."

"It doesn't matter. You shine on him, and it will warm him up. Whether he wants it or not."

I consider this, at last saying, "Yeah, alright. I'll do it. As a favor to you."

He kisses me. "Thank you, baby girl."

I smile. "I thought that was my stripper name."

"You *are* my baby girl. I'll always take care of you."

I never wanted to be taken care of. It's not a nickname I would have liked. But everything is different with Adrik. Black becomes white, and wrong becomes right. He's so powerful…it means something to be protected by him.

I lie back down on his chest. Each breath in his lungs raises and lowers me by several inches.

"Jasper's whole family is dead," Adrik says.

"I didn't know that."

"They were killed when he was eight. His father's lawyer took custody of him. He shipped Jasper off to boarding school."

"Oh yeah…same school as Chay Wagner, right? And Rocco Prince."

"Yeah. When I met Jasper at Kingmakers, I was a senior, and he was a freshman. He was a fucking mess. Angry, aggressive. Drinking too much. Getting in fights every week. It was like he wanted every-one to hate him. But I saw something in him."

"Like you did in me," I say quietly.

"Exactly. I was his friend. I protected him. But then I graduated, and he fell in with Rocco and the rest of those assholes."

"Half of them are dead now," I tell Adrik. "Did you know that? Wade Dyer by accident—Rocco Prince on purpose."

"Yeah, I heard. I don't think it was good for Jasper. When I saw him in Moscow again, he was so fucked up I thought he'd been sick or something. He was skin and bones."

I know he's trying to make me feel sympathy for Jasper. Unfortunately, it's working.

"Okay, okay," I say. "I'll even consider being nice to him."

Adrik pulls me close against him. "When you turn on your charm, no one can resist you."

I laugh. "And when I'm a dick, nobody can stand me."

He squeezes me tighter. "I can."

———

When Adrik falls asleep, I'm still awake in the dark.

It's not because I'm agitated. Actually, I'm still suffused with warmth. More comfortable than I've been since I came to Moscow.

But my brain is firing madly, not at all interested in going to sleep.

As carefully as I can, I slip out from under the weight of his arm and roll out of the bed, landing on the floorboards naked and barefooted. I grab Adrik's T-shirt off the floor and pull it over my head. It comes down almost to my knees.

Taking my phone off the nightstand, I creep out of the room, trying to avoid the places where the floor creaks.

I head downstairs to the kitchen, thinking I might eat the rest of that burger.

The house is silent. Even Andrei and Hakim have gone to bed.

I heat up the food in the rickety old microwave and wolf it down.

When I'm finished, I scroll through my messages.

I've talked to my mom twice since I've been here and my dad just once. The conversation wasn't pleasant. It went something like this:

Dad: "You need to get your ass home *immediately*."

Me: "That's not happening."

Dad: "I'm not playing with you, Sabrina. You cannot fuck with the Bratva. You get yourself in trouble over there, and I can't save you."

Me: "I don't need you to save me. I can take care of myself."

Dad: "We tangled with the Bratva in Chicago, and not the high table either. We fucked with someone's cousin's cousin's cousin, and my father was killed and our house burned to the ground. Something I didn't witness 'cause I was in the hospital with six bullets in my back. You are in the heart of Moscow begging for these people to skin you alive for the fun of it."

That's when I lost my temper.

"I've heard that story a hundred times. Stop trying to pin your mistakes on me! I've got my own life to live, my own choices to make. I'd rather die by my own decisions than live by yours."

He was quiet on the other side of the line, so quiet I thought he'd hung up. Then he said, "You don't know what that means. You've never felt real pain. You've never been tortured. You've never made a mistake that haunts you the rest of your life—if you even live long enough to experience that particular hell."

My guts were churning. He was scaring me—not as much as he wanted to but some. I hated what I was putting him through, him and my mom. She cried on the phone, begging me to come home.

All I could say to my father was, "I'm happy here. I'm not coming back, not anytime soon."

The "happy" was a bit of an exaggeration. Sometimes, I'm very happy in Moscow. Other times, I'm exhausted and frustrated.

I'm pretty good buds with Hakim at this point. Chief is friendly, and Andrei is always down for mayhem. But I've made basically no progress with Vlad or Jasper—even after bribing them with high-end escorts.

As I scroll through my phone, I see a message from my aunt Aida.

> **Aunt Aida:** Thinking about you today. It was raining and I remembered how much you loved jumping in puddles when you were little. You never seemed to feel the cold.

I text her back.

> **Me:** I felt it. Just thought it was worth it, I guess.

She calls me a moment later. I'm surprised to see she's awake until I remember it's only dinnertime in Chicago.

"Hey, Auntie."

"Hey, love. How are you doing?"

My aunt's voice is like stepping into a warm bath. I can picture her so clearly: the smile lines around her eyes, her look like we're sharing a secret, the way she holds her shoulders like she's barely suppressing a laugh.

I was feeling kind of stressed and shitty, but now I can honestly reply, "Not bad."

"How's the Russian coming on?"

"Medium."

"And the roommates?"

"Oh, they still hate me. Well, half of them anyway."

She laughs, a laugh that's very like my own, though probably a little nicer.

"Give it time."

It occurs to me that Aida has her own experience with hostile roommates, having married into a family that feuded with ours for about two hundred years prior to the wedding. She had to live in their house. Eat at their table. My aunt Riona was probably ten times meaner than Jasper could ever dream of being.

Somehow, Aida made them love her.

People say I'm like my aunt. But I know the truth. While we can both be funny and wild, Aida is warm at heart. I have cruelty in me and spitefulness. I'm more like my father—and everybody hated Nero.

Just because I'm like him doesn't mean I have to behave like him.

"Can I ask you something?" I say to Aida.

"Yeah, shoot."

"You were a stranger in a strange land…how did you do it? How'd you get the Griffins to accept you?"

She lets out a soft sigh. "Well…are you a visitor? Or is this home?"

I have to think about that for a minute.

I've come to realize that none of the Wolfpack has family they want to return to. Jasper has none at all. Hakim's parents think he's a criminal who's disgraced their name. Chief is the product of a failed marriage, both parents having moved on, remarried, and had children with their new families. Andrei was raised by his grandparents, one now dead, the other in a retirement home. And Vlad is a Petrov himself, though only distantly related to Adrik.

When Jasper accused me of playing a game here while intending to return to Chicago, he wasn't entirely wrong. I do still think of Chicago as home.

But I want to build my life here with Adrik. I've committed to that. More than I've ever committed to anything before.

"I don't know," I say at last.

I can hear my aunt's gentle breath on the other end of the line, listening, not judging.

She says, "They'll accept you as family if you treat them as family."

"I do," I say. "Mostly."

She laughs.

"Just remember this, little love. I'm a Gallo...but I'm also a Griffin."

That's hard for me to imagine.

When my mother married my father, she was swallowed up by the Gallos. I've been defined by that name all my life. My uncles and aunts and cousins are powerful figures, known to everyone I know. I'm compared to them, taught by them, shaped by them.

It's hard to imagine trading that identity for another or even sharing it.

"How long did that take you?" I ask her. "To really feel like both."

"It's bonding to your partner that does it. When you're truly partners, you become as one person. Your goals are the same. Your desires are the same. Everything you do is for both of you. You're not selfish anymore."

I can't picture that either.

I don't know if I could ever be that way. I *am* selfish. It's always been about what I want.

"I'm not as good as you," I say to Aida. "I don't know if I ever will be."

She laughs. "I'm not *good*. But I am happy. And I hope you'll be that."

"I hope so too."

"Sabrina...you have so much fire in you. Give that passion to someone, really give it to them, holding nothing back, and see what happens."

"Like you did with Uncle Cal?"

"That's right. I gave it all to him...after a little resistance."

I laugh, quietly so I don't wake anyone up. "Gallos don't do anything the easy way."

"No," Aida says. "But it always works out in the end."

That's why everyone loves Aida. Because she never gives up hope. She could have her neck under a guillotine, and she'd still laugh and say, *I'll figure something out.*

Maybe she's right. If the blade comes down on your neck, crying about it won't change a thing. Maybe it's better to die happy, believing life is good and will go on forever.

"Thanks, Auntie," I say. "I love you. And I miss you."

"I miss you too. But not as much as your mom. Make sure to call her."

"I will," I promise.

I end the call and throw the remains of my burger in the trash.

As I'm about to head back upstairs, I hear music coming from the other side of the house. It's light and soft, so faint that at first I think I'm imagining it.

I pad down the hallway, passing the closed doors belonging to Andrei and Hakim.

The last room is Vlad's. His door is slightly ajar. I assume, he's listening to music, but then a note fumbles, and I realize he must be playing himself.

Peeking in the room, I see Vlad cross-legged on the bed, holding a tiny ukulele in his massive hands. Even a normal guitar would look small compared to him. The ukulele is comically under-size, like a toy. Yet he's making lovely music with those sausage-size fingers.

After a moment, I recognize the song—one of my mom's favorites, "La Vie En Rose."

I can't help lingering just outside the door, listening. It brings back my parents' kitchen so vividly: my grandpa Axel sitting in his favorite hideous green chair in the corner, his head nodding because he could never sit in the sunshine without falling asleep. My mother making empanadillas. She's so good with her hands, everything she touches comes out just right. My brother, Damien, stealing one from the first batch, sitting down to eat it while he reads. Unlike me, he can read for hours and hours, oblivious to all distractions.

And then my dad. Coming into the kitchen not for the food

but for my mother. Lifting her hair off the back of her neck so he can kiss her there. And then, when that's not enough, turning her around, kissing her again, not minding that her floury hands are getting all over his clothes.

Then dancing with her to this song. When he dances, he doesn't limp. He shows that grace, that lightness that must have accompanied every movement when he was young. When he holds my mother in his arms, you'd never know he's in pain.

It's not a glamorous kitchen, like one out of a magazine. My parents' house is small, comfortable, messy at times. My mother doesn't care to decorate, and my father doesn't care to spend money on anything without wheels. The rugs are from Puerto Rico, the tiles on the floor in the same cheerful prints, laid by my grandpa when his knees were still good.

My eyes are hot, my throat tight.

I'm very alone in the dark hallway, even with Vlad on the other side of the door.

I shift in place, forgetting about the floorboards. Vlad hears the creak and stops playing.

I could run away, but that would be stupid.

Instead, I push the door open, saying, "Sorry. I really like that song."

Vlad looks at me, silent, unsmiling.

"It's my mom's favorite."

"Hm," he grunts. "Mine too."

"Do you know the words?"

"Yeah. Can't sing for shit, though."

"Me neither."

He plucks the strings with his thick fingers, beginning over again.

I lean against the doorframe, closing my eyes. Letting the notes float around me in the air.

Even though I really have no voice, I softly sing along:

Hold me close and hold me fast,
This magic spell you cast,
This is la vie en rose.

I sing the whole song, imagining my mom singing it the way she does, much sweeter than I could ever manage.

When it's over, we both stay quiet a moment, letting the last vibrations fade away.

"How come the ukulele?" I ask Vlad.

"I went to Hawaii once. Only time I ever went on a trip with my parents. It felt like we flew to literal paradise. Not like here. It didn't seem like the same planet at all. Every place we saw was more beautiful than the last. More peaceful. I heard the ukulele, like angels strumming on harps. It was men playing it, big men. I was already a big kid. I thought, *I could do that. I could make it feel like heaven everywhere I go.* It's not the same when I play it here. But it's a little the same."

This is the most I've ever heard Vlad speak at once. Especially sober.

"It was heaven," I say. "For a minute."

Vlad lets out a puff of air. He's not smiling, but he's also not glowering at me like usual.

"Why are you awake?"

I shrug. "Sometimes I get wired and can't sleep even when I'm tired."

He nods. "Me too."

"Well." I lift one hand in farewell or maybe a salute. "Thanks."

As I leave, I hear him strumming the chorus one last time.

CHAPTER 24
ADRIK

WE START SELLING SABRINA'S DRUG IN EBAN FRANKO'S STRIP CLUBS. It's an immediate success. Sabrina recruits the most popular strippers to sell for us in the private rooms. Their clients pop a pill, and an hour later, they're having the best night of their lives. The girls love it because Molniya makes their clients cheerful and generous, shoving so much money down their G-strings they can hardly keep hold of it all.

Before we've even made a deal for the nightclubs, Vlad and Jasper are inundated with orders from street dealers who have heard of the new product. I have to be careful not to step on the wrong toes, but I let a couple of independents sell in open territories.

The big fish is Avenir Veniamin and his collection of high-end nightclubs. He already has an agreement with Yuri Koslov, but they're on bad terms because Koslov has been late handing over his cut and possibly shorting Veniamin his agreed-upon percentage. Veniamin has offered us access to half the clubs, with the understanding that we can sell in all of them if the drug performs as well as I promise.

While I'm negotiating with Veniamin, Sabrina is hard at work on additional formulations.

"Molniya is for dancing and partying," she says. "I want to make another version for concerts and another for sex."

"It already makes us want to fuck like rabbits."

She grins. "Wait till you try this."

She holds up a tiny pink pill in the shape of a heart.

"What's that?"

"I'm calling it Eliksir."

I give her a suspicious look. "What's in it?"

"LSD on the front end, MDMA after. And tadalafil. But that gave me a stuffy nose, so I had to add a decongestant."

"What's tadalafil?"

"It increases blood flow. It was a heart medication, but then the men who took it noticed a useful little side effect—you can stay hard for hours and fuck again right after you just finished."

"Does it work on women too?"

She laughs. "We're about to find out."

We pop the pills and lie around watching porn for a while, waiting for it to kick in.

Sabrina picks the porn, because when I get to pick, I always choose the videos of her and me. She's made several for me now. I don't even watch normal porn anymore, because nobody's as hot as her. And nothing's as hot as watching me fuck her. I've probably watched the one of her riding my face four hundred times. I know it all by heart, every flick of her hair, every flex of her back. She looks like a jungle cat, sleek and ferocious.

At the moment, she's put on some shit with a girl possessed by a demon. This demon is apparently horny as fuck, because as soon as the girl's roommate comes home, they start fucking in exorcist positions.

"Why do you always pick such weird porn? Why does she need to be possessed?"

Sabrina shrugs. "Everybody watches porn one step past what they're experiencing."

"That's the line for you these days? Literal possession?"

She laughs. "I dunno. It doesn't seem that crazy to me. I'd fuck a demon if he looked like you."

"Aww. Thanks, babe."

I'm starting to feel the first effects of the drug. I'm hot and definitely aroused, though that might simply be the effect of Sabrina lying naked on the bed with no blanket on top of her. Her body is sleek and brown, soft in all the right places and tight in others.

At the same time, I'm noticing how white her smile is, with lovely straight teeth. Just what I'd expect from an American.

Everything about her is healthy and strong. Her skin glows, and her curls spring up with wild energy. Even her fingernails are pink like the inside of a seashell, neat and unpolished.

I swear there's a halo of light around her. Is it the sunshine on her body? The drugs? Or is it just how I feel about her?

"You're not human," I say. "You're something better."

She laughs. "You're high."

"How dare you."

She's giggling, rubbing the arches of her feet against my legs. It feels phenomenal.

The girls on the laptop screen are making horrible demonic noises.

"This is awful," I say, clicking to the next porn in the queue.

I scroll ahead to the good part—which turns out to be a beautiful blond girl giving herself a bubble bath in her backyard. Her tits are covered in soap suds. Her skin looks soft and clean and pink from the heat.

"There, see?" I say to Sabrina. "Isn't this nicer? Look at those bubbles. Look at her tits."

"She's gorgeous," Sabrina agrees.

"Yeah, she's top shelf. They asked this girl if she wanted to do demon porn, and she said, "No thanks, I'm busy that day. If you want, you can come and take a video of me in my backyard. I was gonna be doing this anyway.""

Sabrina convulses with giggles. I love making her laugh. It's the most beautiful sound, rich and full and totally uninhibited. She'll laugh at anything when she's in a good mood, which is almost always.

She closes the laptop and pushes it aside, rolling on top of me, looking into my face.

"No one would guess how funny you are. When you're supposed to be a big bad gangster."

"I'm bad. When I have to be."

"Is there anything you wouldn't do?"

I think about that for a minute.

"It depends on the circumstances."

"What if I did something terrible? Would you hate me?"

"Like what?"

"What if I was a cannibal? And I killed Jasper and ate him."

"Jasper's too skinny."

"Vlad, then."

"Then I'd be like, 'Whoa, babe. Ask next time. I'll get you a burger.'"

She snorts. That turns into a full-fledged laugh, helpless giggles that come in waves as she rolls against my chest.

"I think this one's too much," I tease her. "It's supposed to be a sex drug. All you got is the gigs."

"Oh, fuck off," she says, grabbing my cock. "It works perfectly."

She's right—I'm rock-hard, even with that awful porn and all this talk of cannibalism.

It might have happened anyway. Sabrina smells like heaven, and her skin is silk as it slides against me.

She slithers down my body, taking my cock in her mouth. It feels like I'm chocolate melting in the sun. I'm a puddle of warm goo, and all I know is pleasure. Every stroke of her mouth, every flick of her tongue is the most exquisite thing I've ever felt.

Sabrina is kindest in bed. She's a generous lover, sensitive to what I like. She loves giving me pleasure as much as she loves receiving it herself.

At the same time, she's filthy and naughty. There's nothing she won't try, nothing that's over the line. I can whisper anything I want when we're fucking. The more dark and depraved, the more ravenous it makes her.

I've never felt so free with someone. There's no judgment, no rejection. She knows it's all playful, all for fun. In bed, we can be whatever we want, whoever we want. We live a thousand lives in sex.

Sometimes we pretend she's a sex robot, obeying my every command. I make her ride me faster, slower, in different positions. I order her to moan and even tell her when to come.

Sometimes we pretend I'm a doctor examining her. I act as if I'm giving her a breast exam, as if I don't know I'm touching her in a way designed to arouse. Once, I wore latex gloves and forced her to spread her legs like they were in stirrups. I could feel her pussy shivering against my fingers, even through the gloves. By the time I slid one finger in her, she was already mid-climax, shaking, trying to stifle her groans, red-faced with embarrassment.

I act out her fantasies, and she acts out mine. What she likes becomes instantly kinky to me, surpassing my own favorite games.

This is our recreation. Hours spent in this dark room, this low bed, linked in our bodies and our minds, giving each other experiences beyond our wildest dreams, beyond what we ever imagined possible.

I've never known what it means to fuck someone you love. Sex with a stranger is a handshake by comparison. Not even on the same planet.

After twenty minutes of Sabrina's slow, sensual blow job, we swap positions.

I massage her body with my free hand while I eat her pussy. She's incredibly susceptible to massage. It puts her in a trance state. This is doubly true today, under the influence of the Eliksir.

The drug makes her chatty. While I'm licking her pussy and

massaging her breasts, she stares up at the ceiling, talking to me in a soft, dreamy voice.

"Do you know what I love about you, Adrik?"

I lift my head for only a moment. "What?"

"Everything."

I chuckle, going back to work on her.

"I'm serious. I love how soft and thick your hair is when I run my hands through it. I love how heavy you feel on top of me. I love how your body is a furnace, radiating heat in me. When I'm tired, when I'm stressed, I lie on top of you, and your warmth recharges me like a battery. I can't feel upset when you're touching me. And you're smart, so fucking smart. I've never met anyone whose brain works as fast as yours. You see everything."

"You're smarter than me," I tell her. "I never thought that about anyone until I met you. It's intimidating."

"You're not intimidated. You're not afraid of anyone."

"I'm not afraid. But I want to impress you."

"So do I," she says softly. "I want to perform for you. I want you to be proud of me."

"I am proud of you, baby girl. So fucking proud."

She starts to come, so gradually that I don't even know it's happening at first. Until I feel her thighs shaking and I hear her teeth chattering together like castanets.

"I've never heard you make that sound before."

"Keep going," she begs.

I keep licking her pussy, soft and slow, like I'm lapping cream out of a saucer.

"I love your hands," she whispers. "I love the way you touch me. I love how you're the light in the room. Everyone wants your attention. Everyone wants to be close to you. But you want to be close to me."

"That's right. You're my favorite person in the world."

"I am?" Her voice cracks slightly.

"Yes, baby. Always you."

She starts to come again, her teeth chattering with every exhale, her breath coming out low and throaty.

I make her come again and again, for over an hour. All the while, she's complimenting me, adoring me, stroking her fingers through my hair...

We've never had sex this gentle, this tender. It's not a sex drug. It's a love drug.

At last, I climb on top of Sabrina and slide my cock inside her, looking down into her beautiful face, those luminous gray eyes looking up at me, thick black lashes all around, the only eyes like them in all the world.

I slide in and out of her, slow and sensual, experiencing every inch of her, the scent of her hair, her soft breath on my face...

When I start to come, it draws out forever, easy, warm, and blissful. I don't have to try for it at all.

It's an orgasm like none I've ever known.

Because I've never come from how goddamn much I love someone.

CHAPTER 25
SABRINA

I'VE BEEN SHOPPING AT GUM, WHICH IS THE MAIN DEPARTMENT store in Moscow. It's really more like a mall, with a lovely glass dome roof, high-end boutiques, and fancy eateries. It faces Red Square, which is currently not red but white, blanketed with the first snow of the year.

That's why I had to shop—to get warmer clothes.

I model my new outfit for Adrik—bright orange fleece joggers, a white hoodie, and a pair of Stan Smiths that are probably counterfeit but an excellent fake. They even have the little green tabs on the tongue with Stan's portrait.

"Orange looks amazing with your skin." Adrik gives me an appreciative up and down. "You have good style. It's fuckin' sexy."

"Thank you, thank you," I say, posing for him.

"What's this for?" he says, tugging at a little stretchy string on the butt.

The joggers have several pockets and zips with no apparent purpose.

"I dunno," I say. "Don't pull on it."

"I think your pants are on backward."

"No, they're not! Knock it off!"

Ignoring me, Adrik pulls the strings out about a foot. "That's the drawstring! They're definitely on backward."

I twist around, trying to look at my own ass.

"Goddammit."

His shoulders shake with laughter. "Don't worry. I won't tell anyone you did that."

"I won't tell anyone you thought I looked stylish as fuck!"

"Watch it," he growls, seizing me and pulling me close.

He's trying to put his hands down my pants and up my shirt simultaneously. I smack him away.

"I don't have time for that. I have to meet Zigor."

I throw that at him like an accusation, because it's his fault that I'm going on this stupid errand. This is my third time tagging along with Jasper for a supply run, and each adventure has been worse than the last. Not because of Jasper surprisingly—because Zigor Zakharov really is a fucking moron. His only genius seems to be finding new and creative ways to annoy us.

He brings his two favorite goons along with him everywhere he goes. Jasper and I call them the Bookends, because they look exactly alike, and they flank Zigor like he's the president instead of a two-bit gangster so incompetent that his father only uses him for babysitting.

I'd much rather be at the lab with Hakim. I'm almost finished the third formulation, the one for concerts.

When I head down to the kitchen, I tell Hakim, "Don't work on the new pill without me."

"I can't work on shit," he says. "We're out of supplies."

"I know. Jasper and I are picking up a double order today."

We've been continually increasing our orders from Lev Zakharov, but it's not even close to enough to keep up with demand. Now that we're selling in Veniamin's nightclubs, we've had to scramble to keep up with production. We've got Andrei pressing pills and Vlad delivering orders to our dealers. Adrik's making agreements to supply my sex drug Eliksir to all the brothels.

Chief is probably working hardest of all. He's got to handle the money and balance the books, an increasingly impossible feat. Adrik is intent on expanding as quickly as possible. We're operating on minuscule margins, taking all the cash we make and rolling it into bigger and bigger purchases of raw materials.

Adrik and I argued last night. I told him we should have a ninety-day cash reserve. He said we didn't need it.

"We're vulnerable," I told him. "If something goes wrong—"

"Nothing's going to go wrong."

"If we took twenty percent of the profits—"

"We can't. Business is booming. We have to grab all the market share we can before someone figures out how to make their own version of the product."

I scoffed. "They'll fuck it up. And by the time they copy Molniya, I'll already have made five more formulas."

"If doesn't matter if their drugs aren't as good. I'm already seeing counterfeits popping up. Not everyone is as discerning as you. They'll buy whatever's cheapest and easiest."

I glared at him, arms folded. "You said we'd make decisions together."

"We do. All the time."

"Unless you disagree with me."

"When two people disagree, you still have to make a choice."

"And it's always your choice."

"I've let you do whatever you wanted with the drugs," he snapped at me.

"*Let* me?"

"The supply chain is my business."

"All of it is *our* business!"

"There's still division of labor!"

"I'm not talking about labor! I'm talking about organization and planning—"

"When we're in a better position, we'll have a reserve. We'll have so much money rolling in, you can fill a vault with cash and swim around in it like Mak Dak."

"We can't wait for that!" I cried. And then, "Wait, what did you just say?"

"I said we'll do it when we're in a better position."

"No...the part about swimming around in the vault."

"Yeah—like Mak Dak. You know—the little duck with the spectacles."

I started laughing. "Are you talking about Scrooge McDuck?"

"Yeah! Mak Dak. He's very popular here in Russia. There's a whole restaurant chain named after him."

The argument was derailed by the urgent need for Adrik to pull up photos of said restaurant chain so I could marvel at the Russian custom of ripping off American brands to decorate every kiosk in town.

I had already observed shawarma shacks with upside-down McDonald's Ms in place of the W in Waurma. If that's not enough cachet, they also slap a Nike or Adidas logo on the side of their restaurant for no goddamn reason at all.

Adrik and I spent an hour happily employed in that manner, our debate forgotten.

My irritation swells all over again when Jasper slouches into the kitchen, equally annoyed at the errands Adrik's been assigning us.

"Let's get this over with," he says, surly and sulking.

We have to drive because there's too much snow on the ground for the bikes.

It doesn't improve Jasper's mood to sit in a car with me for over an hour, driving out to a trucking depot in the Mozhaysky District. I put on my favorite song, and he deliberately switches to the next one right when it gets to the best part. I spend the ride fantasizing how I could shut Jasper in a crate and nail it shut and ship it to Mongolia by the slowest route possible.

Zigor is already waiting when we pull up to the low, cement buildings, teeming with trucks pulling in and out and forklifts unloading the cargo.

"*Privet druzhbani!*" Zigor cries, coming over to slap us both on the back. He smacks me so hard that I stumble forward. I have to restrain myself from popping him in the nose.

"Is the truck en route?" Jasper asks.

"Nice to see you too," Zigor says, in English for my benefit.

Jasper ignores this, waiting silently for Zigor to answer his question.

"*Da, da,*" Zigor assures him. "Everything is good. The driver call me. He comes in ten minutes."

Zigor refuses to use any names for his mules or provide more details than absolutely necessary. He knows that if we had our own connections to the suppliers in Thailand, we wouldn't need him at all.

Even if Zigor is an idiot, his father is no fool. Lev Zakharov has flawlessly navigated the complexities of switching trucks and altering manifests so the origins of the shipments are less suspicious to the border guards. He pays out all the bribes along the route and seems to have designed several ingenious systems for hiding the drugs from anyone who hasn't been paid off. So far, I've witnessed sliding double walls in the shipping containers and false roofs and floors in the trucks.

These measures are necessary because the bribes we pay are already ruinous. We shell out thousands at each checkpoint, including here at the depot.

Jasper has cash on hand for that purpose. He leaves me alone with Zigor while he goes to make our "donation" to the depot master.

Zigor looks me over, smirking.

He's on the wrong side of thirty, big and soft-shouldered. He has an unfortunate coif, thinning with suspicious blond streaks, reminding me of every time they try to give Bruce Willis hair in a movie.

"Is better when Adrik sends you," he says. "Next time, maybe no need for Jasper at all."

I throw him a filthy look.

"Nobody sent me," I lie. "I'm here to get what I need."

"Why you need so many different things?" Zigor asks. "Keep it simple. I get you good *geroin* much easier. You make more money too."

"Not interested."

Opioids are the one drug I won't touch, and I'm not interested in selling them either. I want willing customers, not slaves.

Tweedledum and Tweedledee stand on either side of Zigor, hands clasped over their crotches, staring at me from behind the lenses of their *Matrix*-style sunglasses.

"Don't you get sick of those two gargoyles breathing down your neck?" I say to Zigor.

"*Nyet.*" Zigor shrugs. "They carry all my things for me. What not to like?"

I shift impatiently, checking the time on my phone. Jasper better not be dawdling in the depot office so he can avoid Zigor's jokes.

"How much longer till the driver gets here?" I ask.

I want to get back to the lab.

"Ten minutes."

"You said that twenty minutes ago."

In response, Zigor pulls out a toothpick and starts picking his teeth. He does this with maximum smacking and clicking sounds, leering at me the whole time.

"Where you get those pants?" he says. "I like."

"Honestly, Zigor, your approbation is an insult. Knowing you like them makes me like them less."

He stares at me a minute, then bursts into braying laughter. The Bookends smile too, but only because they think they're supposed to. I'm pretty sure neither one of them speaks English.

"Funny girl," Zigor says.

Luckily, Jasper reappears before Zigor can ask me on another date. He's been trying to pressure me into coming out for a drink every time I see him. I told this to Adrik, hoping he'd murder him, but Adrik's shocking lack of jealousy continues. He only laughed and said, "Zigor's a lightweight. He'd probably pass out on the table after two shots."

At last, our truck arrives. We've paid for the use of the most distant loading bay, the one where the cameras don't work.

Jasper drives the SUV right up to the back of the truck.

The Bookends help with the unpacking. This takes longer than expected because this time, the product is hidden inside the frames of several treadmills. We have to take the machines apart using wrenches and Allen keys.

When we're finished, Jasper and I climb back into the SUV, planning to drive the product back to the lab.

Zigor jumps in the back seat. "I come with you."

"That's not necessary—" Jasper starts.

"Filipp and Georgiy will follow," Zigor says placidly.

Seized by an evil impulse, I ask Zigor, "What's your favorite song? I'll DJ."

"You have Hard Bass School?"

"Of course." I find them on Spotify. "They're Jasper's favorite."

I play what is commonly known as the *gopnik* national anthem at top volume. It's a pounding, repetitive, ass-fuck of a song, the Russian equivalent of "Gangnam Style" if it were sung by squatting thugs in tracksuits.

Jasper turns and stares at me silently.

I promised Adrik I would be nice to Jasper…but I also promised myself not to let opportunities pass me by. And this is the perfect opportunity to give Jasper an aneurysm.

"You want it on repeat?" I say to Zigor.

"*Da!* This song best song. Can never play too much."

"I couldn't agree more."

Narkotik ne klass.
Ya yedu na hard bass!

Zigor and I sing along as loud as we can while Jasper pulls out of the depot, his right eye twitching.

CHAPTER 26
ADRIK

On Christmas Eve, I broker a deal with the Markovs for twenty-five thousand doses of Molniya. The Markovs own the largest slice of Moscow, and they don't let anyone else sell in their territory. They used to buy from the Chechens, but Sabrina's pill is the new hotness. Everyone wants it.

Sabrina's coming along with me for the handoff because Ilsa will be there. Their friendship survived the breakup, though Sabrina's been too busy to actually meet up with Ilsa since she came here.

I find her in the living room, trying to help Chief with his Tinder profile. Andrei sprawls on one of the beanbag chairs, shouting out opposite advice: "You need a pic where you look tough, manly. Doing something impressive. Maybe holding a big wad of cash."

"He's not trying to attract *you*, Andrei." Sabrina rolls her eyes. "He wants an actual human woman."

"Women love money."

"He's not looking for a sugar baby. Here, Chief. This should be your profile pic."

She points to one of Chief working on his bike, his coveralls down around his waist, only an undershirt on his upper half, his hair messy and grease all up his arms.

"I'm dirty," Chief protests. "I look like a scrub."

"You look competent," Sabrina insists. "Look at your hands, your forearms..."

"Forearms!" Andrei scoffs.

"You're gonna get swiped by girls who want to be touched," Sabrina says, ignoring Andrei.

"I'm wearing my glasses. Glasses aren't popular in Russia."

"You look intelligent. You gotta be yourself on dating apps. There's no point trying to look like one thing and showing up as another."

"He won't get any matches as himself," Andrei warns.

"What do you know?" Sabrina snorts. "I haven't seen you go on one date since I've been here."

"I'm busy."

"Yeah, busy losing to Hakim in *Dr. Mario*."

"I don't *always* lose," Andrei says with dignity.

"What's your caption?" Sabrina says, turning back to Chief.

"It says, 'If you want to get to know me, then ask.'"

"That's terrible."

Chief grimaces. "I was trying to be mysterious. I don't know what to write."

"You need to write the line that gets you what you want. The right bait for the right fish. You don't want just any girl—you want the right girl. That's why it's best to be genuine all along. How about 'Match with me, and I'll make the first move.'"

"What girls will that get?"

"Curious ones. I know how funny you are on your keyboard. Go through their profile, find something interesting about them, and come at these girls like you know them, the way you text me. You're the funniest person in our group chats."

"That's true," I back her up.

Chief is far more confident through text than in person. Sabrina is smart to compliment his strengths—it's what I would do. In fact, it *is* what I do when I'm trying to build him up.

"Not in person, though," Chief sighs.

Sabrina says, "Let them meet the best you first. Here, show me your matches."

Chief shows her the only girl who's swiped right on him: a nervous-looking blond whose profile pic is mostly the giant black cat sitting on her lap.

"Okay, so look through her pics," Sabrina says. "What do you think she wants you to notice in this picture?"

She points to an image where the blond girl is standing under a tree in Gorky Park, wearing a red summer dress with buttons down the front.

"She looks…pretty," Chief says.

"That's good," Sabrina encourages. "But let's compliment more than her looks. Let's compliment her taste. Something like, *I bet when girls think they want to wear a pretty red dress, this is what they picture in their heads.* You're telling her that she's stylish and iconic. That she created a moment. That other girls would admire her if they saw this pic."

"Alright," Chief says, typing out the message.

Andrei watches with interest.

Chief hits send.

"Let me know if she replies," Sabrina says.

"You ready to go?" I ask her.

"Wait!" Andrei cries. "What about *my* profile?"

Sabrina laughs. "I'm gonna need a lot more time to fix yours. I'll do it when we get back."

"You should be charging for your services," I tell Sabrina as we climb in the car.

"They can't afford me," she says airily.

"I see the effort you're making." I lay my hand on her thigh. "And I appreciate it."

"Yeah, we're getting on alright. Even Jasper has his good points. I mean, not his personality or behavior or mood…but something."

I try not to let her see me smile.

"He's punctual. You can say that for him," Sabrina says, as if it pains her to admit even that.

"He's a lot more than punctual."

"Sure. He also makes the best coffee."

I pretend to be hurt. "I thought you said I made the best coffee?"

"Well, you had just made me come three times when I said that."

"Four times, actually."

"I'm glad one of us keeps track."

We're driving into the Presnensky District, where the Markovs have the majority of their hotels and restaurants. The Markovs control their territory with an iron fist, because the majority of their income comes from *krysha*. Those who pay for protection expect business to run smoothly. In a sense, the Markovs are both landlord and security force. They're cautious about what product gets trafficked on their streets and in their properties.

Because this is the first of hopefully many such transactions, I'm doing the deal in person. Neve Markov will be representing her family. We're meeting at the Aurora Hotel on the bend of the Moskva, close to Krasnaya Presnya Park.

I've dressed a little nicer than normal, in slacks and a black wool coat.

Sabrina eyes me as I toss the keys to the valet.

"You clean up nice."

"Likewise."

She's all in white today—white trousers, a white turtleneck, and a white coat belted at the waist, with the collar turned up against the cold. As she stands in front of the ornate stone facade of the hotel, thick flakes of snow drifting down around her and settling in her dark hair, I think how exotic she looks yet perfectly at home.

"Ready?" I say, taking the briefcase from the back seat.

"Of course."

She tucks her hand in the crook of my arm, and we ascend the steps together.

We take the elevator to the eighteenth floor where we meet Neve Markov in a private suite overlooking the river.

Ilsa opens the door. I think she intends to greet us with a handshake, but the moment Sabrina sees her, she throws her arms around Ilsa's waist and hugs her hard. Ilsa can't help smiling and hugging her back.

"Good to see you," she says. "You know my sister, Neve, and this is Simon Severov."

"*Rad nashei vstreche,*" Simon says to Sabrina. *Nice to meet you.* He shakes her hand and then mine, though we've met before.

"Please sit down." Neve gestures to a small, striped sofa. She and her fiancé sit opposite us. There's room for Ilsa on the same couch, but she takes the armchair to the left of us instead.

I set the briefcase on the table between us and open it, turning the case so Neve and Simon can see the neat packets of pills shaped like yellow lightning bolts.

"And what exactly is in this?" Simon asks. His accent is thicker than Neve's, but his English is good for someone who went to school here in Moscow.

"It's proprietary," Sabrina replies.

"Then how can I test it?" Simon says, his upper lip curling slightly.

Ilsa shoots him a look, her jaw tight. I suspect she's more annoyed by the fact that he's speaking for her sister than by the questions themselves.

"It's already been tested in the best clubs in the city," I say calmly. "We're selling out faster than we can make more."

"Will there be a problem getting consistent delivery?" Neve inquires.

Neve Markov has a low, clear voice that seems to cut through the space between us. She has an air of calm authority, a way of sitting still with her hands neat and immobile in her lap, only her eyes moving. I've heard other Bratva speak disparagingly of her, laughing at the idea of a female *pakhan* with her sister as lieutenant. I doubt they'd talk the same way if she were in the room. There's nothing laughable about her, not in person.

I assure her, "If we make a deal for regular transactions, you'll get your orders."

"Good." She nods. "Once a month then, to start. Is that agreeable?"

It's more than agreeable. The Markovs are flush with cash. A steady order will help fund our operation as we grow.

"Forty a pill?" I say. "American dollars?"

She nods.

Molniya resells for sixty dollars each, an astronomical price compared to the Netherlands or the UK, but that's the cost of party drugs in Russia. The materials are difficult to smuggle in, the bribes ruinous, the penalties draconian if you're caught. We could all receive a life sentence in Siberia just for meeting here today.

Ilsa hoists the black duffel bag next to her chair, setting it on the coffee table. She unzips the bag, showing me the stacks within. I can count the money at a glance—a hundred bills per strap, $10,000 per stack, a hundred stacks total, for a cool million in cash.

American dollars are more convenient than rubles. They take less space and can be used in payment cross-border. Anyone will take them happily.

Our business complete, Sabrina takes the money and Ilsa the pills. Neve brings the tea service from the side table, setting it out between us.

The large silver samovar is filled with traditional Russian caravan. In the old days when the camel caravans took sixteen months to bring tea from China, it would arrive flavored with smoke from the campfires along the route. Nowadays, the flavor is added intentionally via oxidization.

Neve pours the concentrate into each of our cups, to which we add the desired amount of hot water. I make mine dark as creosote and Sabrina's the color of her lovely tan skin. She hasn't come to appreciate our tea quite yet, not at full blast.

Simon drinks his the old way, with a cube of sugar held between his teeth.

We chat as we eat the stacks of sandwiches and tiny pastel-colored cakes. Or I should say, Neve, Simon, Sabrina, and I chat, while Ilsa sits in near silence. She's in a somber mood, though not because of me and Sabrina, I don't think.

Neve is telling Sabrina all about her wedding venue, an old estate in the countryside outside Moscow.

"I'll send you and Adrik an invitation, of course."

"Do you do bridesmaids in Russia?" Sabrina asks. "This is your chance to make Ilsa wear pink."

Neve smiles. "No bridesmaids. Ilsa will be my witness—it's like a maid of honor. She gets a sash."

"And Neve will wear a crown," Simon says. "As is fitting for my queen."

He lifts her hand, pressing her knuckles to his lips.

Ilsa doesn't like that phrasing one bit. Her eyes narrow, and she sets her cake back down on her plate without taking a bite.

As we all set our plates aside, Neve says, "If you'd like, I've reserved the suite for your use tonight. There will be fireworks over the Moskva. You'll have a perfect view."

I would never stay in a room overnight after a normal business meeting—especially not with this much cash on me. But I've known the Markovs all my life. I consider us friends as well as allies.

Besides, Sabrina has no poker face. I can see how this idea excites her. If only so we can fuck as loud as we want without the Wolfpack overhearing.

"*Spasibo*," I say. "That's very generous."

"I'll send the staff for the dishes," Neve says, shaking our hands in farewell. I see Simon's diamond glittering on her finger, bigger than one of our pills.

"We should go for lunch together," Sabrina says to Ilsa. "If either of us ever takes a day off."

"I'd love that," Ilsa says.

I think it's the only sentence she's spoken the whole meeting. Sabrina is going to have to meet Ilsa one-on-one if she wants to actually talk to her, because it's pretty clear Ilsa despises her sister's fiancé and isn't going to say shit when he's around.

In a reverse of our entrance, Neve, Ilsa, and Simon depart, leaving Sabrina and me alone in the suite.

"What should we do?" I ask Sabrina.

She bites the edge of her lip, looking me up and down.

"I can think of a few things…"

———

Several hours later, we're lying on the bed in the dark. The only light comes through the large windows overlooking the river. The clouds have cleared away enough that I can see the flat disk of the moon, cold and silvery, looking down on its twin rippling in the dark water below.

I hear a faint popping sound. A small flare shoots up into the air, then bursts into thick purple sparks, like a chrysanthemum blooming in the sky. It's followed by a dozen more flares. Our window erupts in color.

The fireworks glisten on Sabrina's naked body. They tint her skin in brilliant bursts of blue, gold, silver, and green. The sparks reflect in her eyes.

"I got you something," I tell her.

She sits up on one elbow, her sheaf of black hair tumbling down, trailing across the rumpled sheets.

"What is it?" she asks, eager as a child.

I take a flat box from my coat pocket, opening it to her view.

The diamond collar is colorless as ice, but it glows like flame as another firework erupts.

Sabrina's mouth falls open.

She stretches out a hand, stopping just short of the glittering jewels, afraid to even touch them.

"Put it on," I say.

She turns obediently, lifting her hair off the nape of her neck.

I drape the diamonds around her throat, fastening the clasp behind her.

Sabrina slips her feet back into her shoes, abandoned next to the bed. She stands in front of the window, naked except for her heels and the diamond collar. A firework detonates above her left shoulder, drenching her in a shower of silver light.

She's so fucking beautiful.

I can't breathe. I can't speak. All I can do is stare.

I wish I could capture this moment and freeze it forever in time.

I lift my phone and snap a picture of her, though I know it could never do justice to her living, breathing beauty. Or to the way she makes me feel.

Sabrina touches the diamonds at her throat, her eyes glinting just as brilliantly.

"We're really doing it, aren't we?" she says.

Her face is flushed with triumph—the diamonds, the penthouse suite, the two of us here together...

"Nothing can stop us," I say. "I'm invincible with you."

Sabrina grins, her teeth a flash of white in the dark between fireworks. She grabs the bag of cash and takes out a stack, ripping off the band. Throwing the money up in the air, she lets it drift down around her. The bills flutter through the air, illuminated in bursts of gold and green.

Sabrina grabs another stack and another. She's pulling them apart, throwing them at me. The money covers the bed, the floor, the side tables. She jumps on the bed and flings cash in the air, jumping up and down, bouncing the money on the mattress, creating a blizzard of bills.

She's laughing maniacally, making a hell of a mess. Her naked breasts bounce on her chest, her hair buoyant, the diamonds sparkling on her throat, the money floating like a thousand papery butterflies.

I gather up an armful of cash and fling it up. The money is a joke, barely real to me. It's what it represents: ambition, success, Sabrina's genius and mine in concert together. I kiss her as it rains down on us.

Sometimes you work and work toward a goal, but when you finally achieve it, it fails to provide the happiness you thought you would feel.

This is the opposite of that.

For all the thousands of times I imagined how it would feel to have the world at my feet, I never could have imagined it like this.

Everything is better with Sabrina by my side. She charges every moment. She bursts me open like a firework. I'm flaming with light and color and pure, electric bliss.

We're jumping on the bed together, naked and out of our minds. With each leap, another firework bursts, booming outside the window like a cannon blast. I'm holding her hands, looking in her face. She's laughing wildly, her eyes brighter than stars.

This is the happiest I've ever been. Maybe the happiest I ever will be.

It's because of her that success comes so early and tastes so sweet.

There's no end of dreaming with Sabrina. No end of believing. It's the most American thing about her—she really thinks she can do anything. And so do I when I'm with her.

Sabrina wears the diamond collar all night long. She keeps it on while we fuck and wears it with her robe while we order room service, sampling the Markovs' burgers and fries.

Sabrina is quickly converting me to her love of cheeseburgers.

She eats them at least three times a week, and I'll admit, they're satisfying. Especially when you've been exerting yourself all night long.

I pour us each a glass of Riesling.

"Not as sweet as Vietti," I tease her. "But not bad."

Sabrina takes a massive bite of her burger, washing it down with wine.

"It'll do," she says. And then, "I got something for you too."

"You did?"

I didn't expect anything. It's my job to spoil Sabrina, not the other way around.

Sabrina retrieves her coat, pulling a small, paper-wrapped package from the pocket.

"I picked it up yesterday," she says. "I was afraid it wouldn't come in time."

I rip open the paper, revealing a switchblade like Sabrina's, only more expensive-looking. The scrimshaw handle is richly oiled, the blade shimmering with waves of layered Damascus steel.

"That's fossilized mammoth bone," Sabrina says. "In the handle. I thought it was cool."

I hold the knife up to the light so I can read the engraving, so small I almost missed it:

You. Always you.

It's what I said to her from down between her thighs the night I pleasured her for hours. She's saying it back to me because it meant something to her.

Sabrina is not sentimental. She rarely shows tenderness in this way.

It affects me more than I want to let her see.

Her own knife is probably her favorite belonging. She carries it with her everywhere and uses it even for tasks she probably shouldn't, like opening envelopes and cutting tags off clothes.

I slip the knife in my pocket, knowing that every time I touch it or use it or feel its weight, I'll think of her. A little piece of her with me all the time.

"I love it," I say, pulling her close.

"Well, I didn't know you were gonna upstage me with this." Sabrina touches the diamonds at her throat.

"That's how it should be. I'd be ashamed if you gave me a better gift."

"What if I want to give you the better gift?"

"Then you should date Andrei. He'd love a sugar mama."

Sabrina snorts, but she's shaking her head at me, mildly annoyed. "But what if I—"

I silence her with my mouth.

"You *are* the gift, Sabrina. You're what I want."

CHAPTER 27
SABRINA

It's two weeks after Christmas, and I'm putting the finishing touches on Opus, the third formula of my hybrid party drug. This one is for concerts. It has the highest concentration of LSD to make music sound phenomenal. Adrik and I tested it out at a live show of Cannons in a tiny dive bar in Danilovsky.

The night started out horribly. We got doused in freezing rain waiting to go inside. Adrik and I were both soaked to the skin, my makeup running down my face, stinging my eyes. Inside, the venue was packed, standing room only around the stage.

I hadn't realized there wouldn't be any seats, so I was wearing thigh-high suede boots with staggering heels. I didn't know the band that well, only that it was my cousin Anna's favorite. I almost said we should go home right then, but Adrik and I had already taken the Opus, and I needed to try it out at a real live event.

Seeing how hard I was shivering, Adrik bribed the bouncers to let us into the upper balcony, which was supposed to be for season ticket holders only. There were two seats free, right against the railing. We sat down and ordered a drink. Adrik put his arm around me, holding me close against his side until heat radiated from his body into mine.

The whole venue warmed up fast once it was packed with people. A sea of heads bobbed below us. The stage set looked more like a play than a rock concert. The facade resembled a café in Paris—working windows with shutters, flowers in the planter boxes, and vines dangling down from the roof.

The opener came onstage—another artist I'd never heard of. He was Russian, and I could only catch about half of what he was calling out to the crowd, despite all the studying I've been doing in my off-hours. Their goddamn language is so difficult to learn, especially with how fast people speak and the various regional accents. This guy sounded southern, maybe from Belarus like Jasper.

As his backing track began to play—a lovely rhythmic remix of an old Temptations song—I felt the Opus kicking in hard. Video screens illuminated behind him, pulses of color flowing like waves of lava in sunset colors of pink, orange, and peach. The venue was warm, Adrik's arm even warmer around my shoulders. The music seemed to float up to me in waves. I could see it, edged with color and light. The sound waves washed over me, over and over with each repetition of the chorus.

"*Spasibo shto vi preshli na segodnyashniy vecher. Nadeyus vi poluchite udovol'stiviye ot uslishannovo,*" the performer called to the crowd.

Thank you for coming tonight. We're here to feel something together.

In that moment, I felt deeply linked to every person in the room. We were all swaying to the music, our hands in the air. Even though I could only understand half the song, I felt every word of it, every emotion. I felt the humanity of the performer. The spark of life inside him, calling out to the spark of life in all of us.

I turned to Adrik. His mouth was open like mine, his eyes a vivid, liquid blue.

"What the fuck..." he whispered.

Neither of us had to say anything else. We both knew what we were feeling, together at the same time. Our minds buoyant on the music, linked to each other like we were holding hands, floating down a river together.

My body relaxed. I was peaceful and so happy I could have cried if I knew how to let myself do it.

When the performer finished, he threw money into the crowd, the bills floating down like the night Adrik and I made a blizzard out of the Markovs' money. It probably wasn't much—maybe $100 or $200 in American dollars—but the message was clear. He was giving back to his fans, sharing his success with them. It made me want to do the same. I wanted to be generous and open, sharing what I have with strangers just for the joy of it.

Then Cannons came onstage, and I heard the first refrain of the song that Anna plays incessantly, "Love Chained," the one that will always make me think of her.

I'd heard the song dozens of times, driving in her car or watching her dance. But I'd never heard it like this. I felt like I was drifting through time, through a haze of memories that came clear and then faded away again like buildings in fog.

I saw Anna laughing with Leo in the front seat of his car, his arm slung across the back of her seat. I saw Leo watching her dance in their high school gymnasium, Anna standing out from the other girls not only because of her sheaf of white-blond hair and her black-painted lips but because of that inimitable grace she possesses that won't let you tear your eyes off her. Leo certainly couldn't. I saw how the two of them always sat together at every family dinner, how Leo's gift was always her favorite at her birthday parties, how they always seemed to be smiling at each other at some private joke I could never understand, not only because I was so much younger but because no one could understand the secrets the two of them shared.

I finally understood the hopeless longing in that song. I understood that Anna loved Leo all her life, long before either of them knew it. She was chained to him and always would be.

This was her siren song to him. She played it over and over and over, calling out to him. Begging him to see her, all of her.

I looked at Adrik, and I thought, *There's so many other people he*

*loves. His parents, his brother, the Wolfpack. Could he ever love me like
Anna does Leo? Like they're the only two people in the world?*

Do I even deserve that?

Adrik touched my cheek with his hand.

"You're a fucking genius," he said. "I've never felt anything like
this."

It was true—the Opus was powerful.

Maybe too powerful. My chest was so tight I could hardly
breathe. Too many emotions all at once.

I've dialed back the dosage just a touch. Now it's manage-
able. Anyone can take it without having a breakdown at a concert.
People don't want too many epiphanies, not when they're trying to
have fun.

Hakim makes the hand sign to me to take a break. I follow him
outside so he can smoke and I can lean against the filthy brick wall,
pushing my goggles up on my head and breathing the air that seems
cleaner, even tinged with Hakim's cigarette.

Jasper pulls up in the SUV a moment later. He's wearing an old
bomber jacket with a sheepskin collar. The effect is a little disturbing
with his skeletal hands and neck—like he went down in flames in
World War Two, and now he's back to haunt us.

He hauls several duffel bags out of the trunk, bringing them
around to us.

"What's all that?" I ask.

"Supplies," Jasper says, as if it's obvious.

I didn't know we were getting another shipment. I help him take
the bags inside, unzipping them to check the contents.

It's a fuck ton of isosafrole and MDP2P. Way more than we've
ever gotten at one time before.

I frown at the neatly wrapped packages. "How did you get all
this?"

"From Zigor," Jasper says, looking at me like I'm an idiot. "What
do you think?"

My heart is pounding double speed in my chest. I strip off my hazmat suit, flinging it aside.

"Take me back to the house," I snap. "Now."

Jaspers drives me back to the Den, his hand pale on the dark wheel. I'm not speaking to him or messing with his music like I usually would. I'm only thinking one thing: *Where the fuck is Adrik?*

The moment we pull up to the house, I jump out of the car. Jasper follows after me, knowing something is up.

I storm inside, stomping room to room until I find Adrik down in the gym, lifting with Vlad.

"Did you spend every fucking penny of that money?" I shout at him.

Adrik sits up from the bench. His black tank sticks to his skin, wet with sweat. He grabs a towel and rubs it down his chest, his muscles swollen and flushed.

"Can you give us a second?" he says to Vlad.

Vlad raises an eyebrow, curious, but he leaves the room without speaking. Jasper stays exactly where he is.

Adrik sets the towel down, standing up from the bench. I forget how much taller he is until he's looking down at me, his chest an inch from my nose. He's making me tilt up my chin to look at him. His jaw is stiff, those pale blue eyes burning with anger. Adrik has a temper too. Even if he keeps a lid on it, it's always there, simmering under the surface.

"You want to try that again?" he says quietly.

"Did you spend all the Markovs' money?" I demand.

"It's not the Markovs' money. It's *our* money. I used it to buy raw materials."

"All of it?"

"Yes, all of it."

He's unashamed and unrepentant.

I'm so fucking furious, I'd like to slap him.

"You made me a promise! You said when we were in a better position, we'd keep a reserve—"

"It's not time yet."

"Who the fuck says?!" I shout.

"I say!" Adrik points his finger in my face. "I do."

He's trying to make me take a step back, but I won't fucking do it. I'm sick of him making decisions without me, in direct opposition to what we agreed.

My face is burning, my eyes too, though there's no fucking way I'd let a tear fall. It would make me look weak, womanish. Everything he thinks about me when he makes these kinds of decisions over my head.

"What makes you think you know better than me?" I hiss.

"This is my country. My people. I know what we have to do to take territory."

"Well, I know business! You don't have a ninety-day cash flow. You don't have contingencies—"

"I have what I need," he says. Cold, arrogant, autocratic. He's a fucking dictator in a country of dictators.

"You're vulnerable," I tell him.

"*I'm* vulnerable?"

Now his voice has dropped even lower…a soft and dangerous rumble deep in his chest. Adrik steps forward, closing his hand around my throat and spinning me around so I'm facing Jasper, my back pressed against his chest.

Jasper watches us, his dark red hair falling down over one eye, his mouth thin and pale.

"Let me tell you something about Sabrina," Adrik says, speaking to Jasper, not to me. "She likes to use sex as a weapon. She uses it to control men and women too…but she's a dealer who gets high on her own supply."

I try to twist away from him. His arm is iron across my chest, his fingers clenched around my throat. I'm burning with pure, flaming rage.

Adrik takes his other hand and slides it up my waist.

"She's the biggest addict of all," he says. "She's completely controlled by it."

He's groping my breast, right in front of Jasper. Lifting it. Squeezing my nipple through my shirt.

Jasper watches, pale and immobile. His eyes drop to my chest, and then he jerks them up again, a little color coming into his cheeks.

I'm so fucking angry I could scream. But at the same time... heat flushes through my body. My thighs squeeze together. There's a throbbing low in my guts.

Adrik pulls down the front of my top, baring my breasts to Jasper. My nipples stiffen in the cold air of the basement gym. Adrik brushes his palm lightly over my breasts, his fingertips trailing over the hard nipples, sending sparks up and down my spine.

I'm clenching my teeth tight together, my breath coming out in pants.

Adrik slips his hand down the front of my pants, inside my underwear. He slides his middle finger back and forth in the cleft of my pussy lips, across my clit.

Jasper's arms tighten. He drops his gaze to the ground, only for his eyes to rise again and fix on me, unable to look away.

Adrik dips his finger inside me and lifts his hand, fingertips shining in the low light.

"See?" he murmurs. "See how wet she is? She's fucking furious right now, but she can't stop wanting it."

He tucks back my hair and leans in to whisper right in my ear.

"That's why I'm in charge, Sabrina. Because you can't even control *yourself.*"

He releases me. I whirl around and hit him in the face, as hard as I can. This is no slap like in sex. It's a closed-fist punch. I split his lip, the blood running down his chin, dripping slowly to the floor.

Adrik doesn't stumble. He didn't even try to block it. He'd probably let me hit him again.

His eyes flick over to Jasper. "Get out."

Jasper leaves without a word.

Now it's just Adrik and me, facing off in the damp gym, deep in the basement.

"Don't you *ever* talk to me like that in front of my men."

"I thought they were *our* men," I hiss. "*Our* friends. And *our* money."

"Call them what you like. But don't undermine me. If you have something to say, you say it to me. Alone."

"Undermine you?" I let out a laugh of pure outrage. "What do you think you just did in front of Jasper? You fucking humiliated me!"

His lip curls up in a snarl. "You push me, Sabrina. You push me and fucking push me."

"Oh yeah? And what happens when you snap?"

He seizes me by the throat again. For a second, I think he's going to strangle me, until our mouths crash together and he's kissing me with all the rage built up inside him. Making me taste the blood from his lip. Making me take his tongue all the way in my mouth.

He shoves his hand down my pants again, thrusting his fingers inside me, fucking me with his hand. I'm still enraged, but that blazing heat is all concentrated in one place, and my body isn't taking orders from my brain. It's caught up in the need, the fucking command, to impale myself on his fingers.

The urge is irresistible. I'm already halfway there, my arms around his neck, one leg hooked around his hip, fucking his hand.

I'm an animal. Adrik is right. I have no control over myself.

I fucking hate him in this moment, but I can't stop needing him, not even for a second.

I'm humping his hand, pressing my whole body against him, clinging to his neck, whimpering and moaning. It's fucking pathetic. And still it's not enough. I kiss him wildly so I can taste his mouth, so I can inhale his scent.

He flips me over, bending me over the bench, ripping my jeans down around my knees. He puts his palm in the middle of my back, shoving down, and thrusts into me from behind. His cock tears into me, stiff as a pipe. He's fucking me hard and vicious, his hips slapping against my ass.

I need it hard. I want it harder. I'm gripping the edge of the bench with both hands, my knuckles white.

He fucks me and fucks me, my tits swinging, our bodies slapping together. Now he's gripping my hips with both hands, plowing into me, punishing me with his cock.

I want the anger. I want the violence. I want to rip and throw and smash everything in this room. I want to pour gasoline around the basement and set the house on fire.

I'm angry, and I'm fucking frustrated. I want to be respected, and I want to be worthy of respect, but I'm ruled by my temper and my emotions, and I don't know how to stop.

I'm already starting to come, crying out loud enough that Jasper will hear it upstairs. Everyone will hear it. They'll know I'm just a whore who likes to be fucked, bent over like a beast.

Adrik lets out a roar, giving one last thrust deep inside me. His hands shake, his fingers digging into my hips.

Then he lets go of me and takes a step back. His cock pulls out of me, his come running down the inside of my thigh.

I pull up my jeans, my fingers trembling too much to do up the zipper.

I can't look at him. I can't meet his eye.

Maybe Adrik is embarrassed too. He's quiet, dressing quickly, finding my shirt and bringing it over to me. He pulls it over my head, dressing me like a child.

Still without speaking, he scoops me up in his arms and carries me upstairs.

I turn my head against his chest so I won't have to see Jasper or anyone else.

Adrik carries me up to our room. He lies me on the bed. I hear the pipes shuddering as he runs water in the tub.

It takes several minutes for the tub to fill. I lie on my side on the bed, looking at the wall, trying not to think about anything. I wish I could shut my brain off like a computer. I wish I could wipe my memory.

When Adrik returns, he undresses me once more. He carries me to the huge old copper tub, much larger than a normal bath. He places me in water so warm that my skin immediately turns a rich, ruddy sienna.

Sometimes I feel like there are two people inside me: one who's relatively reasonable and one who's completely insane. When the madness passes, all I can do is look around at the wreckage and wonder who that other Sabrina was. Where does she come from, and where does she go? And which one of us is the real Sabrina?

I'm afraid it's her. This person who sits in a bath, calm and lucid, is only an illusion. A mask I wear until the real Sabrina returns.

My arms float in the water like they don't belong to me. I'm dissociated, watching while Adrik lathers a sponge and begins to wash me, starting at my feet, moving up my body. He washes every inch of my skin, gently and carefully.

When he's done, he tilts up my chin and pours a little water over the crown of my head, letting it run backward around my ears.

He takes the shampoo from the shower, squirting a little into his palm. He begins to massage it into my scalp with slow, deep circles. His hands are strong. The pressure is immensely relaxing. I lean my head back against the copper rim of the tub, eyes closed, hearing the seashell sound of his palms passing over my ears.

Adrik rinses off the shampoo, pouring the water over my hair from the glass he uses when he's brushing his teeth. He scoops the water out of the tub, gently pours it over my head, keeping his hand pressed against my hairline so no water runs in my eyes.

When he's done with the shampoo, without me asking, he

retrieves the conditioner and runs it through the lower two-thirds of my hair. Even in my strangely distant state, I note how observant he is. He knows not to use the conditioner on the roots, not because I ever told him but because he watches me in the shower. He watches how I treat my hair. He knows my habits and my preferences.

That's what makes it so painful when he goes against what I want. It's intentional. Adrik doesn't do anything by accident.

He uses his fingers to separate the tangles, no easy task in hair as long as mine. Then he lets the conditioner sit for three minutes, gently stroking my head with his palm while we wait.

He rinses my hair once more before lifting me from the tub and wrapping me in the biggest, fluffiest towel. He sits me on his lap, my head on his shoulder.

"I'm sorry," he says. "Can you forgive me?"

I'm quiet for a moment, wondering how truthful I should be.

At last, I admit, "I'd forgive much worse than that."

It's not good to write someone a license to treat you any way they please. Yet I'm only telling him what we both already know. We've tested each other's boundaries and found that they are far outside the norm. They hardly exist in some places.

What Adrik and I value, what we accept, is not like normal people. That's what draws us together. But also what makes us so incendiary.

We're a combination of elements that hasn't been tested before. Will we create something revolutionary together? Or will it all blow up in our faces?

I don't know. And I hardly feel that I have a choice. I can't disengage from Adrik, even if I wanted to. Every day, I'm pulled deeper and deeper.

This is why I've never fallen in love before—it opens the door to all kinds of madness.

CHAPTER 28
ADRIK

I really fucked up with Sabrina.

Maybe the pressure is getting to me. Navigating the complexities of the underworld in Moscow is like running a dozen games of chess in my head—if there were hundreds of players swapping in and out and all those players would shoot you in the back given the chance.

Meanwhile, I'm supposed to direct the six other people in this house. I've got to keep them all safe and motivated. I've got to play to their strengths while shoring up their weaknesses. I'm a fucking babysitter and therapist and boss all rolled into one.

I've got to keep Vlad from bullying Chief and stop Andrei from irritating everybody else. I need to find another assistant for Hakim and figure out how to thaw the cold war between Sabrina and Jasper.

I have to keep the cops out of our business and a constant ear to the ground for the backlash coming our way from our legion of rivals, as the success of Molniya draws way too fucking much attention.

I know Yuri Koslov is pissed at us. Veniamin has cut him out, giving us full access to sell in his clubs. Koslov is a member of the high table and not someone I would have wanted as an enemy. Unfortunately, while I believe in abundance when it comes to making money, power is a zero-sum game. For one to gain, someone else must lose.

The Wolfpack is on the rise. Several of the old guard are declining.

Moscow is in turmoil. Two of the *kachki* got in a conflict no one seems to quite understand. Some say it was over a woman, others that it was a refusal to pay a gambling debt. Whatever the real reason, Boris Kominsky put a dagger in the eye of his old friend Nikolai Breznik. Even the high table isn't exempt—Savely Nika had his mansion raided, $48 million in cash and jewels carried out by the cops. Nika himself is sitting in a prison cell, an unheard-of humiliation for a Bratva boss. Apparently he got on the wrong side of the minister of energy over a bad oil deal.

Chaos creates opportunity but also risk. Everyone is on edge, violence breaking out in Solntsevo and Kapotnya over what should have been minor disputes. The Chechens and the Slavs are closer to war than they've ever been.

The distribution deal with the Markovs is crucial. They're a powerful ally. I'm sure the Chechens and Yuri Koslov would love to squash the Wolfpack before our drugs get any more popular, but now they risk tangling with Nikolai Markov and Simon Severov's family as well.

I had to roll that cash back into more product; I feel confident it was the right choice. Yet I do respect Sabrina's intelligence. She's not wrong—I'm taking a risk running such a thin margin. A calculated risk.

I did promise her to make decisions together. But at the end of the day, there can only be one general.

Still, I don't feel good about any of this. I don't feel in control.

I had so much confidence in my ability to do everything at once. Reality is messier.

Jasper is loading up the last of our ready-made product for Andrei to take to the distributors in the clubs.

I bring the totals to Chief so he can record the debts and the credits, tracking the ever-evolving centipede of our finances, devouring on one end and eaten up on the other.

Chief works out of a tiny office in the back of the house, the quietest space when Andrei and Hakim are playing video games at top volume or when Vlad is blasting his music.

The accounting is complicated by the fact that anything written down in the ledger has to be recorded in code, on the off chance our records are ever used against us in court.

Of course, if you actually find yourself in the judge's docket, something has already gone terribly wrong—as evidenced by Nika. A full thirty percent of our earnings goes to the police and various government officials to keep them dutifully uninterested in what we're doing.

When I finish with Chief, Jasper is lurking out in the hall. We haven't spoken since the incident down in the gym.

Jasper already resents Sabrina's presence the most of anyone in the house. He believes she's warping my decisions. I had to show him that she's no succubus bewitching my mind. I had to demonstrate that I'm the one in control.

Jasper may need a lesson of his own.

As soon as he sees me, he says, "I think Sabrina should stay in the lab."

Both Jasper and Sabrina hate picking up the raw materials together. This isn't the first time one of them has tried to get out of it.

"Not happening," I tell Jasper flatly.

"She's volatile," Jasper says. "Unpredictable."

"She's also useful," I remind him. "I'm not keeping her locked in the house."

"You saw how she lost her temper over nothing. What if something really pisses her off? She could get us in serious shit."

I turn and face Jasper, filling the hallway with my shoulders, blocking his path. Letting him know I'm fucking serious.

"Sabrina is a tiger. One of a kind, nothing else like her. And no, a tiger can't be tamed. Who would want it to be? All its power comes from the fact that it's wild. You can't cage a tiger. You can only try to be its master. Nobody wants a tiger that's a shell of itself. You want the most powerful fucking tiger you can get. And that comes with dangers. If you have a German shepherd, that dog will lay down its life for you. With a tiger, if you don't feed it and you don't respect it, it will eat you."

Jasper considers this, eyes narrowed, hands stuffed in his pockets. At last, he says, "Am I the dog in this metaphor?"

"I don't know," I reply. "But I can tell you, the tiger doesn't ask what it is in the metaphor. It already knows what it is."

Jasper smiles thinly, accepting the reproof.

He may not like me taking a slap at him, but he can't deny that Sabrina is valuable. She already proved her worth. The hybrid drugs were her idea. Hakim helped with the execution, but the formulas were her creation. She was the one bold or reckless enough to experiment on herself. She's the one who knows how to create an experience.

The pills are selling beyond our wildest dreams, and Sabrina's branding makes them recognizable and highly covetable in the open market. Imitators pop up every day, but the packaging is distinctive enough that the devotees will only accept the real deal. Molniya, Eliksir, and Opus are becoming as legendary as Orange Sunshine in the '60s.

I have to keep my focus on the mob of rivals jealous of our success.

Jasper and Sabrina will keep working together. It's good for both of them. They'll realize that soon enough.

CHAPTER 29
SABRINA

JASPER AND I ARE WAITING FOR ANOTHER SHIPMENT IN THE ASS crack of nowhere. This time, the product is coming up the Moskva River. We're waiting in a shack two hours east of the city so we can waylay the goods before they fall under the purview of the port authority.

This wouldn't be so bad, except that it's cold as hell in our little hidey-hole—no heating whatsoever and cracks in the walls as wide as a finger. The wind blows through in whistling gusts, stirring the old newspaper scattered across the floorboards.

More incessant than the wind is Zigor's endless chatter. He can't stand a two-minute stretch without anyone talking. Since his companions are the perpetually silent Bookends, the sulky skeleton Jasper, and me—currently wondering if I could stuff my ears with bits of newspaper without Zigor noticing—he's got an uphill battle keeping conversation going.

He keeps disappearing to answer the "call of nature," returning a few minutes later sniffing and rubbing his nose, twice as talkative as ever. I assume he's taking bumps in private not for Jasper's and my benefit but to avoid the Bookends whose job is surely to report on him to his father as much as to protect him.

It must enrage Lev Zakharov having a son this stupid. Adrik told me that Lev clawed his way up from abject poverty, selling stolen goods out of a briefcase in Rostov-on-Don, eventually opening his own pawn shop, then a whole chain of them, and finally expanding into the world of black-market goods.

Lev is notoriously cheap, a ferocious bargainer, ancient and wrinkled as a grasshopper. When he was sixty-two, he made the one frivolous decision of his life and married a nineteen-year-old waitress. Zigor was the result. According to Adrik, the waitress soon realized she had not secured the life of luxury she hoped—Lev was so stingy that he counted the squares of toilet paper she used and forced her to run hot water through the same coffee grounds three times in a row before she could grind more. The waitress fled to Azov, leaving Zakharov with a chubby toddler to raise.

Of course, this is all legend and rumor, so who knows how much of it is true. I could ask Zigor, but then I'd have to talk to him.

Jasper has commandeered one of the only chairs in the shack. Zigor has the other, but he keeps hopping up to pace around the room or take another stroll down to the empty dock to "look for the boatman."

The two Bookends have seated themselves on upturned buckets. The buckets are so low that their knees jut up around their chests. They look like a pair of crouching spiders, especially with those ridiculous sunglasses they refuse to take off even indoors.

I'm sitting on a rickety three-legged table. As long as I sit cross-legged right in the middle, I don't tumble off.

"We should have waited in the car," Jasper complains, blowing on his hands. "It'd be warmer."

"You need eat more!" Zigor tells him, slapping his own stomach. "I never cold."

"Yeah, but then I'd look like you," Jasper says.

"Is good for man to be big. Bigger the better, yes?" Zigor waggles his eyebrows at me suggestively.

"Yeah," I say in a bored tone. "Whenever I enter a room, I look at who's tallest, and then I fuck that person immediately."

I pretend to scan the room, squinting at each of the men in turn.

"Looks like Tweedledee wins," I say, nodding to the left Bookend. "Better luck next time, Zigor."

"Ho ho! Time to get busy, Georgiy!" Zigor chortles.

The left Bookend, apparently named Georgiy, turns his head toward me, scowling behind his sunglasses. "Who this Tweedledee?" he demands.

"He's a famous rock star," I say. "I'm surprised you haven't heard of him."

I could swear Jasper almost smiles before remembering to be miserable.

He's in a worse mood than usual. Adrik pulled me aside before we left, asking me to take it easy on Jasper.

"How come?"

"It's a bad time of year for him," Adrik said.

I assume he means this is when Jasper's family died—the kind of anniversary no one wants to celebrate but you can never forget. That would make sense, because for the last week, Jasper has barely left his room. He looks so fucked up that even I feel sorry for him—hair not combed, face unshaven, shadows under his eyes dark as bruises. So thin and pale that he truly does seem determined to starve himself down to the bone.

He obviously hasn't been sleeping. He's keyed up and twitchy. Every time Zigor makes a loud or abrupt noise—about every two minutes—Jasper jerks in his chair. If glares could kill, Zigor would be on his twenty-eighth resurrection. I'd be on my sixth or seventh.

"How much longer?" Jasper demands of Zigor.

"How I should know?" Zigor shrugs. "No cell service."

"He was supposed to be here an hour ago," Jasper says, checking the time on his phone.

"You know boats..." Zigor says, making a vague gesture in the air.

To irritate Jasper, I say, "I don't know boats. Can you explain them to me?"

Jasper shoots me my eighth fatal glare.

"Boats…" Zigor says wisely. "Sometimes fast, sometimes slow."

"Wow." I nod. "You're so right."

Another ten or twenty minutes pass in silence. And by silence, I mean no one is speaking but Zigor is making a clicking sound with his tongue against the roof of his mouth. He's managing to do it at precisely the irregular interval you can't get used to. Every time he clicks, Jasper's eye twitches. Jasper's leaning forward on his knees, hair falling into his face, clutching his head.

"You have headache?!" Zigor booms at top volume.

I take back what I said before—Zigor's growing on me. The enemy of my enemy is, if not exactly my friend, at least a useful annoyance.

The Bookends break out a pack of cards.

"*Vy khotite igrat'?*" Tweedledee asks Zigor.

"*Nyet,*" Zigor says, looking sulky.

The Bookends bet heavy, and I'm guessing Zigor already burned through his allowance. He's been making the strippers of Moscow rich and happy.

"*Vy?*" the right Bookend says to Jasper.

He shakes his head.

They don't ask me to play. That annoys me, not because I want to play but because they would have asked if I was a man. The Bookends treat me like furniture or actually more like a yappy little Pekingese brought along by Jasper for no discernible reason.

Zigor watches the Bookends methodically turning over cards on the upturned milk crate between them. With a dramatic sigh, he stomps outside again, returning a few minutes later flushed and glassy-eyed.

"We play real men's game," he announces, pulling his revolver from his pocket. He holds up the gun so the steel muzzle glints in the greenish light of the shack.

"Put that away," Jasper snaps.

We're all armed, but it's bad form to pull out your gun and play with it. Bad form to even acknowledge it's on your person.

Too bad, because Adrik made good on our bet—he bought me a P30L with a custom compensator, which really is the handgun from the first John Wick movie. I'd love to blow Zigor's mind by telling him that Keanu Reeves gave it to me.

Ignoring Jasper, Zigor snaps open the drum of his revolver, letting the bullets fall to the floorboards one by one until only a single .38-caliber bullet remains. He spins the drum, flicking it back in place.

"You know this game?" Zigor says. "Very famous."

"Oh yeah," I say blandly. "Mongolian roulette."

"You know is Russian game!" Zigor shouts. "You make me angry with these jokes. Mongolian! *Pah!*"

He spits on the floorboards.

"Put it *away*," Jasper hisses. He's still seated, but his body is stiff, turned toward Zigor now, his lips as white as his skin.

The Bookends are barely paying attention, still absorbed in their game. I doubt this is the first time Zigor's gotten high and pulled out his revolver.

Zigor points the gun at me.

"Simple rules. We pull trigger once each. God will decide who is good and who has been naughty."

Jasper's fingers dig into his thighs. He's so tense he's almost shaking.

"Quit fucking around," he barks.

Zigor swings the gun around so it's pointing at Jasper instead. He takes a few steps forward, closing the gap between them.

"You want go first, Jasper? Better odds."

"Don't even fucking think about—"

Jasper is cut off by the distinct click of Zigor pulling the trigger. Nothing happens—the chamber is empty. But Jasper leaps to his feet with a howl of rage, snatching the gun out of Zigor's hand and pointing it right in his face.

"You think that's funny?!" he shrieks. "What were you gonna do if it went off?!"

Without thinking, perhaps without even meaning to do it, Jasper's finger jerks on the trigger.

Instead of the same empty click, the gun fires.

A small, dark hole appears in the center of Zigor's forehead. Zigor's expression is one of pure astonishment, mirrored in Jasper's shocked face. He falls backward, crashing to the floorboards with a thud that shakes the shack.

The two Bookends look up, mouths open in surprise.

I rip my gun from my waistband and shoot them each in the head, one after the other.

Zigor's bodyguards topple off their buckets, their playing cards scattering across the floor in a flurry of hearts and spades, clubs and diamonds.

Jasper turns to me, paler than paper, mouth open in shock. "What the fuck?!"

"What the fuck? You what the fuck!" I shout back at him.

We're both frozen in place, staring at the carnage around us. In less than twenty seconds, we went from utter boredom to three men dead on the floor, blood slowly spreading outward in bright halos from the holes in their heads.

"This is so fucking bad," Jasper says. "Why'd you shoot the other two?"

"'Cause they would have put ten bullets in your chest and brought your head back to Lev. And if I didn't let them do that, they'd sure as fuck rat you out."

Jasper stares at the fallen bodyguards, absorbing the truth of this.

"You're right," he says at last. And then a moment later, very quietly, "Thank you."

"It's fine," I say brusquely. "But what the hell are we gonna do now?"

Jasper casts a swift look down the dock, checking the time on his phone.

"We need to get out of here before the boatman shows up."

"What about the supplies?"

"We could wait till he gets here," Jasper says. "But then we'll have to kill him too."

Neither of us particularly likes that idea. It's one thing to cap someone who's about to shoot you and quite another to murder the equivalent of a drug Door Dasher.

"We'll have to leave without it," I say. "We gotta get out of here. The longer we stay, the less plausible deniability we have."

"And what, just leave them here?" Jasper says, looking down at the bodies.

"I'm not gonna chop 'em up and bury 'em. That's a six-hour job for Zigor alone."

Jasper seems to come to a decision. "Wipe down anything you touched," he says. "Don't leave anything behind."

We look around the shack once more to see if there's anything we missed. The wind sounds eerie and ominous in the dead quiet, no chatter from Zigor anymore. Not even the gentle flick of playing cards turning over.

"Let's go," Jasper says.

We practically sprint back to the SUV, pulling out of the dirt road and speeding back to civilization.

As we drive, I say to Jasper, "Quick, text Zigor."

Jasper stares at me blankly. "He's not gonna answer…"

"I'm aware. Text him something like *Where are you?* Then do it again in an hour."

"Oh," Jasper says. He pulls out his phone, typing the message one-handed while holding the steering wheel with the other. He presses send, then says, "I don't think Lev is gonna buy that."

"What else are we supposed to do? He's got no proof of what happened."

"He won't need proof," Jasper says darkly.

That's too true to argue. It's not a court of law, and it's pretty fucking obvious something hinky went down.

"Drive faster," I say. "We need to tell Adrik."

Jasper presses the gas, even though both of us are dreading that conversation.

CHAPTER 30
ADRIK

THE PHONE CALL I'VE BEEN EXPECTING COMES TWO DAYS AFTER Jasper shot Zigor.

I pick up, trying to keep my tone casual.

"*Privet*," I say.

"Adrik Petrov." Lev's voice is low and rasping. Every time he takes a breath on the other end of the line, I hear a rattle deep in his chest. It should give the impression of age and sickness, but instead, the sound is menacing, like a diamondback slowly shaking its tail in warning.

Preempting him, I say, "I'm glad you called. I haven't been able to get hold of Zigor. We missed a shipment."

There's a long silence on the other end of the line.

Then, low and furious, Lev hisses, "*Don't fucking lie to me.*"

I wait to hear what he knows.

His anger is palpable. It seethes through the line, a heat I can feel against the side of my face.

"I'm going to give you one chance," Lev says. "And one chance only. Give me the man who shot my son. Turn him over to me, and he will receive his punishment by my hand. That will be the end of it. I'll seek no other revenge. I know it was one of your Wolfpack."

I pause for what I hope is the appropriate amount of time to indicate shock and confusion.

"I have no idea what you're talking about. Zigor is dead?"

I hear a creaking sound—perhaps the phone shaking with rage in his hand.

"I thought better of you, Adrik. I thought you had honor."

Now my temper rises.

"What kind of honor is that? Handing over one of my men to your pliers and blowtorches? Never. I'm sorry for what happened to your son. I truly am. But these are my brothers. Even if one was responsible, I wouldn't sacrifice him to you."

"Is that your final answer?"

"All my answers are final."

"Then I hold *you* responsible, Adrik. It will be *your* head."

"Come and get it."

I hang up the call.

Sabrina is sitting cross-legged on the bed. The book she was reading lies flat on her lap. She's pinching the skin between her thumb and forefinger, hard enough that her nails dig in.

She certainly heard my side of the call and possibly Lev's as well.

"How does he know?" she asks.

"He doesn't know for certain, but he's sure enough."

"What's he going to do?"

"I don't know. Put a hit on me maybe."

"We should go to Rostov-on-Don right now, today," Sabrina says at once. "Kill him before he can kill you."

"I can't. I've got way too much shit to do here. We're going to need a new source. We owe orders to Franko and the Markovs, not to mention our own dealers."

"You won't need a new source if you're dead."

"Sabrina, please." I cup her chin, tilting up her face to look at me. "Give me some credit. I'm not that easy to kill."

She's unsmiling, her eyes huge in her strained face.

"You're not invincible either."

I kiss her softly on the mouth. "Yes, I am. As long as I have you."

She doesn't look convinced, so I continue. "Look, I'll keep an ear out. Threats aren't action. Lev is pissed right now, but that doesn't mean he actually believes that Zigor is worth starting a war over. We'll wait and see what he does."

Sabrina chews on the edge of her lip, too hard.

"Don't," I say, touching her lip with my thumb. "You'll hurt yourself."

"Why are you taking the heat for Jasper?" she says. "He fucked up bad."

"That's what it means to be the boss—I'm responsible for what Jasper does. Besides, there's power in the pack. I'd rather fight Zakharov with seven of us than give up a brother."

She's frowning, her dark eyebrows giving poignant expression to her face. I want to smooth out the little lines of worry. I want to take all her fears away.

"You wouldn't turn Jasper over to be tortured and killed. No matter how much you hate him."

"I don't hate him," Sabrina sighs. "And no, I guess I wouldn't give him to Lev. Not really."

"Good." I smile. "Then for once, we agree."

For a week, nothing happens. I think maybe Zakharov will let it go. Zigor was his only son, but I'm sure he was a hinderance to Lev's business as much as a help. Zakharov spent a lifetime building his small horde of money and influence. He's still only a bit player. Revenge could cost him everything.

Then Mykah calls me. Though Apothecary is neutral ground, Mykah and I have been friends a long time. We were at school together—not only at Kingmakers but also in St. Petersburg, in our middle and senior classes. He often passes me information, and I do the same for him.

"Bad news, my friend," he says without preamble.

"Oh?"

"Lev Zakharov is in town. And he's hired Cujo."

"What for?"

"No one's saying it openly. But I think you can guess."

I certainly can. Cujo has been breaking knees and slitting throats a long time. He's one of the best, and he doesn't come cheap. I wish Zakharov had picked a different time to be extravagant.

"Thanks for letting me know."

"Watch your back, my friend."

I hang up the call, wondering if I should say anything to Sabrina. This isn't going to help her stress levels. On the other hand, it's dangerous for her not to know that Lev is here in Moscow, hunting me down with the help of the city's premium enforcer.

In the end, I gather all the Wolfpack together and tell them to be on their guard.

"No one goes anywhere alone. Keep your mouths shut, and watch your backs. Especially you, Andrei."

"I haven't told anybody what Jasper did!" Andrei cries, offended.

"*Nobody?*" Vlad says, suspicious. "Not in some comment on Reddit? Not a whisper to your favorite stripper?"

"No fucking way! I'm offended you would even ask."

"You did spoil Vlad's birthday surprise," Sabrina remarks.

"And you told Adrik who dented his bike," Hakim says.

"And you called Eban Franko's wife by his mistress's name," Vlad adds.

"Those were different!" Andrei protests. "This is way more serious."

"Franko's wife tried to cut his balls off. That was pretty serious to him," Chief says.

Jasper has been sitting quietly this whole time, his skin green-tinged and sickly looking. He's got a bandage along his jaw from the most recent addition to his tattoos.

"Never mind," I say to make them stop. "Just remember what I said. Stay together. Don't go near the *kachki*."

"You got it, boss," Andrei says virtuously.

I glance over at Sabrina. She looks about as cheerful as Jasper.

"You too," I say to her gently. "Don't go anywhere alone."

"I never do anyway." She shrugs. "Hakim and I are headed to the lab right now."

"Why don't you take Jasper with you? Just in case."

"Sure," Sabrina says without even a grimace or a word of argument. "He can keep an eye out while we're working."

CHAPTER 31
SABRINA

Hakim and I work for several hours, using up all our remaining supplies. We're going to need more raw materials, fast. Hakim and I couldn't make enough to fill even the orders we promised to the Markovs, let alone everyone else.

As we strip off our protective gear, I say to Hakim, "You going to Neve Markov's wedding?"

"Yeah," he says. "She invited all the Wolfpack. Which is nice, since I don't know her personally."

"How 'bout you, Jasper?" I call, tossing my goggles onto the messy heap of my hazmat suit and gloves in the trunk of the SUV.

Jasper is smoking moodily, sitting on the filthy curb behind the brewery. He doesn't seem to care that the cement is wet and icy or that he probably shouldn't be smoking so close to a fresh tattoo. He gives a little start when I call out to him, looking up at me with those pale green eyes ringed with black.

"I don't know," he says. "I don't like weddings."

"This one's gonna be a who's who of Mafia royalty, though," I say. "It's the Mafia Oscars."

"That sounds fuckin' awful." Jasper stubs out his cigarette on the curb, dropping the butt in the gutter.

"Winter weddings are stupid," Hakim says. "They should wait for summer."

"Maybe they don't want to wait." I shrug. "Everybody says they're crazy about each other."

"Yeah, give it six months," Jasper says.

"You should write greeting cards, Jasper," I say. "For people who want to ruin their loved one's day."

"Happy birthday," Hakim says. "The endless nothingness of death is one year closer."

"Happy anniversary," I say. "I've only cheated on you twice in twenty years, and I feel like that's pretty good."

"Happy Father's Day," Hakim says. "All my worst traits come from you, Dad, yet I look like Mom, and that bothers you ever since the divorce."

"Fuck off," Jasper snarls.

I have at least six more Jasper greeting card ideas, but I decide to save them to tell Adrik later. Jasper really does look like shit, and it's not as much fun to tease him when he's all fucked up.

"Come on," I say. "You gotta try Shake Burgers."

We drive around the purse factory, even though it would only take a couple of minutes to walk.

Jasper looks around at the turquoise vinyl booths, checkered tiles, Formica tables, and the old jukebox in the corner.

"Looks like that *Pulp Fiction* movie," he remarks.

"You like Tarantino?" I say. "I didn't know that."

"I like all movies," Jasper replies. "But his are some of the best."

"You want me to put on 'You Can Never Tell'?" I grin. "We can dance."

"Jasper can't dance," Hakim informs me, plopping down on the stool closest to where his crush is furiously slicing tomatoes. "*Dobryy den*, Alla."

Alla glances up at us but offers no greeting other than a long-suffering sigh.

"*Gde Misha?*" I ask. *Where's Misha?*

"*V shkole*," Alla grunts. *At school.*

"Oh, right." I check the clock on the wall. "We're early today."

"Doesn't anyone else ever eat here?" Hakim asks, looking around the empty restaurant.

"*Nyet*," Alla says. "American diner is stupid idea. My father was idiot."

"But your food's so good," I say.

"I hate cooking."

"What do you like doing?" Hakim asks her.

"Not cooking."

Jasper slouches over to one of the booths. Usually I take a spot at the counter next to Hakim, but some impulse of sympathy or maybe just the desire to talk about Tarantino prompts me to sit opposite Jasper instead.

"What's your favorite movie?" I ask him.

He's silent so long that I think he isn't going to answer. Then I realize he's considering the question with more deliberation than I would have expected.

At last he says, "*Predator, The Mirror, Inglourious Basterds, The Big Short*, and *The Irony of Fate*."

"Not bad," I say. "I love *The Big Short*, but I feel like nobody else has watched it."

"I watch it every year," Jasper says. "To remind me what happens when people get greedy."

"Yeah, and what do you watch *Predator* for?" I grin. "So you know what to do when aliens start hunting us?"

To my surprise, Jasper smiles just a little. "That one was my brother's favorite."

I've never heard Jasper mention his family before.

I want to ask him about his brother, but I don't want to step in anything when we're finally getting along at least a little bit.

Alla brings us a couple of burgers without waiting for us to order. She already knows what I like, and I guess she figured Jasper would want the same.

Jasper lifts his burger and takes a bite, chewing gingerly because of the plastic wrap along his jaw. He just expanded his skeleton tattoos, covering the left side of his face with a perfect approximation of the lower mandible and teeth beneath.

"Shit, that's really good," he says.

He puts his burger down a moment later, looking out the window listlessly.

He's been a wreck since the thing with Zigor.

"I have a brother too," I tell him. "Damien."

"I know. I've heard you talking to him on the phone."

"He's younger than me. He goes to Kingmakers next year."

"Isaak was older," Jasper says quietly. "I idolized him."

"What was he like?"

"Smart. Confident. Aggressive. He wasn't a dick though—even though I was five years younger. He protected me."

That sounds a lot like Adrik. Many things are becoming clear for me in this moment.

I should probably shut up now. But I can't stop myself from saying, "Adrik told me what happened to your family. I'm sorry."

"Don't give me sympathy," Jasper says, looking at his hands in his lap. "I don't deserve it."

"Everyone deserves sympathy."

Jasper gives a bitter laugh. "Adrik didn't tell you everything."

"He said…he said there was a car bomb. That your mom and dad and brother were all inside."

"Did he tell you why?"

I shake my head.

"My father worked for a don named Kazimir Anisim. Have you heard of him?"

"No."

"He was the big man in Belarus at the time. My father was his accountant."

Jasper cracks the joints of his fingers mindlessly, compulsively.

Crack, crack, crack, each pop sharp and distinct in the quiet of the booth.

"My brother was brilliant and good at everything. Not me. It was a struggle to get my parents' attention. I wasn't popular at school. My marks were shit. Over the summer holidays, I was always underfoot, driving my mom crazy. So my father would take me along with him on errands. Sometimes he took me to Anisim's house. He'd go into the boss's office, and I'd sit out on the patio, playing with Anisim's dogs. He had two cocker spaniels."

He pauses again, making a face as if he's in pain, as if his stomach hurts.

"Anisim would come out to watch me with the dogs. He said they liked me better than anyone. I knew he was important and my father's boss, so at first, I was scared of him. But he looked kindly, like a grandfather with white hair and blue eyes and round gold-framed spectacles. He wore tweed suits and smelled like peppermint. He used to give me peppermints and tell me that he could see I was clever and observant. He'd ask me things like did I notice the new painting in the hall? When I said I did and described it to him, he praised me for it."

It all sounds so benign, yet a feeling of dread creeps over me. Jasper is still looking down at his hands. I can tell he's not seeing his fingers or anything else in the restaurant around us. His eyes are glassy, his skin bleached whiter than ever.

"He started asking me other questions. What was my mother's favorite flower? What did my brother like to do for fun? I thought he was curious or testing me. Maybe he meant to send my mother flowers or take my brother to the movies. I was eight and an idiot."

"All eight-year-olds are idiots," I say softly.

Jasper hardly seems to hear me.

"My father would ask me afterward, 'What do you talk to Anisim about?' And I'd say, 'Nothing. The dogs mostly.' I didn't want my father to stop bringing me along or to stop his boss talking to me. I loved the attention. Soon the questions became more specific. Strange questions I didn't always understand—Did your father go anywhere Thursday night? Does he have another cell phone? I knew there was something off about it. Maybe I even knew I was spying on my father. But it seemed harmless."

My stomach is churning, though no more than Jasper's I'm sure. I want the story to stop while I'm compelled to hear every word of it.

"Anisim was right about one thing: I was observant. I reported many things to him. Things my father wouldn't even know that I'd know. That my father was drinking too much, that he was sneaking out of the house at night when my mother was asleep."

Jasper sighs.

"What I didn't know was what had happened six months earlier. My father was driving home one night in the rain. He hit a woman crossing the street. She was a nurse, walking to the bus stop from the hospital. My father knew he'd be charged, so he fled the scene. He didn't know the *militsiya* had him under surveillance. They saw the whole thing. They'd been looking for an in with Anisim. The hit-and-run was a gift from heaven. They cornered my father. Threatened him. Swore that Anisim would never find out where they'd gotten the information. And maybe he wouldn't have."

Jasper's face contorts. His fingers clench into fists and then lie still on his lap.

"But he did suspect a mole. I gave him all the information he needed to confirm it was my father. His lieutenant put the bomb in the car. It was Sunday morning. We were all driving to brunch. I was in the back seat with my brother. My mother turned her head and said, 'It's a long drive. Did you use the bathroom?' I ran back into the house. We had a big house with a detached garage. My father started the engine so he could drive the car close to the door and pick me up out front. I stepped outside right at that moment. I heard the key turn and saw the car explode in front of me. The blast blew me backward into the house."

My hand is over my mouth. I can't speak.

"It knocked me out for a minute. When I came to, I stumbled outside. The car was a ball of fire and smoke. The windows had shattered. I could see all three of them, black and melted, their faces on fire. My mother and father in the front. Isaak in the back seat."

"That's awful, Jasper. God, I'm sorry."

I'm feeling deeply guilty for every moment I resented him, for every stupid remark I've thrown his way.

Jasper looks at me, eyes narrowed.

"Don't pity me. *It was my fault.*"

He passes one skeletal hand over his face as if to wipe away his own emotion.

In that moment, I finally understand his tattoos. They're penance for what he did—the mark of death all over his body. The reminder of his family, burned to the bone. Perhaps a desire to join them.

And the tattoo on his face—that's penance for Zigor. For endangering his new family once more.

I want to say something to Jasper. What, I'm not sure.

Misha comes bursting through the door, throwing her backpack down next to Jasper and plopping beside me in the booth.

"You're early today!" she chirps.

Jasper is making a face like he's never seen a human child before.

"Who is this?"

"Misha," I say. "She's the manager."

"More like the janitor," Misha mutters, casting a mutinous glance at her sister.

"Did you finish *Ender's Game?*" I ask her.

"Yeah, last night!"

"Perfect." I pull a battered paperback from my coat pocket. "I brought you the next one."

"There's a sequel?"

"Sort of. It's the same story but from Bean's perspective. You might like this one even better."

"Cool!" Misha says, immediately opening the book and beginning to read.

"You done?" Jasper says to me, returning to his usual chilliness.

"Yeah," I say. And then to Alla, "Can I get another box?"

No sense letting Jasper's burger go to waste.

CHAPTER 32
ADRIK

WE'RE SUPPOSED TO BE GOING TO NEVE MARKOV'S WEDDING IN AN hour, but nobody is ready.

Sabrina comes in from the garage, oil embedded all the way under her fingernails and in every little crack and line of her hands, streaks of grease on her face and in her hair, which is twisted up in a knot on her head with pieces coming down all around her face.

She's wearing a pair of Chief's coveralls. When she grins at me, her teeth are the only clean thing on her filthy face.

"I did it!" she exclaims triumphantly. "I got that *fucking* bike fixed!"

The feeling I get seeing her like this is a hard, twisting jolt in my guts. I like her this way better than almost any other. I knew when I saw that first picture of Sabrina in the garage that this is her essential self—clever, industrious, loving to get her hands dirty.

"Jasper's bike?" I ask.

Jasper has taken it back to the dealer three times with no success. They tell him the rattle is sorted, and it seems to be, until he passes fifty kilometers an hour.

"It's fixed this time," Sabrina says. "I'm sure of it."

I'm sure she's right.

"I did it, Jasper!" Sabrina shouts as he comes out of the kitchen into the hallway.

Jasper looks startled, until slow understanding spreads across his face.

"You were working on my bike?"

"Yeah! Fucking fixed it! Those lazy shits didn't want to take the whole thing apart, but Chief helped me. The chain was too long. It was slapping against the bottom of the guide."

Jasper stands in place, hands in his pockets, mouth moving as if he's not quite sure what to say.

"Well…thanks."

Sabrina grins. "I knew I could get it."

"You better shower," I tell her.

"What?" She looks down at herself. "You don't want your date smelling like motor oil?"

"Actually, I love when you smell like that," I say, low enough that only she'll hear.

Sabrina gives me a wicked smile. "I know you do."

"You gonna take that wrap off your face?" Andrei says to Jasper, likewise coming out of his room.

Andrei isn't dressed either. I'm the only one who's put on a suit. The rest of these idiots are going to be standing in freezing water when they all try to shower at once.

"I guess," Jasper says. "It's been long enough."

Gingerly, he peels the plastic wrap from his jaw. We all crowd around to admire the new tattoo.

"Did you go to Gasleys?" Andrei inquires.

"Yeah."

"They're the best." Andrei nods. Then, elbowing Sabrina, he says, "When you gonna get your patch?"

"Never." Sabrina tosses her head. "My body's perfect exactly the way it is."

She doesn't have any tattoos. And it's true—her skin is so flawless, it's hard to imagine improvement. Like painting over marble, what would be the point?

"We all have a wolf," Jasper says.

Even Jasper got one inked over the humerus bone tattooed on his right arm.

I never asked any of my men to do it, but they all did, one by one, after joining me.

"You have to," Andrei says.

"No, she doesn't," I interject before Sabrina can argue.

Sabrina throws me a look that's far from grateful. She doesn't want me to fight her battles for her. Especially not in the house.

"You better hurry before we run out of hot water," I prod her.

"Yes, Dad." She rolls her eyes. "I'm going."

I know she's being sarcastic, but it sends a pulse of heat through my chest all the same. I want to take care of Sabrina much more than she wants to receive it.

Following her up the stairs, I say, "You'll be the most gorgeous woman at that wedding."

Sabrina pauses halfway up, turning toward me.

"Are you worried about going when Zakharov is still looking for you? He knows you're gonna be there."

"He's not invited, and even if he was, there's no way he'd start shit today. Nikolai Markov would skin him alive if he ruined his daughter's big day."

"When are we going to deal with him?"

"Soon," I promise.

Our biggest point of conflict is how we prioritize what needs to be done. We're in a constant state of triage, bleeding out in a thousand places. All we can do is plug the most critical holes first. The order of those actions is where Sabrina and I disagree.

Things have been tense between us.

She thinks I lied to her, luring her out here under the promise of partnership while putting myself in a position of authority over her.

She's not entirely wrong. I need to find a way to show her how much I value her intelligence and her initiative, even if I don't always agree with her.

She's integrating with the group, but she's not just another soldier.

I have to show her how much she means to me.

We haven't even had time to hook up the last few days. I'm aching for her. We need that physical contact to keep us connected. It's crucial to our relationship.

While Sabrina showers, I run through a list of potential suppliers Jasper brought me.

He's found a dozen different options, but none of them are great. None can provide all the ingredients we need, and I have to discard half the list on price, availability, or conflicting arrangements with rivals.

Sabrina emerges at last, lips painted, eyes smoky and catlike, hair piled up in cascading ringlets like Aphrodite. She's wearing a plum-colored gown, draped and silky, the material clinging to her luscious curves by a few thin straps.

I haven't seen her dolled up like this in weeks. She's ravishing. My mouth waters, blood rushing into my cock.

In an instant, I'm up from the bed, seizing her by the shoulders and tearing the dress off her.

I've ripped Sabrina's clothes plenty of times before. She loves when I'm ravenous for her. She loves when I'm rough.

This time, she shrieks with outrage, shoving me away.

"*What the fuck are you doing?*"

She's never pushed me away before. She's never stopped me from fucking her, not even in the most inappropriate or hurried moments.

I'm off balance, confused.

She lifts the dangling shoulder strap, torn from the dress.

"You ruined it!"

"I'll buy you another dress."

"I don't want another dress! I loved this one. There isn't a hundred of every beautiful thing. Not everything is interchangeable!" Her cheeks are flaming, her shoulders shaking. "I want to be seen in this dress. I don't want it ripped off me."

I can see I made a mistake, which makes me feel stupid and angry.

"You always liked when I ripped your clothes before. You want me to be aggressive. I can't read your mind. I'm just guessing."

Sabrina's lip quivers. She looks young and vulnerable in a way I've never seen before.

"You always guessed right before. When you care about something, you get it right."

That hits me harder than any slap.

Sabrina glares at me. "I want to be your partner, not a sex object."

I'm struggling to control the negative emotions swirling inside me. This is unfair, when sex has always been a keystone of our relationship. When I've always seen much more than her looks.

Fighting to keep my voice calm, I say, "I wouldn't desire you if I didn't respect you. From the day we met, I've only had eyes for you, because I respect you the *most*."

Sabrina blinks hard, several emotions battling on her face.

At last, she says, "I hope that's true."

She returns to the wardrobe to pick another dress.

I wait downstairs for her this time. She emerges twenty minutes later in a long black gown with gold chains at the bust and shoulders. To me, she looks just as stunning as before. But her expression is subdued, and she hardly meets my eye.

She rebounds a little at the wedding.

Neve Markov and Simon Severov are married at the Bykovo Estate. I assume they picked this location instead of a more conventional luxury locale like the Four Seasons because its remoteness allows the Markovs to arrange intensive security for their infamous guests.

The estate was long abandoned. Despite its recent renovation, there's still an air of neglect in the overgrown forests of the grounds and park. The dark trees with their blanket of snow give a fairy-tale feeling, lovely and menacing all at once.

The ceremony takes place in a white stone church with tall black spires and ornate bell towers.

Neve is a czarina in her fur cloak and gown, her twenty-foot train carried by several giggling flower girls.

Simon can only keep his haughty expression in place until he sees his bride proceeding up the aisle. Then he breaks into a smile that gives me an unexpected jolt of jealousy.

I look at Sabrina, upright and somber in the chair next to mine. I see the bare hand lying in her lap, and I wonder what would happen if I offered her a ring. Would she accept it? Or would she see it as a manacle on her finger? One more way that I want to control and dominate her...

She's not entirely wrong. The more attached I become to her, the less I want her in danger. Her encounter with Zigor's bodyguards makes me sick when I think of it. Had they been more on their guard, she could have caught a bullet just as easily as Jasper.

Love and business were never meant to mix.

I look at my parents, seated across the aisle from us.

My father protects my mother. He would never let her take the risks Sabrina takes.

Then there's Ivan and Sloane—partners in even their darkest and bloodiest endeavors.

I thought I wanted a relationship like theirs, but when it comes down to it, I don't know how they do it. Ivan is the boss ultimately, isn't he? When the Malina attacked their house, he threw Sloane to safety while he stayed behind.

Do they argue like Sabrina and me? Have they ever?

How can I get what I want when it changes every day?

Sometimes, I want Sabrina with me every moment. Other times, I want to lock her away in a tower where only I can visit her. Where she'll always be safe.

She would hate that worse than anything.

All I know is that I want her, more than anything else in the world.

I picture her walking down the aisle toward me, more beautiful than Neve Markov or any other bride...

I want her bound to me forever.

I seize Sabrina's hand, the left one, and squeeze it tight, murmuring in her ear, "That should be us at the altar."

She turns to look at me, her eyes strangely clouded.

"I only just turned twenty. I'm not planning to get married any time soon—if at all."

It feels like she took out her favorite knife and stabbed it in my side.

She's young, I know that. I always forget how young.

But fuck, does she really mean that? She doesn't know if she'd ever marry me?

The more I try to pull Sabrina closer, the more I push her away.

She's my little tiger—wild and ferocious.

What do tigers want?

To eat men alive.

How can I make her want what I want? How can I bring us into alignment?

I barely follow the ceremony, my head full of contradictory thoughts. What to do about Sabrina, what to do about Zakharov... how to salvage my business, how to keep us all alive...

The priest crowns the beaming couple, and they share their cup of wine.

Ilsa Markov stands next to her sister, wearing the silk sash of a witness over her pale-blue gown. Simon's brother stands on the opposite side in the same position.

Nikolai and Nadia Markov and the two Severovs offer their children crystal glasses, which they smash with all their might on the tiles of the chapel floor. Everyone cheers at the hundreds of glittering fragments, each one representing a year of happy marriage to come.

The ceremony complete, we all proceed to the reception in the grand hall.

I introduce Sabrina to everyone who hasn't met her yet. Her Russian has improved so much that I hardly have to translate for her anymore. She's been studying late into the night. She works feverishly at every task, sometimes staying at the lab for fourteen hours in a row when she's in the middle of a new formula. I never thought I'd meet someone more driven than me.

We chat with my parents. It was only a few hours' journey from St. Petersburg to Moscow, much farther for Ivan and Sloane, who only arrived this morning after an all-night flight. You'd never guess it. Sloane looks sleek and elegant in her black gown, Ivan the dark shadow always beside her. He kept the beard and longer hair he grew in that Kazakh prison cell, now carefully trimmed and groomed. It suits him.

My mother looks like Nefertiti in her gold gown, her hair cut in a blunt bob. She hangs on my arm, happy to see me after several months' absence.

"Do you feel at home yet?" she asks Sabrina.

"*Bol'shuyu chast' vremeni*," Sabrina replies. *Most of the time.*

"*Ochen' khoroshiy!*" my mother cries, delightedly clapping her hands. *Very good!* "You've been practicing!"

"A little," Sabrina says.

"A lot," I correct her.

"Did I tell you my mother was Italian?" Mom says.

"No." Sabrina looks at me, surprised. "I didn't know that."

"She was a Fratto from Sicily. My father was Armenian."

"That explains why Adrik is so dark."

My mother laughs. "His hair when he was born—I'd never seen anything like it. A full shock of jet-black hair, three inches long, sticking straight up off his head."

Sabrina smiles. "So basically the same as now."

"Yes, exactly." My mother reaches up to ruffle my hair. I sigh and let her do it. It wasn't going to lie flat anyway.

"Do you ever go back to Sicily?" Sabrina asks her.

She shakes her head, the smile fading from her face. "My mother died when I was young, my father shortly after Adrik was born. My brother too. Dom is all I have. And the boys, of course."

"I'm sorry," Sabrina says.

"Dynasties can fall in an instant, no matter how powerful they may seem."

"Your father had it coming," my dad says, angry after all this time. If my grandfather were here in this room, my father would kill him all over again for how he treated my mother.

"Sabrina's father is Italian, but her mother is Puerto Rican," I say to change the subject.

"It's good to intermarry," my father says. "Keeps the bloodline strong."

"Of course you'd say that," my mother laughs, kissing him lightly on his scarred cheek. "You're completely biased."

"Too bad Kade couldn't come," Sabrina says.

"Kingmakers is so strict." My mother scowls. "They should at least let them come home for Christmas. Or you should have." She shakes a finger at me.

"We were working."

"I've heard about your work." My father raises an eyebrow at me. "Not exactly what we discussed."

"I think you know I'm always going to exceed the mandate."

"Is that what you call what happened with Zakharov? Exceeding the mandate?"

"We're not here to talk business," my mother says, laying her hand on his arm.

"I don't need you checking up on me," I tell my father, my temper rising.

If I wanted to be under his thumb, I would have stayed in St. Petersburg.

Sabrina slips her hand into mine, standing close by me.

"Adrik is doing incredible things here," she says. "No one's ever grown a market as fast as him. Every one of his men is brilliant and loyal to the bone. He'll handle Zakharov like he handles everything else—like the man you taught him to be."

I look at Sabrina, my throat too tight to speak. She's meeting my father boldly, her tone respectful but her words impossible to mistake. She won't stand anyone criticizing me.

My father is surprised though not entirely displeased.

"Indeed," he says. "Adrik has always been a son I could be proud of."

As my parents move on to congratulate the Markovs, I pull Sabrina tight against my side.

"Remind me not to piss you off."

"If only you *would* take that lesson to heart," she says, sipping her champagne.

"And what about you?" I say. "Queen Shit Stirrer."

She smiles. "What fun would it be if I always behaved?"

"I can't even picture that."

"You'll certainly never see it."

We part shortly afterward, pulled into separate conversations. I shake hands with Simon and his new bride and give Ilsa Markov a congratulations she accepts with brittle thanks.

The Markovs are popular as well as influential. Almost every gangster of note is here to pay their respects.

I see the several of the *kachki*, including Cujo himself, who watches me impassively from the other side of the room. If he really has been hired by Zakharov to seek revenge on his behalf, it must irk him to stand so close without being able to take action.

While I'm keeping an eye on Cujo, Yuri Koslov sneaks up on me.

"Adrik," he hisses.

"Yuri."

He's tall and shaped like a rectangle, with thick dark hair combed forward in a Caesar. His heavily hooded eyes have a bluish tinge to the lids, crowded close to the bridge of his hooked nose. He wears a heavy gold watch and ring on his right hand.

"Congratulations are in order," he says.

"I'm not the one who got married."

He smiles thinly. "More the home-wrecker type."

"I wasn't aware you and Veniamin had officially tied the knot."

"We had a successful partnership for six years until you showed up."

"That's funny. Veniamin seemed only too eager to make a new arrangement. But isn't that always the way? The husband is surprised when the wife files for divorce."

"Especially when someone's fucking her on the side."

"That happens when the husband isn't getting the job done."

His mouth twists in a sneer, upper lip almost touching the bottom of his nose.

"Arrogant as ever, I see."

"Arrogance is an exaggerated sense of one's own abilities. I'm accurate."

"You might want to reevaluate your perceptions. You've under-estimated the sway I still hold. I'm not the only one displeased with your attempts to jump the ladder in Moscow. The Petrovs think they can spit in the face of the high table? We haven't forgotten the events of the last year."

"Nor have the Petrovs," I say quietly.

I haven't forgotten who conspired against us. Danyl Kuznetsov may be dead, but Foma Kushnir is still a member. And I doubt those two acted alone. At minimum, they had the tacit consent of the other *pakhany*, including Koslov.

"I thought you came to Moscow to renew the bonds of friend-ship," Koslov says. "Instead, you steal from me."

"I can't steal what you never owned. Those are Veniamin's clubs. He was free to make a new deal."

Koslov's heavy lids drop lower than ever. "A deal that should have included me. You're making enemies, Adrik. It's not too late to make a friend."

I know a shakedown when I see one.

"Friends bring something to the table. Come to me with an offer instead of a threat, and perhaps I'll consider it."

Koslov's sallow face flushes with rage. He would love to punish me for my insolence, but he knows as well as I do that I possess a resource everyone wants. That gives me power. I build my allies by the day, as well as my enemies.

If he knew how precarious my position actually is, we'd be having a very different conversation. Luckily, I'm not stupid enough to show the slightest sign of weakness.

"You speak to me as if we're equals," he seethes.

I'd like to tell him that I don't see him as my equal at all.

But my father is close by, and that reminds me to practice at least some level of diplomacy.

Softly, I say, "Time will show."

I've barely seen the back of Koslov when Avenir Veniamin saunters over.

"Is he gone?" he laughs.

"For now."

"Still salty, I suppose."

"As a pretzel."

Veniamin laughs. "You've already doubled his sales volume, and you actually pay me on time. The results speak for themselves. I'm hearing incredible things about this Opus. I want the whole lineup."

"It will sell just as well."

I don't tell him that I have literally no pills at the moment and no way to make them.

Across the room, I see Sabrina speaking with Krystiyan

Kovalenko. She's gesturing with her hands, her face animated. He's leaning in close, his thumb sliding slowly up and down the stem of his champagne flute.

Heat rises up my neck.

"Excuse me," I say to Veniamin, cutting him off in the middle of more effusions on our future prospects.

I stride across the room, pushing my way through the crowd. When I reach Sabrina, I grab her by the arm.

"Adrik!" she says. "Have you—"

"Let's go," I bark.

"Adrik." Krystiyan gives me a shit-eating grin. "It's been too long. I was just talking to your lovely partner here. It seems we can help each other."

I turn on him, practically snapping in his face.

"Help each other? Like you helped Mykah? No fucking thank you. I wouldn't take a pint of blood from you if I was dying in the street. I'd rather bleed out than have any part of you touch any part of me."

"Mykah?" Krystiyan laughs in such a convincing way that I could almost believe him—if I were a fucking idiot. "You got that all wrong. I had nothing to do with that."

"Save it. When your loyalty was tested, you showed everyone who you were."

He doesn't like that. His smile strains, pulled thin at the edges.

"Like when Ivan was taken," Krystiyan says softly. "And it showed everyone how weak the Petrovs really are."

I step in close, close enough that I could rip out his throat with my teeth.

"Yet Ivan's here today, at this wedding, because of what we were willing to do to bring him home. Someday, you'll learn the difference between a brother and a hired gun."

Grabbing Sabrina by the arm again, I march her away from that smarmy fucking snake before I do something I'll regret.

Sabrina allows me about four steps before she rips her wrist out of my grip.

"*What the fuck?*" she hisses at me.

"We're not working with Krystiyan."

"Perfect!" she snaps, throwing up her hands. "'Cause we have so many other options and so much time to get what we need. Oh no, wait—we owe six different people massive orders of drugs with no possible way of fulfilling any of them."

"Keep your voice down."

"Are you fucking kidding me right now?"

"You have no idea who he is or what he's like."

"No, why would I? You haven't shared that information with me. It's so much easier to interrupt my conversation and drag me away by the arm like a fucking child on a playground following a predator to his car."

"Stop behaving like a child, and I'll stop treating you like one."

"You're the one holding some old grudge from school!"

"It's not my grudge. Krystiyan was the Miles Griffin of our school—he was the connection for contraband. And he had a partner—Mykah Leonty. You remember him from Apothecary?"

She nods.

"They got themselves in hot water selling tainted product. A girl in our class OD'd on fentanyl. Somehow Krystiyan walked away without so much as a slap on the wrist, while Mykah lost two fingers and was expelled from school."

"You're saying Krystiyan sold him out."

"He's a backstabber. And I'll tell you something else—he's connected to the Malina. Whether he was involved in what happened to Ivan or not, he fucking knew about it. We are not *ever* working with him, under any circumstances."

"Understood, *boss*," Sabrina says, tossing back the last of her champagne.

"Don't be like that."

"How do you want me to be, Adrik? You act like I'm independent until the moment I'm not doing exactly what you want. We make choices together until I don't agree with you. Stop the charade already."

Before I can reply, she's set her empty champagne flute on the tray of a passing waiter and turned and walked away.

Perfect. I've managed to alienate the high table, turn away a potential supplier, and seriously piss off the woman I love.

Well done, Adrik. That's got to be some kind of record.

CHAPTER 33
SABRINA

I'M SO FUCKING FRUSTRATED I COULD SCREAM.

I head to the bathrooms to calm down, but several minutes of pacing the powder room only make me more agitated. The candy-colored room feels like a padded cell, if Marie Antoinette were in charge of decorating. The gilt mirrors, upholstered walls, and frilled furniture press in on me from all sides, the air heavily perfumed with the scent of overblown lilies.

I feel powerless and hamstrung—tasked with impossible feats, my legs cut out from under me every time I gain traction.

Adrik acts like he's so rational, but he makes emotional decisions like everyone else. We work with people we don't like or trust all the time. Why is Krystiyan any different? Adrik made us partner with Zigor, and look how that turned out.

As I'm silently fuming, washing my hands over and over at the sink, Sloane comes and stands at the mirror next to mine.

I look at our twin reflections: both of us dark-haired, olive-skinned, wearing black gowns with a slit up the thigh. I could be looking at myself thirty years in the future.

Sloane's eyes meet mine in the mirror.

"Trouble in paradise?" she says.

Ever the spy. She was probably watching Adrik's and my entire conversation.

Adrik respects Sloane more than almost anyone. Probably more than he respects me. If I were going to be jealous of anything, I should be jealous of that.

"I might have made a mistake coming here."

"Maybe you did," Sloane says evenly.

I turn to face her, anger rising all over again.

"You don't think I could do what you do?"

Sloane picks up a folded towel, drying her hands with easy grace.

"You haven't put in the time, and you haven't done the work. You want to be a queen, and you don't even speak the language."

"I'm learning as fast as I can," I hiss.

"This isn't a classroom. There's no room for mistakes."

"Yet you've made a few of your own," I snap back at her.

Sloane doesn't rise to the bait. Her calm is a steady vibration that fills the room, pressing against my eardrums. Her eyes hold mine, bright and clear and hypnotic.

"You think I came to Russia to kill Ivan with guns blazing, *pew pew*, I'm a fuckin' gangster? When I broke into his monastery, I knew my life was stretched out like a thread across a pair of shears. I made one tiny mistake, and the tide turned against me in an instant. If Ivan didn't happen to have a tiny kernel of humanity inside him, I would have met a horrific end. If you think any of these other men are Ivan, they're not. They will skin you alive. They don't care that you're beautiful. They don't care that you're special. You're nothing to them."

I lift my chin.

"I've never needed anyone to save me yet."

Sloane looks me up and down. It's hard not to shrink before that stare, especially when I know she's seeing every last detail: the dark circles under my eyes, the motor oil under my nails, the little red marks on my arms where I pinch myself when I'm stressed.

Sloane says, "I was a lone wolf once too. You feel strong when you think you don't need anybody, but the truth is you just don't have anybody."

I'm stripped in front of her. Exposed.

I don't have my family here. I don't even have Adrik's support.

Enemies on all sides, friends who barely tolerate me...

I *am* alone, and I don't know how to be any other way.

"Ivan treats you like an equal," I say. "You'd never put up with less."

"Actually," Sloane says, her voice gentler than I've heard it before, "I escaped from Ivan the first chance I got. Then I came back to him naked in rain boots, asking for his help. Our relationship changed when I allowed myself to be vulnerable."

This is hard for me to understand. Hard for me to even picture.

"I don't know how to do that," I say.

"Then practice," Sloane says. "While you're working on your Russian."

She leaves me in the powder room, the air dull and void without her.

I sink down onto an overstuffed chaise, thinking for a long time before returning to the party.

The tension is thick during the car ride home. Adrik drives slowly through the snow, the puffy flakes driving relentlessly toward the windshield, the wipers parting the snow like a curtain and sweeping it to both sides.

Jasper and Hakim sit in the back. Hakim rolls the window down an inch and sticks his nose out for a breath of fresh air, because he drank too much and now he's carsick.

"Can you close that?" Jasper says waspishly. "The snow's blowing all over me."

"If you want me to puke," Hakim groans.

"If you even think about puking in this car, you're walking home," Adrik warns him.

Dark trees pass by my window, branches weighed down with inches of heavy snow, some bent low enough to almost touch the ground.

"Jasper agrees with me," I say.

I'm still looking out the window, but I can feel Adrik's eyes on the side of my face.

"Jasper knows Krystiyan is a piece of shit."

"He'd still rather have the product."

Jasper is silent in the back seat. His silence is concurrence. He'd contradict me otherwise.

Adrik doesn't care if Jasper agrees or not. His anger is all pointed at me.

"You don't know the players, and you don't know the history," he snarls. "And you don't have the clout to keep someone like Krystiyan in line."

"You think he'd try to take advantage of me."

"I know he would."

"That's the real truth." I turn to glare at him. "You don't trust me to handle him."

"You seemed pretty sucked into his bullshit at the wedding."

"I can read people just like you can! I can do what needs to be done."

"In Chicago, maybe," Adrik says sourly.

He's in a black mood, probably because I disappeared the whole second half of the reception, sitting alone in the powder room, lost in my own thoughts. Now his face is darker than I've ever seen it, and he grips the steering wheel with unnecessary ferocity.

"What's that supposed to mean?"

"It means this isn't fucking Chicago."

"Enlighten me."

The windshield wipers make a repetitive swish and clunk that's agitating in the small space of the car, like the ticking of a clock.

Low and challenging, Adrik says, "You'd kill a man if you had to?"

"Yes."

"What about his wife and kids?"

I shoot him a look, trying to gauge if he's serious with this asinine line of questioning.

"This is Russia. If your enemies even suspect you won't go after the family, you might as well paint a target on your back. You exterminate everyone. That's the rule. That's table stakes. You snuff out the dynasty so they don't rise up in the next generation. The Griffins and the Gallos would not still both exist in Russia two hundred years later, because one of those families would have put the boot on the baby that became your grandmother."

I've never heard him talk like this. He's staring straight ahead, knuckles white on the wheel, face black and bitter.

"You don't have to murder people's kids to be scary. Get the fuck out of town. That's not how you do business."

"You have no idea what I'd do."

He's being an asshole because he doesn't want to admit we need Krystiyan's product and we don't have any other choice.

"You didn't exterminate the Malina," I say quietly. "That's what you're really mad about. You're salty 'cause they gave you a black eye."

"*Watch it*," Adrik growls.

I fall silent, listening to the irritating *swish, thunk, swish, thunk*. There's no need to say anything else.

I've already made my decision.

CHAPTER 34
ADRIK

As soon as we get home Sabrina goes right to bed, and in the morning when I wake, she's already gone.

It's unusual for her to wake up first. She's obviously avoiding me.

I come downstairs to the main floor, noting the still silence of the house. Andrei and Hakim are still asleep as usual, and no one else is around.

I start to make breakfast on the old stove, taking a pack of bacon and a carton of brown speckled eggs out of the fridge. Before I've even set out the skillet, I find myself walking out the front door, checking the carport where—as I suspected—the black SUV is nowhere to be seen.

Chief is stumbling into the kitchen when I return, his hair sticking up in all directions, pushing his glasses up so he can rub his eyes with the back of his knuckles.

"Where's Sabrina?" I ask.

"I dunno. I just got up."

Vlad comes up from the basement a moment later, sweaty and red-faced.

"Where's Sabrina and Jasper?"

He shrugs. "I haven't seen anybody."

I pull out my phone, launching the app that lets me track Sabrina's phone. I find her little blue dot in Izmaylovo. Instantly, I know what she's doing.

"Where are you going?" Chief says as I switch off the stove.

"I'll be back in an hour."

"Aren't you gonna make bacon?"

"Make it yourself."

I tuck my gun inside my jacket and grab my helmet, roaring off on my bike even though the roads are wet and slushy.

I head straight to Izmaylovo, to the dingy little restaurant I've deliberately never visited. Written across the plate-glass windows in faded script, I see the promise *Svizhi Pyrohy! Fresh Pierogies!*

The restaurant isn't open yet, but the door is unlocked. A goon in an overcoat lurks inside, sitting at one of the unset tables, fucking around on his phone.

"Where are they?" I demand.

Unconsciously, he glances toward the kitchen. I stride off in that direction while he shoves back his chair and almost trips over his own feet trying to chase after me.

I shove open the swinging doors. Four faces turn in my direction, each bearing a completely different expression: Sabrina's is a flash of surprise that quickly turns to annoyance, Jasper looks like a kid with his hand in the cookie jar, Krystiyan's henchman shouts something at the other goon in Ukrainian—probably *You were supposed to be watching the door, you dumb shit*—and Krystiyan himself gives me a smirk so enraging that my hand twitches to shoot him right then and there.

"Adrik. Nice of you to join us."

"Out," I say, pointing at Sabrina. "Right now."

Sabrina doesn't move an inch. She crosses her arms over her chest, coolly replying, "I'm not going anywhere."

Jasper would happily leave if he weren't literally in the midst of handing a big bag of our cash over to Krystiyan. He's frozen in place, unable to complete the deal right under my eye and likewise unable to take back what's already been set in motion.

It's Krystiyan's goon who moves first, reaching into his jacket.

He's about ten times slower than he'd need to be for that maneuver to go anywhere. Before he can pull his hand out, I've got my gun in his face, hissing, "Don't even fucking think about it."

"The deal's already done," Krystiyan says, smug and satisfied.

"Then it can be undone."

I pick up the black duffel bag at Sabrina's feet and fling it in Krystiyan's face hard enough that he stumbles backward. His hair is disarranged, his cheeks blotchy with anger.

"Keep the money," I say to Jasper.

"What the fuck do you think you're doing?" Sabrina cries, stepping between Krystiyan and me, getting right in my face. "We need that product!"

"Not from him."

"You're being insane! I—"

Before she can say another word, I stoop and seize her around the thighs, throwing her over my shoulder and bodily carrying her out of the kitchen.

She shrieks like a harpy, hitting my back with all her might, screaming, "What the fucking fuck?! Are you serious right now?! What the fuck, Adrik! Put me down or I'll—"

"Let's go," I bark at Jasper.

I don't wait to see if he follows. I'm carrying Sabrina out of the restaurant, back to the car, where I fling her in the passenger seat and close the door in her face.

Jasper is right behind me, loading the money back in the trunk.

"Bring my bike home," I order, trading him keys.

Sabrina is still screaming at top volume as I climb in the front seat.

"How fucking dare you—"

"How dare *you*?" I bellow back at her, twisting the key so hard I almost snap it off the fob. The engine roars to life, and I peel away from the restaurant, my hands shaking on the wheel. I don't know if I've ever been this angry. "You take my lieutenant and make a deal behind my back after I forbid you to do it?"

"Forbid me!" Sabrina sneers. "You're not my father, and you're not my fucking boss! This is my business as much as yours, my fucking product! I need those supplies, and you blew it up for nothing, because you're paranoid, because you want to be in control!"

I'm weaving through traffic, speeding way too fast. So angry that I could jerk the wheel and send us both careening into a semitruck just to spite her.

"How did you even know where we were?" Sabrina demands.

"I put a tracker on your phone."

She stares at me, mouth open, face pale with rage.

Then she pulls her cell phone out of her pocket, unrolls the window, and flings it out onto the road. Her phone smashes on the pavement, the pieces run over immediately by a delivery truck.

"Really fucking clever!" I shout at her.

She's breathing shallowly, chest hitching, no color in her face. Her lips are ashy and her eyes wide and unblinking, burning with cold fire.

"I can't believe you," she hisses. "You put a chip on me like a fucking dog?"

"And I'll do it again," I say coldly.

We're already almost back at the Den.

I've never seen Sabrina so angry. Part of me knows I should de-escalate, but the other part of me is feeding off her rage, building and building like a firestorm in high wind.

Maybe it's time we had this out once and for all.

CHAPTER 35
SABRINA

ADRIK PULLS INTO THE DRIVEWAY. I LEAP OUT OF THE CAR, STORM-ing toward the house.

A moment later, I hear Jasper pulling in behind us, the tires of Adrik's bike crunching over the loose gravel.

I spin around and march right back again, shouting, "Back me up, Jasper! Tell Adrik we need that product. You know I'm right!"

Jasper stops, still straddling the bike.

He gives me a look—half guilt and half apology—before saying, "What Adrik says goes."

I could fucking kill him. After I just saved his ass! After he agreed with me this morning that we should get the deal done!

"This is what you want?" I sneer at Adrik. "A lapdog who agrees with everything you say? Even when he *knows* it's the wrong choice! But no one will call you out because they also know you're a stubborn fucking *dictator* who won't listen to anyone but himself!"

"I should string you up by the ankles for what you did," Adrik snarls, his voice low and vicious.

"You *humiliated* me!" I scream back at him. "I made a deal, I gave my word, and you carried me out like a toddler! You think Kovalenko's gonna keep that to himself? He'll tell the whole fucking city! No one will respect me, because my own partner doesn't!"

The memory of Adrik throwing me over his shoulder makes my

whole body burn with a heat that's painful, that feels like it'll swallow me whole. I wish it fucking would. I've never been so embarrassed or so hurt.

I see the tiniest flicker of shame on Adrik's face—acknowledgment that what he did was wrong. But he won't fucking say it. He won't admit it or apologize.

I'm so tired of the lies. Tired of the bullshit.

I want the truth, once and for all.

Pointing my figure at Adrik, I say, "Are you going to treat me as an equal or not?"

Adrik looks at me, his jaw flexing.

"I'm always going to do what I think is right. For all of us."

"So that's a no?"

"I'm not going to go against what I know is best for me and my men."

"Then you should have told me that in Dubrovnik!" I scream at him. "I was honest with you from the beginning! I told you exactly who I was and what I wanted! And you deceived me! You let me think things were going to be one way when I came out here, and they're not. They never have been!"

Adrik pauses. His jaw works, his narrow blue eyes little more than slits against the cold winter sun. In a quieter voice, he says, "I had to have you. Can you blame me?"

I wanted him to admit it, but now that he has, it only makes me angrier.

"I knew it! You fucking lied to me! You *never* planned to make me your partner! You just said what you had to say to get me out here!"

"You wouldn't come any other way. And it's good. We're doing great together!"

Adrik spreads his arms as if to indicate all we've achieved. It's meaningless to me when I own none of it, when it all belongs to him.

"It's good for *you*! You don't care what I want! You don't care what I feel! You think you're smarter than me, stronger than me? You're fucking *not*! If we went head-to-head, you'd learn a thing or two about what I can do."

Adrik tosses his head contemptuously. "You wouldn't last one day out there without me."

"Fucking try me!"

"You'll be crawling back here."

I think I loathe him in this moment. I look at his handsome face, and all I see is a liar and manipulator who played on my emotions, who found my weaknesses and exploited every one.

"I wouldn't come back to you if you crawled over broken glass to beg me. I'm promising you that, Adrik…and unlike you, I never break my word."

"Calm down," he says. "You're being ridiculous."

I am a human torch of burning rage. Every word Adrik speaks is pure gasoline poured on the flames.

"I'm not gonna fucking calm down! It's fucking *over* between us! Do you understand me? Over! We're not lovers. We're not even friends!"

"Think about what you're saying—"

"I'm saying exactly what I feel—not like you, you fucking liar! I *always* tell the truth. And I'm telling you we're done."

Adrik makes a scoffing sound. He really doesn't think I'm serious.

He stands there, arms crossed over his broad chest, while I march into the house. He's still standing there a minute later when I stomp back out with my backpack slung over my shoulder.

It's not until I jump on my bike that he looks mildly concerned.

"Now don't go roaring off in a tizzy—"

He thinks I'm blowing off steam. He expects me to at most drive around an hour and then come back again.

Well, he's going to be waiting a long fucking time.

"Sabrina—" Adrik calls while I rev the engine. "Wait—"

I'm already peeling out of the carport, spraying Jasper with gravel as I pass.

Adrik tries to chase after me, but Jasper's still straddling his bike. By the time I hear the Ducati's engine sparking to life, I'm flying away down the road.

CHAPTER 36
ADRIK

"Get the fuck off the bike!" I shout at Jasper, like this is his fault.

Jasper scrambles to pass it to me.

Too late, much too late. By the time I reach the end of the driveway, Sabrina is gone.

I try to call her twice before I remember that she pitched her cell phone into traffic.

"Fuck!" I bellow, fighting the urge to chuck my own phone across the road.

How the fuck did that get so out of hand?

It already feels like a nightmare, surreal and exaggerated, nothing that actually could have happened.

Fuck fuck fuck fuck fuck!

I can't believe I let my temper spiral like that. It's fucking Sabrina. She amplifies every emotion. When we're good, I'm on top of the world, happier than I've ever been. But when she turns that aggression on me, she unleashes the animal, and I become this fucking monster, completely out of control.

I roar back up the driveway to the house. Jasper is still standing in the yard, looking guilty as hell.

"Did you find her?"

"Does it look like I found her?"

Jasper flinches, a little kid getting screamed at by his abusive stepdad. That's me. I'm the piece-of-shit stepdad.

"I'm sorry," I say. "It's not your fault."

"Yeah, it is. I went behind your back."

My teeth grind together so hard they make a creaking sound.

"Well, we were in a shitty fucking position, weren't we? And now it's worse."

I stalk into the house, Jasper at my heels, stumbling under the weight of the bag of cash he and Sabrina planned to exchange for raw materials.

Chief, Vlad, Hakim, and Andrei are all lurking in the living room, pretending like they weren't watching out the windows as Sabrina and I screamed at each other in the yard.

"What are we gonna do?" Hakim asks.

"We're going to find her. Check the airport, the train station, the bus depot, every place she might go. Call Ilsa Markov. Go to her house. She and Sabrina are friends. That's who she'd call here in Moscow."

If she had a phone, that is…

"On it," Jasper says, heading for the door at once.

"Wait," I say. "Stay in pairs. Zakharov's still in Moscow, and he's still got Cujo on the payroll last I heard."

A sick chill runs through my guts, like I just drank a gallon of ice water. I hope to god Sabrina is smart enough to stay the fuck away from those two.

We split up, Vlad with Jasper, Andrei with Hakim, and Chief staying at the house in case Sabrina returns.

"Call me the second you see her," I say to Chief. "That goes for all of you."

I'm expecting to find her within a couple of hours.

But by nightfall, there's no sign of her at all.

I'm coming unglued, shouting at everyone.

"How are we supposed to find one girl out of twelve million people?" Andrei complains.

"She's a gorgeous American. How hard can it be? Fucking find her!" I yell.

We don't find her.

My phone remains dark and silent—no messages and no missed calls.

CHAPTER 37
SABRINA

I FEEL LIKE SUCH A FOOL. EVERYONE TOLD ME NOT TO COME TO Moscow. My family *begged* me not to come. The idea of returning to Chicago, disgraced, a failure, is more than I can bear.

What the fuck am I going to do now?

I doubt Kingmakers will let me back in, even if I wait until next year.

And honestly, I wouldn't want to go back anyway.

I've had a taste of freedom, adulthood, empire building. Most of the time, I really fucking loved it.

Our business was accelerating by the day. That's what really pisses me off—Adrik and I built something incredible. Now I guess it's *his* business. He gets to keep it all while I walk away with nothing.

All I've got in my pocket is a couple thousand in cash. I don't have my phone because I threw it out the window. I wouldn't have done that if I'd known I was going to leave twenty minutes later.

Knowing that Adrik had been tracking me, spying on me, made me feel slimy and exposed. I wouldn't have minded sharing my location if he'd asked me first or if it was mutual—the ability to find each other makes sense from a safety perspective. But as usual, he did whatever the fuck he wanted with no consideration for what I think.

My mind twists around and around in a cyclone of negative

emotion. I'm alternately furious, regretful, resentful, and afraid. I have no idea what to do. I hate all my options.

I'm not going back to Adrik, I'd rather curl up and die than eat that kind of crow.

And I'm not going back to Chicago either. That would be admitting defeat.

There has to be another option.

I park my bike at Brateyevskiy Park and walk around the frozen pond for almost two hours, until my toes are ice inside my boots and I can't even see my breath floating on the air in front of me because I'm too fucking cold.

I skipped breakfast this morning so I could meet Krystiyan Kovalenko before Adrik woke up—not that it did me any good. I should have set the meeting for four in the morning. Then I'd have made the deal before the sun came up, and none of this would have happened.

Maybe it wouldn't have mattered.

This was all going to blow up in my face sooner or later. Adrik never intended to share power with me. Our conflict was inevitable.

I'm starting to get hungry, even though my guts are twisted up tighter than a slinky. I've got to get some food.

I find a little restaurant in Maryino, quiet and almost empty. I order a plate of *kotlety*, but when the food comes, I can hardly eat it. I'm miserable, sick to my stomach, my hands shaking with anxiety. I feel like a rag doll, beat up and coming apart at the seams.

I took almost nothing from Adrik's house—none of the new clothes I bought, no toiletries. All I've got is one extra outfit, some cash, my favorite gun, and a few packets of pills I was using for testing purposes.

I ask the waiter to bring me a drink. Even though it's barely past lunchtime, he drops off a double vodka and soda without so much as a raised eyebrow. God bless the Russians and their acceptance of day drinking.

I down the liquor too fast, forgetting how empty my stomach is. It hits me hard, the warmth in my chest pleasant and soothing, the dizziness in my head less enjoyable.

Most importantly, it anesthetizes me a little. This aching, wrenching pain inside me is unbearable. Pressure like I'm being slowly crushed under a pile of stones, like they used to do to witches. Every time I think of the look on Adrik's face, disdainful and dismissive…every time I think how shameful it felt to be thrown over his shoulder like a fucking sack of potatoes, my ass in the air, all my pretensions laid bare…

I could fucking kill him for that.

Yet I miss him. I miss him already. I miss how I felt with him—elated, euphoric, invincible. The whole world illuminated with beauty and infinite possibility.

But it was a lie, all a fucking lie.

And that makes me angrier than anything. I hate that he tricked me. I hate that he created this attachment between us. He sewed us together down every limb, and now that I'm trying to pull away from it, it's ripping me apart. It feels like I won't survive it.

I order another drink and then another. The waiter brings them, not caring how drunk I get in the corner of his restaurant, so long as I'm quiet and I pay my bill afterward. When he's not serving me, he sits at the bar, slowly working his way through a crossword puzzle.

The more intoxicated I get, the more I come to a conclusion that may or may not be batshit insane: I'm not fucking leaving.

I came to Moscow to make my mark. I'll be goddamned if I'll walk away after all the work I put in.

I don't know how I'm going to do it, but I created Molniya, and I'm going to keep selling it.

Adrik said he always wants me on his team?

He's going to see what it looks like when I'm not.

Five hours later, I give the waiter a tip much larger than I can actually afford, and I stumble out of the restaurant.

Way too blitzed to ride a bike, I leave my motorcycle in the alley and hail a cab instead.

I need a new ally.

There's only one place to find them.

The cab pulls up in front of Apothecary, the driver squinting at the faded wooden sign.

"Vy uvereny, chto eto pravil'noye mesto?" You sure this is the right place?

"Nope," I grunt, stumbling out of the back seat.

I try to pull myself together enough that I won't look like a blazing hot mess, checking my reflection in the dark-tinted windows covered over with iron bars. The effect is disturbing—like I'm looking at myself inside a Russian prison cell. Eyes hollow, hair deranged.

"Fuck's sake," I mutter. "Didn't I use to be hot?"

I try not to sway like I'm on sea legs, heading down into the dim, smoky club.

Mykah is behind the bar as usual, mixing up cocktails for the girls clustered along the bar, showing off their legs on the high stools. I wave to Polina. She gives me a wink in return, sipping her mai tai.

"Adrik pridet?" Mykah calls to me. *Is Adrik coming?*

"He's meeting me here in an hour," I lie.

Mykah has Adrik on speed dial. He would 100 percent rat me out if he thought Adrik was looking for me.

Though for all I know, Adrik is happy as a clam at home. He and Jasper and Vlad could be toasting at the kitchen table, glad to be rid of me. Thinking how they're going to spend their money now that they only have to split it six ways. Ungrateful motherfuckers.

I slide onto the stool next to Polina. Tonight, she's wearing a silvery dress with a fringe around the hem, which makes her look like a flapper. Her black bob is a shining cap, her lips painted hot pink to match her shoes.

"*Kaz biznes?*" I ask her. *How's business?*

"Slow."

"Well, lemme buy you a drink at least."

"Somebody bought you too many drinks," she laughs.

"That somebody was me. I'm tryna take advantage of myself," I slur.

Mykah brings me a Moscow mule before I even have to ask.

"You really do make the best mules here," I tell him. "The name is deserved. One more for Polina too."

I toss a crumpled bill down on the bar.

"You keep that in your underwear?" Mykah snorts, trying to smooth out the bill.

"I don't wear underwear. Would you keep your gun in a ziplock? No. You gotta keep the important things accessible."

"If you sit at the bar, the men will think you're selling something," Polina warns me.

"Maybe I am…primo drug chef for hire. Going to the highest bidder."

I lean back against the bar, scanning the room through the thick haze of smoke. Ismaal Elbrus is puffing up a storm, surrounded by his usual bevy of beauties. A few of the *kachki* are here, though luckily not the one they call Cujo. If he's looking for Adrik, I sure as fuck don't want him to catch sight of me. I don't know if Zakharov knows I was present when his son was shot or even if he'd recognize me. I'd rather not find out by getting chucked in the trunk of a Soviet bodybuilder.

The club is relatively quiet, since it's only a weeknight. The most commotion comes from a table in the back where a motley assortment of gangsters are playing Texas Hold'em.

My ears perk up when I hear a familiar voice barking, "*Ya skazal tebe, Klim. Nikakikh grebanykh zastol'nykh razgovorov!*" *I told you, Klim. No fucking table talk!*

Craning my neck, I see the dark hair, broad shoulders, and unmistakable outrage of my favorite ex-girlfriend.

Her antagonist, the chatty Klim, is a scrawny Slav with earrings in both ears and an unlit cigarette hanging from the corner of his mouth. He throws an amused look to his compatriot across the table, remarking, "I'm allowed to make conversation."

"Not about your cards," Ilsa snaps.

"Take it easy."

"I'll take it easy when you pay me what you owe me from last week."

"Last week! You got a miracle ace on the river. That was a bad beat, and you know it."

"It's not a miracle. It's probability, you dumb shit. And you're still gonna pay me."

Ilsa's face is flushed, her voice low and guttural. If I'm not mistaken, for once in her life, she's drunker than I am.

Because they're speaking in Russian all the way across the room, I lose the thread of the argument whenever they lower their voices. From what I observe, the two Slavs are trying to take advantage of Ilsa's inebriated state to win back some of the money she's taken from them. They're communicating across the table in hints and signs while Ilsa grows more and more indignant.

Fair play is everything to her. If you really want to piss her off, the quickest way to do it is to cheat.

I don't know which straw breaks the camel's back, but Ilsa leaps to her feet, upending the table, sending cards and chips and cash scattering everywhere. The Slavs howl in outrage, along with the other four players at the table. There's a mad scramble for the muddled money, the players snatching up everything they can reach and stuffing it in their pockets. Klim is shouting in Ilsa's face. Steel flashes as his buddy pulls a knife.

I'm running over. Mykah is faster, putting one hand on the bar and vaulting over it before I've taken two steps.

"I told you, Ilsa, if you flip one more fucking table—"

"I've got her!" I interject, grabbing Ilsa by the arm. "I'm taking her home."

"What about my money?" Ilsa cries.

"Leave it," I hiss in her ear. "They want to shank you."

"Fuckin' try it!" Ilsa hollers, leaning over my arm to swing at Klim. "You skinny little bitch baby bastard—"

"Alright, he got the message," I say, hauling her away while Mykah blocks the Slavs from stabbing us in the back on our way out the door.

Ilsa is both taller and heavier than me, and neither one of us is sober. Trying to help her up the stairs is like a piece of spaghetti trying to lift a meatball. We're not meant for this.

I'm hurrying her along while doing my level best not to puke. All this exertion makes my head spin. The street tilts back and forth like a teeter-totter.

I wave down the nearest cab. It pulls up to the curb, covered in so many scrapes and dents that I'm wondering how our driver still has his license. Not the best advertisement for his services. Worried the Slavs might come up the stairs looking for us, I shove Ilsa in the back seat and fall in after her.

We're a tangle of arms and legs, looking for seat belts that apparently don't exist.

"What's your address?" I ask Ilsa.

She mumbles it to the driver. Hopefully he understands her better than I do, because he starts driving.

Giving up on the seat belts, Ilsa and I slump together in the back seat, her against the window, me with my head on her shoulder.

I'm taking slow, deep breaths, pretending it smells nice in here and not like old cigarette butts and take-out shawarma.

"They're always fuckin' tryna cheat me..." Ilsa mutters. "He owes me ten K already."

"Why do you keep playing with him?"

"Who else am I gonna play with?"

"Not me. I've already lost enough money to you in cards."

"That's 'cause you get bored and stop paying attention."

"I might have ADD."

"You've got something." She looks at me as if really seeing me for the first time. "What are you doing here anyway?"

"In Moscow?"

She snorts. "At Apothecary."

I take another breath and let it out slowly, wondering how much to tell her.

"I split up with Adrik," I say at last.

It doesn't feel good to say it. Actually, it feels fucking awful. Real in a way it wasn't before.

"I kinda figured that would happen."

I lift my head to glare at her. "Could you try not being honest for once in your fucking life?"

Ilsa shrugs. "You're a terrible girlfriend, and you're both volatile as hell."

I guess that was obvious to everyone but me.

A dark wave washes over me, so heavy and cold that I sink all the way down in the battered back seat. I close my eyes, wishing I could just drown.

"Hey," Ilsa says, resting her hand on my thigh. "I shouldn't have said that. I drank too much."

"It's okay." I'm blinking hard. "I just…really liked him. I thought it was going to be different this time."

Liking Adrik doesn't even begin to cover how I felt about him. But I can't explain that to Ilsa, because I can't even stand to think about it. And what good does it do now? It's over.

It was never going to work. To believe that I could have what my parents have…I was delusional. I'm not my father, and I'm sure as fuck not my mother.

I'm just a person who destroys what they love.

I was always going to end up alone.

After a minute, Ilsa says, "I guess I split with my sister too."

"What do you mean?"

"It's fuckin' Simon. Ever since she met him, she's a different person. It's all *Simon says this* and *Simon thinks this*...like he's the fuckin' boss instead of her. Letting him speak for her, letting him handle our business. She was the genius. She was the one with ambition. Now she thinks the sun shines out of his ass."

"He's pushing you out?"

"He acts like he's not, but he wedges between Neve and me. Always whispering in her ear. We agree on one thing, then she comes back the next day after talking to him. *Simon thinks maybe we should...*" Ilsa imitates her sister savagely, giving Neve a soft and prissy voice quite unlike her real tone. "The Severovs are fucking *nothing*. They can't wait to get their hands on what my father built."

"You think he doesn't care about her?"

"Sure he *cares* about her." Ilsa rolls her eyes. "Neve's gorgeous. He knows he's got a catch. And she's dick drunk—all giggly and twitterpated. I swear to god, he's brainwashing her."

"With sex?" I laugh.

"Yes!" Ilsa cries. "And she's falling for it! I can't believe I used to respect her. She was my Xena. Now I find out she's just another Ariel."

The disgust in her voice makes me snicker. Also the fact that Ilsa has apparently watched both *Xena: Warrior Princess* and *The Little Mermaid*.

Her antipathy to all things love and romance is maybe the only thing that could cheer me up in this moment.

"So...what are you going to do?"

"I'm not fucking working for him, I can tell you that," Ilsa says darkly. "I was supposed to be Neve's lieutenant. Simon doesn't want me, and I wouldn't do it for him anyway."

"You living with her still?"

"I've got my own place, thank god. It's up there." She points, mostly for the cabbie's benefit. He's struggling to see the numbers on the dimly lit street.

"Thanks for the ride," I tell him, doling out a little more of my limited cash.

Ilsa steps out of the car, forgetting that she's drunk, almost eating shit on the curb.

"Who put that there?" she mumbles.

"Stalin."

She laughs her loud, barking laugh. "I did miss you."

"Yeah?" I say, feeling the first touch of warmth in my chest not attributable to too many shots of liquor. "I missed you too."

We climb the metal stairs to her fourth-floor apartment. She's not exactly living large in this old cinder-block building. When she unlocks the door, I'm hit with the familiar scent of her favorite soap and the faintest hint of gunpowder.

Her apartment is clean and perfectly organized. The walls are bare brick, the floor tile with only a couple of rugs under the couch and table. She doesn't have a TV. A gray cat sits in the windowsill, next to several flourishing plants. Her view is the equally depressing building across the street.

"Jeez, times are tough," I tease her.

"You know I don't give a shit about decorating."

"Do you like heat and light? 'Cause I'm not sure you have those either."

Ilsa flicks the switch. A lamp illuminates, casting a golden glow over half the room.

"Happy?" she says.

"I will be once you pour me a drink."

"I think you've had enough."

That's what she says, but she's already heading into the kitchen, taking the vodka out of the freezer.

My favorite thing about Ilsa is how easy it is to tempt her. She's the most disciplined person I know...until I convince her to be otherwise.

She brings back the bottle, no glasses.

I take a swig, the liquor colder than ice, burning all the way down my throat like it will freeze me from the inside out. I swallow more, hoping it will numb everything I don't want to feel.

"Gimme that." Ilsa takes the bottle partly to stop me drinking more and partly so she can drink a few swallows.

We're sitting on her couch, each of us sprawling back against an opposite arm, our legs meeting in the middle. I've kicked off my shoes, and the arch of my foot rests against the curve of her calf.

"I can't believe you left school," Ilsa says.

"Don't rub it in."

"You regret it?"

"I don't believe in regret."

"Still the same old Sabrina, then."

I sit forward to grab the bottle, inverting it and letting the vodka run down my throat in three long swallows, wiping my mouth on the back of my arm. "I wouldn't say that."

"Oh? What's different?"

"Well." I take another pull. "I speak Russian now. So it's gonna be a lot harder for you to talk shit without me noticing."

Ilsa smiles without showing any teeth, just a sideways quirk of her mouth. Ilsa is what in the olden days would have been called a "handsome woman." She's all bold lines, dramatic eyebrows, the bone structure of a queen. When she's angry, she's fucking terrifying. When she smiles at you, you feel like she's bestowing a favor. It's hard to make her laugh, really laugh. When she does, it's loud and satisfying.

"Anything I have to say, I'd say to your face."

"I know."

There's a long pause. I lean my head back against the armrest of the couch, listening to the rush of cars on the street below the window. The vodka is doing its work. I'm not happy. Actually, I'm still fucking miserable. But that misery seems separate and contained, like a dark cloud in the center of the room. I can skirt around its edges instead of standing right in the middle of it.

My body hardly seems to belong to me. I look at my hands on my lap, and they're someone else's hands. What they've done, what they will do, has nothing to do with me.

I don't have to care about everything so much. I don't have to feel. Nobody else seems to. I can be numb and cold and cruel like the rest of the world.

"Were you happy to see me here?" I say to Ilsa, still looking up at the ceiling.

She's silent for a moment. Then she admits, "Yeah. I did miss you. More than I thought I would."

"What did you miss?"

She lets out a soft, amused sound. "You want me to compliment you?"

"I need it."

She lifts my foot and holds it in her lap, squeezing it with pleasant pressure.

"I missed how I can always tell what you're thinking. What you're feeling. You're easy to know—easy to understand."

"You mean I'm simple and obvious?" I laugh.

She presses the heel of her hand against the arch of my foot, twisting like a mortar and pestle, sending a wave of relaxation all the way up my leg.

"You're genuine."

"No need for the lasso of truth."

She rubs the ball of my foot with both thumbs, smiling that crooked smile.

"You always made me feel like Wonder Woman. Like I could do anything."

"I'm glad I wasn't always an asshole."

"Not always."

Ilsa hooks a finger in the elastic of my sock, slowly peeling it down the length of my foot, baring the delicate skin beneath. My foot looks vulnerable and naked in the low light, toenails unpolished and pearlescent.

"Something else I always liked…" Ilsa says, her voice low and throaty. "How responsive you are."

She brushes her fingertips lightly up the sole of my foot, from heel to toes. The wave of sensation sends a shiver up my spine.

"Well…you always knew how to touch me."

Her hands wrap around my bare foot, close and intimate. The rest of my body is heavy and relaxed, soaked in warmth. She's kneading and massaging, taking control of all of me through the pressure on this most sensitive part.

She looks at me with those blue eyes, not bright and narrow and electric like Adrik's but large and soft and dark, like the ocean at night. Slowly, she lifts my foot to her mouth, running her tongue lightly across the underside of my toes, her tongue soft and wet and velvety.

"Yeah. I know what you like."

She peels off my other sock, then tugs off my jeans, tossing them aside.

The thong I'm wearing is a soft peachy pink, the thin material clearly showing the outline of my pussy lips, the cleft between, and the wetness soaking through the material.

Ilsa touches the wet spot with her thumb.

"Yeah…same old Sabrina…"

I groan, shifting my hips slightly, pressing against the ball of her thumb.

Ilsa pulls my underwear to the side, looking at my pussy, the tip of her tongue slipping out to moisten her lower lip.

"You still have the prettiest pussy I've ever seen."

She rubs her thumb lightly between my lips, spreading the wetness all the way up to my clit, rubbing slow circles around the nub.

Her hands are soft. They give me a floating, melting feeling. They remind me how soft I am too…how relaxed I can be…

My thighs part. My pussy opens like a flower.

Ilsa brings her fingers to her lips, tasting me, licking my wetness off the ball of her thumb. Her lower lip glistens, full and red and ripe and delicious.

She slips her middle finger in her mouth, wetting it. Then she slides it inside me, just once, pushing it in and pulling it out with exquisite slowness.

I let out a long moan.

"You like that?" she murmurs.

"Yes."

"Ask me to do it again."

"Please…I need it…"

She pulls my thong down my legs, her fingertips tracing a long line from my hips to my ankles.

"Close your eyes," she says.

I tilt my head back on the armrest of the couch, eyes closed, lips parted, taking slow, deep breaths.

I feel the cushions sink as Ilsa leans over me, her long, dark hair a curtain around my face. Softly, ever so softly, she strokes her fingertips on my pussy in a motion almost like tickling but so much lighter.

"Relax," she whispers.

My thighs are wide open, everything exposed. I'm not clenching, not squeezing. I don't have to protect myself. I submit to the delicate sensation of her silky fingertips sliding over me, over and over, in soft, cascading raindrops. It's warm and sensuous, never invasive, never too much. I can give in to it completely. I can let it carry me away…

"Your cheeks are flushed," she murmurs.

Her warm breath is inches from my mouth. I feel it on my open lips. Even though my eyes are closed, I know Ilsa is watching my face, watching each gasp and flutter of my lashes. She loves watching me come.

The orgasm spreads over me like warm liquid poured across my body. It diffuses down my limbs as I let out one long, wavering sigh.

Ilsa strokes my pussy like her own little pet.

She presses her lips against mine, once.

"Good girl."

I look up into her face.

"You haven't lost your touch."

"I should hope not."

She stands up from the couch, pulling her shirt over her head, stepping out of her pants, revealing that powerful body I've always envied. Her breasts are small and high like they wouldn't dare get in her way, shoulders like a swimmer, a tattoo of an olive branch on her ribs. Thighs that could crush you, that have crushed me, many times.

She comes around the arm of the couch, leaning over me, pulling my shirt off as well. I wasn't wearing a bra. My nipples are already hard, standing up on my chest.

Ilsa bends over, taking my breast in her mouth. Her mouth is warm, her tongue flicking against my nipple, sending sparks of heat through my chest.

Her breasts are right above my face. I tilt up my chin, licking her nipple with the flat of my tongue, massaging her other breast with my hand. I suck on her tits with deep, slow pulls, trying to get as much in my mouth as I can.

Her flesh is petal-like against my cheek. I nuzzle against her chest, inhaling her perfume. Thinking how remarkable it is that Ilsa has skin this soft hidden under her clothes.

Ilsa moans against my breast, switching to the other side, sucking just as hard.

I arch my back, grabbing her under the ribs. I pull her down on top of me, her weight heavy and satisfying. I nose her underwear to the side, my hands on the backs of her thighs, pulling her legs apart.

I latch my mouth onto her pussy, licking her clit with long strokes, sucking on it gently, tasting her, breathing her in. Oral on a woman is so much more intimate than on a man, so much more like kissing.

Ilsa's head is between my thighs, licking and lapping in just the same way. We fit together so well, every part of us soft and smooth and meant for sliding. There's no stubble on her face, no roughness. I can grind against her while she grinds against me, her scent in my mouth as rich and feminine as my own.

Touching her is like touching myself. I know what feels good. I lick her clit and stroke it with my fingertips. What she does to me, I do to her—when she increases her speed and pressure, I follow suit. We're grinding together in tandem, building our orgasms at the same time.

I grip her ass in both hands, licking and licking at her clit. I use the flat of my tongue, giving her more and more pressure, while I'm spreading my thighs, riding her tongue.

She pushes two fingers inside me. The way she touches me is delicate, exploratory—feeling with her fingertips, dipping them in and out.

I do the same to her, feeling the intense heat, the rhythmic squeezing, the intimacy of being inside someone.

She's panting now, *huh, huh, huh,* and I know she's about to come.

Her pussy clamps around my fingers, tighter than you'd ever believe. Her thighs shake on either side of my head. I'm caught in a vice, the tremors running down my body. It makes me come too, clenching and vibrating, crying out with her pussy pressed against my tongue.

I roll away from Ilsa, falling off the couch, feeling like toothpaste squeezed out of a tube. My ears are ringing, my whole body flushed and pulsing still.

I open my mouth to say something.

My stomach contracts. Without warning, without any ability to stop it, I vomit all over Ilsa's rug.

"Are you fucking kidding me?" she says.

I fall forward into the puke, slamming my head on the floor.

When I wake up, I'm in Ilsa's bed. Sunshine pours in through the window, cruel and garish. Someone honks their horn on the street below, and it stabs into my ear like a deliberate assault.

I sit up, then immediately regret it. My head feels swollen and wobbly on my shoulders, aching with every beat of my heart. I trace the worst throbbing to the lump on my forehead. Just grazing it with my fingertips sends another bolt of pain through my head, worse than the car horn.

It takes me a minute to actually get out of the bed. Black mist sweeps over my vision, and I have to cling to the footboard of the bed, hunched over, until it passes.

When I stumble out to the living room, I must look like walking shit, because Ilsa's head snaps up and she barks, "If you puke on my floor again, I will fucking kill you."

I'd tell her *I'm not gonna puke*, but I really don't trust myself to open my mouth. Instead, I hobble over to the kitchen table and sit down across from Ilsa, pulling the hem of her oversize T-shirt down over my knees. She dressed me in her Pussy Riot shirt, so I know she can't be completely pissed at me.

"Could you please yell at me *after* I have some aspirin," I croak.

Ilsa takes a slow bite of her toast, frowning at me while she chews.

She pushes away from the table and disappears into the kitchen, rummaging in the cupboards deliberately loudly. She takes an ice tray out of the freezer and bangs it against the counter like she's setting off depth charges.

"*I'm sorrrrrryyyyy*," I moan, hands over my eyes.

Ilsa gives the ice one last decisive bang, then quiets down, bringing me a glass of tomato juice and a bottle of seltzer with four aspirin on a plate.

"Thank you," I say humbly, scooping up the pills and swallowing them down with a fizzy rush of seltzer.

I take about five seconds to breathe, imagining the seltzer diffusing into my dehydrated veins. Then I push the tomato juice an inch toward Ilsa, saying hopefully, "Little hair of the dog?"

"You are so…"

"Irresistible?"

"Intolerable."

"I've heard that."

Ilsa splashes a shot of vodka into my tomato juice, probably because she knows I'll die otherwise.

She watches while I gulp it down, yanking the bottle away when I reach for more.

"You're worse than I thought."

"I'm fine. I'm gonna be completely fine."

"You're a fuckin' mess."

I cast a quick glance across the table at the vodka bottle, wondering if I have any chance in a fight against Ilsa at this moment. Maybe if I really surprise her and get her in a headlock and choke her out…

"You're on the rebound. I'm not gonna be your backboard," Ilsa says.

My eyes snap from the bottle to her face, heat flushing across my collarbones.

"I'm *never* going back to Adrik," I tell her. "I'll cut his heart out of his chest before I give him mine again."

Ilsa gives an irritated snort.

"He still has it. Fucking look at you. I've never seen you like this."

I bet I look like a literal lunatic. My hair has never been my friend in moments like this. It's the worst tattletale of my mental state, probably frizzy and matted and feral. If I were dumb enough to look in a mirror, I'd see the bloodshot stare of a coked-up cult leader.

But none of that matters right now.

I need to persuade Ilsa to do me a really big favor. So I need to sound sane and convincing.

"Ilsa…do you have a lot of guns and a flamethrower?"

"Oh my god," she groans, thrusting both hands into her hair like she's going to pull it out.

"Hear me out! Adrik has something that belongs to me. I need to get it back."

"What do you think you're going to do?"

"Not me…us. As partners. Equals. Two people who won't fuck each other over or lie or get married to some asshole named Simon."

"We don't have any muscle or money…no agreements, no alliances…"

"It doesn't matter. We've got the recipe for the goodies everyone wants."

Ilsa stuffs the rest of her toast in her mouth, not convinced.

"I can't fall into your black hole again," she says.

"What's that supposed to mean?"

"It means you're insane and unreasonable. Nothing's ever enough for you. You want more more more more more."

"Okay. But don't we deserve more? Isn't *more* the most fun?"

Ilsa lets the tension stretch out, really sticking it to me.

At last, she says, "I'll help you. But I'm not gonna fuck you."

"Gross! I would never."

She laughs. "I'm serious."

"Me too. I learned my lesson mixing business and sex."

Ilsa shakes her head, like she can't quite believe she's agreeing to this.

"What do you need from Adrik?"

"He kept all the money," I say. "I want my equipment."

An hour later, we meet at the front door, both of us showered and dressed, my headache fading to a dull throbbing at the temples.

Ilsa is wearing a black suit and boots, her shirt unbuttoned at the throat, hair loose behind her. I'm in my favorite orange sweatpants.

"No fucking way," she says.

"What?"

"I'm not going out with you like that."

"Why not?"

"Because if someone shoots us, I'm not gonna be identified lying next you on a slab wearing that fucking outfit. No, it's too embarrassing. My father will be like, *I really think she should have seen this coming.*"

I roll my eyes. "So sorry. Let me go find something business casual in my backpack."

"You can borrow something of mine."

"I could if you had better clothes."

"You own sequin pants and two jackets with fringe on them. *Two.* I've seen them."

"That information was privileged."

"We were never married. I've told your secrets to everyone."

"That explains some looks I've gotten."

We grin at each other, flushed with the adrenaline of what we're about to do.

"I could maybe borrow an outfit," I concede. "Give me a minute."

I reemerge from Ilsa's room five minutes later, wearing her gray suit. She's broader in the back, but I'm bigger in the chest, so it fits better than I expected.

"Discreet enough for you?" I say.

"Yes." Ilsa looks me up and down, her lips quirking up on the right side. "You know how I feel about a woman in a suit."

"You're goddamn right I do."

We drive over to the lab. Because there's no raw materials to work with, Hakim isn't there. I punch in the code, shaking my head when I see Adrik hasn't changed it. He really doesn't know me at all.

Ilsa and I gather up everything I want, stowing it in the back of her car. The most valuable item is the custom pill press. We take anything else that's mobile, bemoaning the fact that some of the best equipment is too large and too permanently attached to move.

As I'm grabbing the centrifuge, I knock a rack of glass vials onto the floor. They explode when they hit the boards, sending glittering glass fragments everywhere.

"Oops," I say. And then, because that actually felt pretty good, I grab another beaker and deliberately smash it on the ground.

Ilsa snorts. "Is that your revenge? You're gonna make Adrik sweep?"

"Yeah," I say, grabbing the rim of the massive sterilizer unit and yanking with all my might. "He's gonna sweep a whole fucking lot."

The unit topples, crashing to the floor.

The noise is immense and invigorating. I'm sweating from the effort of hauling all this shit, face flushed, a dark, furious energy rising inside me.

Standing inside the lab again is painful. I'm remembering the endless hours I worked with Hakim in here, how excited I was when we finally figured out the god-awful process of synthesizing our own LSD, how Adrik picked me up and swung me around when we told him the good news.

He was only excited because he knew how much money I'd make for him.

I was just his fucking employee.

I rip one of the Bunsen burners out of its socket and fling it at the furnace, denting its metal flank.

Ilsa laughs. "You throw like a girl."

She's already grabbed her own burner, winding up. She pitches it through one of the high windows, glass raining down in a thousand vicious points, embedding in the rotting wooden floor.

"Show-off."

She grins.

I'm not smiling. The destruction isn't relieving my anger. I'm only thinking how pithy, how pathetic this is. How little it will matter to Adrik when he has all the money, all the deals, all his Wolfpack around him.

The ugly little demon on my shoulder whispers in my ear:

He never needed you. He never cared.

He's glad you're gone.

Everyone's glad when you're gone.

I wrench one of the drainage pipes out from under the sink and hit the side of the furnace with it as hard as I can. The impact vibrates all the way up my arms, the sound echoing in my ears, hollow and dead. I hit the furnace again and again and again until my hands are aching, until the whole room throbs with a noise like a gong.

Ilsa stands still, watching me. She's not laughing anymore.

After a minute, she grabs a pipe of her own and starts smashing everything in sight—the sinks, the tables, the cupboards, the fridge…

Her eyes are flat and dark, her hair in strings around her face, teeth bared. I don't think she's seeing the lab at all but rather the faces of everyone who let her down. Maybe even my face.

The sounds of destruction pound in my head. My world is crashing down around me.

I'm caught in the frenzy, in the bitter need to see this all the way to the end.

I grab a jug of acetylene and uncork it, pouring it out in a trail on the floor. The fumes are ether-like, and they make my head spin.

"Give me a lighter."

Ilsa pauses, the pipe still clenched in her hands.

"You sure you want to do that?"

"*Give it to me.*"

Ilsa throws me the piezoelectric lighter I always used on the Bunsen burners. I spark it to life, holding it in my hand.

The lighter seems to fall in slow motion. When it touches the ground, nothing happens for a moment. Then a river of bright orange fire flows outward in both directions, sending up gouts of thick black smoke.

The heat hits me. My skin tightens. My eyes burn.

I'm burning all my hopes, all my plans, all my hard work. All my illusions too.

Ilsa lets out a startled whoop, excited by the speed at which the flames rip through the decrepit lab.

I'm not excited. Not even satisfied.

I feel nothing but pain.

CHAPTER 38
ADRIK

AROUND MIDNIGHT, I GOT A TEXT FROM MYKAH THAT SABRINA carried Ilsa Markov out of Apothecary, both of them smashed and stumbling, disappearing into a cab.

I sped over. Of course they were long gone. Sabrina's bike wasn't even there.

My first reaction was relief that Sabrina was still in Moscow with someone who—while not exactly benign—would at least probably keep her safe.

The next news I receive is Hakim's frantic phone call that our lab is on fire.

I drive over with Jasper, Vlad, and Andrei, all of us strapped in case this is Zakharov and Cujo's doing.

By the time we arrive, the firefighters have put out most of the blaze, the red-and-white trucks clustered out front spraying down the last of the smoking embers on the roof. I have to pay the firemen a hefty bribe to leave without making a report.

Once they're gone, I step through the hole that once was the door, surveying the wreckage of the brewery.

The interior space is a hollow, blackened hole—charred beams dangling from the ceiling, windows smashed outward, the floor piled with smoking rubble.

I'm surrounded by the slow drip, drip, drip of ink-dark water from the roof. The stench is overwhelming, smoke and chemical-drenched wood burning my lungs.

Some of the damage is from the fire itself; the rest of the equipment was vandalized intentionally. Pipes ripped off the boilers, tables smashed up, sinks bashed and dented. I see black rivers where accelerant was poured and then set ablaze.

Jasper picks through the ruin on the other side of the room. His shirt is pulled up over his face. He hates the smell of smoke.

Hakim leans against the doorframe, arms crossed over his chest, not bothering to look through the mess. He knows there's nothing salvageable here.

The fire swallowed everything, chewed it up, and spit it out in scorched splinters. A storm of heat and wrath and madness.

Jasper comes to stand by me, lowering his shirt, his eyes pale and fierce, the teeth and bone tattooed along his jaw making him look particularly grim.

"Sabrina did this," he says.

"I know."

Vlad whips his head around, lip curled in a snarl. "That filthy fucking bi—"

I turn a look on him that shuts him up mid-shout, the words dying in his throat.

"*Don't*," I hiss. "When she comes back, you don't want to have said anything you'll regret."

"Comes back?" Vlad stares at me, blinking slowly. "She destroyed our fucking lab! We should kill her for this. We'd kill anyone else."

"She's not anyone else," Hakim says from the doorway. "She built this lab in the first place."

"And then fucking burned it down!" Vlad scoffs.

"She's angry," I say.

"You think?" Andrei laughs.

I shoot him a look almost as mean as the one I gave Vlad, making him duck his head and scuttle away from me like a crab.

"She took some of the equipment," Hakim says.

Jasper side-eyes me. We can both guess what that means.

"She's setting up her own shop?" Jasper says.

"Possibly."

"With who?"

"Maybe Ilsa."

"You think the Markovs are cutting us out? Poaching our chef?"

"I don't know."

I don't know if Neve Markov is a part of this or only Ilsa. It's no secret there's been friction between the sisters since the wedding. Ilsa might be disgruntled enough to strike out on her own.

Sabrina and Ilsa won't get far alone. They'll need money and assistance.

"We're so fucked," Andrei says, looking around the wreckage with a level of awe bordering on amusement. Sabrina has put us in a hell of a jam.

We owe drugs to Avenir Veniamin for his nightclubs, to Eban Franko for his strip clubs, to the half-dozen brothels we promised Eliksir, and to our street dealers. To the Markovs as well, though they just dropped to the bottom of my priority list.

"What are we gonna do?" Jasper murmurs.

"Can you make it yourself?" I ask Hakim. "If we get you another lab…"

"I can make Molniya. We hadn't finalized the recipes for Eliksir and Opus."

He means Sabrina hadn't finalized them. I don't know if Hakim can do it on his own.

Molniya is our bread and butter—it's the one that matters most. But we still need somewhere to make it and a new supplier for raw materials.

It's going to cost me dearly to rebuy all this equipment. Sabrina's doing this on purpose—putting the squeeze on me. Turning the screws to prove her point that I should have kept a larger cash reserve. She knows exactly where I'm scraped thin. She knows everything about our business.

I can't stop staring around at the damage. This is Sabrina's rage, directed at me. Destroying everything we built.

The inside of the brewery looks like the interior chambers of a heart—burned, blackened, ruined.

This is how much I hurt her.

Now she's hurting me in return.

———————

Back at the house, Chief, Andrei, Hakim, Vlad, and Jasper argue in the kitchen, a babble of conflicting ideas and warnings.

"We need a supplier—"

"We could go back to Kovalenko—"

"Fuck no—"

"The Chechens could sell to us temporarily—"

"It's a month at least until we're up and running again—"

"Not if we—"

"That's not possible—"

"But what if—"

I push past all of them, heading upstairs.

"Where are you going?" Jasper calls.

"Gonna lie down for a minute."

I hear the silence as they stare at my back, then the shuffle as they all cast looks at one another. Confused. Wondering what's wrong with me.

I head up the stairs alone.

It's pointless to talk this over with them. I already know what needs to be done. We'll have to take on a new partner. The options are few, and I hate all of them, but there's no other choice. We'll burn every bridge we've built if we can't get our product out on time.

I lie down on my bed, hands clasped behind my head, looking up at the ceiling.

I wonder what Sabrina's doing right now, at this moment.

I don't believe for a second that she's satisfied with burning the lab. She took that equipment because she's going to start cooking drugs again.

"If we went head-to-head, you'd learn a thing or two about what I can do."

That's what she shouted at me right before she left.

We were both yelling, both angry. I lost my mind for a minute. I didn't mean any of it.

But Sabrina did.

She's always been more honest than me.

I thought she'd cool off and come right back again. Now I realize this is only the beginning. She sees me as her enemy, her rival. Her betrayer.

I asked her to jump and promised that I'd catch her. Then I let her slip through my arms and fall...

She's been gone twenty-four hours. Every minute that passes is a spoon scooping into my guts, digging out another piece of me. There's a hole in my chest, a deep hollow. If I lose any more, I might collapse.

I miss her. I fucking miss her.

I can smell her shampoo in the shower, the hand soap she bought in Danilovsky Market, the last spritz of her perfume she pressed from wrist to throat before setting the bottle back on the shelf.

I roll off the bed and retrieve the bottle from the bathroom. It fits in my palm like a purple glass grenade, the lid missing or lost. I spray the perfume into the air. The mist settles on my outstretched palm. I cover my face with my hand, inhaling deeply.

Sabrina.

Sabrina...

The ache in my chest is too much.

I lie down on the bed once more, pulling out my phone. Starting at the beginning, I scroll through every photo I have of her.

The very first is the one she sent me after Dubrovnik, crouching at the wheel of her bike, working the wrench. Looking back over her shoulder, eyebrow raised in mild surprise, a smile breaking out as she catches sight of whoever stood there holding the camera— probably her mom, or maybe her dad or brother or grandpa. Grease streaked under her eye like a baseball player, hair tied back by a filthy bandanna, little curls coming down. Her upraised palm gripping the wrench, bicep tensed like Rosie the Riveter, cheeky and fierce.

Next the photo of us in Cannon Beach, her arms wrapped around the waist of the ridiculously oversize teddy bear I won for her, head thrown back, mouth open in laughter. I can hear that laugh. I can see the color in her cheeks, hot from all our battles. She was still egging me on, trying to get me to play her in *Halo* again. I was determined to win her that bear. I aimed for those targets with a clarity of mind I've never known before or since, like it was the most important task in the world. Goddamn if I didn't hit every one, even with that shitty rigged rifle.

Next is a video of her running on the beach with Nix, racing each other across the sand. Nix looks like Artemis, thighs flashing in the sun, barefoot and fleet, red hair streaming behind. Sabrina sprints with all her might, then flings herself into a cartwheel, whirling head over heels, before eating shit in a tidal pool, salt water splashing everywhere, soaked to the waist, laughing and rubbing sand out of her eyes.

"Who put that there?" she cries.

Her voice is so distinct, it's like she's in the room with me.

I close out of the video, pressing the heel of my palm against my eye. Pushing hard until I see sparks.

I swipe through the images faster and faster—a selfie of the two of us on Arbat Street, Sabrina modeling her hazmat suit, a picture of her half-asleep at the kitchen table, chin on her palm, nodding off during dinner after one too many late nights at the lab. Then Sabrina in the diamond collar and heels, standing by the window, fireworks bursting into bloom over her shoulder, her naked body bathed in colored sparks. So beautiful that I never would have believed my own memory if I hadn't taken a picture, if I weren't looking at the image right now...

I had everything in that moment—everything I'd ever dreamed of and more.

How did I lose it so fast?

I swipe again, finding one of our last pictures together, taken at Neve Markov's wedding. Sabrina's looking at the camera, unsmiling, wearing the black dress that was only her second choice. Her eyes are dark, full of unhappiness.

I stand next to her, grinning, holding her tight against my side. Totally oblivious to the look on her face.

It's good for you! You don't care what I want. You don't care what I feel.

Sabrina's voice echoes in my head—furious, indignant, pained...

I switch folders, scrolling through our sex videos.

I find my favorite, the very first she ever made for me.

The camera jostles as she adjusts my phone on the bookshelf, angling it toward the bed. Then Sabrina crosses the frame, naked and bronze, hair a wild mane down her back.

I slip my hand down the front of my jeans, resting it on my cock.

Sabrina climbs atop my prone figure, straddling my face. Her thighs are strong and shapely, and her hands grip the headboard.

She settles her pussy down on my mouth, arching her back, sliding her clit across my tongue.

I remember her scent and her taste. I lift my hand to my mouth, inhaling her perfume...

The Sabrina on my phone moans softly. She presses her bare breasts against the headboard, palms flat, fingers spread on the wood as if I were standing behind her, pushing her up against the wall...

Her head turns toward the camera, cheek against the plaster, eyes closed. Her lips part. She lets out a long breath that I feel in my own lungs, my soul coming out in that sigh...

My hand grips my cock, painfully tight.

She's riding my face, slow at first, then faster. Her body rolls like a wave, breasts thrusting forward, ass arching back. She lets go of the headboard to push her hair back with both hands, her palms sliding down her cheeks, down her neck, down her chest, lifting her breasts, grasping them, holding them tight...

I'm stroking my own cock in time with her movement, building and building...

I look at her proportions, sleek and feline...the curve of her waist, the full globes of her ass...

Sabrina is my standard of perfection now, the only thing I'm attracted to. Anyone taller than her is too tall, thinner than her is too thin, paler than her is too pale. I want whatever she is and nothing else. She is beauty and sensuality. She's made for me.

I hear Sabrina cry out—my favorite sound, soft and plaintive, almost begging.

She's coming on my tongue, panting with each roll of her hips, moaning every time she presses against me.

I pump my cock harder, aching to come along with her, desperate for relief.

But the Sabrina on the screen can't fill the emptiness of the room. I need to turn my face against her neck and smell her scent where it's strongest, right against her hairline. That's what I need to come.

The Sabrina on my phone collapses, shivering with pleasure.

My hand grips my cock, the head purple, my knuckles white.

I can't fucking get there. I can't fill the hole inside me. I can't wash away the sickness in my guts.

I stand up from the bed, pent up and shaking, clenching my phone. My cock throbs, but I'm already losing my erection, the little pleasure I could grasp slipping away in a moment.

I close the video, staring at the home screen.

No messages. No missed calls.

In despair, I hurl my phone against the wall, smashing it to pieces.

CHAPTER 39
SABRINA

I'M LYING BY KRYSTIYAN KOVALENKO'S VAST INDOOR POOL IN THE depths of his mansion in Rublyovka. The space is damp and cave-like, the domed roof covered in hand-painted tiles, white and blue, with images of thistles, cathedrals, stags, and birds. Images of the outside world in this deep hole in the ground.

The pool is filled with salt water so brackish that you can only see a few inches below the surface. Anything could be hiding in the dark water.

Ilsa swam laps for an hour. Now she's lying on her back, a towel over her eyes, possibly asleep.

I don't think she's getting rest at night. She tries to stick by my side twenty-four seven, because she doesn't trust Krystiyan or his men. She's supposed to be my partner, but she's reverted to bodyguard, like she used to be for Neve. It's her nature to try to protect the people she loves.

We've been living in this mansion for almost a month.

Our rooms are right next to each other. Once or twice, I've even slept in Ilsa's bed when we've stayed up late talking or I just needed to feel the warmth of her back against mine. We aren't fucking, though Krystiyan thinks we are. He watches us on the security cameras. The nights I stay in Ilsa's room, he's pissy in the mornings.

I let him think what he wants because it helps keep him at arm's length. He's constantly filling my room with bath salts and pink roses and piles of boxes and bags from Moscow's boutiques. He asks me to dine with him almost every night. I stay late at the new lab to avoid him.

Adrik was right about one thing: Krystiyan makes my skin crawl. He has not improved on further acquaintance.

In fact, when I hear his strutting walk echoing across the tiles, I consider rolling into the pool and holding my breath under the water until he's gone.

Instead, I stay exactly where I am, head cushioned on a towel, eyes closed, pretending to sleep like Ilsa.

I'm hoping he'll give up and go away.

His footsteps slow as he approaches. I feel his shadow overlying my prone frame.

"Any more beauty sleep and I won't be able to look at you."

I open my eyes slowly, gazing up at Krystiyan Kovalenko.

He's got his hands stuffed in the pockets of his trousers, face freshly shaven, dark hair combed into a careful pompadour above a high fade. Krystiyan is overly groomed for a gangster. His suits are tailored too tight, and he wears pocket squares and cuff links, diamond studs in both ears.

He's handsome in a *GQ* kind of way—cleft chin, white teeth, strong Roman nose—but he's too slick for my tastes. He definitely plucks his eyebrows.

Then there's his personality—smarmy, manipulative, and envious. His insecurity revolts me.

When Krystiyan insists on engaging me in conversation, I've made it a habit to stare at him, waiting for him to get to the point.

"Your boyfriend's back in business." Krystiyan tosses me a small plastic baggie.

I hold it up to the light, examining the pill inside.

It's small and ovoid, daffodil yellow, stamped with a lightning bolt. That's all they could manage, since I took the custom press.

Heat spreads through my chest. Adrik is selling my product—*my* fucking invention.

I look at Krystiyan. He has to snap his eyes back to my face. He was trawling his gaze over my damp bikini bottoms, the little droplets of water gathered in my navel, and the points of my nipples poking against the triangle top. I want to pull on a robe, but I won't give Krystiyan the satisfaction of seeing me squirm.

Nor will I correct him when he calls Adrik my boyfriend or Ilsa my girlfriend. He wants to be contradicted.

I'm beginning to believe that Krystiyan's fixation on me is nothing of the sort—it's Adrik who obsesses him. He talks incessantly of how they were rivals at school. Every conflict, every interaction, is dug up and recited. Or at least Krystiyan's version of events. Unfortunately for Krystiyan, I spent a lot of time with Adrik. The Adrik Krystiyan portrays—overconfident, arrogant, easily bested by Krystiyan's machinations and Krystiyan's aspersions—bears little resemblance to the man I know.

Stealing me away from Adrik is Krystiyan's greatest achievement.

The only thing that could top it is running Adrik's business into the ground.

"How do we stop him?" Krystiyan demands.

I roll the baggie between my thumb and index finger, making the yellow pill twist back and forth.

"We sell our Molniya cheaper."

"Cheaper?" Krystiyan frowns. "We're barely making money as it is."

"Neither is he. Adrik has to buy materials at top dollar from the Chechens, and he has no cash reserves. We can undercut his price. Drive him out of business."

Krystiyan pretends to consider the idea, like he's the one in charge. I can tell from his smirk he's already on board.

He has the money to do it, flush with cash after inheriting from his father. Davyah Kovalenko was a broker, facilitating the sale of construction contracts to oligarchs. He had a heart attack while fucking his favorite mistress on a yacht in Sochi. He might have survived it if the mistress had called for help instead of robbing his body of watch, rings, credit cards, and cash. Krystiyan told me that he slit the girl's mouth on both sides when he tracked her down as punishment for the theft.

He should have thanked her. Krystiyan loves playing boss, ordering around his motley mix of mercenaries. A few are *kachki*, a few Ukrainian, a few Bratva, though from lesser, lower families. He pays them generously, but they don't respect him. I hear their muttered jokes. I see the looks they give each other behind his back.

"How long do you think it will take to drive him out?" Krystiyan asks.

I shrug. "A month or two maybe."

It'll cost Krystiyan a fuck ton of money, not that he'll notice. He reminds me of a trust-fund kid who purchases a nightclub or a clothing line, hemorrhaging money because they understand nothing about business.

I'll stop the bleed when it suits me.

After I've cut Adrik's legs out from under him.

Krystiyan drops into a squat next to me. Russians have the most remarkable ability to hold that position, even while wearing dress pants and loafers.

"What about the new drug?" he says, looking at me from under his thick, dark brows.

He has an unpleasant way of speaking, as if everything is an insinuation or a double entendre. Especially with me, he uses a soft, intimate tone that makes me want to smack him upside the head.

"It's ready," I say. "I tested it last night."

Krystiyan sticks out his bottom lip in a pout.

"Why didn't you invite me?"

"Maybe next time," I say with zero sincerity.

Krystiyan rests his palm on my thigh, looking in my eyes.

"You'd be surprised how helpful I can be."

"Krystiyan…"

"Yes?"

"Get your hand off my leg."

He smiles at me like I'm joking without moving his hand.

"Are you deaf?" Ilsa barks.

She hasn't moved the towel off her eyes. Hasn't sat up. But her voice cracks like a whip, echoing in the cavernous space.

Krystiyan jerks back his hand, then smooths his hair like that was the real reason he stopped groping me.

"This better work," he says, his voice several degrees colder. "It's an expensive proposition funding your operation."

"You're already selling five times what you ever sold before." I toss my head. "Spare me the complaints."

Putting the squeeze on Adrik is a slow process by which I continually drop the price of Molniya while selling as much product as I can to flood the market. Adrik has to buy materials at the Chechens' exorbitant prices, losing money on every sale he makes. He can't keep it up forever.

Krystiyan complains weekly about the money we're bleeding out twice as fast as Adrik, but I know our reserves can stand it. It's a siege. I'm starving Adrik out of his castle while I still have a storehouse full of food.

Adrik is under attack, yet I'm the prisoner at Krystiyan's house. Not only because I don't want to encounter any of the Wolfpack on the streets of Moscow but because Krystiyan becomes more anxious and repressive by the day. I've strong-armed him into sinking his fortune into this standoff. Everything rests on my head. I'm his gamble—he has to make me pay off, or he loses everything.

There's a distinct sense that his men are watching me, following me, always close. Ilsa hates it. She hates all this. She's always worked with her own family, on whom she could completely rely. We're constantly on edge, not trusting Krystiyan, not even able to trust that his men are loyal to *him*.

Not wanting to be at the house under Krystiyan's eye, I spend as much time as possible in my new lab. It's clean and modern with proper ventilation but also cold and stark and much less cheerful without Hakim's constant remarks on what I'm doing wrong. Ilsa doesn't sit with me. She's always prowling around, making sure Krystiyan's goons aren't up to anything shady.

The lab's other drawback is that it shares a wall with a restaurant owned by Yakim Dimka, another Bratva boss. I can hear the bang of the swinging doors as waiters go in and out of the kitchen, the sous-chef bawling at his staff, and even the dishwasher humming to himself as he sprays down the utensils.

I'm sure Krystiyan rented this space to suck up to Dimka. I doubt it does him much good—the restaurant is too small and shabby for a *pakhan* to eat there himself. We'll never even cross paths.

The sound of people working close by is less dreary than total silence, if occasionally distracting.

I've been making my most brain-bending formula yet. I don't have Hakim to help me with the time release, so I design it to all hit at once, an obliterating blanket of sensation, smothering and intense. I added ketamine for total dissociation. You can float outside your own body and watch yourself walk and talk and move around like an automaton. Like you've become both a robot and the god that operates it from afar.

I test it on myself with Ilsa keeping watch. I spend hours separating my brain from the pain in my chest that beats and beats all day and all night without any rest. That's the only time I don't feel it—when I'm high out of mind.

I take the drug more often than I need to for testing. I take it almost every day because it's the only relief from the hurting.

When I'm on it, I don't want to eat. Ilsa gets us food, and I sit in front of mine, watching my hands touch and pick it up. When I put it in my mouth, it feels like a foreign object, like a penny. I move it around with my tongue, unable to chew or swallow.

My clothes are getting loose. My skin is sallow. I haven't been outside barely at all. I'm yellow and drained.

Each day that goes by turns the screws on Adrik but also punishes me. I hate working with Krystiyan. I hate how stressed Ilsa looks. This isn't how she thought it would be. If it were just her alone, she'd never put up with Krystiyan's bullshit. She stays because she's worried about me.

All I can do is succeed, because that's what I promised Ilsa and what I promised myself.

I work harder and harder while sinking further into misery. Wondering how anybody can feel this shitty and survive.

I call the new drug Mechtat, which means "dream." It's a lie…I'm not dreaming anymore. Not even hoping.

––––––––––

In the sixth week of the standoff, Krystiyan comes into my room while I'm getting ready for bed. He knows he's not allowed in here. Without looking at his stiff gait and white knuckles or smelling how much Stoli he's been drinking, I already know he's angry. The intrusion is the message.

I'm standing at the mirror in a silk slip, slowly wiping my face with a cleansing cloth. I took a double dose of Mechtat earlier, and I'm just at the point where everything looks distant and posed, like a movie set.

I see the pleasant chiaroscuro quality of the light, dark everywhere except the soft golden ring light illuminating my face. When I'm high, I like to spend a solid hour washing, moisturizing, and massaging my face. Telling myself I'm still beautiful, no matter how ugly I feel.

Krystiyan looms up behind me, a pale face floating over my shoulder in the mirror. With his black hair slicked back, in his dark suit, he certainly looks like the devil's bargain.

When he's angry, the edges of his lips go white, and the area around his mouth stiffens like the muzzle of a dog.

"You *said* if we sold the drug cheaper, Adrik wouldn't be able to buy supplies anymore. You *said* he wouldn't be able to fulfill his contracts to the clubs and the dealers, and we'd get them instead."

"That's right." I watch my lips move in the mirror—dusky red, the color of a rose a gangster would lay on a coffin if this really were all part of a movie I was filming. "It's simple math. He'll run out of money first. That's why America is the business giant of the world and not Russia—'cause you don't respect the fucking numbers."

"Well, guess what, John Nash? He's just partnered up with Yuri Koslov. And he *is* filling his orders, and we *are* still losing a metric fuck ton of money!"

By the end of his tirade, Krystiyan is yelling right next to my ear, loud enough to make the hair shift around my face.

I stay perfectly calm. That's the beauty of the dissociative state. Krystiyan can't possibly annoy or upset me. I can't even feel the stress I was feeling before I took the drug. Good or bad, nothing touches me.

Happily, this reads to Krystiyan as confidence. As if I'm certain that what I promised will still come to pass.

"Even better," I assure him. "Now Adrik has to split his profit two ways. And he has to work with someone outside the Wolfpack. He's not in control of his environment anymore. That makes him vulnerable."

It probably also makes him furious. Now we both have a partner we can't stand.

You might miss collaborating with someone you could fuck, won't you, Adrik?

"What's that supposed to mean?" Krystiyan snarls.

"Figure out the weak spot in his new supply chain. Yuri Koslov isn't nearly as meticulous as Adrik. There's bound to be one."

Krystiyan considers this, his mouth working.

After a minute, he leans in close and hisses, "You better be as smart as you think you are."

It turns out I am.

Two days later, Krystiyan informs me that he's discovered the time and location of Adrik's next three shipments.

The bribe he paid for the information was more than half the value of the drugs themselves. Ilsa and I, plus four of Krystiyan's men, successfully intercept the truck twenty miles from its drop point. When I open it up, Yuri's hidden compartments are much less ingenious than Zakharov's. It only takes ten minutes to strip the vehicle of every last gram of illicit material.

Krystiyan is cackling at our theft. All his doubts forgotten, he's right back to thinking he's kingpin of the world, running train on Adrik like a real big boss.

I don't feel good or bad about it.

I don't feel anything at all at the moment.

CHAPTER 40
ADRIK

SABRINA HIJACKING OUR MATERIALS IS A BIG FUCKING PROBLEM.

First, she's not just stealing from me anymore. Yuri Koslov wants to put a bullet in her head. Second, this is a direct attack on my business. Not price manipulation and market flooding—she stole from us. Which means we're going to war.

My feelings for Sabrina over the last six weeks have vacillated from regret to all-consuming rage. I've never been angrier at someone in my life. To position herself as my enemy and rival, after everything we shared…

I spend hours fantasizing about the dark and depraved things I'll do if I ever get my hands on her.

Yet even in my most murderous moments, I can't stand the thought of her catching a bullet from one of Yuri's men.

So when Koslov demands that we retaliate against Krystiyan Kovalenko, I tell him I'll handle it myself. I order the Wolfpack to strap up, and we drive over to Krystiyan's compound in Rublyovka.

All six of us are in the SUV. Hakim and Chief wait in the car. Jasper and Vlad come into the entryway, but Krystiyan's men won't let them any farther.

Jasper wants to stay with me. In fact, he barely agrees to let me go on without him.

"It's okay," I tell him. "I've got it covered."

Alone, I follow Krystiyan's lieutenant into what I can only describe as a villain's lair.

It's a dramatic room painted charcoal gray, with floor-to-ceiling drapes, a roaring fireplace, and an actual Siberian bear rug frozen in a futile roar beneath the legs of a throne-like chair.

The rest of the seating is more conventional. Sabrina sits on a perfectly normal couch, Ilsa on an easy chair. They both look tense and pale.

Krystiyan is the only one comfortable, because he's the only one foolish enough not to understand what's happening in this moment.

He thinks he's in some triumphant position. Four of his men around him, mine out in the hall. Sabrina at his right hand, like a queen taken in conquest. Ilsa her knight, sitting next to her, elbows on her knees, fist under her chin, silent and watchful.

Krystiyan actually grins, lolling in his ridiculous chair. Teeth almost as white and straight as an American, a heavy gold bracelet dangling from one wrist, nails manicured, wearing a $6000 suit. Every inch the king.

I'm in jeans and boots. Same jacket as ever. Same hair. I doubt I've changed to Sabrina's eyes. The differences are buried too deep—a poison spreading below the surface where no one can see.

Sabrina is completely altered. If I believed it were possible, I'd think Krystiyan had been torturing her. I've never seen her so drained of light. She's a fading photograph of what she once was.

Yet there's still a desperate, fragile beauty I feel compelled to save, like a painting that might be restored or a ring that could be dug up and cleaned and made to shine again.

"Adrik," Krystian smirks. "I was wondering when you'd come to see me."

Without even glancing in his direction, I say, "I'm not here to see you."

I haven't taken my eyes off Sabrina for one second since I walked in this room. My stare burns into her, lighting her on fire. I see the color rising up her neck into her cheeks, like a temperature gauge. The longer I stare, the hotter she gets.

I take three long strides toward her. Krystiyan jumps up from his chair, stepping in front of me to intercept.

I put one hand on his shoulder and slice across his throat, opening a gash as thick as a finger with the razor-fine blade of the knife Sabrina gave me.

Whatever Krystiyan intended to say is cut off short, his vocal cords severed along with everything else. There's nothing but whistling silence as he raises his fingers to his neck, his face blank of anything but surprise.

He sinks forward, landing softly on his knees.

The room is utterly still. Krystiyan's men haven't moved an inch. They stare at me impassively, watching their boss struggle and drown without lifting a finger to help him.

All is silence but the pattering of blood from the tip of my knife to the floor.

I look Sabrina dead in the eye.

"Baby...you are really starting to piss me off."

Krystian topples over behind me. Sabrina's wide and startled eyes flutter from his body to his men, still unsmiling, still unmoving, hardly seeming to register their boss on the ground.

"You're wondering why they don't do anything? Let me explain it to you. You see that one behind you there? With the earrings? That's Denis Radmir. We went to school together in St. Petersburg. The one beside him is Yev Tamila. They know who I am. They know that if they even *think* about firing a bullet at me, Jasper will come and hunt them down and cut their throats a month, six months, a year later. And if Jasper doesn't find them, Vlad will. Or Andrei. Or Hakim. Or even fucking Chief. All these men know that. *That's* the difference between a brother and a hired gun."

I see the sick paleness that comes over her, realizing that she really didn't see this coming. Realizing how much she doesn't know.

Ilsa regards Krystiyan's body on the floor with no surprise at all. I could never have done the same to Sabrina without Ilsa intervening, because she wouldn't have left her so unprotected to begin with. She stays right by Sabrina's side.

Ilsa understands how quickly the balance of power shifted.

Krystiyan has no family, no pull beyond his cash. The loyalty his money bought died the moment I cut his throat.

Ilsa's shoulders lower like a sigh.

I'm still holding the knife, my thumb brushing against the inscription Sabrina wrote for me in another time, another world.

You. Always you.

There's only ten feet of space between us. The closest we've been in six weeks. An agonizing, eternal amount of time.

I can feel her heart beating across that space. I smell her scent, high and sharp with adrenaline. Her pupils are pinpricks, her lips damp.

I could take two more steps to reach her, but she's tense and trembling, a rabbit on the grass. If I take a step toward her, she might bolt.

"You're done," I tell her. "It's time to come home."

She stares at me, white as death, eyes flat and metallic.

"Never," she whispers.

The air is full of the iron smell of blood.

It's Kovalenko's, but it feels like it's Sabrina and me who are cut. We've hacked at each other again and again. We're in some kind of contest to prove who has the stronger will. For us to be together, maybe one of us has to conquer.

We'll keep hurting each other until someone begs for mercy.

I point at Sabrina, and I make her a promise. "Come at me again, and I won't pull any punches."

I close the bloody knife and put it back in my pocket.

Krystiyan's men don't speak a word to me. Denis Radmir simply nods as I pass.

I leave the house, the Wolfpack behind me.

The car ride back is silent.

Jasper drives, one hand on the wheel. I see him sneaking glances at me out of his peripheral.

"You okay?" he says at last.

The weight of what I just did is already crashing down on me. I'm replaying every word, every glance between Sabrina and me. Already feeling that it was all wrong, all fucked up.

I don't know what I should have done...but not that.

I can't answer Jasper. All I can do is shake my head once.

Another long silence.

Then, grimacing, Jasper says, "For what it's worth...I miss her too."

We all do. The mood in the house has been dismal the last six weeks, and not only because of me. You don't realize how bright Sabrina shines until the light goes out.

The day she left, Jasper agreed with her. He was afraid to tell me the truth. Yet another thing for him to feel guilty about. And another thing that shows me how blind I can be.

CHAPTER 41
SABRINA

BEFORE ADRIK HAS ENTIRELY LEFT THE ROOM, ILSA PULLS HER gun out, her hand on my shoulder. She backs me out the opposite way, hustling me back to our rooms to pack up whatever we need.

It's not Adrik she's worried about—it's the rest of Krystiyan's men. Now that Krystiyan is dead, they're unallied and disconnected. A roving band of guns for hire until they find their next opportunity.

She's throwing my stuff in a bag, taking too much of the shit Krystiyan bought me, which I would never wear in a million years.

"What are you doing?" I hiss at her. "We need to get back out there. We could still use some of those men."

"And pay them with what? We haven't made a profit. You've only drained half Kovalenko's money—which we no longer have access to. We need to get out of here before those guys realize they're not getting their last paycheck."

She picks up my backpack and forces it onto my arm.

"Why are you in such a rush? We need our equipment at the very least—"

Ilsa wheels on me. "Sabrina, it's over!"

She's not packing anymore. She's just staring at me like we already had this conversation and I didn't hear it.

"What are you talking about? We can find another partner."

"There's not going to be another partner. Adrik's buddied up with Yuri Koslov. He's high table. Nobody else is going to join our vendetta against two of the most dangerous people in the city. And even if they would—" She holds up her hand to forestall me. "*I'm* done. It was fun, it was crazy, it was a much-needed break, but it's time to get back to real life."

I can't believe she's saying this.

"This *is* my life," I hiss at her. "I'm not going back to Chicago."

"Well, I'm going home," she says. "And you should do the same."

She's trying to be brisk and matter-of-fact, but when she sees the look on my face, she can't keep it up. She stops and puts her arms around me for a minute, not saying anything. Just holding me.

It feels like every awful sensation is trying to spill out of me. Ilsa's arms are the only thing keeping me together. I'm a broken vessel that will collapse unless it's cradled just right.

Eventually, she has to let go.

"Come with me," she says.

I shake my head. "No thanks. I never really cared for Simon either."

She looks at me, trying to read my face.

I force a smile. Like I'm not terrified to be alone. Like I'm not minutes from falling apart.

"I'll be fine," I lie. "You can go."

I think I fool her. She's reassured enough to say, "Same old Sabrina."

"Same old Diana."

She smiles and shakes her head.

"See ya, kid."

When she's gone, I can't even take any Mechtat, because there's no one to keep an eye out for me anymore.

———

I spend the night at a cheap hotel in Odintsovo.

For the first time since I came to Moscow, I'm completely alone.

I've got about $6000 in cash, a mix of American dollars and rubles. Also a couple baggies of product, about two hundred pills in total.

I sit on the chintz bedspread and think, playing with my dad's old knife. I twist my wrist to float the blade out and back again, running through the tricks I know mindlessly, repetitively. The blade slices through the air with a sound like scissors, tucking in and out of the handles, flashes of silver in the dark like a coin turning underwater.

The knife feels like a part of my hand. I've had it all my life. I haven't cut myself in years, even when I play with it drunk.

At this moment, I'm stone-cold sober.

I've been using too much. Trying to escape the wave that washed over me the moment I lost Adrik.

I'm trapped in this deep, dark coldness. The drugs keep me asleep. Every time I wake and draw breath, water rushes in, and I drown all over again.

Alone in this hotel room, I'm drowning and drowning and drowning.

Seeing Adrik tore me apart all over again.

He walked in like a warrior, radiating power and confidence. Krystiyan was a fool to step in front of him. Anyone could see that no one could stand before him.

He cut Krystiyan's throat with the knife I gave him. Then he threatened me with that same knife, my fucking gift to him, my words on the handle.

His face was a mask of anger and disdain.

He barked at me to come with him—not a request, an order.

He hasn't changed at all.

Except that he hates me now.

I know how weak I was in that moment. He looked so confident, so ferocious. Everything in me was crying out for his touch. If he had said a word of kindness or apology, if he even said he missed me…I would have melted in an instant.

He didn't say it, because that's not how he feels.

He only wants me back out of pride.

I flick the knife out again. This time, it nicks the edge of my index finger.

I look at the bead of blood, bright as a jewel.

I can't feel the cut, not even when I raise my finger to my mouth and suck on it. It tastes of copper.

I'm going home. You should do the same.

Going back to Chicago is quitting.

I'm a lot of things...but I'm not a fucking quitter.

Adrik thinks he's won? I'm not even close to done yet.

There's nearly full batches of Molniya and Mechtat complete at the lab. The Wolfpack might have cleared it out, but if not...those drugs are worth a lot of money.

I close my knife and set it on the nightstand.

In the morning, I'll see what I can salvage.

CHAPTER 42
ADRIK

I'M LYING IN MY ROOM, ALONE IN THE DARK.

I've been staring at the ceiling for almost three hours, unable to sleep. Replaying what I did over and over and the look on Sabrina's face: desperate, haunted, miserable.

I never stop fucking up when it comes to her.

Maybe that's the real curse of our relationship. With anyone else, I can be calm, calculated, decisive. The moment I see her, a storm surge of emotion hits me, all conscious thought obliterated.

Cutting Kovalenko's throat was reckless in the extreme. I guessed that his men wouldn't do anything, but I didn't know for certain.

In that moment, all I saw was Sabrina. Krystiyan was the barrier between us. I cut him down like a blade of grass.

But when he was dead on the ground, she still wouldn't submit.

It's time to come home.

Never.

What do I have to do to break her?

The answer is I can't.

I can't convince her either.

I wouldn't come back if you crawled over broken glass and begged.

Everything inside me hardens like iron at the thought.

I've never begged in my life. Neither has she. We can't. We won't.

It isn't in us.

This has been the worst six weeks of my life. Worse even than when Ivan was taken. The darkness has swallowed me whole, and I can't see the faintest trace of light.

Sabrina has been applying pressure like a vise around my head. Constantly twisting the screws. Willing to take her vendetta against me far past anything reasonable.

She's put us in an absurdly dangerous position. The longer I allow her to disrupt my business, the weaker I look. She's drawing the jackals all around me, inviting them to finish me off.

Killing Krystiyan will remind them what I can do. But I can't keep allowing her to defy me, publicly and openly. Attacking me without reprisal. Destroying what's mine.

Yuri wasn't happy when he heard that I let her go. I told him it was because of Ilsa Markov—we don't want her father as an enemy. He knows that's not the real reason.

I don't control Yuri. He's petty and vengeful. He's killed men for far less than what Sabrina has done.

Working with him is worse than Zakharov. He's no silent partner, operating from afar. He's right here, constantly in my shit, believing he's the superior in our arrangement because he's high table. While success has made him sloppy, he's no dilettante like Krystiyan. His men are armed and vicious, well paid and experienced.

Still, I'm certain one of his subordinates was the source of the leak when Ilsa and Sabrina hijacked our delivery. It's the only way they could have known the truck's route.

Yuri doesn't believe it.

I told him we need to change the location of the next shipment. He said it's impossible; the product is already en route.

Countless problems, countless hazards. This was true when Sabrina and I were partners, but I didn't feel the weight of it then. It was a challenge I enjoyed.

Now it all feels black and smothering, a fist around my heart squeezing tighter and tighter.

I have to deal with Zakharov too. He's gone to ground, but I know he's still here in Moscow. Waiting to jump out and bite my ankle like the old viper he is.

The night I gave Sabrina that diamond collar, I really believed I could have it all. At the height of my love for her, I even thought I could be a good man.

Now I know that's impossible.

I'm not a good man. I'm not a good partner.

I can't even be a boss like Ivan. He did what had to be done. He never enjoyed it.

I'm full of so much frustration and darkness, I *want* to hurt someone. I want to rip and tear and destroy anything and anybody who crosses me.

I enjoyed killing Krystiyan.

And I'll enjoy killing Zakharov. Cujo too, if he's stupid enough to get in my way.

CHAPTER 43
SABRINA

Krystiyan's lab is located in Nemchinovka, Yakim Dimka's restaurant on one side and a laundromat on the other.

From the front, it looks like an office space—simple and nondescript. The hours are posted on the door, though that door is always locked. I enter through the back, leaving my bike parked in the alleyway.

The lab looks as pristine and organized as ever, lights off, drawers tightly closed. I don't think anyone's been in here.

Even though this place is professionally outfitted with proper vent hoods, double sinks, and a six-burner stove plus an industrial-size refrigerator for all the perishable ingredients, I never really liked it. The lights have an ugly greenish cast, and all the stainless steel reflects bits and pieces of my face back at me.

I miss the raw brick of the brewery, the high windows that sent shafts of light down like a church, and the smell of hops. The whistle that would blow when the shift changed at the purse factory next door and the way Hakim would perk up, saying, "Almost time for Shake Burgers," his voice muffled behind his respirator.

I wish I hadn't burned it all.

I drop my backpack on the counter and unzip it, planning to stuff it with as much product as I can carry.

I take the flat packs of Molniya from the cabinet, already pressed into lightning bolt pills and vacuum-sealed in packs of a hundred. These were supposed to go to Krystiyan's dealers, but they're mine now.

I've been making the product in batches. There's no Eliksir or Opus at the moment. What I have here is still worth a small fortune.

I pull open the fridge, wondering if I should take any of the raw materials along with me—at least the ones that are hardest to source. The refrigerator is double normal size, with one of those hefty metal handles that clicks and unlocks like an old appliance from the '50s. The pale fluorescent light bathes my face as I rummage through the various bins and jars within, each labeled with Sharpie in my own writing, messy but easy for me to read.

My head is deep in the fridge, the containers clinking and clattering as I shove aside what I don't need. No Ilsa keeps watch for me. So I have no warning of my unwanted visitors until I stand upright and realize I'm no longer alone.

Two men stand on the opposite side of the room, firmly situated between me and the exit. One is tall, broad-shouldered, dressed in a royal-blue tracksuit with a gold medallion around his beefy neck. His traps are so thick that his head hunches forward, his small eyes looking up from under a heavy shelf of brow. His swollen fists hang at the end of gorilla-like arms, the nose of a Beretta poking out from the right hand. This is the former boxer, the Olympian turned enforcer they call Cujo.

Which means the older man next to him is Zakharov.

Zakharov doesn't resemble his son. He's smaller, leaner, as brown and wizened as an apple core left to dry in the sun. His eyes are almost colorless behind the round lenses of his rimless spectacles. He's wearing a plain brown suit that looks thirty years out of date, though well preserved. His shoes are likewise old, carefully brushed and polished.

When he speaks, his voice rasps from some place deep in his chest. "Where is Krystiyan?"

Slowly, I step back from the fridge, leaving the door open.

I look from Zakharov to Cujo to the doorway behind them.

The lab is long and narrow, like a bowling alley. Cujo fills almost the entire width of the room. I'm as trapped as a ship in a bottle—no way past.

The distance between us seems to stretch and deform, the light fading as if it only exists at the end of a very long tunnel. I'm halfway to fainting, realizing how completely and utterly fucked I am in this moment.

"Who are you?" I say, striving for the lightest, most innocent of tones while my blood turns to lead in my veins and my knees wobble beneath me.

"Adrik tried to insult my intelligence," Zakharov says quietly. "I hoped you'd be smarter, Sabrina."

Fuuuuuuuck me.

I try to think of a way past them, my brain firing madly, while I stare at the impossible barrier of Cujo and the gun in his hand.

Cujo knows what I'm thinking. He tracks my movement, a smile playing at the edges of his thick lips.

"Krystiyan is dead," I say, inching back from the men, toward my backpack, the cabinets, and the gas range.

"That seems to happen to your partners with surprising frequency."

"I guess I'm unlucky. I'd prefer if they stayed alive."

I'm back at the stove. No more room to retreat. Through the solid plaster behind me, I hear the clinking of plates, the shouts of the expediter, and the sizzle of steaks. I could scream and bang on the wall, but I doubt anyone would come running.

Zakharov tilts his head, the light flashing across the lenses of his glasses so they become opaque and then clear again. His breath rattles in his lungs.

"You're going to tell me everything I want to know."

My back is against the wall. My gun is in my backpack, my knife in my pocket. If I reach for either, Cujo will shoot me.

"I don't know anything." I rest my hand lightly on the stovetop. "I'm just the chef."

"I think we both know that's not true."

Zakharov nods to Cujo.

Cujo barrels toward me like a bull, head lowered.

Instead of diving for my backpack, I reach behind the stove and yank the metal coil out of the wall. The light hiss of escaping gas is drowned by my shout as Cujo grabs my ponytail and wrenches me backward. My tailbone connects with the floor, sending a sharp jolt all the way up my spine, immediately dwarfed by shrieking, tearing pain as he drags me across the tiles by my hair.

He flings me down in front of Zakharov.

Zakharov looks down on me dispassionately, his face as blank as the flat lenses of his spectacles.

"Where is Krystiyan?" he repeats.

"I told you, he's dead."

Cujo backhands me across the face. The force of that slap is like a bomb detonating in my brain. My body flies sideways, my skull slamming against the cabinets.

I come to when Cujo grabs my hair and sets me upright once more. The whole side of my face is on fire, buzzing like I've been stung by a swarm of bees.

"Where is he?" Zakharov repeats.

"In his house, dead on the floor, I told you!"

"Since when?"

"Last night."

Zakharov glances at Cujo. Some silent confirmation passes between them. Possibly they visited Krystiyan's house with no answer, or they've been calling him.

"Where is Adrik Petrov?" Zakharov demands.

"How should I know?" I lie. "I haven't seen him in weeks."

Cujo hits me again, closed fist this time. If I thought the slap hurt, it was a fucking kiss on the cheek compared to his punch. A fist with the size and mass of a chunk of cement comes crashing into my mouth, my lip splitting instantly against the knuckles, my mouth filling with blood.

Little black dots fall across my vision like snow. My head lolls forward.

Cujo slaps me again, brisk and sharp, on the swollen side of my face.

"Wake up," he grunts.

The room comes clear again in painful focus. My blood is on the tiles in bright spatters. I spit a little more, surprised how much comes out of my mouth. I tongue the left side of my teeth. One of the lower molars is loose.

"You're worth every penny, aren't you, big boy?" I mutter.

I swear Cujo smiles just a little. He enjoys his work.

Zakharov takes his phone out of his pocket, thrusting it at me.

"Call Adrik," he orders. "Tell him to meet you here."

I give a low laugh that sprays more blood across my lap.

"Adrik wouldn't answer my call, let alone come here to save me. I burned down his lab and stole his product, and I've been doing my damnedest to run his business into the ground. You're doing him a favor beating the shit out of me."

Another look passes between Zakharov and Cujo as Zakharov tries to ascertain the validity of what I'm saying.

He's been in Moscow for months, digging for the details of what happened to his son. I can see the tension in his face, the built-up frustration of dead end after dead end. He can't guess why Zigor was killed—the truth is too bizarre. All his rage is pointed at Adrik, but Adrik is surrounded by the Wolfpack at all times and now Yuri Koslov and his men as well.

Zakharov crouches in front of me, looking intently into my face. His breath is unpleasantly warm and intimate.

"I had a deal with Krystiyan Kovalenko. He knew the locations of Adrik's next three shipments. Tell me where Adrik will be, and I'll let you live."

I know where the shipments are going. In fact, the next one arrives tomorrow night.

I could tell Zakharov where to find Adrik. I could even draw him a map.

"I'll make you a better deal," I say, squinting at Zakharov as my left eye begins to swell shut. "You tell me how old that suit is, and I'll tell you where you can buy a new one."

Zakharov's upper lip draws up, showing long, gray teeth.

"Very amusing," he says. "Let's see how long you keep laughing."

He stands.

Cujo hauls me to my feet by my hair, driving his fist into my stomach. I double over, retching. When I try to draw breath, it's impossible. He's pummeled the air out of me, and the muscles are too torn to breathe in. My mouth is open, eyes bulging, no air coming in for an agonizing amount of time, until finally, with a horrid gasp and a pain like a knife in my ribs, my lungs slowly inflate.

"Where's the next shipment?" Zakharov demands.

I hold up a finger, still trying to breathe.

Cujo slaps me again, knocking me back down to the floor.

I cough, shaking my head at Cujo.

"Not as good, big boy. I've been slapped by cheerleaders harder than that."

Cujo seizes the front of my shirt, lifting me up and flinging me into the open refrigerator. The shelves collapse around me, sending containers of product tumbling down on my head, glass jars shattering on the tiles.

Blood runs down into my eye from a cut on my scalp. I blink it away, slipping my hand in my pocket, gripping the handle of my knife.

When Cujo stoops to grab me again, massive hands grasping either side of my shirt, I flick out the blade and stab it down into the side of his neck.

There's no boxer like an old boxer. Cujo slipped and ducked

thousands of punches in his prime. He sees the flash of metal in his peripheral and twists, the blade embedding in that thick band of muscle running from neck to shoulder instead of in the jugular.

He roars and stumbles back.

I kick out at his knee, buckling it, then I try to punch him as hard as I can in the balls. He turns, and my fist meets hipbone instead. I howl, cradling my hand. He backhands me across the face, knocking me back into the refrigerator.

His face is the color of brick, right hand shaking as he reaches across his broad body to pull out the knife.

It looks pathetically small in his hand. Cujo tosses it aside, the knife spinning away across the tiles.

His eyes are bloodshot beneath the heavy shelf of his brow. He snarls and lunges for me once more.

"Wait, wait, wait!" I cry, holding up my hands. "I'll tell you what you want to know!"

Zakharov makes a hissing sound, snapping Cujo out of his rage, stopping him short.

"Where will Adrik be?" he demands.

"I'll tell you. I just want a smoke first."

Zakharov's eyes narrow, studying my face.

We both know he's not letting me walk out of here alive—especially not if he plans to ambush Adrik.

Even prisoners get one last cigarette before the firing squad.

Zakharov nods to Cujo. Cujo reaches in the pocket of his track pants, pulling out a crumpled packet of cigarettes. He shakes one out and passes it to me.

"Lighter?" I croak.

Less of a gentleman than Jasper, Cujo tosses me his Zippo.

I put the cigarette between my lips, on the side not split and bleeding.

Leaning back against the broken shelves, I gaze at Zakharov. Spilled product soaks through my jeans, bits of glass digging into my thighs. The chemical stench mingles with the scent of propane.

My right hand is all fucked up from punching Cujo. I hold the Zippo in my left, giving a few experimental flicks at the wheel with my thumb.

Zakharov watches, impatient, his tongue darting out to moisten his lips.

Cujo glowers at me, blood soaking down the arm of his tracksuit, dripping from his fingertips.

If this is my last view, I wish it were prettier.

"I'm sorry about Zigor," I say to Zakharov. "But you have to admit…he was obnoxious as hell."

I flick the wheel, spark the flame, and toss the lighter toward the gas range.

Before I can draw up my legs and pull the fridge door closed, before the Zippo has even landed, the propane ignites in a surging storm of liquid fire. It roars toward us with deafening noise and heat, swallowing up all the air in the room, incinerating everything in its path.

The force of the explosion helps slam the fridge door. I'm closed up in the cold, dark coffin, the refrigerator rocking against the wall as it's blasted backward. I can feel the heat leaking in through the seams. My right arm burns where I reached out to yank the door shut.

The fire rushes past like a freight train.

In its wake, I hear shouts and the distant sound of alarms and sprinklers going off in the restaurant next door. There's chaos and clattering, dishes smashing, people running.

I kick at the inside of the refrigerator door, breaking the latch, forcing it open again.

Now I see why the noise from the restaurant was so loud—the explosion blew a hole in our shared wall. The teenage dishwasher peers through the gap, his face covered in soot, his apron singed.

His eyes widen when he sees me stumble out of the refrigerator into the still-burning remains of the lab. The cabinets are on fire, and the stove is a smoking ruin. Cujo's body was blasted back against the base of the sink. Zakharov lies face down by the doorway—he tried to run.

"*Syuda!*" the dishwasher calls to me, sticking his arm through the gap. *This way!*

I limp over to him, acrid black smoke filling my lungs, blinding me so all I can see is his pale hand reaching through the hole.

He hauls me through. I cry out, my ribs in agony, my right arm screaming at the heat of the burning plaster.

I'm reeling, barely able to stand. He has to half carry me through the soaking spray of the sprinklers, out to the back alley of the restaurant between the overflowing dumpsters.

"*Pozhaluysta, bol'nitsu.*" I rasp. *Please, hospital.*

He throws a look back toward the restaurant, his anxious expression telling me that he knows exactly who he works for and the inherent danger of getting involved in whatever the fuck is going on next door.

"*Pozhaluysta…*" I say again. *Please…*

Lips pressed together, he gives a quick nod. With my arm slung around his shoulders, he hustles me out to his car, a tiny, battered Lada Niva, more rust than paint.

"*Ne samuyu blizkuyu,*" I beg him, curled up against the car door, my face throbbing, my arm feeling like it was dipped in gasoline and set ablaze. *Not the closest one.*

He nods, understanding.

He's young, maybe only sixteen or seventeen. Skinny, with curly dark hair and permanently wrinkled fingers from long shifts plunged in hot, soapy water.

He drives me to a small hospital in the Mitino district, dropping me off at the side entrance.

"*Skazhite im, chto eto blya avtomobil'naya avariya,*" he says. *Tell them it was a car accident.*

"*Spasibo.*" I push a wad of bills into his hand, almost everything I had left in my pocket.

He tries to refuse, but I close his fingers around the money and hold tight.

"*Pozhaluysta, nikomu ne govorite,*" I say. *Please don't tell anyone.*

The hospital hallway seems a hundred miles long. It's hard for me to draw a full breath.

I think, *This is how Houdini died, punched in the stomach by a boxer. Probably a boxer less mean than that motherfucker Cujo.*

I lean against the wall, arms clutching my sides, emptying the contents of my stomach on the freshly washed floors. The vomit is bright red.

He got me good, alright.

And I got him even better.

I hear a nurse shout something in Russian, but I don't understand it. All I see is the floor rushing toward me at lightning speed.

CHAPTER 44
ADRIK

THE NEWS OF AN EXPLOSION AT KRYSTIYAN'S LAB MAKES ME SICK with dread.

I race over there, even though Jasper is sure it's a trap.

The fire was definitely real. It destroyed the lab, the laundromat, and half of Yakim Dimka's restaurant before the trucks arrived.

I won't stop harassing the paramedics until they tell me the only two bodies carried out were male.

The relief that sweeps over me is more enervating than reassuring. It takes the strength out of my legs. I have to sit down.

"More of Sabrina's work?" Jasper mutters, surveying the wreckage of the buildings.

"Why would she burn the lab? Krystiyan was already dead. And who were the men in there with her?"

Jasper shrugs.

"Assistants?" he guesses.

The explanation comes the next day when we're summoned to the Bolshoi Theatre.

This is where the high table meets, or where they used to meet with regularity when they were at the height of their power. Now Ivan has abdicated, Abram Balakin retired, Danyl Kuznetsov is dead, and Savely Nika is in prison.

I'm not stupid enough to think that means they're impotent now.

Animals are most vicious when wounded.

Jasper accompanies me through the long tunnels beneath the theater in which the many ballerinas scurry back and forth, skinny to the point of emaciation in their tights and battered shoes, their hair scraped up into excruciating buns atop their heads. The air smells of wax and sweat and fresh paint from the stage sets.

Jasper is on edge, even though Yuri is meeting us here. He keeps reaching inside his jacket to touch the handle of his gun.

"Don't do that once we're upstairs," I warn him.

We take the elevator to the top floor.

The private suites have a view down to the stage—not that there's any performances this early in the afternoon. Perhaps a rehearsal. I doubt the *pakhany* pay attention either way. None of them are patrons of the arts, unless you count fucking the ballerinas.

Yuri Koslov is already inside the suite, spearing shrimp from a seafood tower with Foma Kushnir. Foma gives me a cold nod, which I return with even less enthusiasm. In the Petrovs' worst and lowest moment, Foma stormed our monastery and tried to kill my father. I'd like to take that shrimp prong and put it through his eye.

Yuri's lieutenant, Rafail Wasyl, sits against the window, watching the door. I don't acknowledge him at all.

Yakim Dimka is here, and Serafim Isidor. Also Nikolai Markov.

Markov is tall and dark-haired like his daughters. We eye each other warily. My deal with Neve fell through once Ilsa and Sabrina defected. No doubt Nikolai is aware his youngest daughter stole a king's ransom in raw materials from me. I'm curious to see what he'll say about it.

Serafim Isidor begins the meeting. Though there's no head of the Bratva, Serafim is the senior member of the high table, both in age and tenure. He's bald and barrel-chested, with a beak of a nose, cheekbones like hatchet strikes, and a mouth that turns down at the corners. Having sat with him in a sauna once, I know he's covered in tattoos from wrist to neck beneath his starched white shirt.

Without preamble, he fixes me with his dark, beady eyes, saying, "Are you sheltering Sabrina Gallo?"

This is not what I expected. I look at all the stony faces staring back at me before replying, "No."

"Were you aware that she destroyed Dimka's restaurant?"

"I heard there was a fire. How do you know it was Sabrina?"

"Employees saw her leaving through the restaurant after the explosion," Dimka says.

"Where is she now?" I demand eagerly.

"That's what we're asking you." Isidor scowls.

"Last I knew, she was with Ilsa Markov." I throw a look at Nikolai, who has remained silent and impassive.

"Ilsa returned home," Nikolai says. "She doesn't know where Sabrina Gallo has gone."

I don't like that at all.

While I felt a certain level of jealousy knowing Sabrina and Ilsa were together, at least I thought Ilsa would keep Sabrina safe. I'm irrationally angry hearing that she abandoned her instead.

Even though I was the one who lost Sabrina first.

Jasper is lurking around the buffet, listening to everything we say. He throws me a quizzical look. We're both wondering the same thing:

If Sabrina's not with Ilsa, where is she?

"Were you aware of the Gallos' history with the Bratva when you brought Sabrina here?" Foma Kushnir sneers.

"If Dean Yenin doesn't hold a grudge against them, I don't see why you would," I say to Foma coldly.

"Because they took our greatest prize," he hisses.

"Alexei Yenin made them pay."

"Not enough."

Serafim Isidor nods slowly, his expression pained. "There is no forgiving the loss of the Winter Diamond."

"That this girl even dares to show her face in our city is an outrage!" Foma cries. "She's disrupted our finest families." He gives Nikolai Markov an obsequious nod. "Stolen from the high table and destroyed our property!"

The fact that none of the wrongs in question were done to Foma himself doesn't lessen his vitriol. It's me he's here to attack, by proxy through Sabrina.

"You brought her here," he accuses me. "She's your responsibility."

"Yes, she is. And I'll deal with her."

"We're past that," Isidor says. "The high table has issued a bounty on her head. She left the restaurant injured. The *kachki* are searching the clinics and hospitals. They'll find her soon enough."

Jasper winces, partly for me and partly for Sabrina.

My hands are cold and sweating. I clench them into fists.

"Cujo was killed in the blast," Dimka says, eyeing me. "Lev Zakharov too. Do you still claim you weren't involved?"

"I didn't know any of this!" I snarl, almost angrier at that fact than anything else.

My stomach churns. If Cujo got his hands on Sabrina, I can only imagine the state she's in.

Isidor fixes me with his dark stare. "Don't test our patience any further, Adrik. Our decision is final: Sabrina Gallo is to be shot on sight. We'll send her head back to her father in a box, to remind him that the Bratva never forget."

I can feel Jasper's eyes on my back, begging me not to react, not to respond. It takes everything I have not to put my hands around the old man's throat.

Foma smirks. "Next time, choose your partners more carefully."

The shame that flushes through me at the word *partners* has nothing to do with Foma's sneer. It's the opposite—I'm not deserving of the word. I never treated Sabrina as a partner. Not really.

The meeting breaks up. I join Jasper by the buffet. He searches my face with his pale gaze.

Speaking low and quiet so we won't be overheard, he asks, "What are you going to do?"

"What the fuck can I do? If I try to protect her, I'll get us all killed. She doesn't want my help anyway. I told her to come home. She refused."

Jasper knows I'm stating the facts while everything within me revolts against them.

On the one hand, there's logic and necessity and the duty I owe to my men, on the other, my desperate need for Sabrina.

Jasper leans in close, his skeletal jaw clenched.

"When things look grim…be the grim reaper."

My guts go cold, wondering if he means what I think he means.

We're interrupted by my new partner.

"Better get going." Yuri smiles. "It's time for the pickup."

I stare at him blankly. In all the madness, I forgot we had a shipment coming in. One we desperately need after Sabrina robbed the last one.

"I'm on it," I say.

"We can drive together," Yuri replies. "I'm coming too."

CHAPTER 45
SABRINA

WHEN I WAKE IN THE HOSPITAL, THERE'S A MAN SITTING NEXT TO my bed. I startle so badly that I almost tear out my IV line before realizing it's my father.

He's sitting bent over, shoulders hunched, face exhausted. I've never seen such dark shadows under his eyes or the lines on his face so deep.

"Jesus, Dad," I croak. "You look worse than me."

"I seriously doubt it."

He's probably right. My right arm is bandaged from shoulder to elbow, three of the fingers splinted and taped. The left side of my face throbs with every heartbeat. My words come out mushy through cracked and swollen lips. I reek of blood and smoke and propane.

I only have to look in my dad's eyes to see that I'm a fucking mess. So destroyed that it hurts him.

I was his baby girl once. I sat on his lap and smooshed his cheeks with my hands and made him laugh.

It was so easy to make him happy then. So easy to be what he wanted me to be.

Now all I do is cause him pain.

Never one to mince words, my father gets right to the point: "The high table has put a bounty on your head."

"How much?" I say. "I don't like to think I come cheap."

His jaw shifts, anger flashing in his eyes. He's never appreciated my comedic timing.

"If I can find you, they can find you," he hisses. "We need to leave. Now."

"I'm not going anywhere. And I don't think you're gonna be able to carry me out of here."

"*Why?*" he cries, his voice anguished.

"I haven't seen it through to the end. I'm not coming home until I do."

"The end is your death. You're never coming home."

I shrug, even that small motion ripping at my side. I think my ribs are broken.

"I'm sorry, Dad. I really am. But you're the one person who can understand. It's not over until I'm satisfied."

He looks at me, his eyes burning in his face.

It's my own eyes staring back at me—full of all the same anger and frustration and longing for all the things you can never quite grasp.

Through time and change and circumstance, he's still the same Nero, deep down inside.

And I'm the same Sabrina.

He knows there's no way to make me leave. No way to convince me.

I'm stubborn and reckless, just like my dad. Born of his blood, for better and for worse.

"I brought you something," he says.

He reaches in his pocket, taking out a handkerchief wrapped around something hard.

He presses it into my palm.

When I open my hand, the silk handkerchief falls away like the petals of a flower, revealing the stone within.

It glitters even under the dull hospital lights, its facets reflecting infinitely like a hall of mirrors, as deeply blue as arctic ice.

The Winter Diamond.

"The Bratva believe it has power," my father says. "They treasure it over anything. If you go before the high table and beg for forgiveness…it may save your life."

My father sold this diamond twenty-five years ago. I can only imagine what it cost him to buy it back.

There's a lump in my throat as big as the stone. I can't speak around it.

All I can do is throw my arms around my dad, even though it's agony to press my swollen cheek against his shoulder.

I inhale his scent: bergamot, lava soap, and gasoline. All my favorite things.

"I love you, Dad. And I know how much you love me."

"More than anything," he says, cradling my head with his hand. "More than the whole world."

It's because he loves me, because he understands me, that he leaves me there.

He knows that what I want more than anything is the freedom to make my own choice.

When he's gone, the pain overwhelms me. My face is on fire, my arm even worse. Every breath stabs at my side.

The nurses offer morphine, but I won't take any more drugs. I can't dissociate. I need my mind clear.

I watch the sun setting though the tiny window in my curtained room. It fades quickly as storm clouds crowd in.

There're no walls, no privacy in this underfunded clinic. I can hear the patients on the other side of the curtains, groaning or asking the nurses for water. The beeps of the machines monitoring blood pressure and heart rate are ticking clocks, steadily counting down.

I wanted to rest as long as I could, but I hear a commotion at the end of the hall—two men, burly and broad-shouldered, with the look of athletes gone to seed. I spy them through the gaps in the curtain.

The one in front is Boris Kominsky; I recognize him from Apothecary. He barks something at the nurse, then gestures to his compatriot, who begins wrenching back the curtains, searching the hospital beds.

I don't know if Boris is here for the bounty or to avenge Cujo. I have no intention of waiting around to find out.

Peeling the tape off the crook of my arm, I grit my teeth and pull out the IV. I slap the tape back over the puncture before it can bleed down my arm, then slip out of the hospital bed.

My clothes are folded on an empty chair, still filthy and stinking of smoke. Tucking the bundle under my arm and carrying my boots, I sneak out the back of the ward.

The exit door has no alarm. I race down the staircase barefoot, my gown flapping open behind me.

I'm dizzy and reeling, delirious with pain.

I couldn't tell my father the real reason I stayed: I need to see Adrik one last time.

He won't be back from the delivery yet. I could go to the Den and wait for him.

I pull on my clothes in the alleyway and stuff my feet in my boots, shivering with cold now that the sun has gone down. The snow has melted, but Moscow is still far from warm.

Even this level of exertion wipes me out. I lean against the cinder block, waiting for the black spots to clear from my vision.

Leaving my hospital gown in a crumpled ball in the alley, I head out to the street so I can hail a cab.

A car stops at the curb, as delightfully ramshackle as all Moscow cabs seem to be.

I've barely opened the back door when I hear a shout. Boris Kominsky has stuck his head out the side door and caught sight of me. He comes sprinting down the street, arms pumping, monstrously fast. His fellow *kachki* is right behind him.

"*Idti, idti!*" I shout at the cab driver.

Russians know better than to hesitate when they're being chased. The cabbie stomps on the gas, pulling away from the curb.

To my dismay, Boris's car is parked only a block down. He turns and runs back to it, barely waiting for his friend to climb in the passenger seat before he speeds after me.

CHAPTER 46
ADRIK

THE PICKUP IS IN NEKRASOVKA, NOT FAR FROM WHERE SABRINA and I built our lab. We pass by the purse factory. It's too dark to see the blackened brick of the old brewery, but I spot the silver glimmer of the bullet-shaped trailer where Sabrina loved to eat. My stomach clenches as if I were hungry, though I know I'm not.

Jasper is driving. I'm in the passenger seat, Yuri and his lieutenant behind us.

Rafail Wasyl is former Kadyrovtsy, the paramilitary operatives who protect the head of the Chechen Republic. He kept the buzz cut and the cargo pants when he left service, as well as his extensive training in kidnapping, torture, and murder.

I'm surprised he doesn't work for his countryman Ismaal Elbrus. Maybe the rest of the Chechens hate him as much as the civilians he terrorized in his homeland.

He's nothing more than a mercenary, though an extremely effective one. I don't particularly like him sitting directly behind me. I keep an eye on him via the rearview mirror.

Rafail lounges in the back seat, the window lowered despite the clouds rolling in, so he can hang his arm over the sill. A rose gold AP glints on his wrist. It looks genuine. Even with how generously Yuri pays, that's an expensive toy.

Rafail sees me watching and gives me a smug smile.

"Glad to see the high table only gave you a slap on the wrist, Adrik," he says. "I'd hate to see you get in any serious trouble... especially over a woman."

Rafail's voice is higher and softer than you'd expect from someone so aggressively masculine.

"I wonder who slapped that new watch on *your* wrist?" I inquire. My comment is for Yuri. Telling him to open his fucking eyes. Rafail doesn't even blink.

"I'm well taken care of. If you didn't run your business with your dick, you could buy one for yourself."

Innocently, I ask, "Is that the one Serena Williams wears?"

Yuri doesn't like his lieutenant enough not to laugh.

"Excellent choice," Jasper says, pulling into the back lot of the warehouse. "People say she's the greatest living athlete."

That worked. Rafail fumes in the back seat, unable to deny that Serena Williams does indeed wear his same watch.

Male ego is our greatest weakness.

Jasper brings the SUV up the ramp, all the way inside the warehouse. We'll be packing the product in the trunk so Jasper can take it to the new lab.

The atmosphere in the warehouse is tense. There's ten men here in total, much more than you'd usually need for a delivery.

Soon we'll be thirteen, when Vlad and Andrei arrive with the driver. They rode their bikes out an hour along the route to bring the truck in safe, in case any more unwanted visitors were waiting.

The Wolfpack are armed to the teeth, wearing bulletproof vests despite their complaints of how uncomfortable they'd be. Yuri's men are likewise strapped. If any of Krystiyan's goons had the bright idea to rob us again, they're going to meet a whole lot more firepower than last time.

My men and Yuri's have separated into opposing camps, close enough for conversation but mostly talking to their own brothers in low tones. A few suspicious glances pass back and forth, and hands are close to triggers.

Each of us suspects the others of leaking the information about the first delivery. Yuri's men mistrust me because the supplies were stolen by my ex-girlfriend. I know it was one of them because my confidence in the Wolfpack is complete.

I really do think it was Rafail. He seems like the type of asshole who would have Krystiyan Kovalenko for a friend. While he's worked for Yuri a long time, I suspect his number one client is always himself.

Not that I'm so squeaky clean these days. Everyone knows my last supplier ended up dead, and I just murdered Krystiyan. I'm not to be trusted either.

The warehouse is dilapidated and freezing cold. Thunder rumbles through the holes in the roof.

"The driver better be on time," I mutter to Chief.

"He is," he assures me. "Andrei just texted. They'll be here in ten minutes."

That ten minutes feels like an hour. Rafail keeps roaming around the warehouse, which means I have to watch him constantly. I despise working with people I can't trust.

I came to Moscow for freedom and independence. Instead, I'm partnered with one of the last people I would have chosen, saddled with his even worse soldiers. All without making a dime in profit, because Sabrina has managed to royally fuck me again and again.

She was right—going head-to-head against her fucking sucks.

I always want you on my team…

Every word we spoke to each other haunts me. Her voice echoes in my head all day long.

I'm hollow and empty inside. Even if I start making money hand over fist, I already know I won't enjoy it. I haven't enjoyed anything since she left. I haven't been happy for one single minute.

That's not going to change. Sabrina will go home to Chicago, or she'll die here in Moscow. No matter how clever she is, how resourceful, she can't survive long with a price on her head.

I hope she goes home. No matter how much it would pain me, the alternative is so much worse.

Lightning flashes, illuminating the interior of the warehouse in garish brightness, highlighting the jumble of old crates and broken-down machinery piled around the room. The smell of ozone fills the air.

This place once took shipments of windows and doors. Dusty plates of glass are still stacked against one wall, sending ghostly reflections back at us whenever anyone walks past.

"They're almost here," Chief reports, having received another text.

Rafail slaps the large red button on the wall, raising the bay doors once more.

The wind whistles into the warehouse.

Headlights sweep the room ahead of the truck. It rumbles up the ramp, rocking side to side.

Vlad and Andrei leave their bikes outside, following the truck on foot.

"Safe and sound," Andrei says, pulling off his helmet, running a hand through his blond hair.

"I rode your bike over," Vlad tells me.

I asked him to because I wanted to go for a ride after this—before I knew how miserable the weather would turn.

Tough shit for me, I guess. I'm not sending Vlad home in the rain.

"That thing's a beast," he says. "I could barely hold on to it."

Pain stabs my chest, like it does a hundred times a day.

"Yeah. I know."

We've barely begun unloading the truck when lightning cracks, apparently opening a rip in the clouds. Freezing rain pours down, leaking through the roof onto our heads.

"Couldn't have found a warehouse with shingles?" Vlad grouses. Yuri hears him.

"How many warehouses do *you* own?" he sneers.

His organization is hierarchal. He dislikes when the Wolfpack even speak in his presence.

I clap Vlad on the shoulder. "We'll be done soon, brother. You're working fast."

This is as much for Yuri as for Vlad—a subtle fuck off.

Yuri rolls his eyes and walks away. He hasn't unloaded shit or done anything else useful. He's the worst kind of boss, barely present, allowing a slimeball like Rafail to speak and act in his name.

Vlad doubles his pace.

We've unloaded almost all the product when I hear the sound of tires in the back lot. I straighten up, motioning for Vlad and Andrei to flank the bay door. They obey at once, grabbing their rifles and taking up a position on either side of the opening.

A car door slams, followed by a spray of gravel as a second vehicle speeds in the lot. Rapid footsteps crunch against the rock as someone sprints toward the warehouse.

I pull my gun, barrel trained at the ramp.

I'm expecting Krystiyan's men or maybe the cops.

Instead, a girl bursts into the warehouse.

She looks around, wild-eyed, sweating and panting.

For a moment, I almost don't recognize Sabrina. The entire side of her face is a bruise so swollen and dark that I can barely see the slit of that eye. Her lower lip is double its normal size, with a nasty gash that's barely scabbed over. Her right arm is wrapped in bandages, the fingers splinted. Some of her hair is singed, the rest of it a matted mane around her head. Her clothes are filthy and burned—I can smell the smoke from here.

The sight of her injuries fills me with a rage so all-encompassing that the muzzle of my gun shakes.

If Cujo were still alive, I'd rip the flesh off his bones with pliers, piece by tiny piece.

Sabrina catches sight of me and goes still. She stands there, unmoving, hands limp at her sides.

No one quite understands what's happening until Boris Kominsky and Ippolit Moisey run up the ramp behind her.

Then Yuri hisses, "That's Sabrina Gallo."

Boris and Ippolit are equally surprised to meet a dozen guns pointed at their faces in what they must have hoped was an abandoned warehouse. They pause on the ramp, feet from their quarry but unable to take a step farther.

Rafail Wasyl waggles the barrel of his gun at the *kachki* like a ticking finger, saying in his high, thin voice, "Ah, ah, ah…this is our catch, boys."

He wants the bounty.

Boris and Ippolit are panting, red-faced, furious. They have guns of their own, but they're more than outnumbered.

"We found her first!" Boris snarls.

Rafail thumbs the safety off his Glock.

"You can leave now, or you can join Cujo in hell," he says softly.

Ippolit is already backing down the ramp. It's the realization that his friend is no longer behind him as much as the bevy of weaponry that convinces Boris to do the same.

We wait in silence until the engine growls to life and their car pulls away again.

Before anyone can act, I bellow, "Nobody fucking move!"

I step between Sabrina and all the men behind me, arms spread, trying to cover as much of her as I can.

Yuri's men are on my left, the Wolfpack on my right. I can feel them shifting and creeping around on both sides, Yuri's men so they can get behind Sabrina and trap her in the warehouse, mine so they can triangulate and cover me from as many angles as possible.

The tension is so high I'm afraid a single bolt of lightning will startle us all into firing. The rain pounds against the roof, leaking down in a dozen places. My fingers freeze around the handle of my gun.

"What are you doing?" Yuri hisses at me. "Shoot her."

Sabrina's eyes widen, even the one horribly swollen and bruised. Her lips part, but no sound comes out.

"Nobody move!" I repeat, throwing a swift and furious glance at Rafail, who's trying to creep up on my left side.

Vlad has his rifle pointed at Rafail's chest.

Still, Rafail smirks at me.

"You can't be serious."

I take another step forward until Sabrina and I are barely an arm's length apart. She looks up into my face, terrified and shaking.

"What are you doing here?" I whisper.

Her eyes dart around the room, to all the guns pointed directly at her.

So soft I can barely hear her, she says, "I just wanted to tell you... that I'm sorry."

Her eyes are huge and wet in her battered face. She blinks. Tears run down both cheeks, cold and silvery like the rain. It's the first time I've ever seen her cry.

I stare at her, mouth open, unable to believe what I'm seeing, what I'm hearing. Every sense is keyed to the highest pitch, my nerves so tight they feel like they'll snap. Any moment, I expect to catch a storm of bullets from both sides.

"I fucked up," she sobs. "And you don't love me anymore."

I've lied to Sabrina, misled her. But this is the one point on which I could never deceive her. "There is nothing you could do to make me stop loving you."

She closes her eyes, tears running down her face in a steady flow.

I'd give anything to pull her into my arms, but I can't move. If I even blink, someone could fire.

She looks up at me again, lips pressed together so tight that the split opens, red and raw. It doesn't matter how fucked up her face is—nothing in this world can take away her beauty. It shines out from within, a fire that can't be extinguished. Not even now.

"It's not enough, though," Sabrina says, her voice cracking. "If love was enough, then we would have made it."

Rafail stands directly to my left, halted by Vlad's rifle. Spiderlike in his dark suit, Yuri creeps around behind Sabrina instead. All of Yuri's men have their guns trained on my closest friends.

I point my Beretta at Sabrina's forehead, the barrel an inch from her skin. Her lips tremble, but she doesn't beg. She doesn't even flinch.

"I'm sorry it had to come to this," I say.

"I'm sorry too," she says. "For everything."

Yuri is behind her now, raising his gun.

I glance at Jasper on my right.

Jaw tight, he gives me the smallest of nods.

I take a deep breath and pull the trigger.

CHAPTER 47
SABRINA

I TRY TO KEEP MY EYES OPEN UNTIL THE END SO THE LAST THING I'll see is Adrik's face.

When his finger jerks the trigger, my lids slam shut without my consent.

The gun explodes louder than a cannon shot. I expect a burst of pain and sudden darkness. Instead, something huge slams into me and knocks me backward, my whole body enveloped in heat and mass and a scent that I know better than any other.

Adrik.

He's wrapped his arms around me and taken me to the ground, rolling me over and over as shot after shot fires all around us. Something rips at my arm, a jolt of heat and pain, and something else bites into my calf.

Adrik drags me behind a stack of crates, shoving his gun in my hand.

Without a word, I position myself at the edge of the crates and start firing.

The warehouse is utter chaos. Bullets rip across the room from all angles, tearing chunks of wood out of the crates, ricocheting off the truck, the SUV, and the rusted old forklifts.

The dusty glass panes stacked against the wall shatter, raining broken glass everywhere. Thunder confuses the sound of gunfire, and flashes of lightning blind us all.

Vlad is closest to us. He rips a handgun from his belt and throws it to Adrik before turning his rifle on Yuri's men, firing shot after shot. A bullet rips into his thigh. He drops to one knee and keeps shooting, teeth gritted, sweat running down his face, mingling with the rain.

It's hard to tell where anyone is hiding in the jumble of equipment. Hard to tell who's even on our side.

The driver of the truck pops his head up, and I almost shoot him before seeing his terrified expression as he dives back down on the floorboards, hands cradled behind his head.

I see Yuri's body sprawled like a rag doll on the ramp. That's when I realize Adrik fired over my shoulder, hitting his partner in the face.

The Wolfpack are wearing vests. Most of Yuri's men are not, except the one dressed in military gear. He changes positions like a trained soldier, his aim terrifyingly good. Hakim pokes his head around the trunk of the SUV for a fraction of a second, and the soldier nails him in the shoulder. Hakim drops to the ground.

Andrei roars with rage, emptying his clip at the soldier, only to take a bullet in the center of his vest, knocking him backward. Lucky for him—the next shot from the soldier's gun whistles through the air right where his face would have been.

I follow the soldier's movement with the barrel of Adrik's gun, ignoring the hectic flashes of lightning and the freezing rain pouring down from the roof. Adrik fires at him too, missing as the man ducks under cover.

The soldier pops up to let out three shots, then drops down again. His technique is flawless. I can't get a bead on him. He's strategic and unpredictable.

The rest of Yuri's men are dropping, less coordinated than the Wolfpack and lacking the protection of vests. There's only two left: one barricaded behind the old forklift and the soldier now positioned behind the wheel of the truck. The driver is smart enough to stay hunkered down on the floorboards. In the brief spaces between thunder and gunfire, I hear him whimpering.

Jasper clambers in the front seat of the SUV. He floors the pedal, slamming into the forklift, pushing it back with so much force that Yuri's goon is crushed against the wall. Reversing with squealing tires and crunching metal, the front bumper pulling away, Jasper leans out the window and shouts to Andrei, "Get in!"

Andrei hauls Hakim into the back seat. Hakim is pale and reeling, blood pouring down his arm. Chief helps Vlad into the other side, Vlad limping and leaning heavily, his beefy arm slung around Chief's shoulders.

As Vlad climbs into the back seat, the soldier fires a shot at his head that pings off the car door an inch from his ear.

Adrik fires at him furiously. The soldier ducks back into the wheel well.

He's between us and the SUV. We can't get past him. We can't seem to shoot him either, the slippery motherfucker.

"Go out through the bay door!" Adrik barks at me. "I'll cover you!"

"But—"

"Go!" he roars.

Staying as low as I can, I sprint for the bay door. Adrik provides cover fire as I run for the exit. Still, I hear a bullet zing overhead as I drop down off the side of the ramp.

I'm out, but Adrik is still trapped.

"Chief!" I scream.

Chief unrolls the back window of the SUV, propping Vlad's AR on the sill. He fires a steady stream of bullets at the truck's back tire, puncturing it so the tail sags down.

Adrik runs for the bay door, dropping and skidding down the ramp like he's sliding into home plate.

He grabs my arm and drags me toward his bike.

I hesitate for just a fraction of a second.

"Are you fucking kidding me?" Adrik bellows.

"I'm doing it!" I cry, swinging my leg over the bike, sitting with my back against the handlebars.

Adrik understands. He gets on the bike, revving the engine, his arms on either side of my waist. I point my gun back over his shoulder.

Yuri's last, most indefatigable soldier appears in the doorway, a black silhouette against the lightning flash.

I'm waiting for him.

He crouches at the head of the ramp, protected by his vest. The rifle at his shoulder points at Adrik's back.

Headshots only...

Exhaling softly, I squeeze the trigger.

The shot hits him dead between the eyes. He tumbles backward, his rifle slipping through boneless fingers, clattering down the ramp.

Adrik peels out of the lot.

I cling to his neck, his heart pounding against mine.

Riding backward is fucking bonkers. The balance is opposite, the road racing away behind me disorienting. All I can do is put my arms around Adrik's waist and my head against his chest, holding on tight.

The rain pounds down on us, heavier than ever. I don't know where Adrik is going—only that we can't ride far in this weather. I can't see in front of us. I don't even know if he's following the SUV.

After only a minute or two, he makes a sharp turn, then pulls to a halt in the narrow space between a silver bullet trailer and a filthy brick wall.

I sit up, looking in his face for the first time.

We stare at each other, water running down our faces, shivering, freezing.

Then Adrik seizes my face in his hands and kisses me.

The pain is excruciating. My lip bleeds everywhere. My jaw aches.

Still I kiss him and kiss him, taking in as much of him as I can.

I want his taste and his scent. I'm desperate for it in the drowning rain.

I kiss him like I'll never get enough. I know I never will.

His hands are all over my body, as warm and strong as they've ever been. When he reaches a part that's too painful, I cry out, and he tries to touch me gently, but it's impossible. We've been apart too long.

We don't stop until I realize he's bleeding all down his side.

"You were hit!" I cry.

"So were you."

He points to the deep groove on my left arm.

"It grazed me." I try to peer at the wound through the blood and rain. "Or it went right through."

I remember the bite on my calf and examine that too, but it proves to be only a pencil-thick splinter of wood kicked up from the floor. Adrik pulls it out.

"We'd better go inside," he says. "Before we fucking freeze."

We limp into the trailer, the steps creaking beneath our combined weight.

Jasper, Vlad, Andrei, Hakim, and Chief are already inside.

Once we're up the steps, Misha slams the door behind us and locks it. She turns off the neon sign and most of the interior lights, plunging us into a cozy darkness illuminated only by the lamp over Alla's prep station and the soft golden glow of the jukebox in the corner.

Vlad has ripped the sleeve off his shirt to make a tourniquet around his thigh. He's sitting in a vinyl booth, eating a plate of Alla's fries, ignoring the small puddle of blood around his boot.

Andrei and Alla are fussing over Hakim, who sits at the counter so Alla can examine his shoulder. She clicks her tongue in dismay, trying to roll the sleeve of his shirt up over his shoulder without hurting him. She dyed her hair bright green since the last time I saw her. It suits her.

When she goes hunting for a first aid kit, Hakim throws me the delighted grin of a little kid at his first birthday party. He resumes his expression of pained anguish as soon as Alla reemerges.

Chief sits down beside Misha and starts leafing through her science textbooks, asking her questions so complicated that I can't understand either of them.

Adrik and I sink into Jasper's booth. Jasper regards me wryly, the bones on his knuckles resting against the tattooed molars and mandible on his jaw.

"So you're back," he says.

"Yeah. Is that okay?"

"God, I hope so," he says, jerking his head at Adrik. "He's been a fucking mess without you."

"Have you?" I say, turning to Adrik. "You looked so hot when you showed up at Krystiyan's house. It made me feel like shit."

"I was dying inside, believe me."

"So was I." I take his hand and press his knuckles to my swollen lips. "Every fucking day."

Adrik looks at my bruised face. His expression is so murderous that it sends a chill down my back.

"Cujo's lucky he's dead," he snarls. Then, shaking his head, "How the fuck did you manage that anyway?"

"Oh, it was so rad." I try to grin without splitting my lip again. "I wish you could have seen it. I was like, *da svidaniya, bitch!* And I blew him up."

"You didn't really say that, did you?" Jasper says, looking supremely disappointed in me.

"No," I admit, disappointed in myself. "I wish I did."

Adrik slides out of the booth, limping over to the jukebox with his hand pressed to his side. He feeds in a couple of coins, then scrolls down the list with his finger before making his selection, "Anyone Who Knows What Love Is" by Irma Thomas.

The music fills the tiny trailer, light and silvery and wistful.

Adrik holds out his hand to me.

I join him on the checkered tiles, my arms around his neck, his hands gripping my hips. We're both so beat up that we can't really dance. All we can do is sway.

I lay my head against his chest and listen to his heart beating, low and steady, beneath the music.

Chief and Misha join Vlad so they can eat some of his fries. He pulls the plate away at first, then relents and pushes it closer.

Jasper leans his head against the window, eyes closed, expression peaceful.

Hakim says something that makes Alla laugh. She leans across the counter to brush his curls back from his forehead with the palm of her hand.

Adrik and I sway together, his heat radiating into me, making me truly warm as nothing else can. He kisses the top of my head, then rests his cheek there, his arms wrapped tightly around me.

"Did you think about shooting me?" I ask him.

"Not for a second."

"Not even half a second? After everything I did?"

He looks down at me and slowly shakes his head.

"It really didn't matter what you did. I can't not have you."

The rain beats down on the metal roof of the trailer, turning all the world outside the windows to a watery blur.

Nothing exists outside of us.

> *The world*
> *May think I'm foolish.*
> *They can't see you*
> *Like I can.*
> *Oh, but anyone who knows what love is*
> *Will understand.*

I lay my head against his chest again, hearing that steady beat of his heart.

Softly, so softly that I don't know if he'll hear me, I say, "Thank you for forgiving me."

"I'll always forgive you, baby girl. Just don't leave me again."

"I won't. I can't."

The rain drips down off our clothes, and blood too. Soon there's a pool around our feet, threads of scarlet diffusing across the white and black tiles. Our boots squelch in the puddles.

Our bodies ache, and our heads spin. I've never been in more pain.

Yet I'm happy.

So happy I could die.

EPILOGUE
SABRINA

TWO MONTHS LATER

In the month after the shootout, it felt like everyone in Moscow wanted to kill us. The high table was in a fury, the *kachki* wanted revenge for Cujo, and even Krystiyan Kovalenko had a cousin or two who liked him enough to care that Adrik cut his throat.

Even with the Wolfpack standing by us and Adrik's family backing us up, we would have been in serious shit. It was the Winter Diamond that saved us.

My father was right—the high table's obsession with Russia's most beautiful gem borders on the superstitious. Serafim Isidor seemed to believe that the Bratva had suffered nothing but bad luck since they lost it. He was willing to agree to almost anything to get it back.

My dad came to Moscow to broker the deal and to make amends to the Bratva in person. He can be very charming when he wants to be. After three hours of negotiations, Isidor was placated enough to apologize in turn for Alexei Yenin's betrayal of the blood oath.

My dad stayed afterward to take Adrik and me out for dinner. I think Adrik was nervous—he hadn't seen my father since their car ride together, and the last time my dad saw me, I wasn't exactly at my best.

I arrived at the restaurant shining like a star in a brand-new dress, hair glossy, face immaculate, not a bruise to be seen. I hung on Adrik's arm, overflowing with happiness to have two of my favorite people at a table together.

My father looked more than relieved when he saw me. We talked all through dinner. I could tell he was impressed with Adrik's descriptions of our supply chain and distribution models. When he found out Adrik plays chess, that was almost enough to make him smile. In time, he might accept that I really do love Moscow—maybe even more than Chicago.

The diamond wasn't the only price to wipe our slate clean. Adrik and I have to pay the Koslov family an outrageous percentage of our earnings for the next two years. Since Molniya and the rest of the lineup continue to earn money faster than we could ever spend it, it's not the worst deal in the world.

It helped that Nikolai Markov supported us. Isidor cares what he thinks much more than Foma Kushnir, who flatly refused to vote in our favor. Ilsa probably put in a good word with her dad, or Nikolai simply realized how profitable it would be to renew his contract for our pills.

Ilsa comes to see me weekly to pick up fresh product. She hasn't quite resigned herself to Simon, but she and Neve are as close as ever.

The *kachki* still hate us, not that they have the pull to do much about it. As long as we stay away from their favorite gym, we should be fine.

Krystiyan's relatives likewise hold a grudge. The Petrovs and the Malina already loathed each other, so that's basically status quo.

You're always going to have enemies in our world. All you can do is make it lucrative for people to keep you alive and dangerous for them to kill you.

Hakim and I abandoned Yuri Koslov's lab and returned to the

old brewery. It took a shit ton of effort to make it operational again, but with all the hours we work, it's the only way he can see Alla as often as he likes. He brings her lunch from her favorite places so she doesn't have to cook any more than necessary.

He didn't give me too much shit about burning the lab. All the Wolfpack were more forgiving than I feared, even Vlad. They only had one stipulation.

"It's time for you to get your patch," Jasper says.

I groan, even though I knew this was coming.

I've always liked tattoos but never felt sure I could commit to one on myself. Even though the idea of stamping my arm with the Petrov wolf is not as anathema as it once was, I can't say I'm thrilled about the idea.

"You better take me someplace good," I say. "I don't want hepatitis from some rusty Russian needle."

"Don't worry," Andrei assures me. "Gasley's has the highest standards. They lick the needle clean between every client."

Despite Andrei's best efforts to wind me up, the tattoo parlor is perfectly welcoming. It's located in a neat brick building on Main Street, a large skylight flooding the room with sunshine and cheerful orange tiles on the floor.

I relax a little more when I meet the artist, Jaromira, who has shiny black hair down to her waist and sleeves of beautiful black roses on both arms. She shows me examples of her work, all fine lines and delicate shading.

"All right," I sigh, situating myself on her chair. "I'm ready."

The Wolfpack has come along to watch me take my licks. They rib me and offer sips of vodka from Vlad's flask.

"Try not to cry," Hakim says.

"I never cry," I say scornfully.

"Never," Adrik agrees, giving me a sideways smile.

My cheeks get hot, but I smile back at him, not really minding that he saw me in my lowest and most desperate moment. It was his too. We were both drowning, and we both pulled each other out.

I can't watch when Jaromira sets her buzzing needle against my arm. I thought it would feel like punctures, being stabbed again and again, but really it's more like someone drawing on you with a sharp pen.

After a while, the endorphins kick in. It's almost pleasant. The sunshine is warm, the buzzing soothing.

I lay my head against the rest on the chair, listening to Jaromira's excellent selection of Russian chansons. Much like the Mexican ballads that detail the exploits of drug cartels, chansons are songs about the underworld.

The more vodka Vlad drinks, the more he wants to sing along. His voice is low and gruff but not unpleasant.

"Go ahead," Jaromira encourages him. "It keeps me entertained."

Chief peppers Jaromira with questions about the internal mechanisms of the tattoo gun.

"I didn't build it," she laughs. "I just use it."

"How you holding up?" Adrik asks me. He's sitting directly across from me, backward on his chair with his arms folded over the seat rest. His hair is dark and shaggy around his face, his blue eyes bright under the skylight. Now that summer is coming, his tan is deepening again.

"I can barely feel it," I say, though in truth it's starting to sting now that Jaromira has finished the line work and moved on to the shading. Each pass of the needle bites a little deeper.

I haven't looked at her work. I already know what the tattoo will look like. It's staring at me from six muscular arms all around me—a black wolf, its mouth half-open in a snarl. I could probably draw it in my sleep from all the times I've traced Adrik's tattoo with my finger.

When Jaromira finally finishes, the Wolfpack crowds around to see.

"It's official," Jasper grins.

I try to feel excitement as Jaromira positions me in front of the mirror, wiping the soap off my arm with a soft cloth.

As the rag swipes down, it reveals not a black wolf but an orange tiger. The tiger prowls up my arm, long and sleek and graceful. Like the wolf, its teeth are bared in a furious snarl.

The Wolfpack laughs at the look on my face, Adrik more than anyone.

"Do you like it?" he says.

"I...I love it."

I really do.

Adrik tilts my chin up and kisses me.

"You're one of us," he says. "But you're still you. You don't have to give up your identity. Just be with me."

"Always." I kiss him back.

"Enough of that," Andrei says. "Let's go celebrate."

***

ADRIK

TWO YEARS LATER

One of the first things I did after I got Sabrina back was call Ivan on the phone and ask him how I could make sure I didn't fuck it all up again.

I asked him who was ultimately in charge of his business—him or Sloane?

Ivan didn't hesitate.

"Both of us."

"But who makes the decisions?"

"Sometimes me, sometimes her. She probably makes sixty percent, even seventy. She's smarter than me, you know."

I laughed. "I'm afraid that might be true of Sabrina. It's not so easy, though. I don't know how to put someone else's judgment over my own. I never have."

Ivan grunted on the other end of the line—a sympathetic sound.

"The best thing is to make your decisions together."

"But what if she's wrong?"

"There is no right and wrong. There's being on one side together or being separated. I choose to be with Sloane and her with me. Always."

That sent a shiver down my spine. It's what I wanted too, desperately.

"When will I get a wedding invitation?" Ivan asked me.

I groaned. "Fuck if I know. That's one of our points of conflict."

"Well," Ivan said, "it's best to agree, but sometimes a little trickery is allowed."

I was more than familiar with the bet Ivan made with Sloane to hoodwink her into marrying him. I preferred not to stoop to chicanery to secure Sabrina, but I wasn't ruling it out if her resistance continued.

It took two long years to convince her to marry me. It wasn't that she didn't want to—or at least I don't think that was it.

If I had to guess, the real reason is that the things that matter deeply to her are the only things that scare her. She's afraid to fail when it matters most.

Plus, she has an instinctive distrust of anything conventional.

I promised her the ceremony could be anything she liked.

"You don't have to wear a puffy white dress or stand in a church. Just promise to be with me, and make it legal so it's harder for you to get away."

She laughed. Then, with more seriousness, she said, "Will it make you happy?"

"More than anything."

"Then I'll do it."

SABRINA

THE MORNING OF MY WEDDING DAY, I WAKE UP TERRIFIED.

It's not that I don't want to be with Adrik. I'm more head over heels obsessed with him than I've ever been. And we've been living and working together for over two years now, so it's not like there's any big surprises of what he's really like.

I guess it's the thought of me as a wife that scares me. I never saw myself that way, and I don't know exactly what it means or how I'm supposed to be.

Adrik and I weren't planning to see each other until we meet at the venue.

I text him at 6:20 in the morning, saying:

Sabrina: Are you awake?

He responds a moment later:

Adrik: I am now...
Sabrina: Sorry.
Adrik: Don't be sorry. What do you need, baby girl?
Sabrina: I need to see you.

He picks me up from my parents' house thirty minutes later, driving a rental car. Just the sight of him calms me down immensely. We drive out to the Morton Arboretum so we can take a walk on the forest trails.

I'm still wearing the shorts and T-shirt I slept in, hair up in a messy ponytail. Adrik has on a crisp white tee that shows how tanned he's gotten now that it's fully summertime. His hair is the longest it's been in a while, black and shaggy. When he runs his hands through it, it makes dramatic shapes: a wave swooping down over one eye or two curtains on either side of his face.

He crosses the loamy paths with long, rangy strides. I have to walk quickly to keep up with him, which is the pace I prefer. The pine trees surround us like hundreds of pillars holding up the pale blue vault of the sky. The air smells damp and fresh, still cool before the heat of the day.

We're alone save for the birds in the trees.

The stillness of this place makes me peaceful.

Adrik is right at home. He's always seemed more animal than man. It's the way he moves—graceful, natural, seemingly without effort. The way those narrow blue eyes flick to a wren on a branch or a garter snake disappearing under the brush. And most of all, the way he seizes me and presses his face against the side of my neck, inhaling my scent deeply.

He's never ashamed of what his body wants.

My body wants him, all the time—his breath, his touch, his proximity. The week he's spent at the hotel with his family while I'm at home with mine has been fucking with me. It was nice to sleep in my old bed one last time, but I miss his weight and his warmth curled around me in the night. I miss waking up with his mouth between my thighs. This is why I'm on edge—I haven't had those constant daily contacts that mellow me out.

He holds my hand now, his fingers interlocked with mine.

"Are you having second thoughts?" he asks me.

"No."

"What is it, then?"

"It's just…I don't ever want you to feel trapped. I want us to be together because we want to be together, not because we signed something. And…I don't want to disappoint you." I hesitate, pausing on the path, not quite looking at him. "If I'm not the wife you thought I would be."

He laughs softly.

"Sabrina, I want to be married to you because that's what fits how I feel about you. Calling you my girlfriend is fucking ludicrous. You're the other half of me. I couldn't leave you any more than I could cut myself in two."

"And what about the other part?"

"You think I want some traditional wife? When have you ever been conventional? I want you exactly the way you are and however you'll be in the future. I don't have expectations for you. It's the surprises I love. You always surpass what I could imagine."

I let out the breath I was holding.

"Okay. I don't know why I'm so stressed. Maybe 'cause I haven't seen you enough this week. I'm never unhappy when we're together. When we're separated, I fall apart."

"I know," he says, cupping my face in his hand. "I feel the same."

He bends his head to kiss me.

The towering pines are the pillars of a cathedral. The light falls down in green shafts as if it passed through colored glass. This is our chapel. This is our real wedding, right here, right now. Just the two of us.

Adrik lies me down on the damp moss that smells of everything living and growing all around us.

He undresses me slowly, kissing each part of my body as he lays it bare. My lips, the hollow of my throat, my breasts, my belly. He turns over my hand and presses his mouth against my palm.

He slips off my shorts and underwear until I'm entirely nude. The bits of sun that make it through the canopy of leaves float like flecks of gold on my skin. He runs his tongue across the sun-warmed patches on my thighs.

Gently, he slips one finger inside me, then raises it to his mouth to taste me.

He lets out a sigh. "My favorite thing in the world."

I kiss him to taste myself on his lips. It's warm and musky sweet, like the bark on the ground.

He lies on his stomach, cupping my ass in his hands, lifting my pussy up to his mouth. He runs his tongue slowly up between my pussy lips, soft and wet and warm, pausing at the top to suck gently, ever so gently, on my clit.

He listens to my moans. He watches my face. He worships my pussy with his mouth, treating it like the most delicate, the most sensitive, the most precious thing in the world.

He's relaxing me, soothing me. Knowing this is what I need, this connection, this relief.

The pleasure rolls over me in waves, as warm as the sunshine, as sweet as the ferns and moss and grass all around us.

I look up at the sky through the lacework of branches, coming slowly with a sound like a sigh.

Adrik sets my hips down, then places his hands on either side of me, looking down into my face as he slides his cock inside me. I'm wet and swollen and extremely sensitive. I squirm under him, barely able to stand it.

He pillows my head on his arm, cradling me, thrusting into me slow and deep.

"Tell me you love me," he says.

"I love you so much it hurts."

"Tell me you'll *always* love me."

"I couldn't stop if I wanted to."

"I'll make you happy," he says. "You don't have to be afraid."

"I'm never afraid when I'm with you."

His arm tightens, pulling my head against his shoulder. His body is tight and immensely strong on top of me. Every muscle contracts as he thrusts deeper and harder, driving his cock all the way inside.

"You're everything to me," he groans. "My whole entire world…"

"*Ya tebya lyublyu, Adrichek,*" I whisper. *I love you, Adrik.*

He comes as deep as he can, then relaxes, pressing me into the ground. His body is heavy, warm, and spent.

We lie there, breathing in the same cadence, our hearts beating at the same time.

The wedding will take place on the lakeshore right at sunset.

We kept the guest list as small as possible—just the people who love us most.

I dress in the small bridal suite close to where we'll eat after the ceremony, the tables bearing garlands of fresh ranunculus and olive leaves, covered over by canopies of gauzy white muslin that float in the breeze off the lake.

My mom finds a minute wrinkle on the skirt of my dress and takes it into the back room to steam.

Sloane pokes her head in while I'm sitting at the vanity in my crinoline and bra.

"Come in, come in!" I call to her.

"I don't want to interrupt you—"

"You're not!"

She joins me at the vanity, sinking down on a ruffled pink pouf that could not be more incongruous to Sloane's style.

Her dress is sleek and simple, her dark hair parted on the side and pinned with a bronze clip. The green of her dress pulls out the same color in her hazel eyes.

She takes my hand and squeezes it, smiling at me. Her fingers are strong like my mom's—both capable women who work with their hands.

"I brought you something," she says. "Not for today, just for you to have."

She holds out a little box to me, the velvet patchy and worn.

I open it up.

Nestled inside is a pair of garnet earrings, as rich and dark as pomegranate.

I lift one of the earrings. It dangles from my fingers like a teardrop, heavy and glimmering.

"They're so beautiful," I breathe.

"They belonged to Dom and Ivan's great-grandmother. Ivan gave them to me a long time ago. I thought you should have them now."

Sloane and I have grown closer over the last two years. She's visited us several times in Moscow. When Adrik and I go to Cannon Beach, we play *Halo* on teams—me and Sloane against Adrik and Zima.

Still, this is far beyond anything I would have expected.

I don't quite have the nerve to hug her. All I can say is, "Thank you. I'll treasure them."

Sloane looks at me in the way she has, as if she can see right inside me.

"You impress me," she says.

I let out a nervous laugh. "Never thought I'd hear you say that."

Sloane smiles too. "You figured your shit out faster than I did. I was in my thirties when I met Ivan. You're so young, you have your whole life ahead of you. Just remember, you need Adrik, and he needs you. Whenever I feel the impulse to be alone, I remind myself to draw back to Ivan. I'm always happier when we're in sync. Stay connected. You're both stronger together."

"I'll try," I say. "I'll really try."

She presses my hand before letting go.

"Thank you, Sloane," I say again.

Her smile has a little more mischief in it now. "When you get back from your honeymoon, we should play *Halo* head-to-head. I just hit Diamond rank."

"Oh my god," I laugh. "I'm scared...but excited."

"That's my favorite feeling."

"Me too."

She leaves me to finish getting ready. I did my own hair and makeup—I wanted to look like myself. My hair is loose in big curls down my back. I take off the earrings I was going to wear and put on the ones Sloane gave me instead. They're perfect for my dress, but I would have worn them either way.

My mom returns a few minutes later, the gown laid carefully over her arm.

"I fixed it," she says.

She's smiling with all the same joy I feel when I get something to work.

She's not wearing makeup at all, her hair center-parted and pulled back in a low bun at the base of her neck. Her dress is cotton, a pale lilac color. She looks like someone Frida Kahlo would have painted or dated. Her smile fills me with warmth.

"Thanks, Mom."

She sits down where Sloane was just a minute before, her knees pressing against mine.

"Congratulations, baby. There's never been a more beautiful bride."

I twist the skirt of my crinoline in my hands.

"Thanks, Mom. I know this isn't really what you wanted for me..."

My mom has never loved the criminal life. She fell in love with my father, and she accepts him for all that he is, but this isn't the future she would have picked for me.

She looks in my eyes, tucking an errant curl behind my ear.

"Oh, baby, you're so wrong. This is everything I ever dreamed for you."

Her dark eyes are fixed on mine, clear and honest, yet I can't quite believe her.

"How can that be?"

"My greatest fear for you was that you were never going to find love. I see you looking at Adrik like I look at your dad, and that tells me how happy you'll be."

"Really?"

My mom nods. "I knew your dad a long time before he even noticed I existed. I remember what he was like before we met, and *that's* what I never wanted for you. You are so like your dad...I worried that you would never find your equal. I'm so glad that you did and so glad that I'm here to see it."

Relief washes over me. When I went to Moscow, I don't think anybody besides Adrik and me thought it was a good idea. It feels so much better to have the support of the people I respect the most.

"I'm sorry we never finished the bike."

We'd been working on that old Indian motorcycle for ages. Like the ship of Theseus, I don't think there was an original part left on it.

"Actually..." My mom smiles. "I have a surprise for you."

"What?" I'm not ready to believe what I think she's about to say.

"When you first left, I was worried about you. I had a lot of sleepless nights. I spent them in the garage working."

I wince, full of guilt for everything I've put her through. Starting at about three years old and continuing through the present.

"Sorry, Mom."

She touches my cheek, her hand soft and cool.

"You've always had to go your own way."

Unable to stay depressed for long, I grin and say, "You really finished it?"

"It runs perfectly. You should take it back with you."

For only the second time I can remember, I'm crying. I don't deserve to be loved like this. But I am. I'm truly, truly loved.

It doesn't oppress me. It doesn't make me feel like I owe something I can't possibly repay. I just feel so fucking grateful.

My mom helps me zip up my dress.

I fix my makeup one last time, and we stand by the door, her arm around my waist, my head resting on hers.

"You ready?" she says.

"Yeah. I'm ready."

ADRIK

I wait on the sand for Sabrina.

The sun is just beginning to sink down to the lake, the sky rich with every shade of scarlet and orange above the dark blue water.

Jasper, Kade, and Sabrina's brother, Damien, are standing up with me. Damien strongly resembles Sabrina, something that endeared him to me at once. He's smart like her, and I suspect he shares her wicked streak, though he hides it better.

Nix, Cara, and Ilsa are the bridesmaids, barefoot and dressed in gauzy light gowns. They look like naiads, like they might have just come up from the water and taken human form on the sand.

The waves roll in gently, the breeze soft against my skin.

Everything is perfect. Or it will be when my bride appears.

I watch for her, anxious, shifting in place.

I see her the moment she steps out of the bridal suite. She crosses the grass, her mother helping to carry the train of her gown.

The closer she gets, the harder it is to look at her. The evening light bathes her skin, illuminating every inch of her until she shines like burnished bronze. Her gown is deep crimson, vibrant and alive.

She's so stunning that I can't believe she belongs to me. I can't even believe she's real.

She walks toward me. For the first time in my life, I'm nervous, hands shaking, legs weak.

Then she smiles at me, and everything is right again.

I hold out my hand to her.

She slips her fingers into mine, standing close beside me, holding on tight.

My father performs the ceremony. It's brief and honest—no religion, no tradition, no rote words.

Sabrina and I say our vows to each other:

"I'll always protect you," I promise. "I'll always trust you. I'll always support you. I'll believe in you, and anything you want, I'll make it happen. You have my heart forever. You have all of me, all that I am."

"I'll love you forever," Sabrina says. "You and no one else. I'll stand by you, no matter what happens. I'll be your partner and your best friend."

The sun is at the waterline, sending out one last brilliant slice of light that dazzles on the waves.

I take Sabrina's face in my hands, and I kiss her, her skin warm and golden and bright.

She tastes of salt and smoke and sweetness. She is everything I want and everything I love.

When we break apart, she still clings to me, looking up in my eyes.

"You were right," she whispers. "This is better. This is the best."

CHAPTER 1

SADIE SPARROW

PopPop escaped Hill House again. Now he's roving the vineyard in a moldy velvet robe and a set of pink floral gardening clogs.

I can tell he's wearing the clogs because of the hoof-like footprints they leave in the dirt. I'm trailing those prints through the valleys of soft, dark earth between the grapevines. Unfortunately, I can't yet hear the *flip-flop* of the clogs, which means I'm not close.

But I know he's out here. Lost in the labyrinth that exists mostly in his head…

So it's the worst possible moment to round the corner and find Monroe Beaumont instead.

"Shit!" I squeak, glancing wildly around. *No PopPop, thank god.* "What are you doing here?"

Monroe Beaumont: last seen three years ago drinking out of the Grady Cup, a puck bunny under each arm, celebrating the winning slap-shot of the college championships.

The next morning, still drunk, he spun donuts on the campus lawn and crashed his truck into the statue of Abraham Lincoln.

I'm pretty sure that got him expelled. I can't be certain, because I dropped out of that same adorable little liberal arts college just two weeks later. My reasons were a lot more prosaic: I suck at art, and I wasn't getting any better.

Monroe's still got the hockey hair, black and shaggy, covering his ears. And the tattoos—can't get rid of those; they've only grown more numerous, sprawling down both arms. He's still got the scruff, and those bright blue eyes, and the smile that you'd think was charming. If you didn't know him at all.

"Sadie, Sadie…" He clucks his tongue, shaking his head at me. "It's almost like you forgot this place is as much mine as yours."

I really hate when he points that out.

Unfortunately…it's true.

The Sparrows and the Beaumonts have a long and twisted history that goes back way before Monroe or I were born. But those long-ago events shape every interaction we've ever had. Including this one.

I'm darting glances to the side, no longer looking for PopPop but praying he'll stay hidden. The worst possible thing would be for Monroe to see him—it could ruin everything.

But Monroe, despite cosplaying as a big, dumb jock, is inconveniently clever.

"What are *you* doing out here?" he says, blue eyes narrowing and closely tracking mine.

I lift my nose in the air, trying to sound haughty. "I live here."

Monroe's snort punctures my pretentions. "Since when? I thought you moved to the city, big-city girl."

I know how small our social circles are, and how incestuously linked. But it still makes me flush, this feeling of being watched by him from a distance.

Because if he's been watching…he's been watching me screw up. Over and over again.

I lift my chin a little higher, trying to sound proud instead of humiliated. "I came back."

"I can see that." Monroe raises a thick, black eyebrow, letting his gaze roam down my frame. That's when I remember that my outfit is only slightly less unhinged than what PopPop is wearing.

I was stomping grapes when I heard he got loose. My skirt is still knotted up around my thighs like a diaper, both legs dipped in purple like I've been dancing in dye. Oh, and my hair's a sweaty mess.

"You look great," Monroe says, grinning.

I roll my eyes. "I look like walking death."

"And *is* that the blood of the battlefield spattered all over your legs?" Monroe inquires politely. "Or did you curb-stomp a squid?"

I give him a long, measured look. "I can never tell if you're just pretending to be stupid."

Monroe recoils in pretend horror, hand on his chest. "Oh, sweet baby Moses, don't tell me you were making foot wine."

"It's called grape treading," I say coldly, "which you should know, oh Master of the Vineyard. You should also know that heritage techniques are having a renaissance."

"Wow," Monroe says. "With fifteenth-century science like that, no wonder business is booming."

He gestures to the empty vineyard, choked with weeds and rumbling with bees but otherwise deserted.

Heat flushes up my neck. The grapes are a week past their prime, but we haven't been able to afford the extra hands to bring them in.

Monroe doesn't know that. But he knows something…otherwise, he wouldn't be here.

"Why *are* you poking around?" I demand, crossing my arms over my chest. "Hazel isn't here."

I shouldn't have said that—my nerves are leaking out. I *wish* Hazel were here. Then PopPop wouldn't have escaped. Or at least, we would have found him by now.

Hazel would know what to do about Monroe—how to conceal what he shouldn't see, how to distract him and get rid of him as quickly as possible.

But my oldest sister deserves a weekend off once in a while, and I'm the one who insisted she take it. So now I have to deal with the consequence.

The consequence is my grandfather sprinting naked through the field directly behind Monroe.

Well...naked except for the pink clogs.

Monroe starts to turn his head at the rapid *flipflipflipflipflip.*

"*Pineapple!*" I shout.

It doesn't work. Monroe is used to ignoring entire arenas of screaming fans; he's not going to be distracted by a sexual safe word. Plus, he has excellent peripheral vision.

"Was that PopPop?" he says, still politely amused. Like he did not just witness three full helicopter swings of grizzled gray junk whipping through the summer breeze. "He's in good shape for an old dude."

I'm sweating and possibly about to puke. Not because I saw PopPop naked—I'm way too used to that.

No, I'm about to puke because Monroe is going to blow this whole thing wide open.

"He's...a nudist," I say, sweat slipping down my spine.

"A nudist?" Monroe is so clearly trying not to laugh.

I'm hating him with all my soul, desperately determined to prove the truth of my lies.

"Yes!" I say, wildly inventing. "It's very important to him. For... religious reasons."

Monroe shakes his head at me sadly. "You're terrible at lying, Sadie. You always have been."

"A capital crime for a Beaumont."

"True." He grins that wolfish grin. "*We're* good at everything."

"Except self-deprecation."

"Well, nobody's perfect." He winks at me. My stomach does a little flip-flop like it's a pink plastic gardening clog.

Stop that.

I've known Monroe Beaumont my whole life. I knew him when he had bright blue braces as well as blue eyes, when his feet were too big for his body and he thought it was cool to wear skinny jeans.

So there's no way I should *ever* be getting flip-flops in my belly from this man.

Especially not when you consider the small and insignificant fact that Monroe and his brothers loathe my family. They covet what we have and want to destroy everything we hold dear.

Not that we need much help.

This is the third time PopPop's gotten out this week. Either we're getting more incompetent…or he's getting worse.

Abandoning pretense, I cup my hands around my mouth and bellow, "POPPOP!"

Distantly, my middle sister June echoes, "*PopPop, where arrrrre youuuuuu?*"

"Do you lose him often?" Monroe says.

I whirl around, heart racing, face flaming. "Help me find him, you colossal ass!"

"Sure." Monroe folds his thick arms over his chest. "If you admit that he's nuts."

I'm rooted to the earth, waves of icy fear and boiling anger rolling over me.

"Don't talk about my grandfather," I hiss. "PopPop's in the prime of his life."

"Maybe so," Monroe says, jerking his chin in the direction of the west pasture. "But I think he just stole that tractor."

Even though it's a disaster that Monroe is witnessing all this, I never could have wrestled PopPop out from behind the wheel without his help. I barely manage to pry the keys out of the ignition before PopPop can steer the tractor directly into the pond.

All the struggle goes out of my grandfather when the engine dies. He stops thrashing in Monroe's arms, going limp and dead-eyed instead. His wispy white hair is sticking up in all directions, and he's still wearing the gardening clogs.

I feel so sad when I look at him, gravity seems to double and double again.

"It's okay, PopPop," I say, finding his velvet robe, wrapping it around his bony shoulders. "Let's get you back to the house."

But PopPop isn't looking at me. He's gazing up at Monroe, his mouth slack, his eyes as wide and delighted as a baby's.

"Oh!" he says, "it's you!"

Monroe shifts uneasily. PopPop knows him, of course, but the warmth and eagerness are for someone else.

PopPop's silvery brows draw together, his expression saddening, his lower lip pouting like a child's. "But you never come to see me anymore…"

Monroe glances at me, seeking help.

My face is so stiff and burning, my lips can barely form shapes. "That's not…that's not who you think it is, PopPop. That's Monroe, Lionel Beaumont's grandson."

"Grandson?" PopPop says, shocked and disbelieving. Then he pauses, squinting, examining Monroe. At last, the childish amusement falls away, leaving the confusion of a very old man. "Oh," he says. And then, a little softer, "Oh."

Monroe gives me a look with way too much understanding.

No, no, no, no, no, he's not supposed to understand! He wasn't supposed to see this at all!

June stalks out of the orchard, long-limbed and red-faced. When she spots us, she throws up her hands in relief. "There you are, PopPop! I've been looking ev—"

Recognizing Monroe, she breaks off so suddenly it's almost comical, as if someone pushed a button and froze her in place.

If it were just me and Monroe, I think she'd turn on her heel and march right back into the orchard. June doesn't like normal visitors, let alone Beaumonts. But with PopPop in the mix, she approaches at a cautious pace.

My father comes loping down the hill, too late to stop what's already happened. Worse, he's glassy-eyed and stumbling, his hair greasy and his clothes hanging off his frame, stained with food as well as paint.

I shoot a miserable glance at Monroe. Those bright blue eyes don't miss a thing, cataloguing every detail of my father's appearance, almost as shocking and just as damning as PopPop's.

"Where was he?" my father mumbles. "Dad, you can't…you can't run off like that."

Monroe has gone quiet, watching my father even more closely than he was watching PopPop.

My throat has closed up so tight, barely a whistle of air can get through.

This is very, very bad.

I shoot June a desperate look, but as usual, June is inscrutable. She gazes at Monroe, unsmiling. I'm no longer certain that she recognizes him. June has trouble with faces. And manners.

"Hello, June," Monroe says.

June blinks at him slowly, like a cat. Then she turns to me and says, "What's he doing here?"

"I don't know. He never told me."

June turns back to Monroe. "What are you doing here?"

But now Monroe isn't answering. He's frowning, eyes pinballing between my grandfather, who has just glanced down and loudly exclaimed, "Who took my damned pants?" and my father, mushy as he mutters, "You got lots of pants, Dad. We'll get you pants."

I don't know which one of them looks worse. PopPop's as wrinkled as a paper bag, his hair thin as cobwebs and his arms skinny as broomsticks. But Dad's even more emaciated, with circles dark as bruises beneath his eyes.

"Can you take him back up to the house?" I snap at my father, as if the damage could be undone if they'd just *leave*.

But it's June who has to take PopPop firmly by the arm and steer him up the long slope to Hill House. Our dad is barely sober enough to follow. He stumbles twice before they're out of view, reeling like a sailor not used to solid land.

When I'm alone with Monroe again, the silence says everything.

He knows the truth now; it's obvious. And there's nothing I can do about it.

I suppose I could cry or beg. Not that it would do any good.

I probably just gift-wrapped exactly what he's looking for. I'm sure that's why he's here: to spy on us, to dig up dirt. To get his greedy hands on what he's wanted for so long. On what they've all wanted...

"What are you going to tell your brothers?" My voice comes out raspy, almost hoarse.

To his credit, Monroe isn't gloating. He isn't even smiling.

In fact...he almost looks sad.

He's gazing up at Hill House, the lonely perch that's bleaker than ever against a gray summer sky, windows blank as blind eyes.

My grandfather's prison.

My father's now, too.

Angry and close to tears, I demand of Monroe, "*What are you going to tell them?*"

Monroe shakes off whatever had hold of him, his lazy grin returning. "We already knew PopPop was out of his mind. I'm not here because of him."

I swallow, confused, not daring to hope. "Then why are you here?"

Monroe's jaw flexes; his throat ticks.

"Because *my* grandfather is dying."

ABOUT THE AUTHOR

Sophie Lark writes intelligent and powerful characters who are allowed to make mistakes. She lives in Southern California with her husband and three children.

The Love Lark Letter: geni.us/lark-letter
The Love Lark Reader Group: geni.us/love-larks
Website: sophielark.com
Instagram: @Sophie_Lark_Author
TikTok: @sophielarkauthor
Exclusive Content: patreon.com/sophielark
Complete Works: geni.us/lark-amazon
Book Playlists: geni.us/lark-spotify